THE STAR WARS®

PLANETS COLLECTION

Combining *Planets of the Galaxy, Volumes One, Two* and *Three*

Allen Nunis

Published by

WEST END GAMES®

RR 3 Box 2345
Honesdale, PA 18431

40100

CREDITS

Planets of the Galaxy, Volume One

Design: **Grant S. Boucher, Julie Boucher, Bill Smith**
Development and Editing: **Bill Smith**
Graphics: **Stephen Crane, John Paul Lona**
Interior Art: **Tim Eldred**
Playtesting and Advice: **Greg Farshtey, Dr. Michael R. Fortner, Greg Gorden, Gary Haynes,
Ron Seiden, Ed Stark**

Planets of the Galaxy, Volume Two

Design: **John Terra**
Development and Editing: **Greg Farshtey**
Graphics: **Stephen Crane, Cathleen Hunter**
Interior Art: **Rob Caswell, Mike Vilardi**

Planets of the Galaxy, Volume Three

Design: **John Terra**
Additional Material: **Bill Smith**
Development and Editing: **Greg Farshtey, Bill Smith**
Graphics: **Cathleen Hunter**
Additional Graphics: **Stephen Crane, John Paul Lona**
Interior Art: **Mike Vilardi**

Revised for Second Edition

Development and Editing: **Bill Smith**
Cover Design: **Tim Bobko**
Graphics: **Tim Bobko, Brian Schomburg**
Cover Art: **Lucasfilm Ltd.**
Additional Interior Art: **Paul Daly, Mike Jackson, Allen Nunis, Mike Vilardi**

Publisher: **Daniel Scott Palter** • Associate Publisher/Treasurer: **Denise Palter**
Associate Publisher: **Richard Hawran** • Senior Editor: **Greg Farshtey**
Editors: **Peter Schweighofer, Bill Smith, Ed Stark**
Art Director: **Stephen Crane** • Graphic Artists: **Tim Bobko, Tom ONeill, Brian Schomburg**
Sales Manager: **Bill Olmesdahl** • Licensing Manager: **Ron Seiden** • Warehouse Manager: **Ed Hill**
Accounting: **Karen Bayly, Wendy Lord, Kimberly Riccio** • Billing: **Amy Giacobbe**

CONTENTS

Planets of the Galaxy, Volume One

Introduction 4
Planet Log 7
Planet Generation System 8
Planet Generation Reference Charts 26
Baralou 29
Celanon 35
Essowyn 41
Garnib 47
Gorsh 54
Isen IV 60
Joralla 67
Mutanda 74
Rordak 80
Veron 86

Planets of the Galaxy, Volume Three

Welcome to Elrood Sector! 92
The Elrood Campaign 95
Elrood Sector Overview 99
Elrood 121
Coyn 135
Kidron 146
Merisee 156
Derilyn 164
Kuras II 176

Planets of the Galaxy, Volume Two

Algara II 186
Atraken 194
Carosi XII 203
Ergeshui 211
Fyodos 220
Gacerian 230
Korbin 237
Zelos II 246

■Introduction

An Imperial Star Destroyer looms menacingly into view on the freighter's viewscreen. As wave after wave of TIE fighters closes the distance, an engineer is frantically trying to fix the hyperdrive controls. Buttons, levers, and wires are all manipulated with expert precision. Trails of smoke and sparks of unharnessed electrical energy decorate the control panel.

As the blasts start rocking the nearly helpless ship, a last-ditch desperation yank on the hyperdrive motivator causes the stars to shift and spin. As the ship zooms out of harm's way, one TIE comes so close the engineer can see the Imperial pilot flinch as he prepares for a collision.

Welcome!

The *Star Wars* movies are set against a vast panorama: a galaxy of countless worlds teeming with strange life-forms, exotic locations and adventure. *The Star Wars Planets Collection* provides a glimpse of that amazing setting!

One of the more appealing aspects of the *Star Wars* movies is the sense of the unknown and exploration. Even since the dawn of time, humanity has related stories of "what lies over there," inventing imaginary locations, creatures and beings that populate unexplored areas. The *Star Wars* movies postulate a galaxy of a "thousand-thousand worlds," yet we only visit half a dozen planets in those movies. What lies beyond Bespin, Hoth and Tatooine?

The Star Wars Planets Collection is a compendium of worlds that gives the reader some answers. The planets in this book cover a wide range of settings and situations that are perfect for the roleplaying game. Originally presented in three separate volumes (*Planets of the Galaxy, Volumes One, Two* and *Three*), this combined edition has been fully updated to *Star Wars: The Roleplaying Game, Second Edition* rules.

Using These Planets in the Game

The first planets in this book — from Baralou to Veron — are described in the time frame of the *Classic Star Wars* time period. The Rebel Alliance is beginning its struggle against the Empire, yet the defeat of the Emperor at Endor is years away.

The second section of this book is a complete adventure setting, the distant Elrood Sector (originally presented *Planets of the Galaxy, Volume Three*). Set during the time period of *Classic Star Wars*, the sector's main planets are described in detail, but introductory sections described the history and personalities of the sector, as well as provide brief summaries of the lesser planets of the sector.

The final group of planets (from *Planets of the Galaxy, Volume Two*) — from Algara to Zelos — are described during the New Republic time period. During this time, the New Republic is struggling to wrest control of the galaxy from the fragments of the once mighty Empire.

In each case, the planets introduced are described in enough detail to give the gamemaster a feel for the world while still allowing plenty of room for exploration.

There are a number of ways each world can be used in the game. The most obvious is the "traditional" *Star Wars* campaign, where the player characters are Rebels fighting to undermine the Empire. Other options are available, such as free-wheeling smuggler campaigns, where independent freighter captains try to make money while dodging creditors, pirates and Imperial Customs inspectors. Of course, players will get an entirely different perspective if running a gritty bounty hunter campaign. In each case, gamemasters have intricate settings which can be developed by creating new characters, interesting encounters and additional locations.

Mike Jackson

The Planet Generation System

It has happened to every gamemaster. The soda sits on the desk, a bag of chips opened, a copy of each of the *Star Wars* sourcebooks and galaxy guides at hand, and just as the gamemaster opens his (or her) notebook, waiting for the next great inspiration to strike ... nothing. No adventure, no world, no interesting characters. With your friends due to arrive in just a couple of hours you have drawn a blank.

That's where the planet generation system comes in. The system allows gamemasters to roll up worlds (leaving things to complete random chance) and also gives comprehensive, detailed hints on how to construct exciting and fun planets. This section is filled with tips, comments and examples design to jumpstart a stalled imagination.

The planet generation system assumes that an interesting setting for an adventure is more important to the gamemaster than creating a "realistic" distribution of worlds in a star system. It's assumed that a gamemaster's primary concern is to create a world that is interesting to visit — the other planets in the system, the star type and so forth can be created by the gamemaster later if necessary.

So grab your dice and photocopies of the blank planet log (see page 7) and start creating your own worlds where legends will be born.

PLANET LOG

Planet Name: _____

Eastern Hemisphere

Western Hemisphere

Type: _____
Temperature: _____
Atmosphere: _____
Hydrosphere: _____
Gravity: _____
Terrain: _____
Length of Day: _____

Length of Year: _____
Sapient Species: _____
Starport: _____
Population: _____
Government: _____
Tech Level: _____
Major Exports: _____
Major Imports: _____

System Name: _____   Star Name: _____

Orbital Bodies:

Name	Planet Type	Moons
_____	_____	_____
_____	_____	_____
_____	_____	_____
_____	_____	_____
_____	_____	_____
_____	_____	_____
_____	_____	_____
_____	_____	_____
_____	_____	_____

Planet Generation System

The planet generation system is designed to help gamemasters design exciting and fun new worlds for *Star Wars: The Roleplaying Game*. The system emphasizes the creation of unusual and memorable settings for roleplaying adventures, without requiring the gamemaster to generate reams of technical data. We hope it inspires great new worlds for your adventures …

Ready To Begin

The gamemaster will need several six-sided dice, a pencil, and photocopies of the Planet Log (page 7). It is also advisable to have a notebook set aside to record the ideas that come to mind.

The gamemaster can use the die charts found in this chapter to randomly generate worlds from scratch. Alternately, the gamemaster can use this rules section as a merely inspirational tool, using the descriptions and ideas herein as a baseline from which a comprehensive, detailed world

Tim Eldred

emerges. The second method takes more time and consideration, but is also more satisfying.

Keeping It Space Opera

When dealing with a science fiction roleplaying game, it's very easy to spend too much time designing one planet. After all, from our own experience, our home world is incredibly intricate and immensely interesting and the *Star Wars* galaxy has millions of stars with worlds equally diverse and fantastic.

However, the nature of *Star Wars* necessitates hopping to two, three, four or even more new planets in the course of an adventure. This system is designed to help gamemasters generate the most important and interesting details of a new planet, and makes a number of assumptions:

• The gamemaster will only want to send players to interesting planets and systems. The odds of this game system are heavily weighted toward generating advanced or colonized planets. The civilizations of the *Star Wars* universe have been spacefaring for so many centuries that most advanced civilizations (and a lot of primitive ones as well) have been discovered and assimilated into galactic culture.

• There are isolated sections of the galaxy that offer undiscovered civilizations and other challenges, and they can also be generated with this system. They can exist for whatever reason: they are far out on the end of a spiral arm; or, they are difficult to get to because they are surrounded by gas clouds, near rogue planets or subjected to huge ion storms.

• Only the system's planet of prime importance is fleshed out here. Other worlds can be developed independently, but virtually everything of interest and value is on the prime world.

• This system results in "finished concept" worlds, and doesn't spend much time explaining how a particular planet got a certain way; it just is. An explanation of the culture and history takes a few minutes to formulate, but the results are worth it.

• Completely random rolls on these charts may generate seemingly contradictory results. The gamemaster always has the option of ignoring results that are unsuitable. However, knowing the diversity to be found in the *Star Wars* galaxy, virtually any result is explainable.

• This system generalizes the type of terrain found on the planets. While few worlds have uniform terrain everywhere, this system gives one or two dominant terrain types so the gamemaster can quickly sum up the planet.

• Optional modifiers listed after some results are just that: optional. The gamemaster has every right to fudge die rolls (or just arbitrarily decide upon a result). This system is only a tool for the gamemaster to create fun worlds; the gamemaster need not be subservient to a series of charts. All modifiers are cumulative.

• If an incompatible condition result is rolled, discard it and select a compatible result.

Planet Function

Since *Star Wars* is space opera, and leans heavily toward action and strong story telling,

the most important aspect to players is what can be found or explored on the planet. The following results give some indication as to what types of industries and activities are common on a particular planet. For greater diversity, the gamemaster may roll on this chart multiple times.

To determine the planet function, roll two six sided dice. Read each number separately (this is a six-sided percentile system; do not add them together for a total). This generates totals between 11 and 66. It is best to use two different color dice (say, red and blue), reading one color die before the other. For example, if you're reading the red die first, and you roll a "3" on the red die and a "2" on the blue die, your roll is a "32" (Homeworld planet).

11: Abandoned Colony

This is a planet that was settled by another planet, a company or some other wealthy instituion. Then, for some reason, the colony was left behind: the homeworld could have been struck by plague or war, or the company could have run out of money. The planet might have been evacuated (only leaving ruins), or supply ships just never arrived, in which case the colonists were on their own: they may have devolved into barbarism and anarchy.

Tim Eldred

Mike Vilardi

12: Academic

Educational institutions are what is most important to the economy of this planet. Academic worlds typically have many universities and colleges, which may be private, corporate or state run.

Options for low tech level worlds are varied: the university was purposefully established to remove students from the temptations of modern comforts. Or, the natives may have had some contact with free-traders, and have committed all of their efforts to unlocking the secrets of modern technology.

This result doesn't necessarily mean academic work towards a degree. Trade schools, institutions dedicated to unlocking the secrets of the Force (these will always be well hidden since the Emperor has made it a priority to kill Force users), and survival schools are possible options.

Optional Modifiers: +1 Starport; +1 Tech Level

13: Administrative/Government

This world is bureaucracy at its largest. The main industry is the orderly (or at least managed) operation of a government, business, or other large institution. Imperial sector capitals often qualify for this designation, but the homeworlds of major, galaxy-spanning corporations and institutions such as BoSS (Bureaus of Ships and Services) may also be considered administrative in nature. Low tech level planets could also be administrative, especially if the economy is directed entirely by the government.

Optional Modifiers: +1 Starport; +1 Tech Level

14–21: Agriculture

This planet is dedicated to the production of food. The types of products can include grains, vegetables, fruits, meats, vitamins, dietary supplements, and water. Many ocean planets also rely on agriculture, through fishing or algae and vitamin farms.

Incompatible Conditions: Asteroid Belt, Artificial Planet Type; Barren Terrain

22: Colony

This planet has been established and sponsored by another, more developed planet or corporation. Colonies are generally dependent upon the sponsor for supplies, and typically are subservient to its dictates. Colony worlds aren't independent entities, although there may be a separatist movement. Colony planets generally produce goods only for consumption by the sponsor, and thus are often prevented from developing a self-sufficient economy or acquiring significant wealth. Many colonies are devoted to agriculture and mining.

23: Disaster

Disaster planets have gone through cataclysmic changes that have dramatically altered the world's history. The event could have been a war that used atomic weapons, a plague, an industrial accident, a collision with a large stellar body (such as an asteroid) or a dramatic change in the nature of the system's star (such as when stars balloon into red giants, incinerating all of the inner planets and drastically changing the climate of the surviving worlds).

The disaster could have occurred just a few years ago (generally making the world very dangerous), or it could have happened decades or eons ago (in which case the danger from the actual disaster may have passed, but the aftermath could be devastating).

Optional Modifiers: (If recent calamity) -3 Starport; -2 Tech Level; +3 Atmosphere

24: Entertainment

This planet's business is show business. Holovids, musical groups and the businesses that distribute their works to the general public are dominant here. Some planets specialize in sporting events (such as swoop races), amusement parks, gambling or tourism.

25–26: Exploration

This planet, and the whole system for that matter, has seldom been visited, until now, when the characters have arrived. Exploration planets tend to have primitive technology levels (if there are even sentient species). There are few urban areas, with the emphasis on dangerous wilderness. Lost artifacts from past ages may be on these planets, or there may simply be wandering tribes of aliens who are eager to trade. These planets may be rich in natural resources.

There may be some hint of galactic civilization in these systems, or on the planet in question — perhaps a secretive trader has retired here, or

fugitives may be hiding from the Empire. These locales are excellent for hidden bases, or if near important trade routes, may be a convenient stopover for independent traders.

Optional Modifiers: -2 Starport; -2 Tech Level

31: Hidden Base

There is a base on this planet that someone wants to keep a secret. This immediately sets up a conflict for the characters, since that someone will probably hunt them down to prevent anyone else from finding out about the base.

Alliance and pirate bases are logical choices. Other options may include the Imperial military or corporate interests (possibly a weapons or biological engineering research facility). Wealthy individuals may have a private hideaway.

32–33: Homeworld

This result means the planet is a homeworld for an established alien species. It could be Calamari (home of the Mon Calamari and the Quarren), Sullust (home of the Sullustans), or one of thousands of other homeworlds throughout the galaxy. Most of these planets have modern starports, a sophisticated trader network and a high level of technology. Almost all homeworlds of atomic tech level or higher have already been subdued by the Empire unless the characters are in unexplored regions of space.

34: Luxury Goods

The planet produces luxury goods, such as

Tim Eldred

Mike Vilardi

liquor, finished gemstones (such as the Garnib crystals), spices, art or other goods. This planet may be self-sufficient, or may be devoted exclusively to producing the luxury good (which would requiring importing everything else).

35–41: Manufacturing/Processing

The inhabitants of this planet devote most of their time to manufacturing goods. The goods generally fit into three distinct categories: low tech, mid tech, and high tech. These goods may be for consumption by the planet's own residents, or they may be for export to other planets. They may be finished items, which are shipped directly to markets, or the planet may be an intermediary step, whereby the planet takes in raw materials from one planet, and then processes the material so that it can be used in the production of a finished good, which is manufactured someplace else.

Low Tech

Low tech items are simple manufactured goods, such as handiworks, native crafts, furniture, basic medicines and woven cloth. The goods may be mass produced in factories, or may be made individually by skilled craftsmen.

Mid Tech

More complex items are produced on this planet. Textiles, mechanical weaponry (projectile weapons), pharmaceuticals, paper goods, vehicles, and primitive versions of high tech goods, such as computers and plastics, can be manufactured on these planets. Assembly line factories are frequently necessary to produce these goods.

High Tech

Modern computers, blaster weapons, superhard plastics and alloys like transparisteel, polymers, chemicals, bioengineered life forms, advanced bio-immunal medicines, cybernetics, medical equipment, droids, vehicles and starships are all considered high tech goods. high tech goods almost always require advanced manufacturing methods.

Optional Modifiers: Mid tech Planets: +2 Starport; +2 Tech Level. High tech Planets: +3 Starport; +4 Tech Level

42: Military

This planet is an important Imperial military facility. It has one or several large bases. Sector capitals, planets near strategic trade routes, Imperial ship yards, and weapons manufacturing planets have huge military bases.

Optional Modifiers: +3 Starport; +2 Tech Level

43–46: Mining

Mining planets depend upon the minerals and metals locked beneath the ground. These planets truly drive the Imperial economy, because without the raw materials there would be no starships or vehicles. Blaster gases are also mined, but are taken from gas giants (such as the Tibanna gas mine on Bespin).

Optional Modifiers: +2 Starport; +1 Tech Level

51–55: Natural Resources

These planets utilize naturally occurring resources such as wood (for logging), animal skins, and glaciers ("harvested" for fresh water). Other products that could be harvested are raw materials for medicines and pharmaceuticals, and may be either plant or animal derived. This category differs from agriculture because the products aren't food.

56: Research

These planets are used for scientific and academic research. The world may have abundant resources, but the particular company or university may have an exclusive charter and is allowed to decide who develops the planet. Research may be for purely scientific or academic knowledge, but other planets, like Gorsh, are studied for new chemical compounds with practical applications.

61: Service

Service planets tend to have a multi-classed social system and great wealth. The exclusive higher classes have control over the wealth and resources, and the lower classes provide services and goods to the wealthier individuals. Service planets tend toward direct sale to consumers, or may be devoted to banking, legal services, medical services, or financial markets.

Optional Modifiers: +1 Starport; +2 Tech Level

62–63: Subsistence

A planet with a subsistence economy is working hard just to survive. There is little to send to other worlds to generate income, and if the planet has to import many goods, the debt could be staggering. Another option is a planet that depended upon one product which has lost a great deal of its value, and as a result, unemployment and poverty have grown dramatically in recent times.

64–66: Trade

Trade planets tend to be the most active and exciting planets in the *Star Wars* galaxy. They are blessed with being on a good trade route, and as a result, everyone stops here to sell goods, make deals and purchase goods for resale at other locations. Sector capitals, planets that produce many different products and planets with wealthy populations are often trade planets.

Optional Modifiers: +3 Starport; +2 Tech Level

Government

Government is the means by which a society determines what is permissible and what is forbidden. Governments can regulate business or corporate behavior, or even eliminate entities such as businesses. They can severely curb a citizen's rights, or be very permissive.

The following results determine what type of government has been established on this planet, but it is up to the gamemaster to determine what the government in question believes in — these categories simply detail by what means the government operates. If the gamemaster wishes to generate more variety, roll on this chart multiple times to determine secondary governments or to determine a strong influence within the prime system of government.

One thing to remember is that most planets in the galaxy are under the firm control of the Empire. This chart assumes that the planet is under Imperial control (with the notable exception of the Rebel Alliance result), although many primitive planets (feudal or stone tech levels) have been left alone simply because they offer too few resources or tax revenues to be worth the effort.

Most Imperial planets have been allowed to retain their traditional form of government, but all Imperial worlds have troops and equipment deployed to help the local population remember who is in control of the situation. Many, but not all, planets have Imperial governors who act as liaison between the Empire and the planetary government. On some worlds, the governor has assumed control (an action well within his or her authority). Particularly troublesome worlds are often subdued by Imperial military crackdowns.

To determine the government type, use the six-sided percentile system. This generates totals between 11 and 66. It is best to use two different color dice, reading one color die before the other. For example, if you're reading the red die first, and you roll a "5" on the red die and a "6" on the blue die, your roll is a "56" (Representative Democracy).

11: Alliance/Federation

Several different groups (tribes, nation-states, corporations or whatever else — you decide) have formed an alliance. The degree of cooperation and the vitality of the alliance differs from situation to situation. Typical purposes for alliance include an improved economy, mutual defense, or the arrival of a situation so compelling that the different groups can put aside their problems to accomplish "a greater good." Betrayal is always a possibility, especially if there are other competing alliances.

12: Anarchy

Anarchists stand for the individual and his or her rights above all else, including government. Anarchist governments could conceivably be quite elaborate, but would exist only to insure that each individual has complete freedom.

Anarchism is commonly perceived as a lack of

law and order, and on many planets, that is indeed the truth.

13–16: Competing States

Several nation-states, tribes or corporations are actively competing for control of the planet. The intensity and type of competition varies, and can range from economic competition to open war.

21–22: Corporate Owned

This planet is owned by a corporation, trade guild or other large business interest. Most of these planets produce goods for use or resale by the parent corporation. Other corporate planets are for the pleasure and relaxation of the executives and employees — in essence, giant recreation planets. Residents are almost always employees of the corporation, and have strict guidelines and rules to follow, such as having to pay rent on corporate housing, or being required to purchase goods only from corporate retailers.

The corporation is allowed to do whatever it likes (with the agreement of the Empire, of course). Conditions on planets are widely variable, from harsh and repressive to agreeable and comfortable.

Optional Modifiers: +3 Spaceport; +2 Tech Level

23-24: Dictatorship

Dictatorships are commanded by a single individual, such as a charismatic military officer, or an insane politician who will execute anyone. Dictatorships are almost always repressive and intolerant of divergent political, philosophical and social views.

25: Family

The most important social organization on the planet is the family. There are a variety of possible scenarios, including a pre-tribal state, where families have little or no technology and constantly engage in warfare with each other. At higher tech levels, a small group of elite families could control the government, either overtly or through behind the scenes manipulation of the government in power.

26–31: Feudalism

A multi-structured social system, in which important officials (nobles or royalty) are entrusted with a specific area of land. They must manage the territory, provide tax revenues to higher-level officials and make sure that the commands of these higher-level officials are carried out.

32: Guild/Professional Organizations

The planet is controlled by a guild dedicated to the advancement of a particular occupation or philosophy. Many trade planets are run by trade guilds (see Celanon). These guilds may also control certain portions of the government, and

subtly direct the kind of legislation and decisions that are made.

33–42: Imperial Governor

This is a planet where the designated Imperial governor has taken control, either due to civil unrest, sheer ego, or belief that the previous government was inept, disloyal or unresponsive.

43–45: Military

Military planets are controlled by either the Imperial military or a local military organization. They tend to have governments which perpetuate only the military structure, ignoring the needs and desires of the civilian populations — martial law is a way of life. Harsh, brutal crackdowns can occur with only minor provocation. Civil rights take a low priority when compared to accomplishing government goals.

46–52: Monarchy

A type of government where absolute authority is granted to one individual, often called a king or queen. The leadership position is normally granted by heredity. Planets may have patriarchal (only male rulers) or matriarchal (only female rulers) societies.

53: Organized Crime

A planetary or galaxy-wide criminal organization has established a government loyal to the criminal leaders. Organized crime planets are typically run so that only those who are unswervingly loyal to the criminal organization receive advancement and promotions; opponents are simply eliminated.

Organized crime may also covertly control a government by bribing or blackmailing officials, or threatening their families. These governments are typically oppressive.

54: Participatory Democracy

Citizens vote directly on important issues (some advanced planets have citizens vote on virtually every proposed bill).

55: Rebel Alliance

A government that supports the Rebel Alliance and its objectives. Few planets can risk openly supporting the Alliance (Alderaan is a painful example of what happens to openly rebellious worlds), but several planets secretly shuttle funds to Rebellion coffers, or offer safe passage for Rebel agents, supplies and weaponry. Hidden Rebel safe worlds also qualify for this designation.

56: Representative Democracy

Planets with a representative democracy have citizens choose officials, who are then charged with representing the "public interest." These type of governments can experience radical shifts in goals and policy if the population is unsatisfied with performance and threatens to remove the representatives from office.

61: Ruler by Selection/Rite

The ruler is chosen by a series of trials, physical, mental or both. While these governments are often found on more primitive planets, advanced civilizations may use complex testing methods to determine who is most fit to govern a planet, nation or locality.

62: Theocracy

A government run by a religious organization. Typically, the citizens are required to participate in certain religious rites and profess faith in the tenets of the religion. Theocracies may be highly tolerant of divergent views, but some are also quite repressive.

63–66: Tribal

Tribal governments seldom control more than a small portion of the planet. Tribes are groups of many families who have banded together for mutual survival, or who share common beliefs. Tribes are often precursors to city-states and nation-state governments, but many highly advanced and sophisticated tribal governments are found on planets throughout the *Star Wars* universe. Tribes can be nomadic, depending almost entirely upon hunting and foraging for food, or they can settle, which indicates the development of agriculture.

Planet Type

The following table determines the basic type of world that the civilization in question has developed on. Roll 2D and find the results below.

2–9: Terrestrial

The planet is a typical ball of rock and metals orbiting a sun. Most terrestrial planets have atmospheres, and many have developed life. Move on to the "Terrain" section below.

10: Satellite (Normally Gas Giant)

This world is a moon orbiting a gas giant (much like Yavin Four as seen in *Star Wars: A New Hope*). Since there is a civilization here, it probably has a breathable atmosphere and supports life, or there were important resources too valuable to pass up. Move on to the "Terrain" section below. Satellites are almost always tide-locked to the gas giants they orbit.

11: Asteroid Belt

Asteroid belts are either the remnants of planets shattered by collisions with large stellar bodies or merely portions of stellar material that never coalesced into a planet. Settled asteroid belts are often rich in minerals and metals, and their small size prevents them from supporting an atmosphere. Most asteroid belt civilizations are either subterranean or have sealed and probably domed buildings built on the surface. Since asteroids are naturally airless, civilizations require regulated environments. Read the sidebar labeled "Regulated Environments" and then move ahead to the section labeled "Starport." Asteroid belt settlements required a tech level of atomic, information or space to be established (if the settlement was abandonned, the civilization may have devolved and lost tech levels).

Optional Modifiers: -2 Population (initial roll only)

Incompatible Conditions: Agriculture, Homeworld Planet Function

12: Artificial

Artificial results indicate orbiting space stations, domed cities built on planets with toxic atmospheres, and great floating complexes built in gas giants (such as Cloud City). All artificial settlements need some means of sustaining themselves (such as huge repulsor engines to keep Cloud City aloft, or sealed domes to keep the toxins out of the city). Since artificial planets require a regulated environment, read the "Regulated Environments" sidebar and then skip to the section labeled "Starport." Artificial settlements require a tech level of information or space.

Optional Modifiers: -2 Population (initial roll only)

Terrain

The gamemaster must determine the dominant terrain for the planet. There can be many different types of terrain on a planet, but the dominant terrain is the one that the characters will interact with most often. Diverse planets may have several major terrain types. Additionally, the planet's terrain may be a combination of types (such as mountainous forest).

While these classifications provide basic information as to the terrain types, the gamemaster must customize them to match the unique nature of the planet. Each terrain entry has a listing of compatible conditions, which is where these terrain types are most likely to be found. Some terrain types also have incompatible conditions, where they will seldom be found. If a quality isn't listed (such as a Moderate Hydrosphere, for example), the conditions are neither particularly favorable for the terrain, nor do they preclude the existence of the terrain type. If the gamemaster rolls incompatible terrain results, he may opt to discard the results, or reason through a really unusual situation that allows this result (this is the most entertaining option).

To determine the terrain type, roll on the six-sided percentile system.

11: Barren

Barren planets are typically Arid, possibly with hostile atmospheres. The ground is extremely hard, dry and is hostile to most forms of life. There may be large rocks on the surface or embedded in the rock hard ground. Minerals and metals may be found. Barren planets are predisposed to unbreathable atmospheres.

Compatible Conditions: Arid, Dry Hydrosphere

Incompatible Conditions: Moist, Saturated Hydrosphere

Optional Modifiers: -2 Population (initial roll only); +3 Atmosphere

12–13: Cave

The planet is dominated by an immense network of caves running throughout the crust. These caves are often caused by volcanic activity, and if the activity is ongoing, areas can quickly become dangerous as lava and toxic gases return to fill the caves they created. Cave planets almost always have Type II atmospheres.

Example: Sullust

Optional Modifiers: +2 Atmosphere; -2 Population (initial roll only)

14: Crater Field

Crater fields can occur in virtually any other type of terrain, and they are the result of continuous impacts from meteorites, resulting in huge cratered areas on the planet. The impacts could

Seasonal Changes

The seasons on a planet are caused by the amount of axial tilt. If the planet's axis of rotation is perfectly "vertical" (perpendicular to the plane of its orbit) there are no seasons, and the temperature is constant year round. However, there will still be temperature changes due to weather.

However, if the axial tilt isn't "vertical," the planet experiences seasons. The greater the degree of tilt, the more extreme the seasonal change. Planets with a high degree of tilt experience extreme seasons. One side of the planet will have brutally cold winters, with continual darkness. At the same time, the opposite side of the planet will experience a sweltering summer and continual sunlight, with temperatures well above boiling. As the planet circles the sun, there will be a brief period of moderation, and then the side of the world that was previously locked in the grip of winter is now exposed to searing sunlight and the side that was experiencing a deadly summer is now exposed to the cold and dark of space. As the planet swings back around the sun, there again is a brief moderate period, before the planet returns to the seasons originally described.

No Axial Tilt — No Seasons
Slight Axial Tilt — Produces Seasons
Extreme Axial Tilt — Extreme Seasons

have ended millions of years ago, or they may still be ongoing. Large enough meteors could cause significant climate changes on a planet by throwing huge clouds of soil into the air or causing earthquakes. Planets with light gravities are favorable for crater fields.

Example: Essowyn

Incompatible Conditions: Thick atmospheres

15–16: Desert

Deserts are typically found on dry and arid planets, and support only a minimum of life due to a lack of moisture. Deserts can be found in any temperature zone. Warm desert areas can be very dangerous because travelers can easily become dehydrated (an exposure suit will prevent dehydration).

Example: Tatooine

Compatible Conditions: Arid, Dry Hydrosphere

Incompatible Conditions: Moist, Saturated Hydrosphere

21–24: Forest

Forests occur most commonly in temperate zones, but they can also occur in very cold or warm areas. If they receive a great deal of precipitation in tropical areas, they are called rain forests. Forests may be active year round, or may be seasonal (most of the plants go into hibernation during cooler seasons). They generally receive ample rainfall.

Example: Endor

Compatible Conditions: Moderate, Moist Hydrosphere; Hot, Temperate, Cool Temperature

Incompatible Conditions: Arid Hydrosphere; Frigid, Searing Temperature

25–26: Glacier

Glaciers are huge, frozen sheets of ice that can be several kilometers thick. Icebergs are chunks of glaciers that have been broken off and now float in oceans. Glaciers grind the land beneath them, constantly reforming it. Glaciers can occur on land, or above ocean.

Example: Hoth

Compatible Conditions: Moist, Saturated Hydrosphere; Cool, Frigid Temperature

Incompatible Conditions: Arid, Dry Hydrosphere; Searing, Hot, Temperate Temperature

31–32: Jungle

Jungles are any area overgrown by plant life, and often include low-lying wetlands that support many forms of plant and animal life. They are often warm at least a substantial portion of the local year. The ground can be moist or dry. They are excellent incubators for life, from plants to insects and animals. They require ample water, but can be warm or cool.

Example: Veron

Tide Lock

Tide locked planets are trapped with one half of the planet continuously facing the sun and the other facing out into space. They cannot rotate, and thus there is no day/night cycle. These planets are *almost* always uninhabitable, but there are exceptions (some planets have a habitable zone on the boundary of the night and day sides). If a planet is tide locked, ignore the effects of axial tilt.

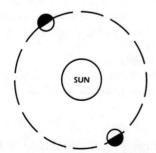

The same side of the planet faces the sun at all times.

Elliptical Orbits

Some planets orbit their star in unusual orbits, with one part of the orbit coming much closer to the sun than the rest of the orbit. These elliptic orbits account for huge seasonal variations, and the lengths of seasons are not equal. In extreme situations, the planet is locked in a deadly cold winter for years at a time, but as it swoops in close to the star, the planet quickly thaws and life returns, all within the span of a few weeks.

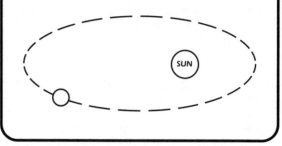

Compatible Conditions: Moderate, Moist, Saturated Hydrosphere; Searing, Hot, Temperate Temperature

Incompatible Conditions: Arid, Dry Hydrosphere; Cool, Frigid Temperature.

33–34: Mountain

Mountainous planets have been (or still are) home to a great deal of geologic activity. The mountains can range from small hills (under a kilometer tall) to huge peaks several kilometers tall. Depending upon the planet's atmosphere, plant life, and soil, mountain areas can support a variety of plant forms from trees to grasses. Peaks of mountains on temperate and cold planets may be snow capped. Snow capped mountains can be quite dangerous because of avalanches.

Example: Ryloth

Incompatible Conditions: Saturated Hydrosphere

35–41: Ocean

Ocean planets are dominated by huge bodies of water or other liquid. The oceans can be very deep, or merely large and shallow, depending upon whether or not geologic activity has created great mountainous regions (islands are often the peaks of small mountains that emanate from the ocean's floor). These planets may be searing to frigid, although frigid oceans will often be covered by huge glacial sheets of ice.

Example: Baralou

Compatible Conditions: Moderate, Moist, Saturated Hydrosphere

Incompatible Conditions: Arid, Dry Hydrosphere

Planetary Weather

Meteorology is one of the most difficult of the sciences to understand, simply because there are so many factors involved in determining the weather of a planet. Weather is defined as any type of wind or precipitation, whether is in the form of rain, sleet, ice, ice shards, or something even more exotic.

In general, weather fronts are created by the spin of the planet and the mixture of different temperature air masses (such as when cool air from a great water body collides with warm air from the interior of a continent). Weather can be amplified by the presence of satellites, an unusual planetary orbit (such as elliptical), local geographic

conditions (there tends to be more rain when a weather front hits a mountain chain, since the clouds must lose moisture in order to rise above them) and the effects of galactic civilization (climate control is used on many advanced planets).

Precipitation might be measured in centimeters per year, or even meters per day, depending upon the amount of moisture in the air and climate. The strength of winds might be barely noticeable, or so strong that buildings must be securely anchored or they will be blown over.

The scope of this work doesn't allow for detailed weather mechanics, but with all of the options available to gamemasters, the sky's the limit.

Optional Modifiers: -1 Population (initial roll only)

42–44: Plain

Plains areas are simply huge, flat expanses of life, typically supporting grasses and bushes as primary forms of plant life. Grasslands can be found in virtually any hydrosphere and temperature range, but they are most common in tropical and temperate dry regions. Very cold, dry grasslands are often called tundra, and very warm, dry grasslands are often called savannahs.

Example: Celanon
Compatible Conditions: Dry, Moderate, Moist Hydrosphere; Hot, Temperate, Cool Temperature
Incompatible Conditions: Arid, Saturated Hydrosphere; Searing, Frigid Temperature

45–46: Plateau

Plateaus are large sections of mostly flat land that are elevated above other portions of nearby land. They typically occur in the interior of continents. On a plateau, virtually any type of terrain can be found.

Incompatible Conditions: Saturated Hydrosphere

51–52: Urban

This result means that most of the planet is covered by artificial constructions, typically huge city sprawls. This is indicative of a very high population, and most so-called urban planets concentrate on trade, manufacturing or administration. Agriculture can sometimes be conducted in huge hydroponics factories, or beneath the surface if the plants don't require sunlight (typical of mosses and fungi). Urban terrains can be layered on top of most other terrain conditions, such as plateaus, mountains, and plains. In addition to habitable cities, urban results may indicate huge factories and refining faciltes.

Aside from buildings, many urban settings will

have extensive cultivated areas for agriculture. This classification can include any developed area that isn't wilderness.

Example: Kari (see *Galaxy Guide 6: Tramp Freighters*)
Optional Modifiers: +1 Population (initial roll only)

53–61 Wetlands

Wetlands are moist low-lying wet areas, and play a vital role in most eco-systems. They can take the form of ponds, marshes, or swamps, and support bushes, trees, grasses and many different forms of life.

Example: Gorsh

Regulated Environments

Space stations, asteroid belt cities, domed cities and other artificial environments are called regulated environments. It is assumed that these environments are set for the most comfortable conditions for the species that built the environment, or in the case of Humans, a temperate temperature, Standard gravity, and a day/night cycle hovering abound 20-25 standard hours.

However, should there be a catastrophic disaster, the natural environment may come rushing into the facility, or things such as oxygen reprocessors or repulsorgrav generators may fail. If the regulated environment is a domed city or a construct within a gas giant, the immense gravitational forces and atmospheric pressures may cause the facility to collapse. Filters could fail, releasing all kinds of toxins into the environment. While accidents should be rare, the potential for disaster is enormous.

Incompatible Conditions: Arid, Dry Hyrdosphere; Frigid, Searing Temperature

62–63: Volcanic

Volcanoes and lava pools cover the planet, indicating a very high level of geologic activity. Volcanic planets often have high levels of ash and toxic gases in the atmosphere, and the lava, of course, is very dangerous. However, these planets often have high quality metals in their crust. Volcanic planets often have hazardous atmospheres.

Incompatible Conditions: Type I atmospheres
Optional Modifiers: -2 Population (initial roll only); +3 Atmosphere

64–66: Special Terrain

These are unusual terrains that demonstrate the incredible versatility of the *Star Wars* universe. These terrain types can also explain seemingly contradictory terrain rolls. What follows are some examples:

• Crystal forests and fields. The crystals may be immensely valuable, or merely scenic. They may also be a hazard if they magnify incoming sunlight, possibly blinding careless travelers.

• Planets with ammonia oceans, where the land masses are actually rock-solid ice fields. This type of condition requires very low temperatures and often has a Type IV atmosphere.

• Underground forests, found in great subterranean caverns. The trees and bushes derive most of their energy from the geothermal energy released by the interior of the planet.

• Huge canyons cover the planet.

• A planet where most of the water is trapped on high plateaus, and the lowest sections of the planet are actually parched deserts.

• Planets like Kashyyyk, with several distinct "bio-levels," where the type of creature and its behaviors is distinctly different based on the altitude. This can be accomplished through use of mountains, huge trees, or even planets where there are many lighter than air gases and many flying and gliding creatures have internal bladders for constant lift.

• Planets that are covered with toxic and radioactive pools. They may have been mining planets that were just tapped out and converted to waste dumps. Whole new lifeforms (and hardy ones at that) could evolve in these conditions.

• A planet with an unusual substance that mixes with water, turning into a jellied goo at temperatures up to 80 degrees Celsius. In warmer seasons, there are huge flowing oceans of the muck, while in winter, the goo hardens, expands and covers much of the planet (much like a hot-weather glacier).

Temperature

This classification represents the average temperature on the planet's surface. Most planets have several varying temperature bands, from the coldest (polar regions) to warmest (equatorial region). The "true" temperature of an area can be altered by local geographic features. Seasonal changes also greatly alter temperature (see "Seasonal Changes" sidebar). Some planets are trapped in what is called tide lock (see "Tide Lock" sidebar). Still other planets have elliptical orbits (see "Elliptical Orbits" sidebar).

All of these possible combinations give the gamemaster a great deal of diversity and choice when designing the planet. These special results are not incorporated into the random tables so that the gamemaster can choose exactly which effects are most useful. Roll 2D to determine the average temperature.

2: Searing

Searing planets average 60 degrees Celsius or more, and are hostile to most life forms, although standing bodies of water are possible as long as the average temperature isn't near the boiling point (100 degrees Celsius). Most civilizations will tend to cluster near the more moderate polar regions or underground.

3–4: Hot

Hot planets average between 30 and 56 degrees Celsius, and while generally uncomfortable, are not nearly as hostile as searing planets.

5–9: Temperate

Temperate planets average between -5 and 29 degrees Celsius, and are in the most comfortable temperature bands for Humans and other life forms.

10–11: Cool

Cool planets average between -20 and -4 degrees Celsius. Most cool planets do not support a huge number of life forms, but life can still adapt to planetary conditions. Plant life may be common if it contains compounds that prevents vital water-based fluids from freezing.

12: Frigid

Frigid planets average -21 degrees Celsius or less, and are often inhospitable. If the hydrosphere is Temperate, Moist, or Saturated, the planet may be covered with ice glaciers.

Gravity

Star Wars: The Roleplaying Game uses four classifications to indicate the gravity of a world. As indicated before, most regulated environments will have a gravity of Standard.

Zero Gravity

Asteroids, comets and other very small stellar bodies have effectively zero gravity, which also eliminates the possibility of an atmosphere (barring the use of technology, such as energy screens). Space stations that lose power may also lose their repulsorgrav generators, effectively throwing the whole station into a zero gravity situation.

In zero gravity, things and beings float unless thrust is somehow provided. On the other hand, once something begins moving, it doesn't stop until something else stops it (such as a collision with a wall). The applies for vertical, horizontal and even twisting movement since there truly is no "up" or "down."

Characters in zero gravity can float up to five meters per round and have no control over direction unless they have something to push off against, in which case they float 10 meters. Increase the difficulty of all *Dexterity* or *Strength* checks by 2 (excluding checks to resist damage). Combined actions are not possible. Characters attempting full *dodges* will smash into any object in their path (taking 3D stun damage). Each *dodge* counts as two actions. Characters will be able to control their direction of flight by firing blasters or projectile weapons as a means of propulsion, but this requires a Moderate *Mechanical* roll to control direction. Similary, characters who fire weapons in combat will be pushed away unless they are braced against a wall.

2–4: Light

Planets with light gravity allow characters to lift heavier objects, but also throws off physical coordination. They also allow easier movement. There are few inhabited planets with light gravity.

In very light gravities, the gamemaster may want to use the following optional modifiers: +1D bonus to all *Strength* actions (except for resisting damage); -1D penalty for all *Dexterity* actions.

Optional Modifiers: +2 Atmosphere

5–11: Standard

Standard gravity is that which is most common on Imperial worlds, and therefore most comfortable for most species. Standard gravity includes several gradients of true gravitational pull, but is placed within this convenient grouping.

12: Heavy

Heavy gravity planets have a much stronger pull than normal, the effects of which can be merely inconvenient or crippling. Planets with very heavy gravity may make a person's body so heavy that they cannot move. There are few planets with heavy gravity, and most of them are just barely beyond the Standard gravity classification. On these "barely heavy" gravity planets,

even walking counts as an action (it is not "free movement").

Gamemasters can use the following optional modifiers for slightly heavier gravity planets: -1D to all *Strength* and *Dexterity* actions (except for resisting damage). Characters must make a minimum of a Moderate *stamina* check after every minute of heavy exertion, although checks may be made more difficult or frequent at the gamemaster's discretion. Characters who fail these *stamina* checks must rest for a double the amount of time they were active or suffer a -3D penalty to all actions except resisting damage in combat. Additionally, when the character suffers damage from collisions or falling, increase the damage by a minimum of 1D.

Optional Modifiers: +2 Atmosphere

Atmosphere

Most stellar bodies of significant size have atmospheres (some planets have had their atmospheres ripped away by a near pass with a rogue planet or some similar cataclysm). Gas giant atmospheres are often composed of methane, ammonia, and various hydrocarbons (Type IV), although a very small number of gas giants have been discovered with a breathable atmosphere within a limited biozone (Bespin being the prime example). Imperial bureaucrats use a very simple classification system for atmospheres. Most ship sensors can determine the type of atmosphere with sensors. However, sensors are not perfect, and may miss trace elements that can be harmful to the ship's inhabitants, so the results of a sensor scan should never be taken at face value. To randomly determine a planet's atmosphere, roll 2D and check the result below.

None

This planet has no appreciable atmosphere and a space suit is required simply to survive on the world. Planets without an atmosphere typically have much greater temperature variations because there is no atmosphere to disperse solar energy (on the sun side) or retain heat (on the night side). Characters exposed to the vacuum of space suffer 4D damage the first round of exposure, and increase the damage by +2D for each additional round in the vacuum.

2–9: Type I (Breathable)

A Type I atmosphere has a proper mixture of oxygen, nitrogen and other gases so that Humans and comparable species can breath it unassisted. These atmospheres may have contaminants that over the long term have a detrimental effect.

Planets with a Type I atmosphere will have life or at least had life recently.

Tim Eldred

10: Type II (Breath Mask Suggested)

Type II atmospheres can support life without use of a breath mask, but either due to too much or too little atmospheric pressure or oxygen, or unusual gases or contaminants, it is recommended that a breath mask be worn. Without a breath mask, detrimental effects, such as slowed reactions, reduced brain activity, poisoning, or a myriad of other effects can begin to occur within just a few hours of exposure. Many alien speciess can comfortably breathe Type II atmospheres without having to resort to breath masks.

Planets with a Type II atmosphere will have life or at least had life recently.

11: Type III (Breath Mask Required)

Type III atmospheres are unbreathable without a breath mask, again due to a number of possible characteristics. The atmosphere could be highly poisonous, or simply not have enough oxygen to breathe. Characters without breath masks can begin to suffer detrimental effects immediately. A small number of alien speciess (and certainly native creatures) will be able to breath these atmospheres unaided.

Type III atmosphere planets frequently support life.

12: Type IV (Environment Suit Required)

Type IV atmospheres are not only poisonous, but they are so reactive that they will cause injury to persons who are exposed to it. Environment suits, space suits or life-support equipment is required to venture through the atmosphere, or characters will suffer burns and other grievous injuries. If the planet is Frigid, a thermal suit

may be necessary. These atmospheres may also be flammable or highly explosive. The gamemaster must customize the effects of the hostile atmosphere.

Hydrosphere

The hydrosphere represents the amount of moisture on or near the surface of the planet. Water is not necessarily the only liquid that can be found. The water may have a high concentration of another substance that makes it unfit for consumption, or the liquid might merely be water-based, but have other components that make it a different compound. More exotic options include huge lava lakes (on planets with plenty of geologic activity), or deadly ammonia seas (on extremely cold planets). Roll 2D.

2: Arid

The planet is 85–100 percent covered by land. The planet has very little or no standing liquid, and there probably is very little moisture in the atmosphere. There may be large lakes and seas, but there are no great oceans. Much of the planet will probably be desert.

3–4: Dry

The planet is 50-84 percent covered by land. The planet has some standing liquid, and the land is probably a mixture of desert, dry plains, tundra, or other terrain types not requiring a great deal of water.

5–9: Moderate

The planet is 15-49 percent covered by land. The planet has large oceans and probably a well developed river network, especially if the planet has large hills and mountains. There are probably many different terrain types.

10–11: Moist

The planet is only 5-14 percent covered by land. Most of the planet is covered by water or another liquid, and the few land masses that do exist are wet. Bogs and swamps are common.

12: Saturated

The planet is only 0-4 percent covered by land. Land only takes the form of islands, which may again be bogs, or swamps. Oceans dominate the terrain.

Length of Day

The length of day for most terrestrial planets not subjected to tide lock or another extreme condition is in the range of 18 to 36 standard hours. Even though tide-locked planets do not have days, it is useful to determine what a likely day length would be so that the length of the local year can be determined. To determine this total, roll 1D:

• If the result is 1-2, roll 2D and it to 10 for a total number of hours.

• If the result is 3-4, roll 1D and add it to 20 for a total number of hours.

• If the result is 5, roll 1D and add it to 25 for a total number of hours.

• If the result is 6, roll 1D and add it to 30 for a total number of hours.

Satellite planets may have days several dozen hours long (as long as it takes the satellite to orbit the gas giant). The local year depends upon the orbit of the gas giant and may be several standard years long.

Length of Year

A simple die roll will generate a suitable total since so many different factors are responsible for the determining the orbital radius and speed of the planet. The total can be increased or decreased by a few days to make the total unique compared to other planets.

To determine this total, roll 2D of different colors. Read the results below and the total of the two numbers equals the length of year in local days:

First Die
Multiply the number x15

Second Die

1	75 local days
2	150 local days
3-4	225 local days
5	300 local days
6	375 local days

Sentient Species

The gamemaster should determine what alien species are on the planet in large quantities. Humans are among the most diverse species in the galaxy and can be found almost everywhere, but other species such as Devaronians, Duros, Gamorreans, Ithorians, Rodians, Sullustans, and Twi'leks are also known to colonize and reside on many different planets. If the planet is similar to a species's preferred climate, or there is plenty of work to be found, other species may be encountered as well. The planet may have a native sentient species, designated by an (N) on this line of the planet log.

Gamemasters must take a few moments to design the native sentient species, bearing in mind the kind of environment the species evolved in. He should decide their biology, culture, history, how galactic civilization changed their society, what common occupations they have and what their personalities are like.

Starport

The Imperial Space Ministry has five different classifications for starports. For random determination of the starport, roll 2D and find the result on the chart below.

2: Landing Field

There may be a flat space on the ground for ships to land. There is no control tower (there may not even be other starships on the planet). Fueling and repair services are probably unavailable at any price.

3–5: Limited Services

This is typically a simple landing field, but there is at least a control tower to prevent collisions between ships in the planet's airspace. There may be maintenance sheds for rent. There may be fuel for sale, but other important supplies are unavailable.

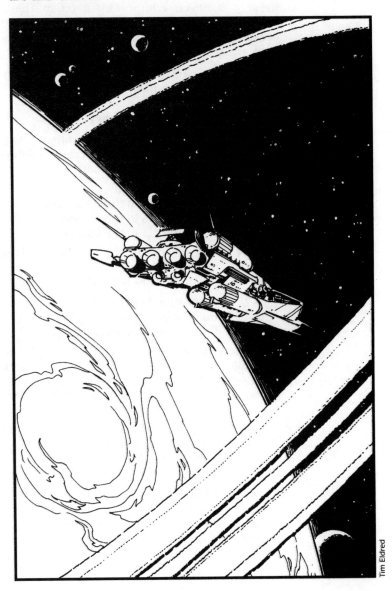

Tim Eldred

6–8: Standard Class

The starport is fully-staffed and equipped. Restocking services are available, and there is a small shipyard for minor repairs and modifications. Prices for repairs and modifications can be up to double normal prices, and take twice as long to accomplish.

9–11: Stellar Class

This type of starport can dock and service almost any class of ship. There are probably several shipyards in the immediate area, and they can handle major repairs and modifications. There is almost always an Imperial Customs office on site.

12: Imperial Class

Modern and luxurious ports with complete storage and maintenance facilities, and a large number of landing fields and docks. A complete menu of services and luxuries are available for the ship and its crew. Important merchants have offices at the starport. The shipyards are capable of rapid repairs and modifications. The Imperial Customs office is well staffed.

For more information on starports, see *Galaxy Guide 6: Tramp Freighters*.

Population

This figure represents the total sentient population on a particular planet. For random determination, roll 1D and use the chart below.

1	Population is 1-999
2–3	Population is in the thousands
4–5	Population is in the millions
6	Population is in the billions

Once the basic range is established, roll 1D to determine whether the population is in single numbers, tens or hundreds for that category.

1–2	Population is in singles (1-9)
3–4	Population is in tens (10-90)
5–6	Population is in hundreds (100-900)

To determine the exact number, roll 1D to determine if the number is 1-5 or 6-9. It is recommended that the population only be determined for two significant figures (i.e., only roll the first two numbers).

1–3	Number is between 1-5 (roll 1D, ignoring 6)
4–6	Number is between 6-9 (Roll 1D, ignoring 5 and 6, and add five)

It is recommended that the gamemaster not allow populations over 100 billion. Any population over 10 billion is very likely to be an urban terrain planet, with a standard class or better starport and an industrial level or higher tech level.

Example: The gamemaster wants to randomly determine the population of a planet. He rolls 1D getting a result of "3" (the population will be in the thousands).

A second die roll yields a result of "5" (the population is in the hundreds of thousands).

To determine the exact number, the gamemaster must first roll the first significant figure. A roll of "1" tells him the number is between 1 and 5, and a second roll of "3" tells him the first number is 3, for a first number of 300,000.

To determine the second significant figure, a roll of "5" tells him the number is between 6 and 10. To get the specific number, he rolls 1D and adds five, ignoring a 5 or 6. He rolls a "1", and by adding 5, gets a total of 6.

This makes the planet's population 360,000.

Tech Level

The level of technological achievement is important in determining what goods the planet can manufacture, as well as what they are likely to be interested in purchasing. Few planets fit directly into one of these classifications.

This classification system, utilized by Imperial bureaucrats, represents the typical level of technology to be found on the planet, but there may be areas where indivduals have developed or somehow acquired more advanced technology. Planets with no sentient inhabitants are considered Stone level by default. Roll 2D.

2: Stone

Stone level civilizations have loosely-knit cultures and the basic social unit is likely to be the tribe. The society makes and uses stone tools and may have developed primitive agriculture. These people do not understand the concept of money, so trade will be by barter. There is no transportation network.

3: Feudal

Feudal planets have a more complex social structure and have begun to produce primitive manufactured goods. They have learned primitive mining and ore-processing techniques. Transportation is normally by ship or caravan.

4: Industrial

Industrial planets are beginning to understand mass production, and have established more complex political and social structures. Windmills, waterwheels, wood or coal furnaces will be used to generate energy. These planets typically want to acquire knowledge to help improve their technology. Motorized transportation, projectile weapons and the beginnings of mass communication are common.

5: Atomic

Atomic planets have advanced, large-scale production of goods. They will be very interested in new technologies. More advanced alloys and plastics become available. Space travel is in its infancy. Established industries, such as transportation, communications, medicine, and business, quickly progress and grow.

6-7: Information

Sophisticated communications, such as computers and satellites, become readily available. Industry becomes more efficient, mechanization is very common, and the precursors of droids appear. Energy weapons are beginning to be discovered, in-system space travel is common and colony ships to other planets are a distinct possibility. Repulsorlift may be developed. Natural resources may become scarce.

8-12: Space

This is the stage of most planets within galactic civilization, and is characterized by hyperspace travel, droids, blasters, and highly efficient industry. Planets at this level are often integrated into the galactic economy, and produce many goods for export, but also import many goods.

For more information, see *Galaxy Guide 6: Tramp Freighters.*

Major Imports and Exports

This should be chosen by the gamemaster only after considering the government, tech level and planet function as a whole. The gamemaster must decide what the planet produces for its own consumption, what it ships to other planets and what it must purchase from other planets. The whole galactic economy is built upon the fact that most planets specialize in producing certain goods and must import goods from other planets for survival.

Imperial bureaucrats group goods within eight general categories. Within these categories, planets may export or import only a few products. The categories are: low, mid, or high technology, metals, minerals, luxury goods, foodstuffs and medicinal goods. For more information see page 16 of *Galaxy Guide 6: Tramp Freighters.*

System/Star Name

Generally, the system and the star are named after the most important planet of the system.

Star Type

The gamemaster should determine the type of star for the system. White, yellow-white, yellow, orange, and red stars could conceivably support habitable planets (yellow and orange are most likely). White dwarfs (which were once red giants) may have once supported habitable planets, but they were burned when the star became a red giant. Binary stars can support habitable planets, and although rare, this is not impossible, as Tatooine shows. This is possible if the stars are close enough to each other so that the planet orbits both stars, or the stars are so far apart that the planet can orbit around only one of the stars (this will almost always be the case). Trinary stars could also support habitable planets, but this is even less likely.

Other Planets

The gamemaster, at his option, can elect to detail the rest of the system. This is a matter of choosing the types of planets and their names, and provided you don't start explaining the detailed astrophysics of the system, odds are likely no one will complain.

In general, terrestrial planets will occupy the inner orbits of the system. Next will be the gas giants, possibly followed by frozen rock planets.

Gas giants will be the only planets capable of supporting habitable satellites. Most satellites for terrestrial planets will be little more than hunks of frozen rock and ice, although they could be a large "companion" satellite. Gamemasters can list other planets on the Planet Log. Moons of particular importance can be listed after the planet they orbit (in the text, listed moons are *italicized.*).

Designing Lifeforms

One of the final steps in designing a planet is deciding the lifeforms that inhabit it. However, for game purposes the gamemaster will never need to completely define the biosphere.

When designing lifeforms, it is most important

Planet Log Terrain Key

Plains		Barren Rock	⋏	Volcano		Water	
Desert		⊛ Craters		⌣ Plateau		Urban/Industrial	
Swamp		⌒ Hills		⌣ Canyon		⊙ City	
Forest		⋏ Mountains		Ice		✦ Spaceport	
Jungle/Rain Forest						▫ Site of Interest	

PLANET GENERATION CHARTS

Planet Function
(Roll six-sided percentile dice)

11 Abandoned Colony

12 Academic
Optional Modifiers: +1 Starport, +1 Tech Level

13 Administrative/Government
Optional Modifiers: +1 Starport, +1 Tech Level

14-21 Agriculture
Incompatible Conditions: Asteroid Belt, Artificial Planet Type; Barren Terrain

22 Colony

23 Disaster
Optional Modifiers: -3 Starport (if recent calamity), -2 Tech Level; +3 Atmosphere

24 Entertainment

25-26 Exploration
Optional Modifiers: -2 Starport, -2 Tech Level

31 Hidden Base

32-33 Homeworld

34 Luxury Goods

35-41 Manufacturing/Processing
Optional Modifiers: Mid Tech Planets: +2 Starport; +2 Tech Level. High Tech Planets: +3 Starport; +4 Tech Level

42 Military
Optional Modifiers: +3 Starport; +2 Tech Level

43-46 Mining
Optional Modifiers: +2 Starport; +1 Tech Level

51-55 Natural Resources

56 Research

61 Service
Optional Modifiers: +1 Starport; +2 Tech Level

62-63 Subsistence

64-66 Trade
Optional Modifiers: +3 Starport; +2 Tech Level

Government
(Roll six-sided percentile dice)

11	Alliance/Federation
12	Anarchy
13-16	Competing States
21-22	Corporate Owned
23-24	Dictatorship
25	Family
26-31	Feudalism
32	Guild/Professional Organizations
33-42	Imperial Governor
43-45	Military
46-52	Monarchy
53	Organized Crime
54	Participatory Democracy
55	Rebel Alliance
56	Representative Democracy
61	Ruler by Selection/Rite
62	Theocracy
63-66	Tribal

Planet Type
(Roll 2D)

2-9 Terrestrial

10 Satellite (Normally gas giant)

11 Asteroid Belt
Optional Modifiers: -2 Population (initial roll only)
Incompatible Conditions: Agriculture, Homeworld Planet Function

12 Artificial
Optional Modifiers: -2 Population (initial roll only)

Terrain
(Roll six-sided percentile dice)

11 BARREN
Compatible Conditions: Arid, Dry Hydrosphere
Incompatible Conditions: Moist, Saturated Hydrosphere
Optional Modifiers: -2 Population (initial roll only); +3 Atmosphere

12-13 CAVE
Optional Modifiers: +2 Atmosphere; -2 Population (initial roll only)

14 CRATER FIELD

15-16 DESERT
Compatible Conditions: Arid, Dry Hydrosphere
Incompatible Conditions: Moist, Saturated Hydrosphere

21-24 FOREST
Compatible Conditions: Moderate, Moist Hydrosphere; Hot, Temperate, Cool Temperature
Incompatible Conditions: Arid Hydrosphere; Frigid, Searing Temperature

25-26 GLACIER
Compatible Conditions: Moist, Saturated Hydrosphere; Cool, Frigid Temperature
Incompatible Conditions: Arid, Dry Hydrosphere; Searing, Hot, Temperate Temperature

31-32 JUNGLE
Compatible Conditions: Moderate, Moist, Saturated Hydrosphere; Searing, Hot, Temperate Temperature
Incompatible Conditions: Arid, Dry Hydrosphere; Cool, Frigid Temperature

33-34 MOUNTAIN
Incompatible Conditions: Saturated Hydrosphere

35-41 OCEAN
Compatible Conditions: Moderate, Moist, Saturated Hydrosphere
Incompatible Conditions: Arid, Dry Hydrosphere
Optional Modifiers: -1 Population (initial roll only)

42-44 PLAIN
Compatible Conditions: Dry, Moderate, Moist Hydrosphere; Hot, Temperate, Cool Temperature
Incompatible Conditions: Arid, Saturated Hydrosphere; Searing, Frigid Temperature

45-46 PLATEAU
Incompatible Conditions: Saturated Hydrosphere

51-52 URBAN
Optional Modifiers: +1 Population (initial roll only)

53-61 WETLANDS
Incompatible Conditions: Arid, Dry Hydrosphere; Frigid, Searing Temperature

62-63 VOLCANIC
Incompatible Conditions: Type I atmospheres
Optional Modifiers: -2 Population (initial roll only); +3 Atmosphere

64-66 SPECIAL TERRAIN

PLANET GENERATION CHARTS

Gravity
(Roll 2D)
2	Zero Gravity
3-4	Light
	Optional Modifiers: +2 Atmosphere
5-11	Standard
12	Heavy
	Optional Modifiers: +2 Atmosphere

Hydrosphere
(Roll 2D)
2	Arid
3-4	Dry
5-9	Moderate
10-11	Moist
12	Saturated

Temperature
(Roll 2D)
2	Searing
3-4	Hot
5-9	Temperate
10-11	Cool
12	Frigid

Atmosphere
(Roll 2D)
2	None
3-9	Type I (breathable)
10	Type II (breath mask suggested)
11	Type III (breath mask required)
12	Type IV (environment suit required)

Population
Basic Range
(Roll 1D)
1	Population is 1-999
2-3	Population is in the thousands
4-5	Population is in the millions
6	Population is in the billions

(Now, roll for within that range if the population is in single numbers, tens, or hundreds for that category. Roll 1D)

1-2	Population is in singles (1-9)
3-4	Population is in tens (10-90)
5-6	Population is in hundreds (100-900)

(For exact numbers, roll 1D to determine if number is between 1-5 or 6-9. Determine to two significant figures. Roll 1D)

1-3	Number is between 1-5 (roll 1D, ignoring 6)
4-6	Number is between 6-9 (roll 1D, ignoring 5 and 6, and add five)

Length of Day
(Roll 1D; the result is in standard hours)
1-2	Roll 2D, add 10
3-4	Roll 1D, add 20
5	Roll 1D, add 25
6	Roll 1D, add 30

Length of Year
(Roll 2D; the result is in local days)

First Die
Multiply die roll x15; add it to the result from the second die.

Second Die
1	75 local days
2	150 local days
3-4	225 local days
5	300 local days
6	375 local days

Starport
(Roll 2D)
2	Landing field
3-5	Limited services
6-8	Standard class
9-11	Stellar class
12	Imperial class

Tech Level
(Roll 2D)
2	Stone
3	Feudal
4	Industrial
5	Atomic
6-7	Information
8-12	Hyperspace

to remember the relationship the lifeform will have with other organisms in its environment. The following general concepts should help you develop interesting and unusual lifeforms.

Life

Animals are life forms that must secure food already organized into organic (carbon-based) substances. In other words, they generally cannot derive their sustenance from sunlight or soil, but rather must hunt down plants and other animals.

Plants are lifeforms that manufacture their own food from inorganic substances. Often they draw energy from sunlight and nutrients from soil; in nutrient poor environments they may consume other plants and animals.

Bacteria are single-celled life forms. They can be both useful and harmful to other life forms.

Viruses are pure genetic material wrapped in a protein coating. When a virus is introduced to a new life form, it replaces the host's genetic material and starts replicating itself, spreading throughout the host.

Relationships

Commensal relationships are ones in which one organism coexists with another. The first organism derives some benefit from its coexistence, while the second organism is neither harmed nor benefits from the relationship.

Parasitic relationships are ones in which one organism coexists with another. The first organism derives some benefit from the relationship, while the second organism is harmed, but not killed, by the relationship.

Predator relationships are ones where the first organism benefits from the second organism, but also kills it, meaning that the predator must continually hunt down new forms of prey.

Symbiotic relationships are ones in which two organisms coexist, and both of them benefit from their association with the other organism.

Intelligence

Non-intelligent organisms are controlled by their genetic code and the nature of their environment. They are merely reactive.

Physical reflex organisms respond to external stimuli in variable ways. This is not a cognitive process, however, but a pattern of innate and learned response to external stimuli. For example, these creatures back away from hot objects after they are burned. They cannot learn in advance that "hot is bad," for example.

Emotional reflex organisms can feel content, sad, and other emotions on a rudimentary level. They do not literally think "I am sad," but instead respond with behavior modification when things are going well or poorly. These creatures can challenge for a mate, battle for territory, "feel" hungry, or get angry when they haven't eaten.

Associative thought organisms can associate one occurrence or action with another one. This allows for learned behaviors. For example, a hungry animal can chose to wait to hunt until nightfall because it has learned to associate nightfall with better chances of success when hunting. These creatures can feel loyalty, hurt, angry, loss, remorse, or happiness to the same levels as more intelligent creatures, but cannot grasp ephemeral ideas like love and war. There is no "good versus evil" for such creatures; they only understand "beneficial to me" and "harmful to me."

Sentient organisms are the highest state of intelligence known in the *Star Wars* galaxy. The organism has the ability to imagine, dream, divine the consequences of events based on past experiences and gauge the probability of future success given previously acquired knowledge. Emotions can be tempered, instilled, altered. The culture of such beings can define things like good and evil in esoteric ways. These creatures can invent new things, create and test theories, or develop artificial worlds with no basis in real experience. True sentience is a rare development.

The Details

Within this framework, virtually every social relationship between any form of life can be defined. Once the situations are defined, the gamemaster can define how the lifeform moves, any unusual attacks or defenses, the lifeform's social structure and needs, and other factors.

For more information on the nature of lifeforms, see *Star Wars: The Roleplaying Game, Second Edition* and pages 3 and 4 of *Galaxy Guide 4: Alien Races.*

Baralou

Baralou

Type: Tropical ocean
Temperature: Hot
Atmosphere: Type I (breathable)
Hydrosphere: Saturated
Gravity: Standard
Terrain: Ocean, jungle islands, barren rock islands
Length of Day: 22 standard hours
Length of Year: 295 local days
Sapient Species: Humans, Krikthasi (N), Multopos (N)
Starport: Limited services (Aqualis Base)
Population: 500,000 (surface), 5 million (aquatic)
Planet Function: Homeworld, algae harvesting and processing
Government: Solitary tribes (Multopos), feudal and solitary tribes (Krikthasi)
Tech Level: Stone
Major Exports: Foodstuffs (bestrum algae, fish), luxury goods (tropical fish, Krikthasi crafts, gemstones)
System: Baralou
Star: Baralou (yellow)
Orbital Bodies:

Name	Planet Type	Moons
Baralou	tropical ocean	4
Alou Belt	asteroid belt	0
Masalou	barren rock	0
Yaralou	saturated terrestrial	0
Tanalou	frozen rock	0

World Summary

The water-rich Baralou system offers mineral wealth, abundant natural resources and vast trade potential for those who happen upon it.

The most remarkable planet, Baralou, occupies the first orbital slot about the yellow star. The world is covered by oceans, with several chains of volcanic islands protruding from the waters. It is a tropical world, with temperatures ranging from 20 to 40 degrees Celsius. Most of the islands, now stable, are covered by tropical jungle. The orbiting moons help generate the violent storms and tremendous tides that constantly sweep the world.

The Multopos, one of two intelligent species native to Baralou, are found throughout the islands. These creatures are currently engaged in a fierce battle for survival with the marine Krikthasi. Both species have developed stone level technology. Trade with the Multopos and Krikthasi is by barter only.

This world is visited by many independent traders, and is also the location for an important Alliance algae processing complex.

System Summary

The Baralou system has much to offer, yet it is still a backwater world due to its distance from major trade routes. There is no permanent Imperial presence in the system. A few free-traders have profited handsomely from their visits to this world. The Alliance views the Baralou system as an important source of food because of the large algae harvesting and processing facility, Aqualis Base.

Baralou's four orbiting moons create dramatic tides and storm fronts, causing constant flooding of the islands. Another problem is the toxicity of the terrestrial plant life — most fruits and vegetables have traces of a potent poison. In game terms, if a character (Human or alien) has five servings of Baralou vegetables or fruits within three local days, he must make an Easy *stamina* check or suffer 2D+2 damage. For each additional serving, check again and increase the damage by 1D. If the character can go three days without eating any native plants, his system will have a chance to recuperate from the poison. Creatures from this planet can metabolize the toxin, so meat is not dangerous to consume.

System Datafile

Baralou system, star: Baralou, yellow star. Four planets in system with asteroid belt in second "orbit." Baralou (innermost orbit) is the only habitable planet in system.

Planet is a warm, tropical world noted for immense tidal changes. Baralou seems to support an intelligent amphibious civilization. Some independent traders conduct a small amount of trade on this world. Visitors are advised to proceed with caution because this is an extremely primitive world.

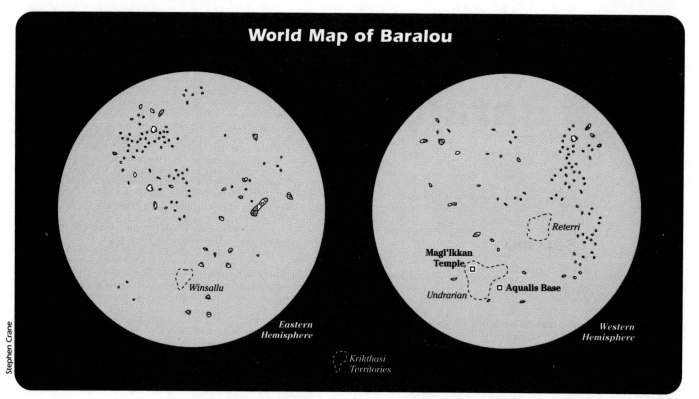

World Map of Baralou

Reterri

Magl'Ikkan
Temple

□ Aqualis Base

Undrarian

Winsallu

*Eastern
Hemisphere*

*Western
Hemisphere*

*Krikthasi
Territories*

Stephen Crane

Tropical Islands

The islands of Baralou support a variety of life forms even though they are constantly assaulted by storms (tides sometimes rise over 50 meters).

The island beaches are a mixture of items washed up from the oceans — soil, sand, rocks and shells. Further inland, and farther away from the most devastating tides, low bushes and trees can be found. Because of the violent changes in conditions, plants on Baralou have very deep root systems. As a defense mechanism, most of the plants secrete some kind of toxin. Most of the plants grow year round.

Many kinds of animals are on the islands, including insects, amphibians, birds, reptiles and mammals. Most have some kind of adaptation to survive the flooding and storms, including gills, the ability to go into hibernation when submerged in water, or flight capability.

A Planet of Riches

The plentiful gemstones of Baralou — sasho gems, kuggerags, rubies, diamonds, jasse hearts — are formed as a result of the tremendous internal pressures of the planet and can be found on nearly every island. The native Multopos are perfectly willing to let free-traders gather as many gems as they wish as long as there is a "fair exchange" of merchandise. Due to their ignorance of the true worth of these gemstones, they are willing to trade a one-kilogram sasho gem (with an open market value of 5,000 credits) for a blaster pistol and a few

power packs. Fortunately for the Multopos and the Alliance algae plant, the traders have been very tight-lipped regarding the source of the gems. If less scrupulous traders and businesses were to ever learn Baralou's location, a more brutal form of exploitation would be sure to arrive on the world.

Majestic and Dangerous Oceans

The oceans of Baralou aren't nearly as turbulent as the surface. While currents are strong, the storms and tidal waves have little traumatic effect more than 40 meters below the surface of the water. Characters caught near the surface when a tidal wave passes will be in for an unpleasant ride, as they feel themselves dragged in a million directions at once, only to be thrown into the air, high above the ocean surface.

Many primitive aquatic plants thrive beneath Baralou's waters, including bestrum algae (which Aqualis Base processes into food) and aquatic grasses. Plankton is plentiful, providing ample food for the fish, mollusks and crustaceans.

The undersea scenery is truly spectacular, with brightly colored fish everywhere. Many of the fish species have evolved specialized defenses and attacks, such as razor-sharp teeth, venoms, poisons or color-changing camouflage.

The sentient Krikthasi are a constant danger. They are just as likely to attack as communicate and will take whatever action is necessary to secure blasters. For all of their hostility and ferocity, the Krikthasi are also useful in warning that a tidal wave is approaching — if the characters see a patrol suddenly dive toward the ocean floor, it is a good idea to follow suit.

■ Treppok

Type: Placid aquatic omnivore
DEXTERITY 2D
PERCEPTION 2D
STRENGTH 6D
Special Abilities:
  Teeth: STR+2D damage. If a character is wounded, he or she must make a Moderate *Dexterity* check to avoid being swallowed.
Move: 45 (swimming)
Size: Up to 30 meters long
Scale: Creature
Orneriness: 4D

The treppok are perhaps the most spectacular of Baralou's undersea creatures. They are large, brilliant red fish, up to 30 meters long. Their tails have six fins, with another six fins at the midpoint of their bodies. They have a flexible, but very strong interlocked skeleton (the Krikthasi build homes from their skeletons). These solitary creatures feed on everything from plankton to fish.

These creatures are peaceful, but the Krikthasi have learned how to manipulate them. Through use of what they call a "treppok call," they are able to produce sounds that terrify the large behemoths. By positioning several Krikthasi kilometers apart, they can force a treppok to swim wherever they want it to go.

Treppok only fight in defense, or unless frightened by the Krikthasi "treppok call." If the latter, they will attack anything that moves. They attack by attempting to bite or swallow whatever they can catch.

■ Grotseth

Type: Aquatic predator
DEXTERITY 3D
PERCEPTION 2D
STRENGTH 3D
Special Abilities:
Teeth: STR+1D damage
Razorded Scales: Grotseth are covered with small, razor-sharp scales which cause 4D damage whenever a character makes contact with the creature and fails a Moderate *brawling parry* or *Dexterity* check to get out of the way.
Move: 16 (swimming)
Size: 3-4 meters long
Scale: Creature

Capsule: Grotseth (the same word is used for singular and plural forms) are the most aggressive and dangerous fish in the oceans of Baralou. They hunt in packs (a normal pack has several full-grown adults and many pups), and they attack any creature that appears weaker or smaller than them. These creatures can be a menace to any being in Baralou's oceans and can be attracted by major disturbances (such as combat between different groups).

Undersea Action

When fights occur underwater, keep the following tactics and tips in mind:

• Lightsabers don't work well under water. They boil up the ocean and spin around, requiring a Moderate *Dexterity* roll to hold onto or pick up.

• Characters use their *swimming* codes for movement and dodging.

• When a grenade goes off underwater, it does 4D damage to everyone within its entire range. Victims at close range can be wounded, but all others take stun damage only. This is because water is tremendous conductor of concussion waves.

• Blasters are not as effective underwater. The difficulty of any blaster shot is increased by one level of difficult, and the blaster does -2D damage.

Multopos

The Multopos are tall, muscular amphibians that populate the islands of Baralou. They have a thick, moist skin (mottled grey to light blue in color), with a short, but very wide torso. They have muscular legs and thin, long arms. Trailing from the forearms and legs are thick membranes that aid in swimming. Each limb has three digits.

Their heads have long snouts, with three sets of gills immediately below the lower jaw. They eat small herbivores and plants. Their large, bulbous eyes are set deeply into their skulls.

■ Multopos

Attribute Dice: 12D
Attribute Minimum/Maximums:
DEXTERITY 2D/4D+1
KNOWLEDGE 1D/4D
MECHANICAL 0D/3D
PERCEPTION 2D/4D
STRENGTH 1D/4D
TECHNICAL 0D/1D+2
Special Abilities:
Webbed Hands: Due to their webbed hands, Multopos suffer a -1D penalty when using any object requiring fine manipulation of controls.
Dehydration: Any Multopos out of water for over one day must make a Moderate *stamina* check or suffer dehydration damage equal to 1D for each day spent away from water.
Membranes: Multopos have thick membranes attached to their arms and legs, giving them +1D to *swimming*.
Aquatic: Multopos can breathe both air and water and can withstand the extreme pressures found in ocean depths.
Move: 7/9 (walking), 11/14 (swimming)
Size: 1.6-2 meters tall

Multopos Tribes

The Multopos form tribes and generally reside toward the center, and thus the safest, portions of an island. They build simple structures out of soil and sand, which they mix with adhesive from certain tree trunks. The resulting buildings are sturdy, but very light and float in water.

Multopos tribes are quite traditional. Indi-

Multopos   Krikthasi

Tim Eldred

viduals stay with the tribe they were born and raised with. There is very little individuality in their society, as each Multopos is wholly dedicated to the tribe.

There is little for these creatures beyond survival. They spend a great deal of time caring for the young (who cannot leave the water until they are about six local years old). If not caring for young, the Multopos spend their time hunting or gathering plants. The tribes are loosely organized; the Multopos normally follow the lead of the tribe member showing the most initiative.

Multopos tribes are isolated from one another, although the species as a whole seems to be curious and peaceful. It is only with the Krikthasi that the Multopos see no potential for peace.

The most important function of the tribe is to raise more Multopos. Because of their amphibious nature, Multopos can only mate in water, and their eggs must be kept in water for the entire development period. This wouldn't be a problem except for the Krikthasi, who steal Multopos eggs for food.

Each Multopos tribe has several canals to keep the eggs alive between storms. Multopos eggs and infants are cared for in these canals, and several adults will watch the canals at all times.

The greatest fear for a Multopos is when a storm floods the island, allowing the Krikthasi to launch an attack. While some of the tribe members try to

bring the eggs and infants to safety, the warriors do their best to fend off the Krikthasi.

The Multopos have had many positive dealings with off-worlders and will be peaceful unless attacked first. They will approach curious visitors and attempt to speak with them in a pidgin version of Basic.

Trading with the Natives

The Multopos have quickly adapted to the galaxy's technology. About the only off-world goods Multopos care for are advanced weapons, such as blasters. While generally not a warring people, they understand the need for a good defense. The traders were more than happy to trade blasters for precious gemstones. Some Multopos tribes with blasters have actively begun hunting down Krikthasi beneath the sea.

Krikthasi

The Krikthasi are large marine mollusks, with long, flexible bodies. The Krikthasi have four small but very well developed eyes, and two openings at the forepart of their bodies. They have four tentacles immediately behind the eyes. One mouth is used for eating, while the other intake forces water into the Krikthasi's body. The water is forced through a series of muscles, and expelled through a group of vents at the rear of the body, allowing the creature to propel itself at speeds of up to 40 kilometers per hour. The other end of the body also has four tentacles, as well as several pairs of dorsal fins (the exact number varies depending upon ancestry).

The creatures are highly intelligent. Their "natural" coloration ranges from black to brown, but they have chromanins that allow them to communicate by changing color. Not only is color important, but the location, speed, pattern and fluctuation of color allows them to express very complex concepts and emotions. Imperial biologists have yet to decipher their language, but they believe that blue and shades of green represent aggression, yellow represents territory and red or orange indicates a willingness to discuss or negotiate.

Krikthasi

Attribute Dice: 11D+2
Attribute Minimum/Maximums:
DEXTERITY 1D+2/4D+1
KNOWLEDGE 1D/2D+2
MECHANICAL 1D/3D+2
PERCEPTION 1D/4D
STRENGTH 1D/4D+1
TECHNICAL 0D/1D+2
Special Abilities:
Color Change: The Krikthasi can change their skin coloration, with precise control over color, location of change, speed, pattern and fluctuation of color.
Swimming: At the time of character creation *only,* Krikthasi receive 2D for every 1D placed in *swimming.*
Water Sensitive: Krikthasi take 5D damage for every minute they are out of water.
Story Factors:
War-like: Krikthasi are aggressive and violent.
Move: 3/6 (walking), 12/15 (swimming)
Size: Up to 2.5 meters long

Krikthasi Society

The Krikthasi are an aggressive, violent and territorial species. Their society is very fragmented, with several large and powerful fiefdoms controlling the majority of the ocean. Each fiefdom, called a *junieuw*, is ruled by an *osi*, normally the most powerful warrior of the territory. The osi's family controls portions of the territory, directing individual tribes. There are also many independent tribes scattered around the oceans of Baralou.

Many times the osis will declare a war in an attempt to capture new hunting territories (the Krikthasi are carnivorous and rely upon schools of fish for food). Border skirmishes are also very common.

The ongoing war with the Multopos has helped the Krikthasi develop their society into its structured and regimented state. Part of the war comes from misunderstanding — the Krikthasi can in no way understand that the Multopos could be intelligent — and partially from a bloodlust that is seldom sated. They also consider multopos eggs a delicious delicacy.

Tim Eldred

The Krikthasi use the interlocked cartilage skeletons of dead treppok for homes, providing a very defensible residence. They carve coral and the bones of dead creatures for spears and primitive tools.

The Undrarian Junieuw

With a territory covering thousands of square kilometers and controlling nearly 20 individual tribes, the Undrarian junieuw, under the control of Osi Hass, is one of the most powerful Krikthasi organizations on the planet. Other powerful junieuws, such as the Reterri and Winsallu, have tried repeatedly to dislodge Hass from his seat of power.

Hass desperately wants to acquire the advanced weaponry used by the Multopos, but so far has had little luck. His proximity to Aqualis Base has allowed him to develop a cozy relation-

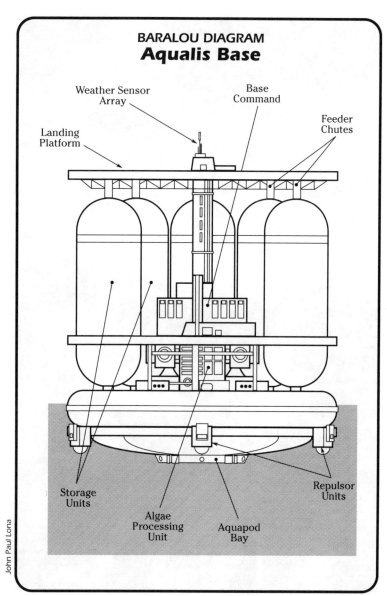

BARALOU DIAGRAM
Aqualis Base

Weather Sensor Array

Base Command

Landing Platform

Feeder Chutes

Storage Units

Algae Processing Unit

Aquapod Bay

Repulsor Units

John Paul Lona

The base has several banks of repulsorlift engines to lift it above fast moving storm fronts and tidal waves.

Since his arrival, Devvol has developed a good relationship with the nearby Krikthasi tribes; he has no reason to bother with the Multopos, and is unconcerned regarding the two species' ongoing war. He also has no qualms about trading weapons for information, gems or assistance, although Rebel High Command would surely investigate his actions if it ever found out what was happening.

An independent freighter, the *Sontor Skipper*, has been contracted to pick up one load of algae every 23 days (Captain Ross, owner of the *Skipper*, normally also trades several blasters for gemstones before leaving the planet).

Magl'Ikkan Temple

This Krikthasi temple is located at the base of a large undersea mountain. It is controlled by the Undrarian junieuw, and is used for ritual combats and important feasts. The base of the temple is built from carved and flattened sheets of treppok bone, with many sculptures of coral. The floor is dyed many different colors.

The temple is constantly patrolled by at least four warriors. Any visitors who approach the temple will be attacked. The Krikthasi will fight to the death to protect the temple. If a celebration is underway, the warriors will fight amongst themselves for the right to attack the "invaders."

Adventure Idea

The characters, in the role of free-traders, arrive on Baralou as a major tidal wave strikes a Multopos tribe. During the ensuing battle with Krikthasi raiders, they are impressed by the valiant but ultimately losing efforts of the Multopos. The Multopos offer to give their gems to the traders if they will only rescue and return their captured eggs.

Adventure Idea

The characters are sent to Aqualis Base for a minor mission and are introduced to the Krikthasi by Devvol. During the meeting, Devvol will supply some weapons to the Krikthasi. Devvol will encourage the characters to make a brief stopover at a nearby island — one with a Multopos tribe that has been attacked by the Krikthasi. As the characters learn more about the Krikthasi's sinister nature, they may be inclined to get involved.

This situation places the characters in the difficult situation of either encouraging needless death on both sides of the conflict, or trying to mediate what appears to be a hopeless situation.

ship with Devvol, the chief administrator at the plant, and Hass has graciously allowed the plant to harvest within Undrian's territory in exchange for information on advanced technology. So far Devvol has given him a small number of weapons (Hass has assured him that they would be used only to repel grotseth attacks) and some help with developing super strong materials from the plants of the ocean.

Aqualis Base

Ostensibly, Aqualis Base (known as Aqualis Baralou Algae Processing Plant #T-18) is owned by the Aqualis Food Conglomerate. In reality, it is an Alliance food production plant. It is managed by Fez Devvol and has a staff of 30 fulltime workers and over 100 droids. The workers harvest the algae with sealed aquapods, while the droids are primarily responsible for maintenance.

Celanon

Celanon

Type: Agricultural plains
Temperature: Temperate
Atmosphere: Type I (breathable)
Hydrosphere: Moderate
Gravity: Standard
Terrain: Plains, forest, urban
Length of Day: 32 standard hours
Length of Year: 187 local days
Sapient Species: Bith, Duros, Humans, Nalroni (N)
Starport: 1 Imperial class
Population: 26 million (permanent), up to 40 million additional transients
Planet Function: Homeworld, trade
Government: Trade guilds (Celanon City), tribal (rural areas)
Tech Level: Space
Major Exports: Foodstuffs, bulk trade goods
Major Imports: Luxury goods, bulk trade goods
System: Celanon
Star: Nalros (yellow)
Orbital Bodies:

Name	Planet Type	Moons
Celanon	agricultural plains	0

World Summary

Celanon is an infamous commerce world and the prime planet for the Celanon Spur trade route. With the rise of the Emperor's New Order, the underground economy has grown to scandalous proportions.

Celanon City is the only substantial city on the world, with a population of over 50 million (only 10 million are permanent residents, including two million Nalroni).

The native Nalroni regulate all trade through Celanon Spaceport and derive tremendous revenues from tariffs and bribes. The Nalroni are some of the most skilled negotiators and merchants in the galaxy, and their merchants guilds and trading consortiums are extremely wealthy and influential throughout the sector. Just about anything can be bought, sold, or stolen in Celanon City.

Outside of Celanon City, the world is dedicated to agriculture. The terrain consists of gentle rolling plains and low hills. An extensive river network feeds the lands of Celanon. Celanon exports many different grains and vegetables.

A World of Contrasts

Celanon has two prime businesses: trade (restricted to Celanon City) and agriculture (to be found everywhere else). A generally temperate world, the huge clan-run farms of the Nalroni cover the continents, producing grains and vegetables for export to hungry and wealthy planets throughout the sector. The world's dominant terrain is rolling fields, with many sections of lush forest.

Most visitors only see the sprawling spaceport of Celanon City. It is the only true city on the planet, standing tall in the middle of simple farms.

Celanon City

"Celanon City — if it's anywhere, it's there."

As one of the most notorious trading cities in the Outer Rim Territories, Celanon City is the one place that everyone seems to be coming from or going to. A free-trader is considered an amateur until he has cut a deal in Celanon City. It is where the smart learn how to survive, and the weak discover it's time to start looking for a desk job.

Celanon City is a sprawling metropolitan complex covering nearly 200 square kilometers. The

---

System Datafile

Celanon system, star: Nalros, yellow star. One planet in system (Celanon).

Celanon's only city, Celanon City, is a major trade center in the Outer Rim Territories. Celanon is an Imperial-allied world ruled by the native species, the Nalroni. Visitors to Celanon are restricted exclusively to Celanon City. Over 50 million people live in Celanon City.

From Celanon Spaceport Central:

"Upon arriving in-system, ships must tune to standard open communication frequency J-33-679-H00 for landing instructions and clearance. Patrol cruisers will direct arriving vessels. Newly arrived ships should prepare for boarding and inspection upon docking."

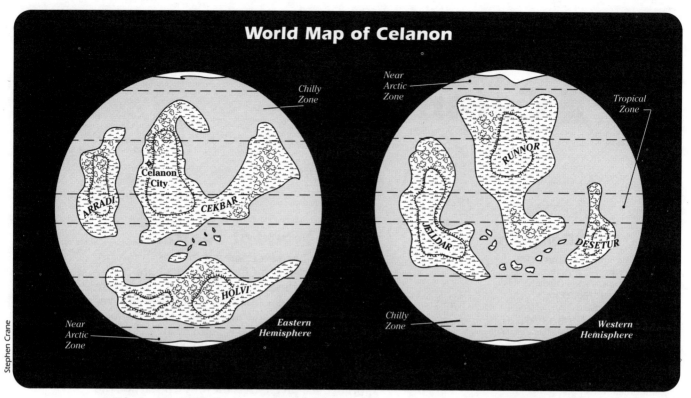

World Map of Celanon

Chilly
Zone

Near
Arctic
Zone

Tropical
Zone

Celanon
City

ARRADI·

CEKBAR

RUNNOR

JELLDAR

DESETUR

HOLVI

Near
Arctic
Zone

Eastern
Hemisphere

Chilly
Zone

Western
Hemisphere

Stephen Crane

city has extended the to property limits proscribed by the charter that established the city, resulting in architects designing taller buildings in order to meet demand for office, warehouse, trading and retail space.

Over 50 million residents of every species make the city a microcosm of the galaxy. It is a place where the very wealthy mix with the very poor, and has a high transient population. Billions of metric tons of goods pass through Celanon's sphere of influence every year.

The streets of the bustling city are crowded around the clock. Like most other worlds, prime business hours are during the day, but nightclubs, street traders and restaurants, located in every corner of the city, keep the pace of life at a fever pitch no matter what the hour.

The city is roughly circular and divided into several distinct districts, including the spaceport, diplomatic section, spacers' section, transient residences, trade consortiums and guilds, Imperial military facilities, market district, corporate zone, and governing zone. The Nalroni are deeply concerned about the prospect of their native culture being contaminated by outsiders, so the outside of the city is ringed by a huge wall, 10 meters tall. Passage to the outside is granted only to Nalroni or special guests under the direct supervision of a Nalroni, and is allowed only through specially designated gates.

Spaceport

The most prominent district of the city is the spaceport region, where all of the small freighters, bulk freighters, and shuttles are docked among thousands of bays. With the ever increasing level of business over the years, the spaceport buildings have been continuously rebuilt. Within the skeletal frames of the spaceport buildings are cantinas, spaceship repair and modification shops, small cargo companies and other businesses dedicated to the needs of spacers. These businesses are more expensive than in other sections of the city, but they are also more convenient than travelling around the city.

Since everyone who visits Celanon City must arrive via the spaceport, this section of the city is always a center of activity. In addition to the traffic of legitimate traders and crewmembers, petty criminals and smugglers comb the streets and alleyways of the district. The spaceport has all of the drawbacks of modern Imperial cities — overcrowding, overpriced goods, and crime. Visitors will also see a large number of Nalroni traders, guild inspectors, and security officers, along with regular Imperial patrols. While the Imperials are present only to keep order, the Nalroni encountered in this section are ever watchful to make sure that the trading guilds are awarded their "fair percentage" for the business that is transacted within city boundaries.

Money Buys Security

Characters visiting Celanon will be treated to the Nalroni way of life even before landing. Visitors landing in the city are asked their preference of facilities — "economy" or "trader" docking bays. Anyone with any experience in the sector will know enough to purchase trader bays.

A berth in an economy bay is 150 credits per local day (pricey by most standards), with standard maintenance and restocking costing about 150 percent of the cost of other spaceports (base fee is 15 credits; see the costs listed on page 30 of *Galaxy Guide 6: Tramp Freighters* for more information). Refueling costs are in-line with other spaceport locations, but the costs of repairs and overhauls are up to five times as expensive as normal (and highly variable, depending upon the model of ship, the local availability of parts and what the mechanic thinks of you).

The basic cost for a trader bay is 250 credits per local day, but maintenance and restocking is available at the standard cost (base fee is only 10 credits). However, trader bays offer something that the economy bays do not — security. Wealth and status can buy anything in Celanon, including the law, and it's well known that trader bays are relatively free of unannounced contraband inspections.

Upon landing in a trader bay, the owner or captain of the ship will be approached by an official Nalroni Trade Representative whose prime purpose is to extort bribes, er, "convince traders of the need to adequately prepare for the security hazards of a bustling trade city such as Celanon City." In other words, for anywhere from 100 to 1,000 credits (for a small tramp freighter, with costs rising proportionally for larger ships), the Trade Representative can assure the characters that no one will pay any attention to the "discrete actions of businessmen such as yourselves." Fees are set according to the number of visits the ship has made to the world (the fewer the number of visits, the higher the cost), whether or not the ship or crew are known to traffic illegal goods (if yes, the cost is much higher) and how much the Trade Representative believes he can convince the captain to pay.

Characters with ties on Celanon will be able to assure themselves freedom from spot inspections and thefts, as well as be able to find reliable mechanics who will do good work for affordable prices.

Celanon Spaceport Control has the unenviable job of making sure that the thousands of ships in orbit and arriving in the city are properly routed to avoid collisions and other incidents. The huge building, nearly 140 stories tall, is constantly abuzz with activity. In addition to traffic control, the planet's customs offices are also based in the building.

Diplomatic Section

This section is dominated by modern buildings of every architectural style. Planetary governments and large corporations have located their headquarters in this section of the city. It is within these large buildings that billions of credits are traded every day, as worlds seek a regular supplier of droids, blasters, food, computer goods or repulsor vehicles, while other planets try to sell off their goods at the highest price possible. This section is big business at its most influential.

The sights and sounds of this section are overwhelming — representatives of the corporations and planetary governments are always on the go and always trying to be the first, the best, and the most noticed. Fashion and attitude are taken to nearly obnoxious extremes, and there are constant social events for these young executives to show off themselves. Luxury airspeeders are the rule, and everyone is dressed in the latest styles from around the galaxy. Imperial troops keep a vigilant eye over these sections, always willing to interfere on behalf of "important people" should disputes arise. The street-level businesses are a conglomeration of shops, restaurants, clothing stores, luxury good shops and service industries geared directly for the well-to-do.

Characters will probably stand out in this section since few of them have the wealth to blend into the crowd and open displays of weaponry are considered rather rude. They are likely to be harassed by Imperial troops or Nalroni security forces.

Spacers' Section

The spacers' section is much like the spaceport section, but it is less expensive and a good deal more dangerous. The open air markets fill every street and alleyway, offering goods of questionable origin, from blasters to used starships. Other common businesses are small trade companies — they are contacted by other companies that need a cargo, no questions as to exactly what please, taken somewhere else, and soon. The trade company then finds a tramp freighter or bulk freighter to make sure that the cargo arrives safe and on-time, taking a healthy commission for their efforts.

Many companies are run or owned by the Nalroni, so deals are seldom generous or entirely upfront. Characters take their chances when securing cargos, but the money is there for those who know how to work the companies and the streets.

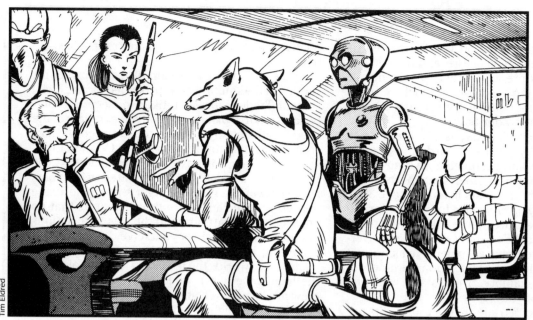

Tim Eldred

People looking for off-world transport, again, no questions asked, are known to frequent this section. Bounty hunters and hired guns are also common, and there are always strong backs willing to trade a few weeks labor for passage to other worlds.

Transient Residences

Celanon City has one of the most fluid populations in the galaxy, and all of those traders need someplace to rest their weary bones. Covering a good chunk of the eastern section of the city, these neighborhoods tend to be overcrowded and expensive. While they aren't dangerous in terms of street crime, they are excellent places to "disappear" from sight for a little while. As a consequence, criminals fleeing the law, Imperial draft dodgers, disgruntled corporate types and others with something to hide tend to end up in these neighborhoods.

Trade Consortiums and Guilds

The trade guilds of Celanon are where the true wealth and authority of the planet are to be found. No deals are accepted, no contracts honored, and no laws enforced or evaded, without a guild's approval. This is one of the few sections where the native Nalroni outnumber the aliens.

The trade guild buildings are sprawling, ornate complexes. Everything is garishly decorated with sculptures, holo-art, and treasures of every description. Luxury airspeeders are everywhere, and richly dressed Nalroni merchants, with assistants to attend to every desire, are constantly on the go.

Characters will seldom visit this section of the city unless under the guardianship of a corporate executive or asked to undertake a mission by the Nalroni (a rare privilege indeed).

Imperial Military Facilities

This is the most restricted section of the entire city. Within the confines of the five-meter tall walls, space-port facilities, troop barracks, ammo dumps, armories and administrative buildings keep Governor Sykar and the Empire firmly in control of the city (or so the Nalroni would have the Empire believe). Five full army battlegroups are stationed within the city at all times.

Market District

An area dedicated to the small trader and merchant, the market district is where small quantities of goods are sold to speculators and consumers. The goods can then be taken on to other worlds and sold at a profit. This section of the city is appropriate for finding illegally modified weapons, cargos of illegal spices, inexpensive droid replacement parts, vehicles and much more. Like the spacers' section, shady and dangerous people cluster in this section looking for profit, no matter how it is made. Undercover Imperial agents are known to frequent this section of the city, but Alliance cells are also common in this sector.

Corporate Zone

While the deals are cut in the diplomatic section, the rank and file workers of the corporations are to be found in this section of the city. The routing of goods is handled by the corporate offices in this sector, as are corporate intelligence networks. Smaller corporations have their headquarters in this section of the city since they can't afford the diplomatic sector. The area is relatively safe, with a moderate Imperial presence. Nalroni will be observing and directing trade everywhere, but it is an excellent section in which to find long-term freight contracts.

Governing Zone

Even the trade guilds need a bureaucracy to enforce their dictates. The governing zone is where all of the petty bureaucrats cluster, and where characters in trouble go to try and get out of trouble.

Of course, the Nalroni character lends itself to corruption and bribery. Individuals who have been particularly offensive are reported to some

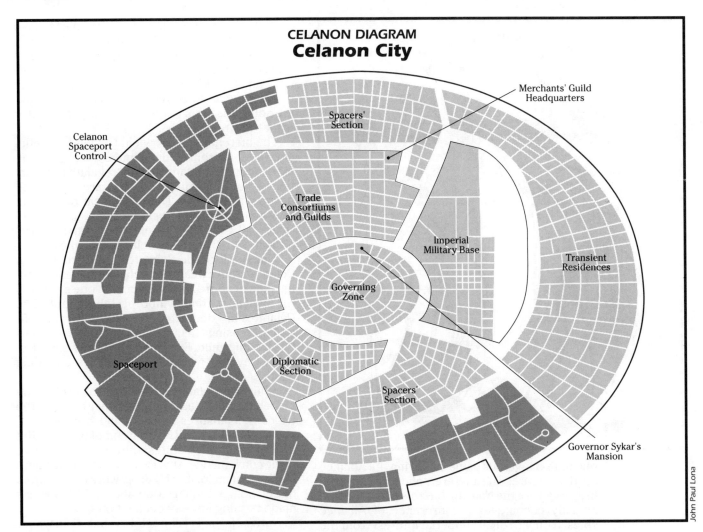

CELANON DIAGRAM
Celanon City

John Paul Lona

institution in this section, and the unfortunate victim has no choice but to watch the bureaucracy grind away until his name has been cleared.

The Gates

The Nalroni carefully regulate the passage of individuals within sectors of the city. The gates are where identification cards are checked, and are also an added source of revenue, since each individual must pay a set fee of two credits each time they pass through a gate. The Nalroni don't allow visitors to leave the city and venture to the countryside. Passage to the farms is only through the gates on the outer boundaries of the city.

An Agricultural World

The beautiful rolling plains and forests of Celanon are seldom seen by off-worlders, yet from this land comes grain, vegetables and meat to feed planets throughout the sector.

There are six main continents (Cekbar, Arradi, Holvi, Runnor, Jelldar and Desetur), providing ample living space and a wide range of climates

(indicated on the planetary map). Weather and temperature on the world is seasonally varied, with fierce storms occurring during seasonal changes. As the world has become more developed and the amount of available forest land has shrunk, many animal populations have dwindled.

Orbital Fleets

The upper atmosphere and low orbit of Celanon is one of the busiest trading areas in the sector. All manner of bulk transports and container vessels constantly circle the world, while representatives from the ship's company try to make a profitable deal. All of this takes place under the watchful eye of the Imperial Navy and the Nalroni planetary patrol. Due to the inordinate amount of traffic around the world, visitors often have to wait several hours before they can be cleared for a flight path to the world.

A Dangerous Doublecross

Just as the Nalroni way of life has always been to keep every option open, so the Nalroni are

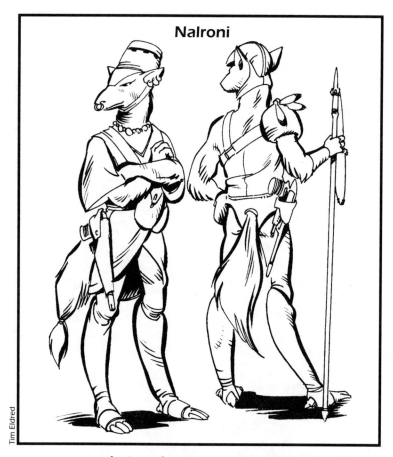

Nalroni

Tim Eldred

graceful in motion. These clever aliens have turned their predatory instincts towards the art of trading and negotiation ("I'm not like the other Nalroni. My side is your side. Trust me."). They have an almost instinctive understanding of the psychology and behavior of other species, and are able to use this to great advantage no matter what the situation.

The merchant guilds wield tremendous influence over Nalroni society, and control the planetary government and strictly regulate the number of Nalroni youngsters who are allowed to become merchants. There is a clear distinction between the urban residents of Celanon City (who call themselves Celanites) and the rural Nalroni who live in large clans and tribes.

Almost all of the Celanites are merchants. A Celanite trader wears the richest robes and clothing he can afford. In their society, one's dress is the most important symbol of status and station. Celanites are dedicated to making a large profit and increasing their status within their respective trading guild. Family and tribal ties are effectively severed when a youth enters a trading guild.

While the Celanites have firm control of the planet, they also distribute the wealth among the tribes. This insures their continued popularity, and while many rural Nalroni complain about the excesses of the Celanites, they are appreciative of the conveniences that their wealth has brought.

The vast majority of Nalroni work on the farms of Celanon. Mechanization and droid labor has made farming an easy occupation.

Native Nalroni architecture is based on wood, clay, and grass, with natural clay pottery and earthenware for dining. With the arrival of the Empire and the new technology, the Nalroni now prefer to live in prefabricated housing units supplied by Imperial merchants, which they then modify and decorate in the old ways.

playing a dangerous game in playing the Alliance off the Empire. The Empire believes it has the firm loyalty of the Nalroni, but this proud people actually encourages the presence of Alliance spies, if only to divert Imperial interest from the huge amount of money the Nalroni are acquiring from their bribes and tariffs. The Alliance regards the Nalroni as useful, but knows that they are not to be trusted. It is not an over-exaggeration to say that virtually everyone in the city of Celanon is a spy (the Nalroni call this double-dealing "being in the hunt"). While the Nalroni do hand the occasional Rebel smuggling ship or spy over to the Imperials (always making sure the blame is squarely placed on someone else's shoulders), it is in their best interest to keep such unpleasantness to a minimum. The Nalroni aren't sure which side will ultimately win the war, and aren't willing to risk being wrong.

Nalroni

The Nalroni are golden-furred humanoids with long, tapered snouts and extremely sharp teeth. They have slender builds, and are elegant and

Nalroni

Attribute Dice: 12D
Attribute Minimum/Maximums:
DEXTERITY 1D/3D+2
KNOWLEDGE 1D+2/4D+2
MECHANICAL 1D/4D
PERCEPTION 2D/4D+2
STRENGTH 1D+2/4D
TECHNICAL 1D/3D+2
Move: 9/12
Size: 1.5-1.8 meters tall

Essowyn

Essowyn

Type: Cratered plains terrestrial
Temperature: Temperate
Atmosphere: Type I (breathable)
Hydrosphere: Dry
Gravity: Standard
Terrain: Cratered plains, cratered low hills
Length of Day: 39 standard hours
Length of Year: 401 local days
Sapient Species: Humans, Saurton (N), Sullustans, Verpine
Starport: 1 standard class
Population: 80 million
Planet Function: Homeworld, mining
Government: Elitist council
Tech Level: Feudal
Major Exports: Metals, minerals, foodstuffs
Major Imports: Foodstuffs, high technology, medicinal goods, spices, herbs
System: Saurton
Star: Saurton (yellow)
Orbital Bodies:

Name	Planet Type	Moons
Kanawyn Belt	asteroid belt	0
Essowyn	cratered plains terrestrial	4
Greawyn Belt	asteroid belt	0

World Summary

The Saurton system is remarkable for its twin asteroid belts, rich with minerals and metals, and its lone world, Essowyn.

Several large mining corporations have facilities located in and near the asteroid belts. The companies are very protective of their claims, and unauthorized travel into the belts is strongly discouraged, although many free-traders visit the mining installations to sell their wares to the miners and their families.

Sandwiched between these two belts is Essowyn, a valuable but battered world that is home to the Saurton, a sturdy species of hunters and miners. The world has become a base of operations for many mining companies, exporting metals and minerals to manufacturing systems throughout the Trax sector. The world is constantly pelted by the debris of the asteroid belts. The civilization is entirely subterranean.

The surface is a combination of plains, mountains and meteorite-created craters. Roaming these

---

System Datafile

Saurton system, star: Saurton, yellow star. One planet, Essowyn, in "second orbit," with two thick asteroid belts in "first" and "third" orbits.

From Platt Okeefe, freelance smuggler:

"Going to Essowyn? Good luck! Essowyn is a revolution waiting to happen. The Saurtons are hardly a homogeneous group, and with the Empire and the mining megacorps jumping into the middle of the fray, tempers are high. This place is going to be a hot spot sooner or later ... and you won't want to be anywhere nearby when the shooting starts. Besides, all the cities are underground — because of continuous asteroid strikes — and filthy, disease-ridden places to boot. In short, just don't go there."

---

plains are huge herds of hoska, great herbivores that are an important source of food on this world.

The System

The Saurton system has two asteroid belts, one inside and one outside of the orbit of its only planet-sized body, Essowyn.

The asteroid belts are rich in ferrous metals, but the system is so far from the major trade routes that only six of the major mining consortiums can afford the cost of operations in the system. Because the companies are fierce competitors, the Empire keeps a close watch over all activities in this system, but allows the companies to vigorously protect their claims: virtually any ship that enters a claimed portion of the asteroid belts will find itself facing a great deal of hostile weaponry.

Each company has at least one space station, and normally several smaller bases on individual asteroids. Container ships visit the system on a regular basis, and several free-traders have been granted permits to sell consumer goods and

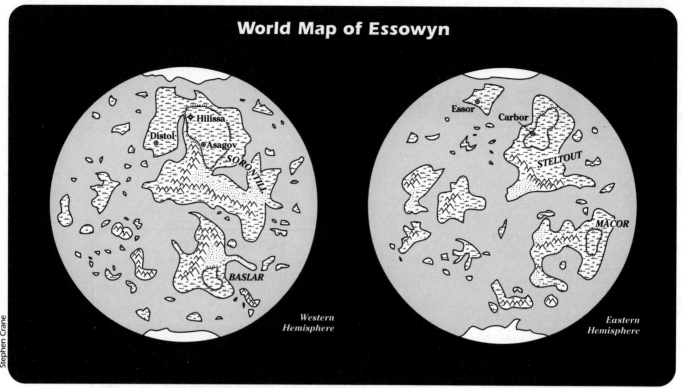

World Map of Essowyn

Hilissa

Distol

Asagov

SORONITII

BASLAR

*Western
Hemisphere*

Essor

Carbor

STELTOUT

MACOR

*Eastern
Hemisphere*

Stephen Crane

other personal wares to company employees. The companies and the Empire have agreed to restrict system access to those with sales permits, so Essowyn is visited only by free-traders who have extra goods for sale.

Essowyn has also been a site for new settlements as the mining companies have developed their interests below the scarred surface of the world. The native Saurton have benefitted from the investment of so many offworlders, and despite the grim nature of the work (and the society as a whole), it is a bustling world with great economic wealth.

Essowyn

Essowyn's many islands and continents are covered with mountains and grasslands. Some forest areas can be found in the mountain areas, but the constant grazing of the hoska herds prevents any but the most meager tree and bush growth on the plains. The world's entire surface is pockmarked with craters from the many meteorites which constantly pelt the planet. Despite a pleasant climate and ample water, the barrage of debris makes the surface almost uninhabitable, requiring all permanent structures to be underground.

Essowyn's atmosphere is turbulent, due in large part to the temperature fluctuations caused by the world's slightly erratic orbit. The four orbiting moons (really little more than captured asteroids) influence the oceanic tides, creating an environment prone to violent storms. These storms rage across the mountains and plains, spooking hoska herds into stampeding. Most of the storms form in the warmer equatorial zones and career wildly across the planet, meandering towards the polar regions of the world, where they dissipate.

Saurton Cities

The underground Saurton cities are dangerous, overcrowded and a health hazard to all but the Saurton. Most cities were established thousands of years ago, and grew out of deep warrens that had existed for many more centuries before then. Huge, multi-layered tunnels are hollowed out of the ground, with massive support beams. Individual rooms and groups of rooms are also hollowed out of the ground. Massive air ducts and water shafts bring fresh air and moisture down into the cities, and each city has a series of connecting tunnels the reach to the surface. Most of the cities are a minimum of 100 meters deep, and are far enough from the surface to sustain only minimal damage from meteorite impacts. With the advent of starship travel, many cities have constructed expansion shafts large enough to accommodate freighters and shuttles, although the majority of visiting ships head to the corporate complexes.

These cities are breeding grounds for many dangerous strains of bacteria because of the squalor and filth that the Saurton are willing to live in. While the bacteria present no threat to the

Saurton, Humans and aliens must be extremely careful in these cities lest they contract a contagious disease (most corporate complexes have decontamination booths which everyone must enter when they return to the complex).

Visitors to the cities will feel the tension of the imminent political showdown the Saurton people are headed toward. Traders do everything in their power to avoid travelling to the cities, instead preferring to deal with Saurton only at mining facilities.

War on the Horizon

Because of the high population density and the warlike tendencies of the Saurton, there has arisen a seemingly irreconcilable conflict between two groups of people: the Quenno (back-to-tradition) and the Des'mar (forward-looking). The planet is on the brink of civil war.

The Quenno have long sought to return Essowyn to the Saurton, and forcibly remove the mining corporations. Since most of the wealth earned for Essowyn is given only to the Council of Elders and not spread to the average citizen, the high poverty level has bred distrust and resentment. Many hunters and craftsmen belong to the Quenno movement and various splinter groups.

The Des'mar are a minority, but they also have the influence of wealth and the full backing of the mining companies. They believe that Essowyn must remain as it is, with the mining companies and continued trade with the rest of the galaxy. Supporters of this movement believe that the people who want to return to the traditional ways are lazy and stupid and should be squashed like grasses under a meteorite. Most mining executives and Council of Elders members are part of this group.

There are several smaller groups with more moderate views, but they are also hungry for power. Mixed into this conflict is traditional nationalism — many people of the once free nations, even centuries after being conquered, believe that the ruling government is too weak to stop a revolution.

All of these factors make the cities very tense places. With so many factions gaining power, and with the tendency of the Saurton to fight over anything, many skirmishes have broken out over the past few years. These skirmishes have even spilled over into the mines, such as the Kussoh Incident, in which a manager called a miner a "lazy coward." The ensuing battle resulted in 15 deaths before the company's security forces could intervene.

Many of the groups are secretly acquiring blasters, explosives and other weapons, and most people believe that warfare will occur within the next year. The mining companies are desper- ately trying to squash the Quenno-sympathetic groups, but they have had little success. The companies have an open bounty on anyone caught supplying weapons to Quennos.

Government and History

When Messert Mines Corporation first stumbled onto the world, the Saurton were organized into several large and constantly warring nations. The company approached the largest nation, Tresycht, and purchased the rights to begin mining in the Thergum Pits. Knowing full well that the area was in dispute with another nation, Messert moved in its equipment and several squads of security forces. With the help of Tresycht warriors, the other nation, Yiszte, was subjugated within a few weeks. Soon, all of the other nations fell under the control of Tresycht, as the nation was armed with modern weaponry and given complete training in combat tactics. Within four years the entire planet was under the control of the Tresycht High Priest, Gellack.

As Gellack tried to establish a government sophisticated enough to control an uncooperative people, he started empowering high priests of the defeated tribes. After several centuries, this simple system has evolved into a form of government that has been able to hold power despite repeated coup attempts. Now, Gellack's ancestors and the ancestors of the other high priests sit on the Council of Elders. The council is responsible for choosing the 35 Saurton citizens (normally wealthy traders or mining executives) who form the *trashur*, or government. The trashur is empowered until a majority of the members die (vacated seats are left unfilled until a new trashur is chosen). This had made for a very inflexible, unresponsive and despotic form of government, which despite its disadvantages, has been able to prevent full-scale warfare amongst the Saurton. However, it has encouraged the development of highly fragmented and often violent factions. The current government is in great peril because the world is teetering on the brink of civil war, yet because of the conflicts within the Council itself, nothing is being done to prevent violence.

The dictates of the Council of Elders are carried out by the Protectors, a combination judge/ policeman/soldier. They are given absolute authority over law enforcement and punishment within given cities, and they are generally aggressive bullies.

Mining Companies

Mining companies establishing operations on Essowyn are granted charters for a set number of years and are given absolute authority over a

Tim Eldred

particular territory, called a Corporate Complex. In return for absolute autonomy, the Council of Elders receives a large percentage of the profit.

The mines produce large quantities of quadrillium and other metals used in starships, vehicles and heavy equipment.

Within the Corporate Complexes, Saurton are allowed to use traditional law and custom (such as beating their fellow Saurton who are lazy), although they must respect company laws when dealing with other species.

The corporations provide complete quarters and facilities for the miners so that they never have to venture into Saurton cities (although many do for the express purpose of causing trouble with the locals). Independent traders can secure permits to bring goods into the complexes.

Many of the operations are run by Saurton who have worked their way up the corporate ladder. This has been most beneficial for the companies since few Saurton will take orders from another species. The Saurton find the other species, particularly the Sullustans, to be weak-willed and lacking motivation.

The mines are dangerous, and quite cramped, with little ventilation and light. Droids do much of the heavy lifting. Boring many thousands of meters into the crust of the planet, cave-ins are common even with the advanced technology employed, and it is not unusual for a whole shaft to cave-in. The pay, however, is excellent so there is never a lack of workers.

The Surface Herds

Hoska

Hoska are immense herd creatures that seem content to mindlessly graze the plains of Essowyn. They gather in herds numbering in the thousands, and when spooked can trample anything that is in their path.

They are huge, hoofed quadrapeds standing nearly three meters at the shoulder and capable of running at speeds of up to 15 kilometers per hour. They are predominantly black, but combinations of brown, tan, yellow, pale red and even white can be found among the hoska population. Each of these huge creatures has a set sharp horns which are used to spear anything that gets in their way.

The hoska herds migrate and stampede across the plains, eating and trampling everything in their path. Few other life-forms have been able to survive in this environment, aside from the Saurton, terecons and a few small, burrowing herbivores.

These animals aren't very intelligent, and will not avoid hazards or dangers, so even if several dozen members of a herd are killed, the survivors will mindlessly continue on. They are also easily frightened. As soon as one creature has been spooked and begins running away, the rest of the herd follows, creating an unstoppable force that sweeps across the plains. Lightning, meteorite impacts, the scent of terecons or a blaster shot are all sufficient to stampede a herd. Hoska are a prime food source for the Saurton.

◼ Hoska
Type: Large grazing herd beast
DEXTERITY 3D
PERCEPTION 1D
STRENGTH 3D
Special Abilities:
Horns: STR+1D damage
Trample Attack: STR+1D+2 damage
Move: 5
Size: Up to 2.7 meters tall at the shoulder
Scale: Creature
Orneriness: 4D

Terecon

The natural enemy of the hoska are the reptilian terecons. These large animals have short, powerful legs. Standing barely a meter tall, these four limbed creatures are found in groups of a least a dozen and can strike out at a hoska herd with amazing swiftness. They are burrowers and bury themselves in the ground while lying in wait for a hoska herd to pass by (they can wait for months between meals). Watching a group of terecons leap from the ground with no warning is an amazing, if horrifying, sight. The mere scent of a terecon can cause entire hoska herds to stampede, a fact which Saurton hunters use to great advantage. Terecons will seldom attack Humans, Saurton or other species unless they happen to be caught in the middle of an attack on a herd of hoska.

■ Terecon

Type: Hunting reptile
DEXTERITY 3D+2
PERCEPTION 2D
STRENGTH 2D
Special Abilities:
Armor: +3D to *Strength* (physical and energy)
Bite: STR+5D damage
Move: 22
Size: 1 meter tall, up to 8 meters long
Scale: Creature

Saurton

The Saurton are thin, golden-skinned, bipedal reptiles. Tall, strong and quick, they possess great stamina and a fierce hunting instinct. They are warm-blooded, and can survive in cool weather, but also lay eggs. They are aggressive and combative, and generally not well-liked by other species. The Saurtons' advanced immune system allows them to avoid the diseases and infections that plague other species. Because of this, the Saurton can reside in unsanitary conditions with no adverse affects, and they are often carriers of diseases.

Due to the continual meteorite impacts upon the surface of the world, these people have developed an entirely subterranean culture. With the abundance of metals, they also developed advanced technology. They had developed radiowave transmission devices, projectile weapons and advanced manufacturing machinery before their discovery by a mining expedition several centuries ago.

Saurton society revolves around immediate family. Children are given a general education from birth until their 12th year, at which time they choose a career and begin intensive training at one of the career academies (unless they choose to become a hunter, at which time they are chosen by a hunting company and receive training in the field). Saurton normally choose their mates from within the same occupation, and normally raise anywhere from eight to a dozen children.

The most prestigious career is that of mining executive because that is the job responsible for producing the most wealth for the planet. These executives receive excessively large salaries and have no lack of luxury goods. The only way to become an executive is to start as a common miner and work one's way up. Other common careers include hunters (a moderate-prestige job), educators (a low-prestige job), craftsmen (a low-prestige job) and traders (a high-prestige job). The Council of Elders strictly regulates the number of openings in each career field to insure that there are always enough workers in a given job.

Saurton

Tim Eldred

Saurton society has no tolerance of failure. Workers are expected to work hard and be responsible. Workers who fail at their jobs are often beaten and sometimes killed by their coworkers and managers. Because Saurton society is so strictly regulated, many fields offer little opportunity for advancement, resulting in even more aggression on the part of the average citizen (Saurton cities are notoriously violent and dangerous).

■ Saurton

Attribute Dice: 12D
Attribute Minimum/Maximums:
DEXTERITY 1D+2/4D
KNOWLEDGE 1D/4D
MECHANICAL 1D/2D+2
PERCEPTION 2D/4D
STRENGTH 1D+2/4D
TECHNICAL 1D/3D+2
Special Abilities:
Disease Resistance: Saurton are highly resistant to most known forms of disease (double their *stamina* skill when rolling to resist disease), yet are dangerous carriers of many diseases.
Story Factors:
Aggressive: The Saurton are known to be aggressive, pushy and eager to fight. They are not well liked by most other species.
Move: 6/10
Size: 1.75-1.9 meters tall

The Black Butcher

Craft: Modified Nova-drive #3-Z Light Freighter
Type: Modifier light freighter
Scale: Starfighter
Length: 28 meters
Skill: Space transports: 3-Z freighters
Crew: 1, gunners: 2
Crew Skill: See Vin Feal
Passengers: 10
Cargo Capacity: 150 metric tons
Consumables: 1 month
Cost: 48,500
Hyperdrive Multiplier: x2
Hyperdrive Backup: x15
Nav Computer: Yes
Maneuverability: 1D
Space: 4
Atmosphere: 280; 800 kmh
Hull: 5D
Shields: 1D+2
Sensors:
   Passive: 20/0D
   Scan: 30/1D
   Search: 40/1D+2
   Focus: 2/2D
Weapons:
   Dual Laser Cannons (fire-linked)
     Fire Arc: Front, right, back
     Crew: 1
     Skill: Starship gunnery
     Fire Control: 2D
     Space Range: 1-3/6/10
     Atmosphere Range: 100-300/600/1 km
     Damage: 6D
   Laser Cannon
     Fire Arc: Front, left, back
     Crew: 1 (can be remotely controlled from cockpit at fire control 0D)
     Skill: Starship gunnery
     Fire Control: 1D
     Space Range: 1-3/12/25
     Atmosphere Range: 100-300/1.2/2.5 km
     Damage: 3D

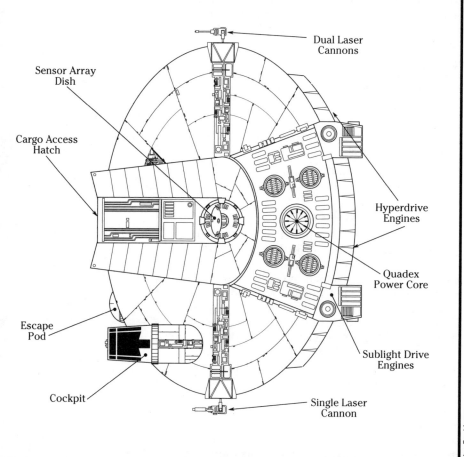

Sensor Array Dish

Cargo Access Hatch

Escape Pod

Cockpit

Dual Laser Cannons

Hyperdrive Engines

Quadex Power Core

Sublight Drive Engines

Single Laser Cannon

John Paul Lona

Adventure Idea

The characters are hired to bring a cargo of blasters to a Corporate Complex, with the understanding that they are for security forces. Upon arrival, they learn that their employer is actually a Quenno organization that is planning to take over a nearby city. Since the transfer is within a Corporate Complex, the characters must try to disguise the nature of the cargo or else they will be gunned down for arms smuggling. They then have a moral dilemma to solve for themselves: Do they want to get involved in the revolution? Should they try and reclaim the weapons so that they will not have to worry about having a bounty placed on their heads? Can they escape the Complex without being discovered? Will one of the Des'Mar groups discover what has happened and attempt to hunt down the characters themselves, or try to attack the Quenno first?

Adventure Idea

A Saurton hunter approaches the characters with a proposition. He would like the Rebels to stop a bunch of traders that have driven the hoska herds away from the city. If they can subdue the traders, he promises that he will be able to sway his

hunting company to join the Alliance's cause, which would help the Alliance acquire new weapons, and raw materials for starships (the company could buy the materials for the Rebellion and then discreetly ship it to a manufacturing world).

The following ship, *The Black Butcher*, can be used as the home base of the troublesome trader. The captain/owner of the ship, Vin Feal, can be used as a continuing villain, especially if the characters are in a tramp freighter campaign.

Feal is a thin Human with close cropped red hair and sidelocks. He wears a bright red matching blast vest and cloak.

Vin Feal. *Dexterity 2D+2, blaster 4D+2, blaster artillery 5D, dodge 4D, melee combat 3D+2, melee parry 3D+1, Knowledge 1D+2, alien species 2D, cultures 2D+1, languages 2D, planetary systems 2D+2, Mechanical 3D, astrogation 4D+2, repulsorlift operation 5D, space transports 6D+2, starship gunnery 6D, starship shields 4D, Perception 2D, con 4D, Strength 2D+1, Technical 2D+2, repulsorlift repair 3D+1, space transports repair 4D.* Move: 10. Character Points: 4. Heavy blaster pistol (5D), blaster rifle (5D), protective helmet (STR+1D physical, STR+1 energy), vibro-axe (STR+2D), cloak.

 # Garnib

Garnib

Type: Glacier covered terrestrial
Temperature: Cool
Atmosphere: Type I (breathable)
Hydrosphere: Saturated
Gravity: Standard
Terrain: Frigid oceans, glaciers, islands
Length of Day: 35 standard hours
Length of Year: 432 local days
Sapient Species: Balinaka (N), Humans, Kubaz, Vernols
Starport: 1 limited services
Population: 100 million
Planet Function: Homeworld, Garnib crystal production
Government: GCC corporate-controlled
Tech Level: Space
Major Exports: Garnib Crystals, fish
Major Imports: Low tech, mid tech, high tech, metals, minerals
System: Garnib
Star: Garnib (blue)
Orbital Bodies:

Name	Planet Type	Moons
Garnib	glacier covered terrestrial	0
Hultomo	ice world	2
Mastala	frigid rock planet	0
Coomputu	frigid rock planet	1

World Summary

The ice world of Garnib, home of the Balinaka species, is the only source of the addictive "Garnib crystals," known throughout the galaxy for their indescribable beauty. The world itself is very cold (by Human standards), with several continents covered by glaciers dozens of meters thick. The Balinaka have carved entire underground cities, called sewfes, with their settlements having a strange mixture of simple tools, ice sculptures and modern devices.

The world is also home to the *wallarand*, a festival lasting for 50 local days in the height of the "warm" summer season. The wallarand is the ultimate expression of the artistic, carefree spirit of the Balinaka people, who find art and joy in the constant struggle against nature.

The gregarious spirit of the Balinaka calls to the hearts of artists across the galaxy, and thousands have emigrated to the frigid world. Within the caves of ice, the artists find inspiration in the

System Datafile

Garnib system, star: Garnib, blue star. Four planets. Innermost planet, Garnib, is terrestrial.

From the Imperial Ministry of Tourism:

Garnib is the homeworld of the Balinaka people, as well as the only source of the famous Garnib crystals, famous for their mesmerizing (and almost addictive) beauty. Though technically an ice world, plentiful hot springs keep inhabited zones relatively comfortable. The planet is owned by Garnib Crystal Creations (GCC), a resident-controlled corporation. Aside from the stunning beauty of the landscapes, Garnib is famous for the *wallarand,* an annual week-long celebration for all residents of the world (tourists are welcome too!).

sculptures and nature itself, while they find a hard, but rewarding living manning the fishing fleets of the world or working in the Garnib crystal plants.

System Summary

Garnib is the only life sustaining planet of the four bodies orbiting the blue star of the same name. Hultomo, Mastala, and Coomputu are all dead, frozen hunks of rock and water. The distant orbits of all of the worlds keep them in a near perpetual state of twilight.

Were it not for the ingenuity of the Balinaka, Garnib would be an ignored and valueless world. However, the Balinakan love for sculpting ice and a chance discovery by Balinaka artists resulted in the fantastic and mesmerizing Garnib crystals. The planet is owned and run by Galactic Crystal Creations (GCC), an employee-owned corporation, so while it is a "corporate world," it is also a world where the people have absolute say over how the company, and thus their civilization, is managed.

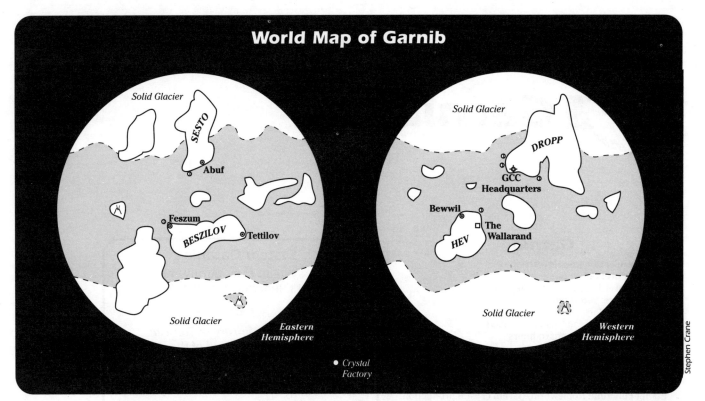

World Map of Garnib

Solid Glacier

SESTO

Abuf

Feszum

BESZILOV

Tettilov

Solid Glacier

Eastern
Hemisphere

Solid Glacier

DROPP

GCC
Headquarters

Bewwil

HEV

The
Wallarand

Solid Glacier

Western
Hemisphere

Stephen Crane

• Crystal
Factory

Over the decades, the crystals have enraptured (some say addicted) millions, with some people owning collections numbering in the thousands. The fame of the crystals and the Balinaka reputation as lovers of art helped make the world an attractive community for artists from all over the galaxy. Many artists arrive with only the clothes on their backs (hardly sufficient for the numbing cold of the glacier winds). Invariably a Balinaka family takes the artist into their home, providing heat, food and support, at least until they establish their own lives. Many of the most respected artists of the galaxy lived on Garnib at one time or another.

Garnib Crystals

Garnib crystals are the end result of a complex manufacturing process that deftly mixes art with science. The Balinaka have excellent vision and are able to see in a much wider spectrum than Humans. Their tradition of making personalized ice sculptures dates back thousands of years, and ever since the first sculpture was carved by the claws of these amphibious mammals, they were judged on the basis of sheer physical beauty and how the sculptures refracted light (of course, most Humans cannot see the slight light refraction variations that to the Balinaka make the difference between a crude sculpture and a true work of art).

The great sculptor Vornest Dep-thesel Digarsarg first incorporated colored pumice and small fragments of gemstones in one of his sculp-

tures, creating a sculpture he called "Crystal of the Stars." When he completed the sculpture and first brought it into the sunlight, he was amazed at the beauty of the light as it filtered through the gems and glass, and found it impossible to turn his eyes away from the remarkable light. One of his trader friends, a human named Abram Zavict, happened upon the scene and also felt the hypnotic effects of the sculpture. He immediately realized that similar sculptures could be sold on other planets for amazing profits, and such was the birth of Galactic Crystal Creations.

The crystal creation process has several steps, all of them requiring the meticulous attention of several skilled artisans. The crystals aren't mass produced, but instead are individualized works of art.

A Balinaka sculptor begins the process by carving the sculpture from a block of ice. The gemmaster polishes, smooths and carves intricate designs in the gems and glass, while the sculptor uses sonic smoothers to put the finishing touches on the sculpture.

The ice and gems are brought to one of the great crystal mills, where a thread master weaves fragments of the gems and glass into a molecular string, that is then sewn into the interior of the crystal. Simultaneously the sculptor and gemmaster set the full-sized gems directly into the crystal.

After several hours of labor, the inlaid crystal is placed in a sonic bath while the team of artisans inspects it for its artistic value and beauty. The final

Crystal Addiction

While Garnib crystals are beautiful and captivating, they represent an "addictive threat" to some. When placed in sunlight, the crystals seem to pulse with a pure white light. Beams of light, brilliant and constantly fluctuating in color, will periodically shoot from the crystal.

A very small number of people seem to become addicted to these crystals upon first viewing, and from that point on insist on purchasing as many different crystals as they can. It is theorized that they are merely overstimulated by the ocular effects of the crystals and develop a psychological need to have more and different experiences. Due to the extremely high cost of these crystals, these addictions are normally quite self-destructive.

The reaction is disturbing enough that several planets have banned the crystals, making them a valuable black market commodity. The Balinaka are greatly upset that something intended to be so beautiful instead has made life so ugly for some, and thus they have an open door policy for anyone suffering from "crystal addiction." If an addicted person can get to Garnib, a family will take the person in, utilizing advanced therapy techniques to help them get over the addiction.

product is sold to GCC, which in turn sells the crystals to tramp freighters and companies (at a tremendous markup) for distribution around the galaxy.

The Crystal Factories

The crystal factories of GCC are small, graceful buildings designed by the greatest Balinaka sculptors. A mixture of sharp angles, graceful sweeping curves and fluid motorized sculptures, they are truly an unusual sight. Each factory is modular, so that rooms and entire sections can be removed and replaced (this is done so that the artists, gemmasters and thread masters can make for themselves the most comfortable and appealing work space possible). Within each factory are a series of rooms called crystal mills, which house the sonic baths for the final shaping of the crystals.

The interior of each room, from crystal mill, to the working studios, to the packaging rooms, to executive offices, are decorated and designed by the user, making each room unique in character.

The factories are positioned near active volcanoes or fissures in the ocean floor. The factory turbines utilize geothermal energy, providing power to every room. All excess energy is freely given to nearby Balinaka communities (in fact, most communities, called *sewfes*, receive their power from the factory turbines).

A Beautiful World

The stark landscape of Garnib is beautiful in its stark brutality. Great glaciers form huge artificial islands and deep valleys, as their bulk grinds and reforms the land below. A great sea of solid white creates a constant blinding glare, with the ice only ended by the vast oceans and the rare volcanic islands.

Few creatures make their homes on the surface of the planet, the Balinaka people being the most prominent. Of the few creatures that do survive, most are amphibious and survive by eating fish or aquatic plants.

The Balinaka make every effort to convey to visitors the harsh realities of Garnib's wilderness — being caught out in the cold typically ends not with rescue, but death.

The Great Caves

The Balinaka make their homes in great ice caverns that they carve themselves. Since each cave is custom built, there is a great variety in style, layout and facilities. The Balinaka are very social creatures, and each home is centered around a common room, which is a workplace, casual lounge, kitchen and recreation area. Most of a family's modern appliances, such as computers, holovid monitors, and sonicooks, will be found in the common room. Each adult family member has a small cubicle for privacy, while children and infants share a common room.

Each cave, aside from the artistic structure of the cave itself, is decorated with ice sculptures, holosculptures, rugs, custom built furniture and other items to reflect the personality of the family.

Artist Communities

There are several artist communities of aliens that have sprung up within Balinaka sewfes. Their caves and lifestyles closely mimic the Balinaka, with a common room and only small cubicles for privacy. Each member has certain, regularly scheduled duties, such as cleaning or cooking. Still, even after a day's work (typically working in a crystal factory or on a fishing ship), most artists have several hours at their disposal for sculpture, song, or writing. These communities are generally not as harmonious as the Balinaka dens, but they are nonetheless close-knit.

Tim Eldred

Fishing Ships

The Balinaka, due to their amphibious nature, have located most of their settlements near the shores of the great oceans. The fishing ships, also owned by GCC, are based in the massive harbors of Garnib and go out every morning to troll the oceans of the world. The work is back breaking (even with most of the work being done by droids), but the pay is high. Many Balinaka are fishermen (regarding fishing as an art form of its own), and many of the artists who have traveled to this world find employment in this industry.

Settlements

All Balinaka families live in one of the sewfes. Being the social creatures that they are, each community has a large open area, called a *heswe*, that serves as a meeting area, playground, market and religious center. Messages to the whole community are posted here, and whenever there is a celebration, artists donate ice sculptures, while lights and holoflashers are placed. Fireworks, live music, dancing, feasts and costume parties are integral parts of many community events.

The Wallarand

Scheduled for the height of the summer season, the *wallarand* is a once a year event that is a combination town meeting, stock holders meeting, party and feast rolled up into one. GCC headquarters selects the sight of the wallarand, and then each community sends one artist to help carve the buildings and sculptures for the temporary city that will host the event. Work begins with the arrival of winter, as huge halls for meetings, temporary residences, and market place booths are carved out of the ice.

As the wallarand nears, all work on the planet ceases, as communities are allowed to begin preparations for the long trek to the city site. Every resident of Garnib, from Balinaka to immigrants, is invited (or more properly, expected) to attend. Over the next four days, friendships are renewed, deals are made, romances blossom. It is a time of constant festivals and parties.

Of course, there is a purpose in it all (aside from fun, which is more than enough of a reason to the Balinaka). Each community selects a spokesman to represent them to other communities and corporate officers. Fishing territories are redrawn, quotas for ice sculpture production are set, and any other differences or needs are discussed and debated (most issues are resolved by the end of the wallarand). At the end of these meetings, every citizen (who is also an employee and stockholder for GCC) is presented with a complete accounting of the financial status of GCC. The citizens then select new corporate officials and vote on what new projects and investments they feel the company should undertake.

The wallarand is where the Balinaka are most painfully reminded that they are Imperial subjects. The Empire seldom interferes with the Balinaka because the corporate officers arrange appropriate income percentages for the Imperial governor.

However, Imperial troops are constantly seen patrolling the grounds of the wellarand, which is a source of tension, anxiety and resentment. It is amazing that open conflict has not erupted between the agreeable but fiercely independent Balinaka and the Imperial officials.

The Imperial Presence

Imperial Governor Verus Carbinol is responsible for law and order on the world of Garnib. He hates cold. He hates ice. He hates the endlessly cheerful attitude of the Balinaka. And, most of all, he hates his life.

Both middle-aged and at what he feels should be the prime of his career, he realizes that this planet is the end of the line for him. However, his world is also quiet enough that he has no overwhelming worries or meddlesome trouble spots; he can just sit back and wait for the money to come into his coffers.

Carbinol is reclusive and seldom leaves his mansion, a gaudy 47-room affair that stands on the coast of the ocean. He will seldom be encountered by the Balinaka or anyone else on the planet.

The only Imperial base, Garnib Station, has a modest three battalions, and is located next to his mansion. However, because the Balinaka are decidedly agreeable and consistently pay their taxes with no complaints, there is virtually no need for them to patrol communities. The troops are dispatched to the wallarand so that Carbinol can assert his authority. Therefore, while being stationed on Garnib is a generally chilly and cheerless experience, it is also an extremely safe and inactive post.

Balinaka

The Balinaka are strong amphibious mammals native to Garnib. Evolved in an arctic climate, they are covered with thick fur, but they also have a dual lung/gill system so they can breathe air or water. They have webbing between each digit, as well as a long, flexible tail. Their diet consists mostly of fish.

Balinaka have very sensitive eyes, being able to see in a visual spectrum far exceeding Human vision. In addition to a high degree of color sensitivity, they have a series of membranes that help them filter and control how they perceive light — a Balinaka can look at a sculpture directly in front of a blinding light and can adjust his perception so that he sees only the sculpture.

The Balinaka are individualistic, but very close to their families and larger community. They are an agreeable people as long as they know that the other people involved are also willing to agree or compromise. They often refuse to debate issues

Balinaka

Tim Eldred

with individuals who are stubborn, selfish or unwilling to see a different point of view. They have gone along with the Empire simply because they realize that fighting is a losing proposition, although they would be willing to fight for freedom as soon as they saw that there was a good chance of winning.

While these people are fun and easy-going, they can be deadly fighters in combat. Their sharp claws can do great damage to those careless enough to anger a Balinaka. They are a playful people, always looking forward to the next celebration. They enjoy dancing, singing, light shows, plays, sculpting and many other forms of relaxation. They are inquisitive and curious — eager to learn new technology and to master new devices.

■ Balinaka
Attribute Dice: 12D
Attribute Minimum/Maximums:
DEXTERITY 1D+2/4D
KNOWLEDGE 1D/3D+1
MECHANICAL 1D+2/3D+2
PERCEPTION 2D/4D
STRENGTH 3D/5D
TECHNICAL 1D/2D+1
Special Abilities:
Vision: Balinaka have excellent vision and can see in darkness with no penalties.
Water Breathing: Balainaka have a dual lung/gill system, so they can breathe both air and water with no difficulties.

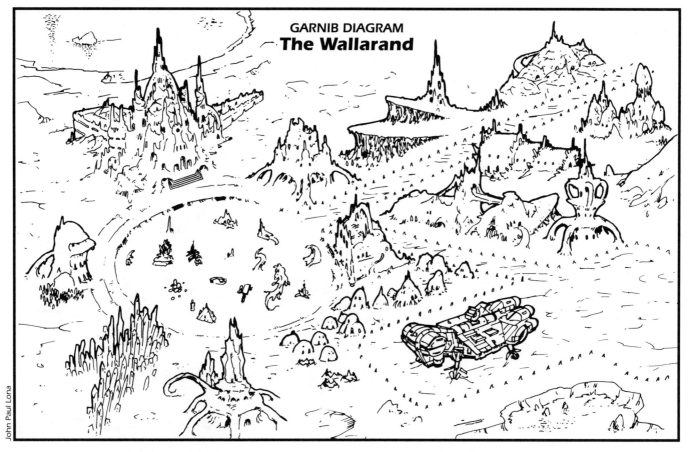

GARNIB DIAGRAM
The Wallarand

John Paul Lona

Claws: Do STR+1D damage.
Move: 12/15
Size: Up to 4 meters tall at the shoulder

Vernols

The Vernols are squat humanoids who have emigrated to Garnib in great numbers. Physically, they stand up to 1.5 meters tall, with blue skin; they have orange highlights around their eyes, mouth and on the underside of their palms and feet. Many of them have come to Garnib simply to become part of what they feel is a safe and secure society (much of their native society was destroyed when a meteor collided with their homeworld five decades ago).

They are natural foragers, adept at finding food, water and other things of importance. Many of them have become skilled investigators on other planets. Others have become wealthy con artists since they have a cheerful, skittish demeanor that lulls strangers into a sense of security.

They are fearful and territorial, but extremely loyal to those who have proven their friendship. Vernols are quite diverse and can be found in many occupations on many worlds. Garnib is the only world where they are known to live in large Vernol communities.

■ Vernols

Attribute Dice: 12D
Attribute Minimum/Maximums:
DEXTERITY 1D/2D+2
KNOWLEDGE 1D/4D
MECHANICAL 1D/3D+1
PERCEPTION 2D/4D+2
STRENGTH 1D/2D+2
TECHNICAL 1D/3D
Special Abilities:
Foragers: Vernols are excellent foragers (many have translated this ability to an aptitude in investigation). They receive a +1D bonus to either *survival, investigation* or *search* (player chooses which skill is affected at the time of character creation).
Move: 8/10
Size: Up to 1.5 meters tall

Adventure Idea

Two Rebel agents on the run from Imperial authorities need assistance getting to Garnib, which would be an excellent place to hide. Everything seems to be working to plan, until the Imperial troops decide that the characters' ship would be a good place to begin spot checking for smuggling. It becomes imperative that the characters somehow convince the Imperials that "these are not the agents you're looking for," or find some means to avoid the inspection entirely.

Adventure Idea

The characters are hired to take a partial cargo of Garnib crystals to the planet Zarsteck. During their stopover on Garnib, an artist suggests that GCC may be willing to offer them a long-term contract (which would mean big profits), however, nothing could be agreed on until the new corporate officers are selected at the wallarand. Unfortunately for the characters, some long-term rivals (such as bounty hunters, a competing freighter, or disgruntled pirates) have followed them to Garnib and want to kill them. The characters must dodge the villains for several days while waiting for the wallarand to begin.

Gorsh

Gorsh

Type: Warm swamp planet
Temperature: Hot
Atmosphere: Type II (breath mask suggested)
Hydrosphere: Moist
Gravity: Heavy
Terrain: Ocean, swampy islands
Length of Day: 64 standard hours
Length of Year: 300 local days
Sapient Species: Humans, Orgons (N)
Starport: 1 limited services (Genetech corporate controlled)
Population: 100,000
Planet Function: Homeworld, biological research
Government: Genetech (corporate-controlled)
Tech Level: Stone/feudal
Major Exports: Medicinal and chemical compounds
System: Gorsh
Star: Gorsh (yellow)
Orbital Bodies:

Name	Planet Type	Moons
Gorta	desolate searing rock	0
Gorlan	searing desert	1
Gorth	warm swamp planet	1
Gartana	poisonous ocean	12
Garsala	corrosive volcanic rock	2
Gortamni	frigid ice	0

World Summary

Gorsh is an obscure system, located in an undeveloped section of the Outer Rim Territories. The world of prime interest, also named Gorsh, is dominated by huge, but shallow salt water oceans. Several chains of volcanic and swamp islands dot the surface. These swamps are home to many kinds of life-forms, including the mysterious sentient plants called Orgons.

Genetech Laboratories has exclusive rights to develop and explore the planet Gorsh, and has established an orbiting research lab. The world has yielded many unique compounds that have been turned into successful pharmaceutical and medicinal products. The company has discovered the Orgons, and has placed a high priority on capture and examination of the creatures, with the ultimate goal of seeing if the plant creatures can be used for scientific research. Only authorized Imperial personnel and Genetech representatives may enter the system.

System Datafile

Gorsh system, star: Gorsh, yellow star. Six planets; third planet, Gorsh, is marginally terrestrial and is the site of an orbiting scientific research space station owned by Genetech Laboratories.

Warning! Gorsh is a privately-owned system. For permission to enter Gorsh system space, contact Genetech Laboratories corporate headquarters on Caprioril. Trespass into the Gorsh system is punishable by a fine of up to five million credits or up to 20 years in a standard Imperial prison camp.

System Summary

The Gorsh system lies in one of the most undeveloped regions of the Outer Rim Territories, well over 30 hours (at hyperdrive multiplier x1) from any settled systems. It was first discovered by an independent scout nearly a century ago, and merely logged as yet another nondescript system; the scout moved on to other systems looking for something that he could easily turn a profit on.

Gorsh is the only habitable world of the six planets orbiting the star Gorsh. Genetech Laboratories financed the first extensive explorations of the system and the Empire granted the company exclusive proprietary rights over everything within the system.

Genetech has a small orbiting research lab, lightly armed and with the bare minimum of supplies. However, the scientists stationed aboard this lab have been able to discover many valuable compounds that have been developed into useful pharmaceuticals and medicines.

Gorsh

Gorsh is a tropical world with a very high moisture content. Most of the surface is open ocean,

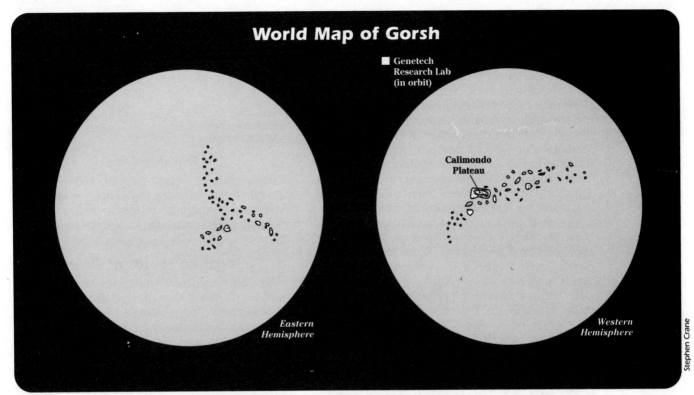

World Map of Gorsh

■ Genetech
Research Lab
(in orbit)

Calimondo
Plateau

*Eastern
Hemisphere*

*Western
Hemisphere*

Stephen Crane

with many large swampy islands. Temperature ranges from 25 to 40 degrees Celsius, with the cooler areas being over the open ocean. The swamps have a very high humidity level, making them muggy and generally unpleasant. Ocean depths average nearly six kilometers, but the maximum depth reaches nearly nine kilometers.

The Swamps

The swamp islands of Gorsh are dangerous and unstable. The islands were formed by the volcanic peaks, volcanic ash, aquatic plant life and sediment. The tallest of the volcanic peaks is only 268 meters above sea level, and the swamps extend away from the mountains for many square kilometers. The islands are crisscrossed by shallow waterways. Plant and animal life can be found throughout the islands.

Trekking through the swamps can be very hazardous. Without some device to measure the depth of water, it is impossible to tell whether or not open pools of water have land six centimeters or six meters beneath. Poisonous creatures, both plants and animals, abound, and many of them have natural camouflage so that they blend into the background until they are close enough to strike. Infectious diseases are spread by insects, sudden storms coming in from the ocean can strike without warning, and there is always the possibility of a dangerous volcanic eruption that can send molten lava, ash and toxic fumes into the air or cause a landslide that will bury anything caught in its path.

Insects and amphibians are the most common creatures. Because of the relatively constant climate, cold-blooded creatures have thrived in this environment. Most creatures have formidable natural defenses, such as venomous bites, large spikes or strong tails for swatting bothersome pests.

Even the plants are dangerous on Gorsh: the Gorshian hands of death is a large (6 meters

---

Gorsh's Atmosphere

Gorsh's high carbon dioxide atmosphere and heavy gravity hamper the activities of beings not native to high gravity worlds. Characters acting without breath masks suffer penalties for high levels of activity. To run for more than two consecutive turns, a character must make a Moderate *stamina* check. A character must make an Easy *stamina* check after every three rounds of fire combat to see if he is winded. A character must make a Moderate *stamina* check after every three rounds of melee or unarmed combat. Finally, for any lifting checks, increase the difficulty by one level. If a character fails any *stamina* checks, he is thoroughly winded and must rest for one minute or suffer a -3D penalty to all actions.

Characters with breath masks can act in the atmosphere of Gorsh with no fear of penalties.

across) carnivorous flowering plant that has crushed more than one careless research scientist. Berries, such as darkkoninns, have a poisonous juice.

Another danger of Gorsh comes from the nature of the land itself. The constantly decaying plant matter creates a huge amount of explosive methane. The methane normally builds in small pockets beneath the surface of the water. The methane compounds are undetectable in the fetid swamp air — unless there happens to be an open flame or a heat source nearby. Exploding pockets of methane have been known to consume an area up to 20 meters in diameter.

However, Genetech has found that where there is danger, there is profit. There are many amazing chemicals produced by the plants and animals of Gorsh that have been discovered by research teams, and they have been refined, developed, analyzed, and ultimately packaged into profitable drugs, medicines and consumer goods.

Flora and Fauna of Gorsh

What follows is a listing of the most dangerous, interesting and important animals and plants to be found on Gorsh. They can be used to spice up any adventure set in the dismal swamps of this world.

Thevaxan Marauder

Thevaxan marauders are large, long lizards, and are brown, black or drab green in color. Their tales make up nearly half their length. They are covered with smooth triangular scales, and a crest of small spikes runs from the tip of their elongated snout to the beginning of the tail. They have long, triangular heads with a large upper skull.

This creature is a solitary hunter, but characters may be unfortunate enough to discover a female's nest, which will have 1-4 eggs or young (about 2 meters long, with *Dexterity 1D, Perception +1, Strength 2D;* tail swipe only does STR+1D damage and teeth only do STR+1 damage). If not raising young, Thevaxan marauders have no nests or lairs and will always be hunting for a fresh meal. When they rest, they bury themselves in muck and water, exposing only their nostrils.

The Thevaxan marauder has many great survival advantages, but stealth isn't one of them. It can be heard plowing through the swamp from quite a distance; it relies on sheer strength to overpower whatever it encounters. The creature is dim-witted and easily tricked or confused.

■ Thevaxan Marauder
Type: Giant reptillian hunter
DEXTERITY 2D
PERCEPTION 1D
STRENGTH 5D

Brawling 5D+2
Special Abilities:
Tail Swipe: STR+2D damage
Teeth: STR+1D damage
Charge: STR damage, plus an extra +1D for every round charging (up to +3D)
Move: 15
Size: Up to 20 meters long, up to 8 meters tall at the shoulder
Scale: Creature
Orneriness: 7D

Darkkoninns

Darkoninns are black poisonous berries that can be found growing anywhere on Gorsh. A Moderate *survival* is necessary to realize they are probably poisonous; if eaten, they cause 6D damage.

Gorshian Hands of Death

The Gorshian hands of death is a flowering carniverous plant that ranges from three to six meters across. These plants are found only in the drier regions of the swamps (such as in the upper elevations and near volcanic peaks). They have spindly stalks that are decorated with five-petaled blue and purple flowers. Any individual who walks across one of the stalks must make a *brawling* or *Strength* check to escape the plant's crushing grasp (it has a *brawling* skill of 3D). If the character fails the check, he or she will be completely enclosed within the stalks and take damage from the crushing attack each round (4D damage); if characters attack the plant, it has a *Strength* of 4D.

Forntarch

Forntarch are dangerous and large carnivorous rodents that lie in trees waiting for a warm meal to pass by. While they typically dine on small reptiles, lizards and mammals, they do attack Humans as well. When a target passes by, they use their powerful legs to leap from the tree. Tumbling down at the unsuspecting victim, they attack with their forelimbs, which are giant razored appendages. Even if the first attack is not fatal, they often impale their victims with one limb, while swinging the other and biting the victim.

■ Forntarch
Type: Aggressive rodents
DEXTERITY 2D
PERCEPTION 3D
STRENGTH 2D
Special Abilities:
Slicers: STR+2D+2 damage
Teeth: STR+1D damage
Move: 4 (crawling), 17 (leaping)
Size: 3 meters long (body), 1-meter-long slicers
Scale: Creature

Tim Eldred

Tesfli Piercers

Tesfli piercers are flying swarm insects one to four centimeters long. Open flame and insects repellants scare them off and exposure to cold will kill them. They cannot bite through clothing, plastics or armor. Their bites cause no actual damage, but anyone bit must make a Very Easy *stamina* check or be infected by a "rotting disease." If a character becomes infected, within one week the infected limb will swell and turn black — if a character seeks medical attention, a Moderate *medicine* or Very Difficult *first aid* roll is necessary to determine the appropriate curative medicines. After two more weeks of untreated infection, increase *medicine* and *first aid* difficulties by one level, and treat the limb as being at -1D for all *Dexterity* and *Strength* actions. After another two weeks, increase the *medicine* and *first aid* difficulties by another level and consider the limb to be at -2D for all *Dexterity* and *Strength* actions. At the end of seven weeks of infection, the limb is totally useless and the infection has destroyed all of the nerve endings and the muscle tissue. This rotting disease can have disastrous (or fatal) effects when one considers how many times a character could be bit by a swarm of tesfli piercers.

Tesfli piercers. *Dexterity 2D, Perception 0D, Strength 0D.* Move: 8. Possible "rotting disease" as described above.

Swarm Bugs

Swarm bugs are blue insects with large ballooning bodies (due to a large internal methane bladder) and fragile, transparent wings. They grow up to 10 centimeters long. While swarm bugs almost never attack other creatures (they feed on plants), they are so numerous that they are a dangerous nuisance. Their unusual digestive tracts create a great deal of methane; if they are ever struck by a hard blow or subjected to high temperatures, they are quite likely to explode in a ball of flame. If they are struck by an object, roll 1D; on a 1 they explode. If exposed to open flame, roll 1D; on a 1–3 they explode. Unfortunately, swarm bugs tend to fly in tightly packed swarms, so if one bug explodes, most of the swarm will also go up in flames. This is an important defense mechanism — while individual (or whole swarms of) swarm bugs may be sacrificed, most other creatures on Gorsh have learned to give these insects a wide berth.

Swarm bugs. *Dexterity 1D, Perception 0D, Strength 0D.* Methane explosion does 2D damage to everyone within a 2 meter radius. Move: 12.

Research Teams

Genetech research teams venture down to the surface of Gorsh on a regular basis, with about one dozen scientists and a few armed guards for protection. The teams are equipped with survival gear, medicines, breath masks, weapons,

Orgons

Tim Eldred

specimen containers, chemical analyzers, pocket computers, biochem synthesizers and field gear to assist them in their efforts. Research teams spend up to two weeks on the planet's surface.

Remote probes are also sent down and can be controlled directly from the lab. If the probe finds anything of note, a followup team is sent to investigate.

In addition to the discovery of new chemicals, the Genetech researchers have recently discovered the Orgons and the company has placed a very high priority on the capture and dissection of one of these strange creatures. The company has kept this discovery quiet, fearing that the Empire or another corporation may decide to investigate their activities on Gorsh.

■ Typical Genetech Scientist

Type: Genetech Scientist
DEXTERITY 1D+1
KNOWLEDGE 3D
Alien species 3D+2, organic chemistry 5D, planetary systems 4D, survival 4D
MECHANICAL 2D
PERCEPTION 2D
STRENGTH 2D
TECHNICAL 1D+2
Character Points: Varies, typically 0-3
Move: 10

Genetech guards. All stats are 2D except: *blaster 3D+2, dodge 3D+2.* Move: 10. Blaster pistol (4D), comlink, datapad, medpac, breather mask, blast vest (+1D physical, +1 energy).

Genetech Orbiting Research Lab

The Genetech Orbiting Research Lab is the home base of the scientists stationed on Gorsh. Housing a total of 40 personnel, it is the only lifeline between this system and the rest of the civilized galaxy. Although cramped and spartan, the space lab and its personnel have been very successful in finding and developing new products for the company.

Orgons

Orgons are the dominant life form on Gorsh. These intelligent and mobile plants have two distinct sections of their bodies. The brain and vital organs are in a round, hardened shell, normally about half of a meter in diameter. The shell is a deep green or yellow color. Trailing away from the shell are anywhere from six to eight tendrils, up to four meters long (the number is dependent upon the age of the individual Orgon).

Each limb is used for mobility as well as absorption of vital nutrients. The limbs are soft and flexible, but incredibly strong, through use of alternating hard armored cells (which provide protection), and cells that perform the same function as muscles in animals. By constricting or loosening these soft cells, the creatures can drag themselves through the swamps or use tools. In order to absorb nutrients, the limbs must be burrowed in the soil. Each limb is also equipped with a very complex nervous system that constantly relays tactile data to the brain. Because of the nature of the hard shells and the flexibility of their bodies, Orgons can better resist damage from blunt (non-bladed) attacks, such as clubs.

They are sensitive to light, and while they don't have vision in the traditional sense of most other carbon-based sentient life-forms, they can "see" light and reflected light within a large area around them.

Orgons are almost always found alone. Because of the slow movement rate of the Orgons, the development of intelligence was the only thing that saved them from extinction. Since they cannot "catch" prey through normal hunting methods, they have learned to make very potent poisons and adhesives, as well as traps. They can then lumber over to the site and consume the creature at their leisure (their limbs also secrete digestive fluids). Orgons need to only eat about three kilograms of meat per standard year.

The creatures communicate with each other by very precise movement of their limbs. The Genetech research scientists have not yet learned how intelligent the Orgons are. Many of the "wonder chemicals" that Genetech has discovered have actually been Orgon compounds.

Genetech Orbiting Research Lab

Craft: Orbiting Research Lab
Scale: Starfighter
Length: 53 meters tall, 22 meters in diameter
Crew: 5, gunners: 1
Passengers: 30 (research scientists), 10 (Genetech guards)
Cargo Capacity: 300 metric tons
Consumables: 6 months
Cost: Not available for sale
Space: Not applicable; geosynchronous orbit
Hull: 9D
Weapons:
   Dual Laser Cannons (fire-linked)
     Fire Arc: Turret
     Crew: 1
     Scale: Capital
     Skill: Capital ship gunnery
     Fire Control: 2D
     Space Range: 1-3/10/25
     Damage: 3D

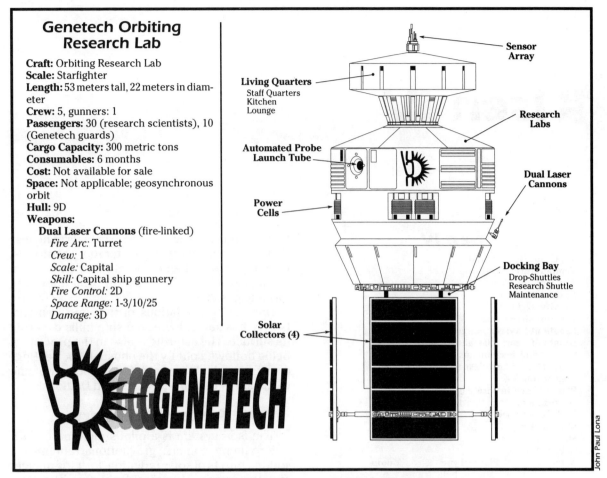

GENETECH

John Paul Lona

The Orgons have learned to shy away from contact with Genetech scientists. They have also developed a very potent poison which they have liberally applied to plants and berries in the vicinity of Genetech encampments.

The worst weapon in the arsenal is a cluster of red goo Humans would name a "skin buster." The sticky substance is filled with an irritant sap which leads to a screaming insane death in only a few short minutes, unless appropriate medicines are applied quickly. The weapon does 6D damage upon initial contact, with 4D damage per turn after the first (a maximum of 10 turns). It only works on exposed skin.

■ Orgons

Attribute Dice: 12D
Attribute Minimum/Maximums:
DEXTERITY 1D/4D
KNOWLEDGE 1D/4D+2
MECHANICAL 0D/3D
PERCEPTION 2D/4D
STRENGTH 2D/4D+2
TECHNICAL 0D/1D+2
Special Skills:
 Knowledge skills:
 Biochemistry. Time to use: Several days. *Biochemistry* is the skill the Orgons use to create new chemical compounds for their own use. Creating new compounds can take days, months or even years.
Special Abilities:
Natural Camouflage: Orgons get +2D to *sneak* in jungle terrain.
Resistance to Blunt Weapons: Orgons get a bonus of +1D to *Strength* to resist damage from blunt weapons.
Story Factors:
Unknown: Orgons are unknown to the galaxy at large; only the Genetech scientists know about these creatures.
Move: 3/5
Size: Up to 1.5 meters tall
Note: It is strongly suggested that players not be allowed to play Orgon characters.

Isen IV

Isen IV

Type: Airless planetoid
Temperature: Frigid
Atmosphere: None
Hydrosphere: Dry
Gravity: Light
Terrain: Airless rock
Length of Day: Not applicable
Length of Year: 740 standard days
Sapient Species: Humans
Starport: Standard class (pirate controlled)
Population: 500
Planet Function: Pirate base, homeworld
Government: Abav Ghart (pirate leader)
Tech Level: Space
System: Isen
Star: Isen (yellow)
Orbital Bodies:

Name	Planet Type	Moons
Kisen	asteroid belt	0
Kossan	asteroid belt	0
Isen	young gas giant	5
Isen IV	airless planetoid	
Kossim	asteroid belt	0

World Summary

The Isen system is in its birth throes, with a still forming star and an endless sea of rock in orbit. Imperial survey teams designated four rough orbits in the supposition that these areas would eventually hold planets. The gas giant of Isen is forming.

The system is constantly bathed in blasts of radiation from the new star, and with the asteroid chunks, is very dangerous to navigate.

These factors have made the system the ideal location for a pirate base — and so, the Void

System Datafile

Isen system, star: Isen, yellow star. Primitive system with three asteroid belts, a proto-gas giant.

Isen is a forming system with no habitable worlds. No known inhabitants. Cursory scouting surveys have indicated modest mineral and metal deposits, but the system is too remote for profitable mining operations at this time.

Demons pirate gang, wanted criminals in no less than 15 sectors within the Outer Rim Territories, have constructed an elaborate hidden base on the planetoid Isen IV, fourth in orbit about the forming gas giant.

Due to the predations of the Void Demons, Isen IV has several wrecked ship hulls covering its surface. The asteroid is also in the process of being hollowed out by the unusual "rock-eating" creatures called the morvak — the legacy of one of the ships captured by the Void Demons.

System Summary

The Isen system is a pilot's nightmare, with free-roaming comets, gravitational anomalies, sudden bursts of solar radiation, forming planets and thousands of asteroid chunks. The lone planet, Isen, is a new gas giant, with five planetoid satellites

Navigating the Belt

The Isen system is so dangerous that ships entering the outer limits of the system must make Moderate *piloting* (whichever skill is relevant) rolls every minute to avoid hitting the hurtling balls of rock and ice. After five minutes of flying time, the characters will enter the heart of system.

Now the characters must a new *piloting* roll every round to avoid hitting an asteroid. Roll one die on the first chart ("Piloting Difficulty") to determine the piloting difficulty. If the characters ever exceed the difficulty by two levels, they have discovered the pirates' path through the asteroid belt, which requires only a Very Easy *piloting* roll every round.

Characters may choose to leave the asteroid belts but they still must navigate a safe path out (since the asteroid belt is a swirling mass of debris, usable paths will constantly be changing). The gamemaster should roll 3D to determine how many rounds will be necessary to leave the belt (this assumes the characters are looking for the quickest path out — if they specifically

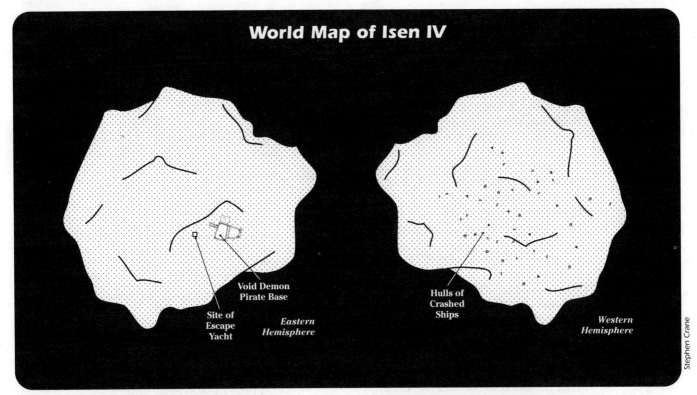

World Map of Isen IV

Void Demon
Pirate Base

Site of
Escape
Yacht

*Eastern
Hemisphere*

Hulls of
Crashed
Ships

*Western
Hemisphere*

Stephen Crane

state they are looking for an EASY path out, then roll 7D for the number of rounds necessary). If taking the quickest path, roll on the "Piloting Difficulty" chart each round. If taking the safest path out, roll on the "Piloting Difficulty" chart each round, but subtract two difficulties from each roll (the minimum difficulty is always Easy).

Failing any of these *piloting* rolls means that the ship has collided with one of the asteroids. Asteroids do a varied amount of damage, depending upon their size. Roll one die and consult the "Asteroid Damage" chart. All damage listings are for starfighter scale.

Piloting Difficulty

Roll	Difficulty Level
1	Easy
2–4	Moderate
5	Difficult*
6	Very Difficult*

* If the piloting total is 40 or higher, the characters have discovered the path through the asteroid belt.

Asteroid Damage

Roll	Asteroid Size	Damage
1	Tiny Meteorite	1D
2	Small Meteorite	2D
3–4	Medium Meteorite	3D
5	Large Meteorite	4D
6	Very Large Meteorite	7D

Void Demon Base

The Void Demon base on Isen IV (the fourth planetoid orbiting the gas giant) is designed to be hard to find and easy to defend. The difficulty of navigating the asteroid belts of the Isen system helps protect the base from exploring ships and wandering tramp freighters. The base's computer systems have a complete log of every individual asteroid and meteor in the system, and are constantly updated by miniature mobile sensors scattered throughout the system. With this complex computer network, Void Demon leader Abav Ghart can instantaneously call up available safe pathways through the asteroid belts.

Ghart has a complete complement of starfighters (all of them "acquired" through his exploits over the years). He also has a highly modified Corellian gunship (also acquired through questionable means) that is used to secure and board vehicles that have been softened up by starfighter assaults.

The base has a series of tractor beam emplacements and turbolasers for defense. Ghart realizes that nothing is ever a sure bet, and has built several entrances into the morvak caves beneath the base. Only he and a few of his most trusted thugs know the route through the caves to an escape cruiser hidden a few kilometers away.

Lore of the Void Demons

This gang is wanted in at least 15 different sectors, for piracy, assault, terrorism, and murder. No less than 50 different incidents of hijackings have been attributed to the Void Demons, and it is believed that their mysterious leader, Abav Ghart, has been made a billionaire many times over. There is a bounty of 300,000 credits for the capture of Ghart (if he is taken alive, the sector governments are offering an even 500,000 credits).

Starfighter Complement

3 Z-95 Mark I Headhunters

A true museum piece, the Z-95 Mark I (or, Z-95Mk1) was the first version of the legendary starfighter. It used a primitive sweep-wing design and a bubble cockpit for greater pilot visibility. These design features were phased out as more advanced technology became available.

■ Z-95 Headhunter

Craft: Incom/Subpro Z-95 Mark I Headhunter
Type: Multipurpose starfighter
Scale: Starfighter
Length: 11.8 meters
Skill: Starfighter piloting: Z-95
Crew: 1
Crew Skill: See pirate pilots below
Cargo Capacity: 50 kilograms
Consumables: 1 day
Cost: 23,000 (in current condition)
Maneuverability: 1D
Space: 5
Atmosphere: 365; 1,050 kmh
Hull: 4D
Shields: 1D
Sensors:
  Passive: 15/0D
  Scan: 25/1D
  Search: 40/2D
  Focus: 1/2D
Weapons:
  2 Triple Blasters (fire-linked)
    Fire Arc: Front
    Skill: Starship gunnery
    Fire Control: 1D
    Space Range: 1-5/10/17
    Atmosphere Range: 100-500/1/1.7 km
    Damage: 3D
  Concussion Missiles
    Fire Arc: Front
    Skill: Missile weapons: concussion missiles
    Fire Control: 1D
    Space Range: 1/3/7
    Atmosphere Range: 50-100/300/700
    Damage: 7D

12 Z-95 I3 Headhunters

The Z-95 I3 ("Improved Model 3") was one of the most popular models of this starfighter and can be found in service on many worlds.

The Z-95 I3 is identical to the Z-95MkI excepted as noted: Cargo Capacity: 85 kilograms, Space: 7, Atmosphere: 400; 1,150 kmh

10 Zebra Starfighters

A basic and inexpensive starfighter that is easy to maintain and pilot. While not very durable, its weapons are potent.

■ Zebra Starfighter

Craft: Hyrotii Vehicle Works Zebra Starfighter
Type: Light short range starfighter
Scale: Starfighter
Length: 12.3 meters
Skill: Starfighter piloting
Crew: 1
Crew Skill: See pirate pilots below
Cargo Capacity: 65 kilograms
Consumables: 1 day
Cost: 65,000 (new), 32,500 (used)
Maneuverability: 2D
Space: 7
Atmosphere: 350; 1,000 kmh
Hull: 2D
Sensors:
  Passive: 15/0D
  Scan: 25/1D+1
  Search: 45/2D
  Focus: 3/2D+2
Weapons:
  2 Laser Cannons (fire-linked)
    Fire Arc: Front
    Skill: Starship gunnery
    Fire Control: 1D
    Space Range: 1-5/10/17
    Atmosphere Range: 100-500/1/1.7 km
    Damage: 5D

11 Gauntlet Starfighters

The Gauntlet starfighter wasn't a resounding success when it was introduced several years ago, but that was due more to the political climate than a lack of engineering excellence. The odd configuration makes for a striking appearance, and it has weaponry to back up its bold lines.

■ Gauntlet Starfighter

Craft: Shobquix Yards Gauntlet Starfighter
Type: Multi-purpose short range starfighter
Scale: Starfighter
Length: 14 meters
Skill: Starfighter piloting
Crew: 1, gunners: 1
Crew Skill: See pirate pilots below
Cargo Capacity: 85 kilograms
Consumables: 2 days
Cost: 165,000 (new), 85,000 (used)
Maneuverability: 2D
Space: 6
Atmosphere: 295; 850 kmh
Hull: 3D+2
Shields: 1D
Sensors:
  Passive: 20/1D
  Scan: 35/1D+2
  Search: 45/2D
  Focus: 5/3D
Weapons:
  2 Laser Cannons (fire-linked)

Fire Arc: Front
Skill: Starship gunnery
Fire Control: 2D
Space Range: 1-3/10/17
Atmosphere Range: 100-300/1/1.7 km
Damage: 4D

2 Laser Cannons (fire-linked)
Fire Arc: Turret
Crew: 1
Skill: Starship gunnery
Fire Control: 2D
Space Range: 1-3/12/25
Atmosphere Range: 100-300/1.2/2.5 km
Damage: 5D

Proton Torpedo Launcher
Fire Arc: Turret
Crew: 1 (co-pilot)
Skill: Starship gunnery
Fire Control: 2D
Space Range: 1/3/7
Atmosphere Range: 50-100/300/700
Damage: 8D

■ Void Demon Base

Scale: Capital
Consumables: 6 months
Hull Code: 3D
Weapons:
8 Laser Cannons
Fire Arc: Turret
Crew: 1
Scale: Starfighter
Skill: Starship gunnery
Fire Control: 2D
Space Range: 1-3/10/17
Atmosphere Range: 100-300/1/1.7 km
Damage: 3D

3 Turbolaser Batteries
Fire Arc: Turret
Crew: 3
Skill: Capital ship gunnery
Fire Control: 1D
Space Range: 3-15/35/75
Atmosphere Range: 300-1.5/3.5/7.5 km
Damage: 3D+2

8 Tractor Beam Projectors
Fire Arc: Turret
Crew: 12
Skill: Capital ship gunnery
Fire Control: 2D
Space Range: 1-5/15/30
Atmosphere Range: 2-10/30/60 km
Damage: 4D

Personnel:
47 starfighter pilots
320 boarding troops
23 administrative personnel
140 droids

Facilities:
12 starfighter bays
1 transport bay
1 landing deck
36 starfighters (various types)

Members of the Void Demons

■ Abav Ghart, Void Demon Leader

Type: Gotal Pirate Leader
DEXTERITY 2D+2
Blaster 5D, dodge 7D, melee combat 4D
KNOWLEDGE 2D
Intimidation 7D, streetwise 5D, value 3D

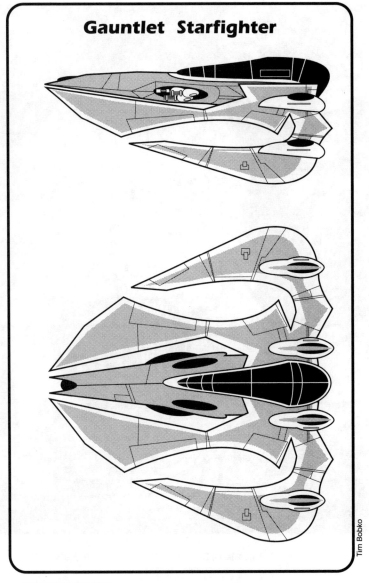

Gauntlet Starfighter

Tim Bobko

MECHANICAL 5D*
Astrogation 6D, repulsorlift operation 6D+1, space transports 8D, starship gunnery 7D+2, starfighter piloting 9D, starship shields 5D+2
PERCEPTION 5D
Bargain 6D, command: Void Demons 7D, con 7D+2, search 7D
STRENGTH 2D+1* *
Repulse-hand 3D
TECHNICAL 1D
Security 3D, space transports repair 2D+2
Special Abilities:
Energy Sensitivity: Gotals are unusually sensitive to radiation emissions. They get +3D to *search* when hunting targets in open areas; in crowded areas, the bonus drops to +1D; in areas flooded with intense radiation, they suffer a -1D penalty to *search*. See page 48 of *Galaxy Guide 4: Alien Races, Second Edition.*
Mood Detection: Gotals are good at reading the intentions of other beings. The Gotal makes a Moderate *Perception* total, and adds the following bonus to all *Perception* skills when making opposed rolls for the rest of that encounter. See page 48 of *Galaxy Guide 4: Alien Races, Second Edition.*

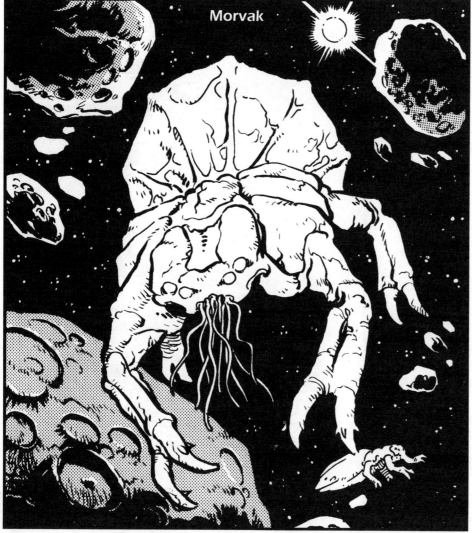

Morvak

Tim Eldred

Roll Misses Difficulty By:	Penalty:
6 or more	-3D
2–5	-2D
1	-1D
Roll Beats Difficulty By:	**Bonus:**
0–7	1D
8–14	2D
15 or more	3D

Fast Initiative: +1D to initiative against non-Gotal opponents. See page 48 of *Galaxy Guide 4: Alien Races, Second Edition.*

* *Motion Interface Package:* Abav has a Motion Interface Package (see page 37 of *Cracken's Rebel Field Guide*) that increases his *Mechanical* attribute far beyond the Gotal species maximum.

** *Repulse-Hand:* Abav has a repulse-hand (see page 41 of *Cracken's Rebel Field Guide*) which does STR+1D damage in combat; he uses his *repulse-hand* skill to attack.

Force Points: 3
Dark Side Points: 6
Character Points: 15
Move: 13
Equipment: Blaster pistol (4D), blaster rifle (5D), vibro-blade (STR+1D+2), comlink

Capsule: Abav Ghart is a two meter tall Gotal who has turned piracy into a frighteningly lucrative occupation. He has obvious cybernetic enhancments, with a repulse-hand and a motion interface package; he relies on their unsettling appearance to add to his ability to intimidate others. He always dresses in expensive, brightly-colored clothing, with a complete array of weapons at his belt. His trademark is an expensive gold pendant he fastens to his belt.

Ghart has been a pirate for nearly five decades and started the Void Demon gang over 30 years ago. He is a cold-blooded fiend of the worst kind. He is willing to do anything or betray anyone if there is a profit to be made. He kills without a second thought — and his henchmen are just as likely to face his wrath as his victims.

Void Demons Personnel

Ghart's prime assistant is a Devaronian named Burnal Terrup. He was hired on by Ghart a decade ago and through subservience, grovelling and behind-the-scenes manipulation, has risen to second-in-command. In Ghart's presence, Terrup grovels to the point of being nauseating. He compliments Ghart on every decision and ridicules anyone Ghart is trying to dominate. Away from Ghart, he is manipulative and seemingly on the verge of psychosis. He wears a worn, tattered blue and orange uniform.

Burnal Terrup. *Dexterity 2D, blaster 4D, dodge 3D, Knowledge 3D, alien species 5D, cultures 4D, languages 5D, planetary systems 4D+1, streetwise 4D+2, Mechanical 1D, space transports 2D+1, Perception 2D+2, command 3D, hide 3D, sneak 3D, search 3D+2, Strength 2D+1, Technical 1D.* Move: 9. Character Points: 6. Blaster pistol (4D), comlink, datapad.

Pirate Boarding Troops. All stats are 2D except: *blaster 4D, dodge 4D+1.* Move: 10. Blaster pistol (4D), blast vest (+1D physical, +1 energy, front and back).

Pirate Pilots. All stats are 2D except: *capital ship piloting 3D+1, space transports 3D, starfighter piloting 3D+2, starship gunnery 3D.* Move: 10. Blaster pistol (4D), comlink, flight suit.

Pirate Gunners. All stats are 2D except: *capital ship gunnery 3D, starship gunnery 3D+2.* Move: 10. Blaster pistol (4D), comlink, flight suit.

The Broken Hulls

Isen IV's surface is a veritable spaceship graveyard of crushed hulls. The Void Demon pirates have stripped the ships of valuable goods and any replacement components they needed for their craft. While most of the obviously useful gear and cargo has been removed, the characters will still be able to access the computer library data banks, providing opportunities to learn of new worlds, valuable lost treasures and other items of tremendous value. Some of the devices on board the ships are still functional, so if characters search the ships long enough they might find something of worth or use to them. Almost all of the ships are tramp freighters or bulk freighters.

Tunnels of Isen IV

All of the tunnels of Isen IV are the result of the incessant tunneling of the Morvak. The interior of the planetoid is completely devoid of atmosphere, and is chillingly cold. The tunnels are about one meter in diameter, and are littered with chunks of rock left floating in the zero gravity environment after the claws of the Morvak cleared away debris. Glow rods can only illuminate a very small radius because of the thick debris and the dark coloration of the rock. It is foolhardy to attempt to navigate the tunnels without complete knowledge of their layout (only Abav Ghart knows the paths within the planetoid). The tunnels wind through the rock at many different odd angles, making for a very complex three-dimensional maze of caverns.

Morvak

The Morvak are unusual creatures that derive all of their sustenance from rock. They require neither gravity nor atmosphere for survival. They have several muscular tentacles that secrete a strong acid, which breaks rock down into basic components. The tentacles then absorb the released oxygen and basic nutrients.

The creatures have two pairs of limbs for movement, as well as two great clawed limbs that

Tim Eldred

are used to carved through hardened rock. Their bodies and limbs are covered with a bony exoskeleton, providing armored protection.

Their tentacles house a sophisticated series of organs that generate vibrational echoes. By placing their tentacles on rock, Morvak can send vibrations into the rock and determine what lies beneath the surface layer of rock. If nutrients are discovered, they will tunnel into the rock. Most areas inhabited by Morvak are riddled with caverns of every size, direction and angle.

The Morvak also have a sophisticated means of camouflaging themselves: they absorb rock coloration into their bodies so that their exoskeletons take on the hue of the rock that they have been dining on. Within a few days Morvak are able to perfectly blend into the area they inhabit.

If Morvak are ever deprived of nutrients, they can place themselves in suspended animation, although they will immediately reawaken if their vibrational sensors sense an influx of nutrients.

Morvak are asexual, and young grow in a pouch on the underside of the creature. The Morvak have several dozen different chromosomes, but activate only a portion of them (the activated chromosomes are different from individual to individual). In this manner, new members of the

ISEN IV DIAGRAM
Void Demon Pirate Base

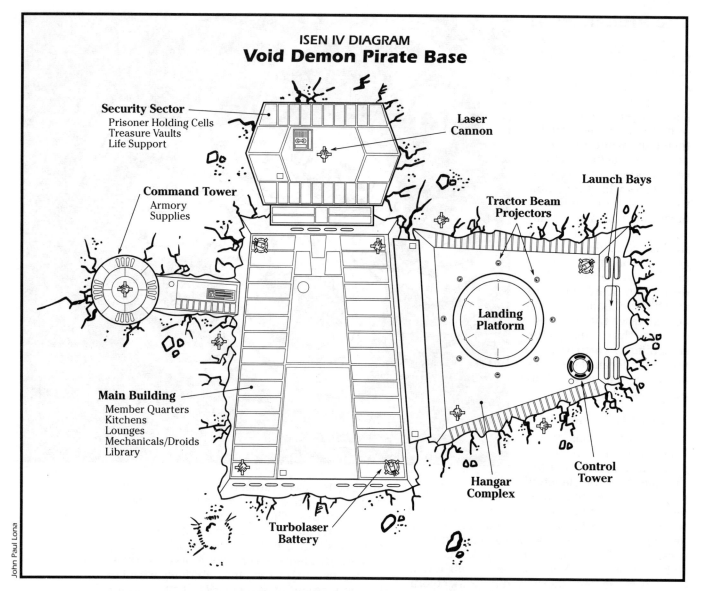

Security Sector
Prisoner Holding Cells
Treasure Vaults
Life Support

Laser Cannon

Command Tower
Armory
Supplies

Launch Bays

Tractor Beam Projectors

Landing Platform

Main Building
Member Quarters
Kitchens
Lounges
Mechanicals/Droids
Library

Control Tower

Turbolaser Battery

Hangar Complex

John Paul Lona

species can be different from their parent, even though there is an identical genetic pool.

The Morvak are social creatures that comb their caves in packs. The are protective of one another and work together to repel invaders and perceived threats. Typical means of defense include collapsing caves on top of or beneath invaders or attacking them outright with their acidic tentacles. If an "invader" refuses to fight or defend itself, curiosity may overwhelm fear, and they may actually attempt to make contact. While their needs and motivations are vastly different than most other carbon-based life forms, they can be quite interesting companions.

■ Morvak
Type: Tunnel creature
DEXTERITY 2D
PERCEPTION 2D
Mineral detection 4D
STRENGTH 5D
Special Abilities:
Armor: A Morvak's hard exoskeleton provides +1D to resist energy and +2D to resist physical attacks.
Claws: STR+1D damage.
Tentacle Acid: 4D damage.
Rock Eaters: Morvak survive by tunneling through rock and ingesting released compounds.
Space Survival: Morvak can survive in the vacuum of space.
Move: 6
Size: 0.7-1.3 meters long
Scale: Creature

Joralla

Joralla

Type: Temperate Jungle
Temperature: Hot
Atmosphere: Type I (breathable)
Hydrosphere: Moderate
Gravity: Standard
Terrain: Ocean, jungle, mountain/jungle
Length of Day: 26 standard hours
Length of Year: 310 local days
Sapient Species: Humans, Tikiarri (N)
Starport: Landing field
Population: 10 million (Tikiarri, estimated), 20 or less (Humans)
Planet Function: Homeworld
Government: Unorganized tribes
Tech Level: Stone
System: Joralla
Star: Jaska (red giant)
Orbital Bodies:

Name	Planet Type	Moons
Manalin	poisonous searing rock	0
Grall	poisonous temperate	0
Joralla	temperate jungle	0

World Summary

The planet of Joralla is dominated by tropical jungles. The red giant star bathes the planet in crimson light.

This world is home to an extremely hostile species known as the Tikiarri. There has been talk of quarantining the planet.

A world of uncommon beauty and peril, Joralla is a monument to temptation. For those willing to take the risk, there are potentially vast mineral treasures to be found, as well as creatures which could command high prices on other worlds. The wise explorer will attempt to come to some arrangement with the Tikiarri to allow safe passage.

System Summary

Joralla, the third planet of the system after which it was named, is a tropical paradise filled with lush trees, wondrous flowers, and incredibly varied species of animals. Joralla's companion planets, Manalin and Grall, have poisonous atmospheres and no commercial potential.

Joralla

The lush tropical rain forests of Joralla tend to conceal a topography that is as lovely as it is diverse. Huge waterfalls cascade from the tops of mountains, pummeling chasms ripped into the very bedrock by earthquakes of unimaginable power. Plateaus hundreds of kilometers wide are dotted with winding rivers and huge forests. Imposing mountain chains cover the three main continents, with volcanoes mixing in with peaks thought long dead. A world of savage beauty, the volcanoes and forests overlook the the expansive, rich oceans of deep blue water.

The atmosphere of Joralla is perfectly suited for oxygen-breathers. Tremendous weather and seasonal fluctuations make for abrupt climate changes from month to month, with temperatures varying from a peak of 50 degrees celsius (at the height of summer in the equatorial zones) to a low of -35 degrees celsius (in the polar regions during winter).

Life Forms of Joralla

The flora and fauna of Joralla is remarkable for its beauty and diversity. The thick jungles are home to thousands of different species of trees, bushes and ferns. Hidden among the lush and colorful plant life are a wide range of insects, mammals, birds and reptiles. The cooler forest

System Datafile

Joralla system, star: Jaska, red giant. Three planets in system. Third planet, Joralla, is terrestrial but has been placed under unofficial quarantine by Imperial Moff Seylas.

Joralla is a dangerous, primitive jungle world with many predators. A local species, the avian Tikiarri, conduct some trade with freighter captains, but their savagery prevents stable trade agreements. The Tikiarri crave high technology weapons; further introduction to standard Imperial technology levels is "strongly discouraged" by the Moff's office.

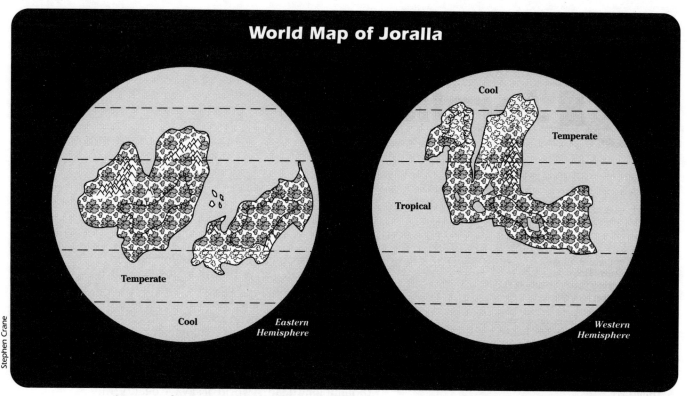

World Map of Joralla

Cool

Temperate

Tropical

Temperate

Cool

Temperate

Cool

Eastern Hemisphere

Western Hemisphere

Stephen Crane

regions are home to many similar species of plants and animals. Joralla's wilderness offers a varied and tasty diet to any who are stranded, with fruits and vegetables in abundance, and many different kinds of wild game.

Some of the most nutritious fruits on the planet are the giant *redspars*. Nearly a half meter across, with a brilliant red skin, these fruits can be found all over the planet. Many of the best-tasting berries come from the *tequa bushes*, which are barely 50 centimenters tall, yet whose branches can be many meters long. Many plants on Joralla have defense mechanisms, such as the brilliant blue *kewafi flowers*, which shoot poison barbs.

■ Wulkarsk

Type: Jungle predator
DEXTERITY 3D
PERCEPTION 2D
Search 4D, sneak 5D
STRENGTH 3D
Special Abilities:
Claws: STR+1D damage
Move: 16
Size: 1.5-2 meters long, up to 1.5 meters tall
Scale: Creature

Capsule: Wulkarsks are six-limbed beasts well-adapted to hunting. They have two distinct torso sections: the lower torso has four legs and provides a low center of gravity. The upper torso has one pair of clawed limbs, with the neck and head at the top of the upper torso. Each limb has three digits, each with a long claw, and a rear claw at the back of the foot or the base of the wrist. Wulkarsk have elongated snouts, with four eyes (two forward looking and two backward looking) and elongated ears

set just above the jawbone but below the eyes. The wulkarsk are the largest members of the family wulkenso, with several closely related animal species also found in the jungles and forests of the planet.

Wulkarsk eat creatures up to Human-sized. They attack without mercy and only flee if severely injured. They are adept at tracking prey through the jungles undetected by their targets.

The native Tikiarri have trained some wulkarsk as hunting beasts. Wild wulkarsk are always found alone, prowling the jungles of the planet. If being used by the Tikiarri, they hunt in packs, and their attack will be followed by the arrival of their masters.

■ Oslet

Type: Climbing herbivore
DEXTERITY 1D
PERCEPTION 3D
STRENGTH 2D
Move: 15 (climbing), 12 (jumping)
Size: Up to 3 meters tall
Scale: Creature
Orneriness: 2D

Capsule: Another creature common to Joralla is the oslet. The large herbivore has three pairs of limbs, but also has a three sectioned torso for great mobility. The lowest set of limbs is long, thick and well-muscled for jumping, while the middle and upper limbs are shorter and better adapted for climbing.

Oslets consume tree leaves, fruits and vines, and they make their nests in the upper limbs of Joralla's towering *sio trees*. They have elongated, flexible necks and small, triangular heads with long snouts. They can turn their heads 360 degrees. They are normally deep red and brown.

The Collapse of the Wasilsi

There is ample evidence that Joralla was once a world that supported two intelligent species. In addition to the Tikiarri, there was a race of humanoids called the Wasilsi. The remains of their villages and religious temples can be found buried in the soil of the world or under plant overgrowth. Many metal artifacts, statues of religious figures, and even parchment scrolls written in a long-dead language have been uncovered. They created many works of art and used gold and other valuable metals.

There is little doubt that the Tikiarri and the ancient Wasilsi people were enemies for many years. Much of the art found on the walls of the ruins depicts the great battles of these two civilizations. Based on skeletons discovered in early research missions, it has been determined that the Wasilsi were much stronger and apparently more

intelligent than the Tikiarri. It is considered highly unlikely that the bird-creatures hunted their rivals into extinction. The question thus remains: what happened to them?

Beyorth Gommdora, a sentientologist with the University of Huvveck, suggests that a plague was responsible for eliminating the Wasilsi. Gommdora's admittedly limited research into the past of Joralla (due to the ongoing conflicts with hostile Tikiarri tribes) shows little similarity between the structure of the Wasilsi and other creatures of the planet. He theorizes that the Wasilsi were somehow "seeded" on Joralla, either as a colony deliberately established, or the survivors of a ship that was forced to crashland on the planet. Thus they may not have had a natural immunity to bacteria or viruses to which the Tikiarri were resistant. If this theory proves to be correct, it is entirely possible that the planet still harbors these germs.

Oslets are easily frightened and will flee rather than fight. They are timid, but are easily trained as mounts (although the Tikiarri have never used them as such, preferring to use wullkarsk to hunt them). They are adept at quickly moving among the trees of the jungle and are a perfect replacement for repulsorlift vehicles, especially since the jungle is often too dense for speeder bikes or swoops.

Current Status

Joralla is seen by most nearby systems, and the Imperial Moff of the sector, as a nuisance. It offers virtually no economic benefit and seems to be at the center of constant controversy. Unable to quarantine the system without approval from his superiors, Moff Debin Seylas has acquisced to the demands of Joralla's neighbors, and has posted a regular patrol of the system. Ships entering the system are warned of the potential danger, while ships exiting the system are often searched to see if they are transporting any of the bothersome Tikiarri. Seylas only wants to do the bare minimum to keep the Imperial governors quiet, without deploying a significant amount of military personnel or equipment to this bothersome system.

Imperial Patrol Craft

Moff Seylas' solution to the so-called "Joralla Problem" is a pair of Skipray Blastboats, which perform regular patrols of the system — normally, a Blastboat is dispatched once per week for a 36-hour rotation.

While Blastboats aren't the most powerful ships in the fleet, they are normally more than enough to contain the independent freighters that sometimes visit Joralla.

Tikiarri

The Tikiarri are a tribally-based avian species whose reputation is sufficiently fearsome to keep the faint of heart from visiting Joralla. While the Empire acknowledges no threat from these creatures, many local systems have had unpleasant experiences with the Tikiarri, who seem to have no respect for the rule of law. Since the Empire has refused to consider requests for an official quarantine of the planet, neighboring systems have found it difficult to control the Tikiarri. On many nearby planets, any ship whose crew mentions it has visited Joralla is promptly searched for Tikiarri, who are either executed or imprisoned, and the ship is forced to depart immediately.

These flying beings can be found throughout the jungles of Joralla. The Tikiarri are perfectly designed for flight — light, hollow bones, large wings, a razor sharp beak and excellent eyesight.

They are carrion eaters, and have come to rely on a predatory animal known as the wulkarsk to provide them with food. The Tikiarri breed the wulkarsk, both for ferocity and for the ability to follow simple commands. The Tikiarri hunt by turning loose a group of wulkarsk, then tracking their progress while gliding on the air currents. Once an animal has been killed by the wulkarsk, the Tikiarri swoop down upon the scene and feast, often bringing scraps back to the nesting area for other members of the tribe.

The Tikiarri are highly competitive both within the tribe and with neighboring clans. Inter-tribal warfare is a constant of life.

Tribes are theoretically ruled by the bravest and most capable male, but in reality the most

Tikiarri

Tim Eldred

Flight. Time to use: one round. This is the skill used for flying. Beginning Tikiarri begin with a flight movement of 15 and may improve their flying Move as described on page 15 of *Star Wars, Second Edition.*
Move: 4/6 (walking), 15/20 (flying)
Size: 1.5-1.75 meters

Adventure Idea

Adriav Kavos, captain of the freighter *Isilia,* has acquired a vital Alliance data disk. He has agreed to meet a buyer on Joralla, where he and his crew will receive a small fortune for their efforts. The characters have been ordered to retrieve the disk, which is hidden inside the modified stock of a blaster rifle.

The *Isilia* made its way to the Joralla system free of incident, and the characters' orders indicate that they have less than one day to recapture the data disk. The following is a timetable for various events in this adventure: the implications and responses to these events will have to taken into account by the gamemaster. All times are "local" for the landing site of the *Isilia.*

• **Late Afternoon:** The characters' ship arrives in system. First priority is discovering the location of the *Isilia* — perhaps the characters were smart enough to check with their contacts before starting out on this adventure. If not, they will have to use a sensor sweep (and during the minutes they will have to stay in orbit, it is highly likely that the *Isilia* will detect them). The *Isilia* has landed in a clearing adjacent to a Wasilsi temple. They may opt to pose as independent traders, making a "friendly call on fellow traders before meeting the locals." The crew of the *Isilia* may actually be friendly upon first encounter.

• **Late Evening:** A nearby and highly aggressive Tikiarri tribe attacks (either the *Isilia,* the characters' ship, or both). They are trying to capture the blasters of the various "invaders." If they are quite successful, they may overrun whoever is holding the data disk and capture the modified blaster rifle in which the disk is hidden. The strength of the attacking force and their persistence should be modified according to the skill of the characters, whether or not they will actually be involved in the combat or be observers, and whether it is desireable for the Tikiarri to capture the data disk.

• **Early Morning:** The buyer of the data disk arrives, with a full complement of gun-toting "assistants." What the characters don't know is that he is actually an Imperial spy who will not only take the data disk, but has called both Skipray Blastboats into the system to capture the *Isilia.*

Naturally, this pattern of events will probably wreak havoc with the characters' plans. This is as it should be. The point of this adventure is to reinforce the notion that everyone, the crew of

devious male eliminates all other contenders and assumes control of a tribe by default. Tribal leaders are extremely fortunate if they survive their first year of rule.

Tikiarri have a natural life span of about 30 local years, but most males die in combat or during hunting by age 20, and most females die before age 20 because they are forced to produce young as soon as they are able (between eight and 10 years of age).

What makes the Tikiarri especially dangerous to visitors is their interest in advanced weaponry. Since a foolish trader introduced the wonders of blaster technology, the avians have spent an inordinate amount of time trying to acquire more weapons. In fact, "hunts" will often revolve around trying to kill off-worlders for their weaponry. Most tribes have at least one or two blaster weapons, always held by the tribe's leader.

■ Tikiarri
Attribute Dice: 11D+2
Attribute Minimum/Maximums:
DEXTERITY 1D/3D+2
KNOWLEDGE 1D/2D+2
MECHANICAL 1D/2D
PERCEPTION 2D/4D+2
STRENGTH 1D/3D
TECHNICAL 1D/2D+2
Special Skills:
Strength skills:

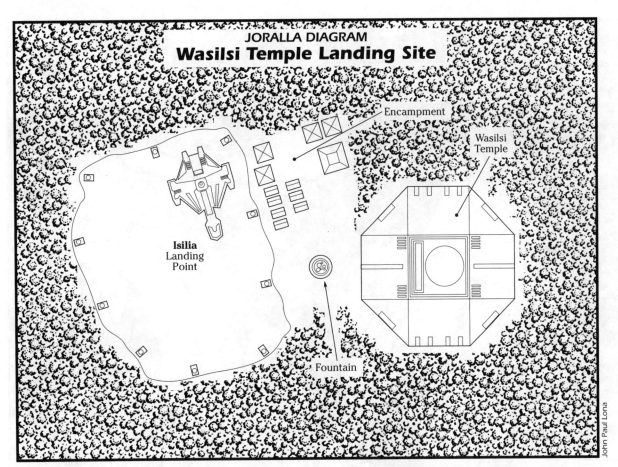

JORALLA DIAGRAM
Wasilsi Temple Landing Site

Encampment

Wasilsi Temple

Isilia
Landing Point

Fountain

John Paul Lona

the *Isilia*, the characters, the Tikiarri, even the Imperial spies, are playing pieces in a deadly game for the fate of the galaxy.

Adventure Personalities

Adriav Kavos

Adriav Kavos is captain of the freighter *Isilia* and has been running the star lanes for years. He's never been too successful, but has never been so destitute that he gave up on cargo hauling. He is a wanderer by nature, lacking direction in business and life in general.

He appears much older than he his true age — years of trying to pay his bills in a very dangerous and competitive business have caught up with him. Kavos is desperately seeking that "one big one" that will allow him to pay off his bills and retire in style (or at least keep him occupied with a steady stream of liquor). He seems to be likeable enough, but he is neither bright, trustworthy nor talented.

He got his hands on the datadisk by having his crew take out some "suspicious looking" tramp freighter crew members in a spaceport on the other side of the sector. They turned out to be Rebels and he realized the disk he stole was worth a fortune. He is obsessed with getting the

deal on this data disk done — and doesn't see the Imperial trap he is about to fall into. He has no respect for the Empire, but doesn't care for the Alliance's cause either.

■ **Adrian Kavos**

Type: Struggling Freighter Captain
DEXTERITY 2D+2
Blaster 4D+1, dodge 3D+2
KNOWLEDGE 3D
Bureaucracy 4D+2, cultures 3D+2, languages 5D, planetary systems 4D+2
MECHANICAL 3D+2
Astrogation 4D+2, space transports 6D
PERCEPTION 3D
Bargain 5D, command 3D+2, con 4D+2
STRENGTH 2D
TECHNICAL 3D+1
Demolition 4D, space transports repair 5D+2
Character Points: 2
Move: 10
Equipment: Blaster pistol (4D), comlink

The Crew of the Isilia

■ **Gezzov-tak**

Type: Arcona Henchman
DEXTERITY 2D+1
Blaster 3D+2, dodge 4D, melee combat 2D
KNOWLEDGE 1D+1
Streetwise 3D
MECHANICAL 1D+2
PERCEPTION 2D+1
Hide 3D, search 5D, sneak 4D

Tim Eldred

STRENGTH 2D+2
Digging 4D+2
TECHNICAL 1D+1
Special Abilities:
Senses*: Arcona have weak long distance vision (+10 to difficulty level of all tasks involving vision at distances greater than 15 meters), but excellent close range senses (+1D to all *Perception* skills involving heat, smell or movement when within 15 meters).
Thick Hide*: Arcona have tough, armored hides that add +1D to *Strength* when resisting physical damage.
Talons: +1D to *climbing, Strength* (for damage with *brawling* attacks) or *digging*.
Salt Weakness*: Gezzov-tak is addicted to salt. He must have 25 grams of salt per day or he suffers -1D to all actions.
* For more information, see pages 15–16 of *Galaxy Guide 4: Alien Races, Second Edition.*
Character Points: 1
Move: 8
Equipment: Blaster pistol (4D), comlink, datapad

■ Nabkess
Type: Ortolan Henchwoman
DEXTERITY 1D+2
Blaster 3D, dodge 3D+2
KNOWLEDGE 2D
MECHANICAL 1D
Starship gunnery 3D
PERCEPTION 2D+1
STRENGTH 2D+2
TECHNICAL 2D+1

Computer programming/repair 4D, space transports repair 5D
Special Abilities:
Foraging: Any attempt at foraging food gets +2D.
Ingestion: Ortolans can ingest large amounts of different types of food. They get +1D to resist any type of poison. For more information, see pages 69–70 of *Galaxy Guide 4: Alien Races, Second Edition.*
Move: 6
Equipment: Sack of food, blaster pistol (4D), comlink

■ Segken Tels
Type: Quarren Henchwoman
DEXTERITY 2D
Blaster 3D, dodge 3D+2
KNOWLEDGE 1D+2
MECHANICAL 2D
Starship gunnery 4D
PERCEPTION 2D+1
Bargain 4D, con 4D+2
STRENGTH 2D+1
TECHNICAL 1D+2
Special Abilities:
Aquatic: Quarren can breathe both air and water and can withstand extreme pressures found in ocean depths.
Move: 10 (walking), 12 (swimming)
Equipment: Blaster pistol (4D), datapad, comlink

■ The Isilia

Craft: Modified Ghtroc Industries class 440 freighter
Type: Modified freighter
Scale: Starfighter
Length: 28 meters
Skill: Space transports, starship gunnery
Crew: 2, gunners: 2, skeleton: 1/+5
Crew Skill: See stats above
Passengers: 4
Cargo Capacity: 100 metric tons
Consumables: 2 months
Cost: 18,500
Hyperdrive Multiplier: x3
Hyperdrive Backup: x15
Nav Computer: Yes
Maneuverability: 1D
Space: 4

Atmosphere: 280; 800 kmh
Hull: 4D
Shields: 1D
Sensors:
   Passive: 12/0D
   Scan: 25/1D
   Search: 35/2D
   Focus: 3/3D
Weapons:
   2 Laser Cannons
      Fire Arc: Turret
      Crew: 1
      Skill: Starship gunnery
      Fire Control: 2D
      Space Range: 1-3/12/25
      Atmosphere Range: 100-300/1.2/2.5 km
      Damage: 2D

Mutanda

Mutanda

Type: Temperate plains
Temperature: Temperate
Atmosphere: Type I (breathable)
Hydrosphere: Moist
Gravity: Light
Terrain: Ocean, plains, hill/forest, forest, jungle
Length of Day: 18 standard hours
Length of Year: 267 local days
Sapient Species: Horansi (N), Humans
Starport: 1 standard class
Population: 120 million
Planet Function: Homeworld, mining
Government: Tribal
Tech Level: Feudal/industrial
Major Exports: Illegally poached animals
Major Imports: Mid tech, foodstuffs, luxury goods
System: Killaniri
Star: Killaniri (yellow)
Orbital Bodies:

Name	Planet Type	Moons
Mutanda	temperate plains	4
Justa	barren moon	
Killaniri	gas giant	15

World Summary

The Killaniri system is one of the largest suppliers of prothium blaster gas to the Empire.

Because of the vast economic worth of Killaniri, the plains world of Mutanda stands ready for startling economic growth. Mutanda's second satellite, Justa, has the only sizeable starport of the system. As such, many workers and goods pass through the corridors of the vast starport, purchasing the wares and services of the Horansi traders.

Mutanda is a rolling land of grasslands, jungles, and natural wonders. The sentient species, the Horansi, are actually divided into four distinct subspecies. In addition to the Horansi, the world has many different species of big game animals, resulting in a booming legalized safari trade. However, the encroachments of poachers may result in the extinction of many species of Mutandan wildlife.

System Summary

The Killaniri system is an important part of the Empire, and sports both a gas giant rich with prothium blaster gas (Killaniri) and a world with its own sentient species (Mutanda). It is a valuable trade system with much wealth, but little political influence.

Killaniri is controlled by outside forces. The great weapons corporations, led by BlasTech and Czerka, have complete control over the gas mining on Killaniri. Therefore, faceless bureaucrats many systems away make all of the decisions regarding the development, management and growth of the system.

As far as Mutanda and Justa are concerned, everyone on these facilities is either in the employ of the weapons corporations, or providing products and services for these people.

The sentient Horansi of Mutanda have found it more desirable to retain a primitive and war-like lifestyle. They don't seem to desire uniting their people, and instead are fractionalized and manipulated by petty criminals, the great corporations, poachers, and untrustworthy but powerful tribal leaders. It seems that Mutanda will simply remain another petty system under the iron grip of the Empire.

System Datafile

Killaniri system, star: Killaniri, yellow star. Two planets in system. Killaniri, a gas giant, is home to an orbiting prothium gas mining station. The inner planet, Mutanda, is terrestrial.

Killaniri's gas mining efforts are controlled by BlasTech Corporation, Czerka Weapons and Blethern Gas Industries, the giant weapons corporations. Due to the strategic value of the prothium deposits, there is a sizeable Imperial Naval presence in the system. Justa starport, the only starport in the system, is owned by the corporations.

Mutanda is home to a sentient species, the Horansi. In order to retain their peaceful way of life while still benefitting from the influx of credits due to the mining, the Horansi authorize many "safari" hunting expeditions.

World Map of Mutanda

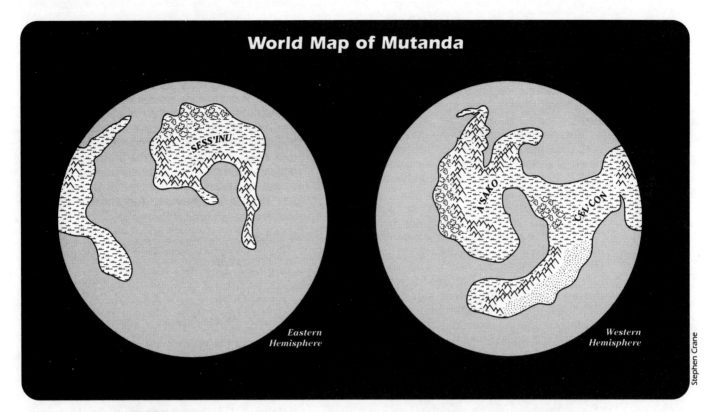

Eastern Hemisphere

Western Hemisphere

Stephen Crane

Killaniri

BlasTech Corporation's prothium refining station floats 40,000 kilometers up from the swirling green, yellow and orange clouds of Killaniri. The planet itself is 154,000 kilometers in diameter, with an atmosphere mixture of prothium, rethen and ammonia compounds. Incredible storms sweep the thick atmosphere, constantly churning the volatile gasses of Killaniri.

Into this mixture fly the gas collectors of BlasTech. Controlled remotely from the space station, and kept in check by droids, the gas collectors are larger than most tramp freighters. Plunging through the atmosphere, the various gasses of Killaniri are passed through huge filters and processing stations, extracting only the prothium.

The prothium is further processed into usable blaster gas at the refining station, as it is passed through a complex series of filters and pressure chambers containing pure rethen.

The economic worth of the system, and the Empire's desire to prevent marauders and Alliance forces from acquiring large amounts of blaster gas, has resulted in a permanent and impressive Imperial presence in the system. The escort carrier *Terrup* and the *Dreadnaught*-class heavy cruiser *Disorver* are stationed on permanent patrol in this system. There are also two Imperial customs corvettes for regular patrol duty. They are serviced by a small Imperial base on the moon of Justa (about 10 kilometers from the starport), which has a troop complement of 600. An additional 600 troops have been stationed aboard Justa starport for customs and law enforcement purposes. This is in addition to the corporate enforcers employed by the companies

Justa Starport

The Justa starport is a great subterranean complex, with surface-level docking facilities for up to 50 light freighters. Larger bulk transports are assigned orbits around the satellite. Jointly owned by BlasTech Corporation, Czerka Weapons and Blethern Gas Industries, this is truly a corporate facility. All of the personnel are dependent upon the corporations and the prothium refining stations for their livelihood. Ships not owned by these corporations are charge exorbitant fees for the services the starport provides (about 200 percent of standard costs).

However, there is also a great deal of opportunity aboard the starport, which is a bustling trade city. The companies generally ignore illegal activities if they are handled with tact and secrecy, and the station has become a haven for mercenaries. Many Horansi have come to the station and can be hired out as scouts, or can be very useful in opening up trade with Horansi tribes on the surface of Mutanda. A great deal of trade is also geared to the many hunting expeditions that come to Mutanda, since most of these tourists have a great deal of disposable income.

Mutanda

Mutanda, like the Killaniri system, has been part of the galactic community for hundreds of years. Primarily, Mutanda is just a planet for exotic hunting vacations and it is easily accessible because of the spaceport on the satellite of Justa.

Mutanda is primarily a temperate plains planet, with wild, open grassland, dotted with copses of trees. The planet is generally warm and arid, with light gravity, few rains and a light but breathable atmosphere (Type I). The arid plains have few rains (primarily at the onset of the cooler winter season), and are often under drought conditions. The rare streams, rivers and watering holes are areas of prime contention amongst rival Horansi tribes and wild animal herds. The mountain and forest regions see much more rain, also primarily during winter, but they are still quite dry and water is a precious commodity.

Many "common" species of the galaxy are also found on Mutanda. Several species grow to larger than typical sizes on this world, and invariably, all of the species are aggressive and dangerous — Mutanda is a harsh world with no room for the weak.

Animals

The great game animals of Mutanda are famous throughout the sector because of their ferocity and cunning. The difficult conditions of the world have bred hardy and crafty creatures that know how to blend into the natural terrain and escape pursuit.

Because of the explosive growth of hunting as an industry, the Gorvan Horansi have begun issuing hunting permits to visitors (the basic fee is 100 credits per hunter per day). These permits are honored by the Empire (especially since the corporations owning Justa starport and the Imperial governor receive a huge share of the permit fees). On the planet, anyone caught hunting without a permit is subject to huge fines (upwards of 10,000 credits) and imprisonment. On Mutanda, the Gorvan spend a great deal of time hunting down poachers, although the other Horansi races harass licensed hunters since the Gorvan permits allow the hunting of other Horansi sub-species. The following are some of the more prominent game animals on the world.

Kalan

Standing a full three meters tall, these brown and yellow herbivores are found in huge herds that roam the grasslands of Mutanda. They have four limbs, with elongated bodies, short necks and broad heads. They have a pair of large tusks.

Unlike many species of herbivores, kalans will not abandon weak members to predators — instead, the herd acts as a unit in defending itself when attacked, making them very dangerous. They work in a group, with two or three individuals which try to lure a predator into the center of the rest of the herd, which then descends on the would-be stalker. As the predator closes in for the kill, the other kalans charge the creature with their tusks, hoping to stampede or gore the attacker. While they are no challenge for powerful ranged weapons, they are deadly in close combat. They are a favorite food of the Horansi people.

■ **Kalan**
Type: Grazing herbivore
DEXTERITY 4D
PERCEPTION 3D
STRENGTH 2D+1
Special Abilities:
Tusks: STR+2D damage.
Trample: STR+2D+1 damage.
Move: 28
Size: Up to 3.4 meters tall at the shoulder
Scale: Creature
Orneriness: 4D+2

Hokami

Hokami are short hunters of the Mutandan plains and one of the chief threats to the kalans. Their bodies can be up to five meters long but they are only about one to one and a half meters tall. With sharp claws and huge teeth, the creatures are quite capable of bringing down most animals on the plains.

They have great skill at sneaking through Mutanda's grasses unseen. They are very aggressive and will attack virtually any creature. They often mistake repulsorlift vehicles for prey.

■ **Hokami**
Type: Stalking predator
DEXTERITY 4D+2
PERCEPTION 1D
Sneak 5D+2
STRENGTH 5D+1
Special Abilities:
Claws: STR+2D damage
Teeth: STR+1D damage
Move: 24
Size: Up to 1.5 meters tall at the shoulder
Scale: Creature

Yeat

The sharp-horned omnivorous yeat are known on many worlds as peaceful grazers, but they have evolved into aggressive predators on Mutanda. More than a few tourists have moved towards a yeat male, an outstretched hand filled with grains, only to feel the steely horns of the beast as it leaves the grain behind for fresh meat.

They are commonly found near the great watering holes on the plains of Mutanda, as well as in mountainous ranges. Their speed is unmatched on Mutanda and their ability to change direction through great leaps gives them great advantages in the hunt.

They have four limbs, with thick black and brown hair. Short, sturdy and designed for speed, they can run through the grasses with amazing quickness. They are found only in mated pairs, or perhaps with young (litters average three to four new pups).

■ Yeat

Type: Omnivore
DEXTERITY 3D
PERCEPTION 1D
STRENGTH 2D+1
Special Abilities:
Horns: STR+1D damage
Move: 29
Size: Up to 1.5 meters tall at the shoulder
Scale: Creature

Horansi

The Horansi are carnivorous hunters who are divided into four distinct sub-species. They share some common characteristics. Bipedal, they walk on two legs, although they run using all four

limbs for locomotion. All Horansi are covered with thick hair of varying coloration, dependent upon subspecies. The Gorvan Horansi have a thick mane of hair trailing down the back of their skulls and necks, while the Kasa Horansi have thick, striped fur and tufts of hair behind their great triangular ears.

All Horansi have excellent vision in low-light conditions, but only the Mashi Horansi are nocturnal. Horansi have an atypical activity cycle, with alternating periods of rest and activity, normally four to six hours long.

Horansi sub-species can cross breed, but these occurrences are rare, primarily due to cultural differences. The Gorvan Horansi are an exception, and have been known to forcibly take wives from other Horansi groups.

Kasa Horansi, the Striped Masters

These orange, white, and black-striped beings are the most intelligent of the Horansi races. They are found predominantly in forest regions. They are second in strength only to the Gorvan.

The Kasa Horansi are brave, noble and trustworthy. They despise the Gorvans for their short-sighted nature. Many Kasa can be found through-

Horansi

Kasa Horansi

Gorvan Horansi

Treka Horansi

Mashi Horansi

Tim Eldred

out the starport on Justa, and a few have even left their home system to pursue work elsewhere.

The Kasa Horansi get along with each other surprisingly well, and inter-tribal conflicts are rare, although they have been known to cross into the plains and raid Gorvan settlements. They have developed agriculture, low technology goods (such as bows and spears), and, through the trading actions of their representatives on Justa, have purchased some items of high technology, such as blasters, medicines and repulsorlift vehicles.

All tribal leaders are albino in coloration. This seems to be a tradition that was adopted many thousands of years ago, but still holds sway today.

The Kasa Horansi are curious about the strange galaxy beyond their home planet. Given the chance, many would be eager to leave their homeworld behind.

■ Kasa Horansi
Attribute Dice: 12D
Attribute Minimum/Maximums:
DEXTERITY 1D/3D
KNOWLEDGE 2D/4D+2
MECHANICAL 1D/3D+2
PERCEPTION 1D/4D
STRENGTH 2D+2/5D+2
TECHNICAL 1D/2D+2
Story Factors:
Technologically Primitive: Kasa Horansi are kept technologically primitive due to the policies of the Gorvan Horansi. While they are fascinated by technology (and once exposed to it will adapt quickly), on Mutanda they will seldom possess anything more sophisticated than bows and spears.
Move: 12/15
Size: 2-2.7 meters tall

Tim Eldred

Gorvan Horansi, the Lords of War

Through strength of numbers and a war-like nature, the golden-maned Gorvan Horansi are the de facto rulers of Mutanda. They actively encourage hunting, and they have no qualms about hunting other Horansi races. Gorvan Horansi are polygamous: a tribe is composed of one adult male, all of his wives and all of the children. As a Gorvan's male children reach maturity, there is a battle to see who will lead the tribe. The loser, if he is not killed in the battle, is free to leave and establish a new tribe. Many Gorvans in recent years have found employment at the spaceport on Justa.

The Gorvan Horansi have purchased many more weapons than the Kasa, but have shown no interest in the other benefits of technology. Through sheer numbers, they are able to control the other Horansi races, but they don't have complete control over the situation. Imperial representatives have only recognized and accorded rights to the Gorvan, or specific individuals from other groups if they are "sponsored" by a Gorvan.

Gorvan Horansi are war-like, belligerent, deceitful and openly aggressive to almost anyone. They dominate the plains of Mutanda and have been able to control the planet and the interactions of off-worlders with the other Horansi races.

■ Gorvan Horansi
Attribute Dice: 12D
Attribute Minimum/Maximums:
DEXTERITY 2D/5D
KNOWLEDGE 1D/2D
MECHANICAL 1D/2D+2
PERCEPTION 1D+2/4D
STRENGTH 1D/3D+2
TECHNICAL 1D/3D
Move: 12/14
Size: 2.6-3 meters tall

Mashi Horansi, the Night Stalkers

Lone, solitary, sleek, and black, the Mashi Horansi stalk the small jungles of Mutanda with great cunning. They are the only species of Horansi that remains nocturnal like their ancestors, and thus have a great advantage over the other Horansi races. They are very quiet and are rarely, if ever, seen by any but the most skilled of scouts and hunters. They mate once for life and the males raise the young. Because of their beauty, stealth, and rarity, their skins are the most prized of all Horansi.

Mashi Horansi make use of technology when it is convenient, but are still uncomfortable with many aspects of it. The Mashi who have moved to Justa have adapted well, discovering a natural aptitude for many skills.

Solitary, superstitious and nocturnal, Mashi Horansi are unpredictable. They are the prime target of poachers on Mutanda and accept this with a mixture of resignation and pride. A Mashi feels that if he must be the target of hunters, let him take a few with him.

■ Mashi Horansi

Attribute Dice: 12D
Attribute Minimum/Maximums:
DEXTERITY 1D/4D+2
KNOWLEDGE 1D/3D+3
MECHANICAL 1D/3D
PERCEPTION 3D/5D
STRENGTH 1D/4D+1
TECHNICAL 1D/2D+2
Special Abilities:
Keen Senses: Mashi Horansi are used to nighttime activity and rely more on their senses of smell, hearing, taste and touch than sight. They suffer no *Perception* penalties in darkness.
Sneak Bonus: At the time of character creation *only,* Mashi Horansi receive 2D for every 1D in skill dice they place in *sneak;* they may still only place a maximum of 2D in *sneak* (2D in beginning skill dice would get them 4D in *sneak*).
Story Factors:
Nocturnal: Mashi Horansi are nocturnal. While they gain no special advantages as a race, their life-long experience with night-time conditions gives them the special abilities noted above.
Move: 11/14
Size: 1.5-2 meters tall

Treka Horansi, the Rock Dwellers

The best trackers on Mutanda are the short-haired Treka Horansi. They are the most peaceful of the tribes, as they are safe from most hunters and Horansi wars in the mountain caves where they dwell. The Treka Horansi do not abide the hunting of other Horansi and will take any actions necessary to stop poachers. Male and female Treka Horansi share a rough equality in regards to leadership and responsibility for the tribe and their young.

The Treka Horansi are the only ones who have allowed offworlders to develop portions of their world. They are very protective of their hunting areas.

Treka Horansi are the most peaceful of the various Horansi races, but they will not tolerate poaching. They are curious and inquisitive, but always seem to outsiders to be hostile and on edge. They make superior scouts and when angered, fierce warriors.

■ Treka Horansi

Attribute Dice: 12D
Attribute Minimum/Maximums:
DEXTERITY 1D/4D+1
KNOWLEDGE 1D/3D+2
MECHANICAL 1D/3D
PERCEPTION 2D/4D+2
STRENGTH 2D/4D+2
TECHNICAL 1D/3D+2
Move: 11/15
Size: 2.3-2.6 meters tall

Adventure Idea

The characters are contacted by a Rebel operative and told that they must venture to Mutanda and capture Sw'isi, a Mashi Horansi who had joined the Alliance, but has now deserted, taking important data disks with him. The agent says that the disks detail an upcoming attack upon an Imperial fueling depot, and he fears that the Horansi is going to sell it to the Imperial soldiers on Justa.

The characters have two possible fronts to cover: the home village of Sw'isi, or the starport on Justa. They may decide to split up, cover only one location, or possibly hire some mercenaries to hunt down Sw'isi.

After several days with no luck, they finally get a lead which indicates Sw'isi has returned to his homeworld, but is actually with an influential Treka Horansi tribe. Upon arrival at the tribe, they discover the Sw'isi is actually still loyal to the Alliance, and returned home to try and rally support for the Alliance amongst his native Horansi. The "Rebel operative" is actually an Imperial agent who knew that Sw'isi was an Alliance member, but could never actually find him. Sw'isi is wanted for several raids conducted on Imperial installations throughout the sector. Unfortunately, the characters have led the Imperial agents, and troops, directly to the Alliance hero.

Rordak

Rordak

Type: Desolate mountains
Temperature: Temperate
Atmosphere: Type II (breath mask suggested)
Hydrosphere: Arid
Gravity: Light
Terrain: Mountainous desert, desert plains
Length of Day: 14 standard hours
Length of Year: 201 local days
Sapient Species: Humans, Viska (N)
Starport: 4 standard class
Population: 5 million
Planet Function: Homeworld, prisoner detention
Government: Caleisk (monarchy)
Tech Level: Space
Major Exports: Metals
Major Imports: High tech, foodstuffs
System: Rordak
Star: Rordak (red giant)
Orbital Bodies:

Name	Planet Type	Moons
Rordak	desolate mountains	0

World Summary

Rordak is the site of one of the most notorious Imperial penal colonies in the galaxy. The world is rich in metals, but the hostile atmosphere, high level of geologic activity and the brutal native species known as the Viska make the world inhospitable.

System Datafile

Rordak system, star: Rordak, red giant. One planet in system, Rordak, which is terrestrial (Humans must use breath masks for long term visits to the planet).

Rordak is the site of several Imperial prison work camps. It is also homeworld to the Viska, who live in a series of repulsorlift cities. Rordak is dotted by a series of orbital nightcloak planetary siege devices, although they are used more for prison camp control (they have no ill effects on the Viska).

Independent ships coming to Viska system must turn to standard Imperial communication frequencies for landing instructions. Visiting ships will be sent to one of four main starports: Dreggusom, Azkulkt, Whosk, or Deggaruls.

Prisoners assigned to Rordak are either forced to work in the dangerous mines or are sold into slavery, laboring at the behalf of a Viska noble. Because every prisoner on the world has been sentenced to life imprisonment, they are considered property of the Empire, to be used as the prisons' wardens see fit.

The native Viska are a cruel, violent species, but because they drink the blood of other creatures, they are terrifying as well. Their society is known for its callous disrespect of the sanctity of life.

System Summary

Rordak is the only planet in its system; originally, there were three inner worlds, but they were all consumed when the star expanded to form a red giant. Only Rordak survived.

Even though that traumatic event occurred millions of years ago, the results on Rordak were dramatic, as seas were scorched, great tectonic shifts occurred, and most life-forms were killed. Over the next few million years, entirely new forms of life evolved, the pinnacle of which are the Viska.

Rordak has been part of galactic society for nearly three centuries, and the stories of the great "blood-sucking fiends of Rordak" (the Viska) are well known throughout the galaxy. The Viska have mined their world for precious ores for centuries, and had advanced to the atomic level of technology on their own. Once Rordak was discovered, they quickly embraced space technology when their system was first visited. The world has been used as a prison world for three decades.

Rordak

Rordak is a small mountainous world, broken and scarred from constant volcanic upheaval. Huge mountains and deep gorges scar the planet's surface. Water is rare on this world, and rains, when they do fall, are highly acidic as a result of

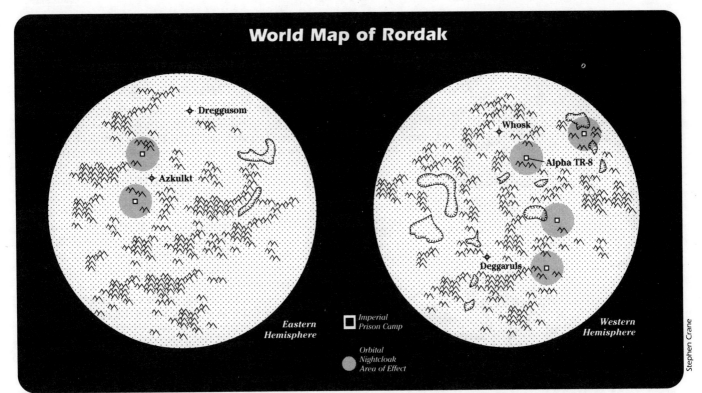

World Map of Rordak

Dreggusom

Azkulkt

Eastern Hemisphere

Whosk

Alpha TR-8

Deggaruls

◻ Imperial Prison Camp

● Orbital Nightcloak Area of Effect

Western Hemisphere

Stephen Crane

the constant volcanic ash which is expelled into the atmosphere. The world's carbon dioxide heavy atmosphere is extremely fatiguing to most new comers. The temperature of the world fluctuates wildly, with an average of 45 degrees celsius during daylight hours, and an average of 5 degrees celsius at night. Seasonal variations can alter the temperatures up to 20 degrees.

The planet of Rordak is populated by very few indigenous species. Plants take the form of stunted trees and brown grasses. A few forms of grazing animals evolved on the planet, and the Viska have learned to feed off these animals. With a constantly expanding population, the Viska must import great amounts of grain and grasses to feed the herds. There are few wild animals remaining on Rordak, and they are found only in the most desolate mountains of the planet.

A Hazardous Atmosphere

The high carbon dioxide atmosphere of Rordak is extremely dangerous to visitors. Several different gases and compounds within the atmosphere make "air poisoning" a distinct possibility. Characters acting without breath masks suffer penalties for high levels of activity. A character must make a Moderate *stamina* check after every three hours of activity (such as running, or hard labor like mining). If a character fails any *stamina* checks, he is thoroughly winded and must rest for one minute or suffer a -3D penalty to all actions. After resting, the character must make an Easy *stamina* check to see if he has contracted

"air poisoning." If the check is failed, he will be paralyzed from the toxins in the air, and pass into a coma for 1D days. At the end of the coma, the character must make another Easy *stamina* check, and if this one is failed, the character dies. Medpacs may be used to counteract the effects of air poisoning — if the roll beats an Easy difficulty, the character has been fully healed and immediately comes out of the coma with no ill effects.

Characters with breath masks can act in the atmosphere of Rordak with no fear of penalties.

Viska Society

The Viska are ruled by a monarch called a *caleisk*, traditionally chosen when the preceding caleisk dies. All of the caleisk's children must battle each other to the death, and the one survivor is declared the ruler of the people. The caleisk then chooses three to six clans, called *lurinn*, to preside over the various repulsorlift cities found around the planet. Each lurinn is ruled by a *calsk*.

Each Viska is a member of a clan, either one of the lurinn or one of the unempowered *calsedra* clans. Whenever a calsk dies, any of the individual's children are eligible to become the new leader, once again through combat to the death with all siblings. Within a particular clan, power is shifted to a new family when a calsk dies without any children. Each family selects a leader, typically through trial by combat, who must battle all other leaders for the right to rule.

The lives of individual Visk are ruled entirely

Tim Eldred

tried to cause the death of someone outside his immediate family). The caleisk and lurinn have absolute authority over investigations into these matters.

Viska Flying Cities

The Viska live in clusters of repulsorlift powered buildings. This tradition came from the need to stay away from the ground, or risk being caught in a volcanic eruption or earthquake. With the advent of modern technology, the Viska began building flying platforms, and have now adapted to a completely aerial society.

All of their structures are huge, open-aired buildings (to accommodate their large wingspans), attached to a huge repulsor column, which is over 500 meters long and nearly 100 in diameter. The cities are built on several levels, reaching many thousands of meters into the air.

The upper levels of the cities are reserved for the royal Viska clans, while the lowliest workers and clans are forced to live on the bottom levels. The middle section is where most manufacturing facilities, trade locations and landing pads are located.

by the clan. The lurinn are granted absolute authority over certain calsedra clans. Within a clan, the calsk has absolute authority over other individuals. Assassination and other destabilizing methods of altering the power structure are regulated through fear — if any individual is proven to participate in an effort to kill someone of higher rank, he is killed (if the individual is within the same family) or the entire family is eliminated in an elaborate ritual (if the individual

Imperial Prison Camps

Rordak is but one of many Imperial prison worlds, but it is one of the most notorious, ranking with the spice mines of Kessel for sheer barbarism. All of the prison compounds are built on the ground, exposing the prisoners to the risks of earthquakes.

Each prison warden is allotted responsibility over one of the many metals mines on Rordak. Forced to labor each day in the dark and dangerous mines of the planet, it is no wonder that few prisoners survive their first few months on the planet (prisoners aren't provided with breath masks). Since everyone sent to Rordak has been given a life sentence, the prisoners themselves are considered Imperial property, and may be sold into slavery, or used as the warden sees fit. They have no rights under Imperial law.

The men, women and aliens sent to this prison camp are the worst the Empire has to offer: murderers, pirates, smugglers, and "Rebel scum" all intermingle in these camps of death. The camps are dangerous, as individuals have reached the point of desperation — the only thing to look forward to is death, and even that will be a relief. Violent battles among prisoners are disturbingly frequent, but the wardens actually encourage these kinds of encounters as a means of keeping the prisoners at each others' throats instead of thinking about rising against the guards.

The insidious nature of the Imperial system blots out hope and kindness. "Privileged" prisoners are often selected to lead other teams of less experienced prisoners and are allowed to use

---

Prison Alpha TR-8

The layout and personnel of prison Alpha TR-8 are presented as a typical facility on Rordak. The layout can be used for other Imperial prison facilities on other worlds as well.

Alpha TR-8 is a camp housing 5,452 prisoners (maximum capacity), with 150 full-time guards and hundreds of service droids. Located just 500 meters from a barthierum mine, the prisoners' daily routine begins at 0400 hours (local time). Each prisoner is to rise, shower and eat breakfast, and be in their mining groups by 0415. With 10 minutes to walk (always under the darkened skies of Rordak), the prisoners work one continuous shift until 0700 (lunch). After the half hour break, they resume work until 1200 hours, at which point they must return to the camp for their rest period (they are allowed six hours of sleep per day).

The camp itself is ringed with guard towers (20 meters tall, with spotlights), infra-red scanners (Difficult *sneak* roll to bypass), proton mines (8D damage) and slicer energy fields (20 meters long, doing 6D damage. Escape is theoretically possible, but Alpha TR-8 has a perfect record.

---

whatever means necessary to meet their quotas. All of the prisoners are under the constant vigilance of the prison guards, who insure that everyone receives a fair serving of abuse.

Prisoners who refuse to cooperate are seldom executed immediately. Instead they are sold to the Viska clans (many end up as vessels for Viska feedings).

■ Major Drummond, Warden, Alpha TR-8

Type: Security Warden
DEXTERITY 3D
Blaster 4D, brawling parry 4D, dodge 4D
KNOWLEDGE 2D+1
Bureaucracy 3D+1, intimidation 5D, languages 3D, streetwise 4D+1
MECHANICAL 2D
Repulsorlift operation 3D+2
PERCEPTION 2D+2
Bargain 3D+2, command 4D+2, hide 3D, search 5D, sneak 3D
STRENGTH 3D
Brawling 4D+1, climbing/jumping 3D+2, stamina 4D
TECHNICAL 2D+1
Computer programming/repair 3D+1, demolitions 3D+1, security 4D+1
Character Points: 5
Move: 10
Equipment: Comlink, blaster pistol (4D), stun truncheon (4D+1 stun), vibro-blade (STR+1D+2), interrogator kit (on belt)

Capsule: Major Drummond is the warden of Alpha TR-8. He is a thin man with a cold and cruel smile; he has thinning grey hair. Drummond began his career as a security guard at the political detention wards of Chromovon. After several years of meritorious service, he was assigned to Rordak, where he quickly worked his way to the warden's position of Alpha TR-8. Drummond cares nothing for his prisoners or even his guards; he only cares about the money that his job brings (based on the amount of ore he can get mined) and the cruelty he can inflict on others. He has been known to take a personal hand in disciplining especially troublesome prisoners.

Average Detention Guard. All stats are 2D except: *blaster 3D, brawling parry 2D+2, melee combat 3D, melee parry 2D+2, alien species 3D, intimidation 4D, streetwise 2D+2, bargain 3D, con 2D+2, command 3D, search 3D, brawling 3D+1, security 3D+2.* Move: 10. Blaster rifle (5D), force pike (STR+2D), breath mask, comlink.

Orbital Nightcloaks

The Empire has used a most effective means of psychological torture to keep order in the prison camps. Above each camp is an orbital nightcloak, which blocks all sunlight. The camps are immersed in one continuous night, and the prisoners are privy only to the constant whistling winds from the mountains. For more information see page 67 of the *Imperial Sourcebook, Second Edition.*

Viska

Viska are flying carnivores native to the desolate world of Rordak. When fully grown, their bodies are between two and three meters long, with a wing span of nearly five meters. They have two large wings, as well as two appendages at the base of the torso. The smaller appendages can manipulate tools, and they have quickly adapted to the use of Imperial technology.

The Viska have long necks, topped by a triangular head. Their eyes are placed well back on the skull, so they have a complete arc of vision, including directly behind them. They derive nearly all of their sustenance from the blood of other living creatures due to a very primitive digestive tract. Their circular mouths house a proboscis called a *blossug*. It is about 40 centimeters long, with several layers of muscle, and a hollow bone with a jagged tip in the center. When a Viska feeds, it extends the blossug, cutting into the flesh of a creature. Through use of the muscles in the snout and a secondary group of muscles beneath the skull, the creature withdraws blood from the unfortunate victim.

The blood is passed through several small organs that extract oxygen and processed nutrients. Because of their biology, the Viska are unable to eat meats or plant life. The Viska are able to absorb the most nutrition from creatures native to their world, including kessarch and drivveb, two kinds of grazing herd animals. A full grown Viska must drink about two liters of blood per day. For creatures not native to Rordak, a Viska must drink nearly three liters of blood and the unusual chemical compounds in the blood stream cause 1D damage (these damage dice are cumulative if the creature has to drink from aliens more than one day in a row). Viska will not feed off one another, although they will sometimes use a proboscis attack as a means of establishing authority over other Viska.

The Viska have excellent infrared spectrum vision, allowing them to operate in complete darkness with no penalties.

Viska expend a great deal of energy, and must rest for eight hours per local day.

Individual Viska are controlled by their clan, and as such, they constantly seek ways to increase their personal status and the status of their clan. Few Viska have ever attempted to leave their native society; those that did escape had to flee elite Viska warriors and hired bounty hunters.

The Viska society is ruled by sheer power alone, so few Viska choose their profession as much as a leader assigns them to a task or occupation. While they take great pride in performing their job well, they also always have an unspoken agenda of moving into positions of more wealth, influence and comfort.

Viska

Tim Eldred

■ Viska

Attribute Dice: 12D
Attribute Minimum/Maximums:
DEXTERITY 2D/4D+2
KNOWLEDGE 1D/4D
MECHANICAL 1D/3D+1
PERCEPTION 2D/4D+2
STRENGTH 2D/5D
TECHNICAL 1D/3D+2
Special Skills:
Strength skills:
Flight. Time to use: one round. This is the skill used for flying. Beginning Viska begin with a flight movement of 12 and may improve their flying Move as described on page 15 of *Star Wars, Second Edition.*
Special Abilities:
Blossug Attack: Causes 4D damage; any attack which causes a wound means the Viska's attack has penetrated the target's skin. The Viska's blood draining attack causes 3D damage each minute.
Infrared Vision: Viska can see in the infrared spectrum, meaning they can operate in full darkness at no penalty.
Story Factors:
Terrifying: Viska are a species that terrifies many other beings. They use this to great advantage (some might say they are even proud of their reputation).
Move: 12/18 (flying), 5/7 (walking)
Size: 2-3 meters long, wingspan up to 5 meters

Adventure Idea

This adventure hook is dependent upon the characters feeling a moral obligation to go upon a suicide rescue mission: perhaps a high ranking informant or officer has been captured and sent

to Rordak. Another option is to have a good friend or even a relative of one of the characters be sent to Rordak for some crime committed against the Empire (maybe even the fact that they associate with known Rebel sympathizers — the characters in question).

The characters can come to the world posing as traders or businessmen who would like to purchase some of the items produced by the Viska factories or some of the metal ores hauled out of the mines. If they choose this option, they will have to either come up with an excuse to enter the prison (such as taking a tour of the mines) or try to sneak through the prison's elaborate defenses.

If the prison alarms are tripped, the entire prison will turn out to see what disturbance has occurred. Naturally the characters may be able to create enough noise and confusion (i.e. explosions) to prevent the guards from discovering what is going on. Once the characters enter the prison, they will want to find their friend. However, they will also face a riot since the prisoners feel that now is time to take whatever advantage one can — some prisoners try to escape, others want to settle grudges "once and for all," still others will try to take down prison guards to get their weaponry. Others, driven insane by months of inhumane treatment, will be entirely unpredictable.

A possible option will be that the person the characters are trying to rescue is being held hostage by some of the other prisoners (perhaps even former Rebels who feel betrayed because they weren't rescued). This puts the characters in the position of trying to negotiate a deal with utter chaos going on all about them.

Finally, after all of the negotiations and combat, the characters have to make their way back to their ship or some preestablished safe location (perhaps a well-stocked cave in the mountains). They may also want to try and steal an Imperial shuttle or small transport from the landing field (if there is one available). From there, they must use guile and stealth to get off-world, since the warden will have alerted all of the Viska cities to the identity of the characters.

Adventure Idea

In a tramp freighter campaign, the characters are hired to bring a load of food to Rordak for the Viska herd creatures, the kessarch and drivveb. While on the planet, they learn the intricacies of Viska culture: slavery, deceit, and ritual combat. While travelling in the city, they will mistakenly offend a Viska noble, who will decide that nothing less than their complete submission to his authority (i.e. selling themselves into slavery) will be appropriate compensation for their disrespectful actions.

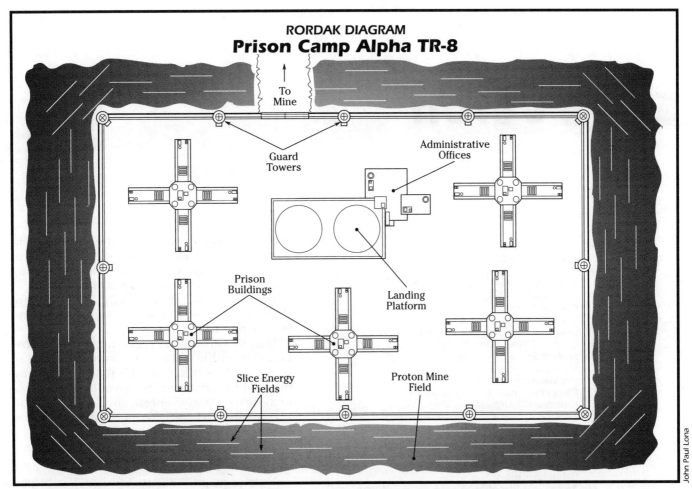

RORDAK DIAGRAM
Prison Camp Alpha TR-8

To Mine

Guard Towers

Administrative Offices

Prison Buildings

Landing Platform

Slice Energy Fields

Proton Mine Field

John Paul Lona

The characters must now seek allies amongst other Viska clans to avoid being hunted down in the city streets while trying to make their way back to their ship. In this adventure, they will be given ample opportunities to further offend the Viska way of life by encountering several Human slaves (former prisoners) who beg to be rescued.

This adventure should take full advantage of the dangers and wonders of the Viska cities: one slip could result in a fall of thousands of meters,

the darkness of constant night because the city is under a nightcloak (the Viska can see in complete darkness anyway), the knowledge that most of the Viska will view the characters as potential meals, and the need to sneak about in a city with a completely alien architecture and design. All of this can help set an exciting tone for this escape-type adventure.

Veron

Veron

Type: Temperate forest
Temperature: Temperate
Atmosphere: Type I (breathable)
Hydrosphere: Average
Gravity: Standard
Terrain: Forests, tropical jungles
Length of Day: 26 standard hours
Length of Year: 367 local days
Sapient Species: Gazaran (N)
Starport: 1 stellar class
Population: 84 million
Planet Function: Homeworld, tourism
Government: Organized tribes
Tech Level: Space
Major Exports: Foodstuffs, primarily fruits and nuts
Major Imports: Mid tech
System: Veron
Star: Noveron, Orell (binary yellows)
Orbital Bodies:

Name	Planet Type	Moons
Sileron	variable seasonal nightmare	2
Veron	temperate forest	0
Trieron	cool research center	0

World Summary

The Veron system, featuring the tropical rain forest world of Veron, is a popular tourist site in the Mektrun Cluster, with a friendly native species and an economy driven by the whims of wealthy visitors. The world's natural beauty has enraptured visitors since it was added to the routes of major cruise lines nearly four decades ago.

The Gazaran settlements have a quaint, rustic ambiance that appeals to citizens of densely populated urban worlds. The cities feature exciting and colorful hagglers' markets, where tourists gleefully pay exorbitant prices for charming native wood crafts and sculptures.

Below the Gazaran cities is the underbrush of the forests, providing an undisturbed playland for amateur naturalists.

Despite a firm military presence, Imperial Governor Ferlem Kie'hintack has allowed the Gazaran to retain their traditional lifestyle and government. The tourist trade has steadily grown even in these days of civil unrest, and Kie'hintack and his bureaucrats have taken more than their share of the wealth.

System Summary

Veron's major industry, tourism, has helped ward off the harsher aspects of Imperial rule. The Gazaran, intelligent gliding reptiles, are among the most eager-to-please hosts in the galaxy. Gazar cities welcome the tourists with open arms, and each visitor is made to feel as if he has become a personal friend of every native he meets. The Gazaran have proven to be a valuable resource for Governor Kie'hintack, who collects a sizeable tariff from the tourist trade and berry exports.

The Rainforests

The tropical rain forests of Veron are known for the fevvenor trees, which cover over three-quarters of the planet's land mass (only the mountains and shore areas don't support the trees). Reaching a height of nearly 50 meters, the trees are merely the crowning feature of a complex biosphere that supports many unusual life forms.

The rain forests are often graced with short, but refreshing rain storms. The planet's low axial tilt allows for consistent weather, with seasonal differences measured more by rainfall variations than extreme temperature change. Temperatures at

System Datafile

Veron system, stars: Noveron and Orell, binary yellow. Three planets, second planet, Veron, is terrestrial.

Veron is a "rustic" trade world which is dominated by forests and tropical jungles. The main starport is named Trelbio and is where most visitors will land upon arriving in-system. The native inhabitants, the Gazaran, have built immense "tree cities" and have actively cultivated the tourist trade.

World Map of Veron

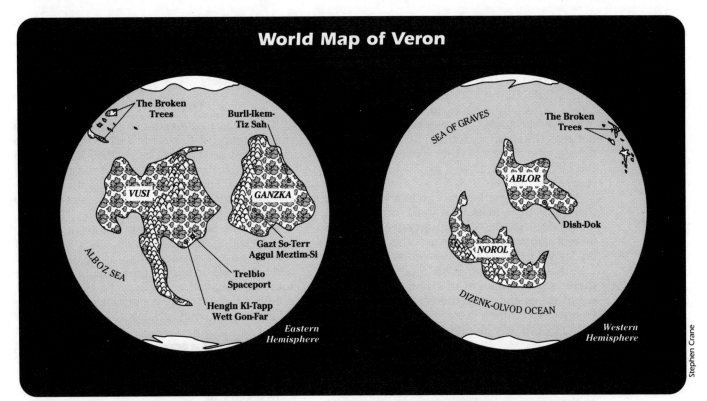

Eastern Hemisphere

Western Hemisphere

Stephen Crane

tree top level are warm by Human standards (rarely does the temperature drop below 35 degrees Celsius, and more often it hovers around the 40 degree mark). Below the tree top level, both rainfall and temperature drop off appreciably. At ground level, the temperature averages 25 degrees Celsius. Because the Gazaran are extremely sensitive to temperature, and their bodily functions are appreciably slowed at the 25 degree mark, they refuse to venture near the ground levels of their world.

Animal Life

Animal life is plentiful and diverse, with insects, small herbivores, avians and large predators all to be found in the forests. Most higher order life-forms are reptilian in nature and are cold-blooded, although the range of tolerable temperature varies greatly depending upon the species. Unlike typical reptiles, many creatures give birth to live young. A curiosity to several biologists that have visited Veron is that many of the creatures thrive on surprisingly small amounts of food (at least compared to creatures of comparable size and activity levels found on other worlds).

Because most of the creatures of Veron are highly sensitive to temperature variations, many creatures will only be found at a certain altitude within the trees. The Gazaran require higher temperatures than most other creatures on the planet and will be found in the tree top regions. Other creatures in the upper trees include small avians and foraging reptiles such as the dressto,

fevvenor toad, and turmil lizard.

The ground level life-forms include many of the large carnivores of the planet, such as the gweraxhai, black behemoths and swamp worms. Since they cannot venture to tree-top level for very long, they pose a minimal threat to the Gazaran, but they have been known to attack careless tourists.

Gazaran Tree Cities

Since Gazaran have sharp claws that can easily penetrate the trunks of the fevvenor trees, they never had a need for ladders, ramps or other artificial constructions. Instead, a Gazar leaps out from a tree trunk, and glides over to other tree trunks.

With the arrival of space travelers, the creatures learned all they could about other societies, taking particular interest in the "extremely large family groups" that tended to form with advances in technology. Since the Gazaran desperately wanted to join the galactic society, they decided to model themselves around more advanced cultures and call their home territories cities.

Each city can have anywhere from about 25 to thousands of members, all living and working together within a certain radius of the respected elder female's home tree. The largest cities are Hengin Ki-Tapp Wett Gon-far (located just to the west of Trelbio Spaceport, with over 100,000 Gazaran), Gazzt So-Terr Aggul Meztim-Si (on the continent of Ganzka, with over 50,000 Gazaran), Burll-ikem-Tiz-Sah (the largest Gazaran city, with

350,000 residents), and Distt Dok. Gazaran cities have been well adapted to fit the needs of visitors lacking the ability to glide.

Although all non-gliding visitors to Gazaran are required to wear repulsor belts at all times, ramps and walkways are a very common sight in cities, especially near open marketplaces and other "public areas." All sales revenues are split between the Gazar merchant and the city's elder female, who distributes the revenue to the rest of the city residents as well as the local Imperial representatives.

Also near the marketplace areas are businesses that cater to tourists who want to explore the underbrush. Outdated repulsorcraft are available for rent, and several Humans and other off-worlders are known to hire themselves out as tour guides.

Although the Gazaran are a peaceful people, there is some amount of crime caused by off-world thugs and small-time criminals. Imperial troops are common in tree cities, although they normally are only involved in crime prevention.

Trelbio Spaceport

Virtually anyone who comes to Veron arrives through Trelbio spaceport. Located on the coasts of the continent of Vusl, the sprawling facility serves dozens of tramp freighters on a daily basis and is a ferry point for tourists coming from space cruiseliners parked in orbit.

The main spaceport, Trelbio Tower, stands 40 stories tall, and contains luxurious hotels and fine restaurants. It is here that visitors will first meet the Gazaran traders, who endlessly wander the corridors of the building in search of customers for their wares and services.

There are over 30 buildings directly supporting Trelbio Tower. Each of these buildings has hotels, restaurants, freight merchants, travel agencies, and tour guide services.

The most influential Gazaran city, that of Hengin Ki-Tapp Wett Gon-far, has complete control over the spaceport, and strictly regulates which other cities may do business within the spaceport and support buildings. Other families must purchase expensive permits to open shops and offer guided tours, although the amount of revenue brought in by these businesses more than offsets the cost of the permits.

The spaceport has the highest crime rate of any location on the planet, chiefly because it is the only place where non-Gazaran will be able to blend into the crowd. Burglaries and baggage thefts are most common.

Gazaran Technology

The Gazaran have learned some aspects of industry and have mastered the use of steam engines, powered primarily by wood, wind or rain. They are developing small-scale manufacturing,

such as mass produced crafts for tourists (primitive glow rods, fire starting kits, climbing gear, short-range distress beacons and clothing). They also use portable steam engines to assist in engineering projects.

Ground Level

The Gazaran culture doesn't even acknowledge the existence of the world below their tree-top cities. They see the area below their homes as an impenetrable dark mist waiting to bring them to an early death. The Gazaran have built up an elaborate and extensive collection of folk tales detailing the horrible monsters that lurk below.

While the Gazaran themselves have no interest in visiting the "dark lands," they know that tourists love a mystery. Exploring the ground level of the world has become a major part of the tourist trade, and as always, the Gazaran have readily adapted: many young Gazar earn a living telling tales of what is below to eager tourists.

Predators of Veron

■ Gwerax-hai

Type: Reptilian hunters
DEXTERITY 4D
PERCEPTION 2D
Sneak 5D
STRENGTH 3D
Climbing/jumping 4D
Special Abilities:
Tusks: STR+2D damage
Move: 16
Size: 1.5 meters tall at the shoulder, up to 3.6 meters long
Scale: Creature

Capsule: Gwerax-hai are lean, strong and quick reptiles. They have a thin torso, with small heads sitting atop a short, squat neck. They have long, curved and very sharp tusks up to 0.6 meters long. They have a long, very thin tail which helps their balance while maneuvering in the trees.

Gwerax-hai are agile hunters, although not particularly fast. They hunt in small groups and try to surround their prey by quietly climbing through the trees of Veron's forest. Once they have injured a creature, they will tenaciously track it through the forests until it has been killed.

They live in groups called "skulks," with five to 15 members. The females care for the young and the males hunt. Their brown and green coloration camouflages them in the forests.

■ Black Behemoths

Type: Predator
DEXTERITY 1D+2
PERCEPTION 1D
Sneak 4D
STRENGTH 5D
Special Abilities:
Armor: Provides +1D against physical attacks
Teeth: STR+2 damage
Move: 9
Size: 2 meters tall at the shoulder, 4 meters long
Scale: Creature

Capsule: Black behemoths are dangerous hunters whose prime advantage is that they know their territory well. Each behemoth has claimed a personal territory and has memorized the location of every tree, pool of water and vine. While not fast enough to keep pace with most creatures, it often feeds after pursued prey becomes entangled in hanging vines or tree limbs. These creatures spend a great deal of time waiting in ambush. Once a black behemoth is aware that food is nearby, it springs to life, ready for the hunt.

■ Swamp Worms

Type: Swamp dwelling predator
DEXTERITY 2D
PERCEPTION 1D
STRENGTH 3D+1
Special Abilities:
Teeth: STR+1D damage
Poisonous Tail: Poison causes 4D damage but can only be used on creatures behind the swamp worm
Move: 15 (wet mud only)
Size: 1.5-4 meters long
Scale: Creature

Capsule: Swamp worms are experts at moving through the thick mud of Veron's surface. They will often bury themselves in a few centimeters of mud and wait for a creature to walk by. Once the vibrations reach the swamp worm's soft skin, it springs to life, attempting to kill with the stinger on the end of its tail.

Swamp worms are dangerous simply because they are usually not noticed until it is too late. They are found in the swamp-like regions of the forest floor. Their appetites aren't large, but they are willing to die in defense of their territory.

The Broken Trees Islands

The Broken Trees Islands are a chain of islands in the northern hemisphere. The Gazaran believe that the islands are the remnants of a large continent which was home to the first great Gazaran civilization. For reasons they do not understand, one day a great storm swept over the continent, destroying many of the trees. After several days of the these storms, most of the land sank, leaving only the peaks of the mountains. Miraculously, some of the Gazaran were able to migrate to the other continents. Scientific expeditions to the islands have found ancient Gazaran artifacts in the shallow waters and many tourists come to the area for aquatic expeditions. Any discovered artifacts are confiscated by the Department of History and Culture, although the tourist responsible for the discovery is given fair compensation. Despite this, the smuggling of artifacts off-world has become a cottage industry for amateur archaeologists.

Gazaran

Veron's consistently warm climate has encouraged the evolution of lifeforms that are cold-blooded. The most intelligent are the Gazaran.

These short herbivores give birth to live young and nurse them out of infancy.

They are short bipedal creatures with several layers of scales. They have a very thin membrane extending from their ribs, feet and hands, which is used to glide among the trees. Specialized muscles line the ribs so that they can control the shape and angle of portions of the membrane, giving them the ability to perform delicate maneuvers around trees and other obstacles. Their bodies are grey or brown in color, and each limb is lined with a crest of cartilage. Sharp claws give them excellent climbing abilities.

The Gazaran are herbivores, subsisting on a diet of fruits, berries and nuts. Because they are cold-blooded, they stay exclusively in the upper levels of the trees.

Females dominate their society for the simple reason that they must be pampered for the species to survive. Pregnant females must relocate to the highest levels of the trees (the warmest areas on the planet) in order to provide optimal conditions for the development of their young, and the males must constantly protect the females from predators. The females are helpless for the entire 133 day gestation period.

Each Gazar city is led by a respected elder female (one who has raised at least 12 litters). Each Gazar has one name, but the name indicates the city, the individual's status within the city and the individual's parents (as a Gazar rises in status, his name will change). The cities seldom engage in open conflict, although each city has several traditional rivals.

Each male is responsible for gathering fruits

and nuts, as well as protecting the females. With the arrival of Imperial technology, many males have also become merchants, educators, engineers for the steam and wind powered engines, tourist guides, workers. Females are primarily responsible for bearing and raising young, although many of them work in the tourist trade as well.

The Gazaran are extremely superstitious, having a particularly pronounced fear of large creatures and the dark. Many Gazaran have nervous habits like stretching their wing flaps, chewing on nearby pieces of wood, and clicking their teeth.

■ Gazaran

Attribute Dice: 12D
Attribute Minimum/Maximums:
DEXTERITY 1D/4D
KNOWLEDGE 1D/4D
MECHANICAL 1D/4D
PERCEPTION 2D/4D
STRENGTH 2D/4D
TECHNICAL 1D/3D+2
Special Skills:
Strength skills:
Gliding. Time to use: one round. This is the skill used to glide.
Special Abilities:
Gliding: Gazaran can glide. On standard gravity worlds, they can glide up to 15 meters per round; on light gravity worlds they can glide up to 30 meters per round and on heavy gravity worlds, that distance is reduced to 5 meters.
Temperature Sensitivity: Gazarans are very sensitive to

temperature. At temperatures of 30 degrees Celsius or less, reduce all actions by -1D. At a temperature of 25 degrees or less, the penalty goes to -2D, at 20 degrees the penalty is -3D and -4D at less than 15 degrees. At temperatures of less than 10 degrees, Gazaran go into hibernation; if a Gazaran stays in the cold for more than 28 hours, he dies.
Story Factors:
Superstitious: Gazaran player characters should pick something they are very afraid of (the cold, the dark, strangers, spaceships, the color black, etc.).
Move: 8/10 (walking), plus gliding (above)
Size: Up to 1.5 meters tall

Sileron

Sileron, the system's inner world, is very hostile and tourists are warned not to visit the planet. It has an extreme axial tilt, resulting in severe seasonal changes. Dangerous storms constantly roll across the world's surface.

The life-forms on the world have developed accordingly. Plants are very active in the hospitable growing seasons, and must aggressively gather enough energy and food for the long winter season. While there are primitive ferns and other simple plants, many have evolved to higher order plants, with active defensive systems. Still others have become carnivorous, consuming insects, arachnids and even small amphibians.

Animal life is aggressive and dangerous. Since animals are also required to gather as much food as possible before the harsh winter, most animals are omnivorous.

Like the plants, many have venoms and poisons that they can use on prey. Most of these creatures have elaborate defense mechanisms as well, such as thick hides, or the ability to camouflage themselves in the natural terrain.

■ Derkolo

Type: Small pack hunters
DEXTERITY 3D+2
PERCEPTION 1D
STRENGTH 3D
Special Abilities:
Armor: +1D against physical attacks
Claws: STR+1D+2 damage
Move: 20
Size: 1.5 meters long
Scale: Creature

Capsule: Derkolo are quick and aggressive killers that hunt larger creatures in packs. They are one of the more common predators on Sileron. They are aggressive and individual creatures seem to have no fear of death. They must consume large quantities of food. In the colder seasons, they hibernate in large burrows; some related species migrate to other other continents on the warmer side of the world.

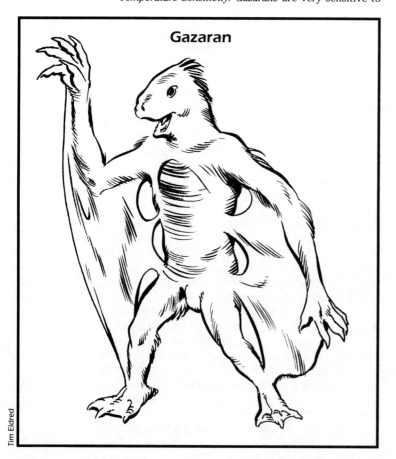

Gazaran

Tim Eldred

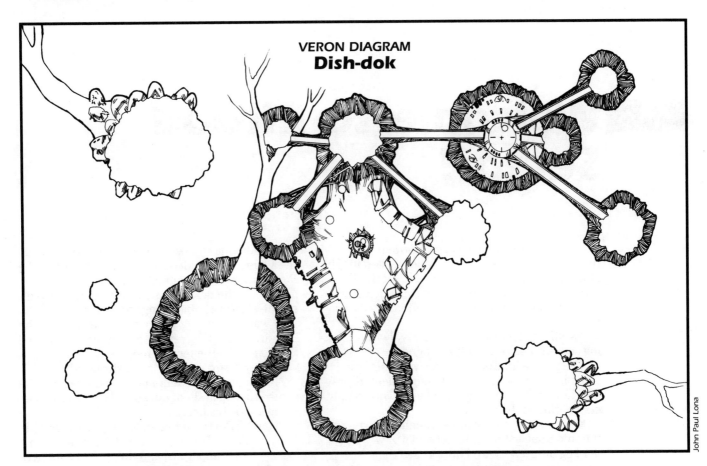

VERON DIAGRAM
Dish-dok

John Paul Lona

Trieron

Trieron, the third planet of the system, is a cool world of oceans and glaciated continents. Aquatic life is plentiful, although land life is rare.

Several academies and universities, including the Academy at Sab Rufo, UnitedChem/SoroSuub University and Metharg's University, have oceanographic research bases on this world.

Adventure Idea

The Rebel characters are sent to Veron to retrieve information from a Rebel agent named Gaylan Della. However, Della misses the meeting at Trelbio Spaceport, and it is up to the characters to investigate his disappearance. They may be able to recruit Gazaran to help with the investigation, especially if it appears that he was harmed near one of the cities on the planet. After questioning several individuals, the Rebels will discover that Della's Rebel cell network had been compromised by Imperial investigators and they must sneak off the world before the characters' allegiance is discovered.

Welcome to Elrood Sector!

The freighter *Blind Luck* shuddered out of hyperdrive as the sublight engines kicked in. The small bridge was bathed in an eerie green glow as the navigational sensors activated and began scanning the area for known navigational reckoning points.

"Well?" pressed Desric Fol, a burly always-frowning scout not known for his patience.

The pilot, a lithe pale Human woman, turned to face him long enough to flash him a silent, reproving glare and return to her business. The computers continued their work.

Klag, a short blue-skinned Humanoid who was the ship's navigator, and chief social powder keg diffuser, cleared his throat. "I think what Desmona is ... trying to convey is that the computer needs time to accurately calculate where we are."

Desric "harrumphed" and sat in an empty chair facing a non-operational console. "Most computers would not only have already figured out where we are, but would also have highlighted likely Imperial interdiction spots, possible trade routes, and projected profit margins besides."

"When you signed on as part of our crew, I had no idea that you were also an accomplished computer expert," Desdemona replied sarcastically.

"Well, how about that! We know where we are!" Klag piped up before the quickly-reddening Desric could explode. "Hmmm. The Elrood Sector."

A young woman dressed in loose fitting white robes bounded onto the bridge, a lightsaber secured to her belt. "I felt us coming out of hyperdrive," she explained. "So, where are we?"

Desdemona reserved a warm smile for Brianna, the young Jedi student who was also part of the *Blind Luck's* crew. Brianna's optimism and friendliness were the glue that kept this team of professional, albeit irritable beings together.

"I was just saying that we have arrived in the Elrood Sector," Klag replied helpfully. He, too, liked Brianna and her effect on morale.

"Never heard of it," Brianna shrugged.

"Nor have I," Desdemona frowned deeply. She turned to Klag in silent question, but the little blue being shook his head.

"I have," Desric rumbled. "Pretty unremarkable place. The locals are stricter than most Imperials, and there's not a lot here ... but there are worse places to spend your life, I guess ... somewhere."

Desdemona absently watched a planet come into scanner range. "We have a place to land if we want to."

"And whoever is down there is scanning us, too," Klag replied. Everyone turned to Desric expectantly. The scout shrugged, caught off-guard that everyone now expected him to suggest the next move. "Well ... until we know which planet that is ..." he began.

"This is Elrood Starport Command," a crisp, clearly enunciated voice came over the com system. "Incoming vessel, please identify yourself, and your intentions. Use standard protocol, please."

Desric placed a hand over his face. "Oh no," he moaned. "Not Elrood proper!" He took his hand off his face and sighed with resignation. "Better fumigate the ship."

"We are the *Blind Luck,* late of Abregado-rae," Klag replied into the com unit. "We request permission to land."

"Permission granted, *Blind Luck,*" the voice replied. "When you land, please observe all standard decontamination procedures. If needed, a decon team will be sent to your vessel to ensure compliance. We will need to see your shipping manifest and cross-verify it with your actual cargo. You will be required to show us your valid pilot's license and ship's ownership files. Our sensors show that your vessel's sublight drive is emitting an ion trail in excess of .54% above the established limit. You will have to have your engines overhauled in order to comply with environmental regulations."

Klag turned the com's volume down. Everyone except for Desric stared at each other in amazement. Even Brianna looked baffled.

"Awfully strict, aren't they?" Brianna ventured with a sheepish grin.

"Is this an Imperial world?" Desdemona asked Desric.

"Nominally. The locals bow down to the Empire, but would like to be independent." He smiled grimly. "The Elrood starport just goes so by the book that …"

"… And lastly, a trained Counselor will be assigned to talk with you about your ship's name. It does not inspire much faith in your competence," the voice concluded. "Land at Elrood Starport 2MZ, Bay 4B. Download code XP-445-T78Y, which is being transmitted now, into your ship's computer upon coming within 50 kilometers of your starport destination. When activated, you will be linked with our navigation beacon and automated landing system. Safe landing, and enjoy your stay."

Desric was now grinning broadly. "Believe it or not, behind all of those rules and regulations is a really nice place. Though I hate to admit it, those rules may be responsible for the generally peaceful nature of the people here. If you can survive the post-landing debriefing, you will find the planet worth your while."

"If we survive it," Desdemona growled.

Klag had this funny feeling that his diplomatic skills were about to get a workout.

Welcome

This section of *The Star Wars Planets Collection* was originally presented as *Planets of the Galaxy, Volume Three.* This section presents the new worlds as part of a larger whole. They all exist within the sphere of space known as the Elrood Sector, an isolated sector far from the heart of the ongoing civil war. This section provides detailed information on the entire sector, including information on important personalities, the history of the sector, and likely adventure and campaign themes that can be used to help bring the sector to life.

Elrood Sector is perfect for a campaign locale. There is enough going on in this corner of the galaxy to keep a group of freedom-fighting, fun-loving characters busy for some time.

Mike Vilardi

The information presented herein is set between the events of *Star Wars: A New Hope* and *The Empire Strikes Back*. A robust, strong Empire has reached the height of its expansion, and it's a grim time for the Rebel Alliance.

The first section of this book is a sector summary, detailing common features found throughout Elrood Sector, including prominent individuals, aliens, Imperial patrols, trade routes, and sector history. This section also includes informatoin on using Elrood as a campaign setting.

What follows are detailed examinations of the most prominent planets in the sector. These sections provide detailed examinations of the cultures, peoples, sights and events that populate these worlds and make them exciting adventure locations.

All in all, Elrood Sector is a strange and exciting place with lots of adventure opportunity. So, drop into sublight and be ready to trade, fight, and make new friends.

Elrood awaits!

The Elrood Campaign

Elrood sector has a little bit of everything: Rebels, Imperials, pirates, worlds to explore, espionage, criminal worlds, and much more. It is quite possible to have a self-contained campaign without the characters ever leaving the sector!

The people of Elrood sector have always had a strong sense of community that crosses planetary distances. These beings all feel a common kinship as residents of the same region of space, and Elrood is a fairly closed community: visitors are treated politely, but they are watched closely. Elrood is the sector capital and Coyn is a major trade world. Derilyn, once the major manufacturing center of the sector, is now under the Imperial martial law, effectively cut off from the rest of the sector.

The occupation of Derilyn has been quite a blow to Elrood Sector. The Empire crushed one world as a lesson to the rest of the sector's planets, and those planets are quick learners. Elrood is a sector free of direct Imperial domination, but nonetheless an obedient holding of Palpatine.

There are two ways of handling an Elrood campaign: the characters either start out as Elrood natives, or they travel here from elsewhere.

There are some tips common to both approaches. Keep the two Imperial Star Destroyers around for as long as possible; their captains should be recurring foes. The captains of the other vessels can also be suitable villains. While the Imperial Star Destroyers are excellent "permanent" villains, the other Imperial ships are defeatable foes (perhaps in the conclusion of the first major plot of a campaign).

Dorok is also a good villain. He is a wily pirate, and has not lasted this long by making stupid mistakes or by not having a backup plan. Grea the bounty hunter can force the characters' to keep a low profile. Lud Chud or Boss Kaggle can be the characters' recurring hassle (much like Jabba the Hutt was Han Solo's adversary).

An individual's reputation in Elrood Sector is important. Since the sector has an undeserved negative reputation, many "Roods" make it a point to foster and increase their own personal reputations. Word travels fast in the sector. Characters will be held accountable for their actions and those who make poor decisions will find it increasingly difficult to find work — or even appear in public.

Because Elrood is a relatively close-knit sector of space, the gamemaster should feel free to add modifiers considering a character's reputation in the sector. For example, a gamemaster might decide that since no one in Elrood has ever heard of the characters, Elrood natives should get a +1D when dealing with the characters. The gamemaster could add an even bigger modifier if she wants to have an "old boys' network" flavor. Examples of this would include *intimidation, bargain, command, persuasion,* or any other character interaction skill. Likewise, as the characters gain experience and a reputation, modifiers should be adjusted. For those who successfully complete jobs for the sector's underworld, they should get a bonus when dealing with the likes of Boss Kaggle or Lud Chud and suffer a penalty when dealing with the self-righteous bureaucrats of Elrood.

Gamemasters should also keep track of the characters' vessel. Ships suffer wear and tear, and after one year of intense use in Elrood sector, the newest Corellian stock freighter will get so banged up it will make the *Millennium Falcon* look beautiful. Make special notes of ship's systems that have taken the worst punishment — perhaps those systems develop chronic problems. These problems can be serious or be minor nuisances ("The ship *always* vibrates that way when we're about to engage the hyperdrive. We've never had a problem … yet!" or "Sigh … the nav computer just winked out again. Um … would you mind just giving that panel a slight kick? With the side of your foot, please, not the toe?")

As far as Imperial influence goes, the Empire officially controls the entire sector, but the only sizable presence is on Derilyn. The Empire's two Star Destroyers are based there. Therefore, the Empire need not be the major villain in an Elrood campaign. However, as the Empire patrols the entire sector, Imperial ships or troops can show up just about anywhere if the adventure demands that kind of obstacle.

For Characters Born in Elrood Sector

While it is overly simplistic to say that every being feels exactly the same way about Elrood, the sector has a distinctive reputation that should be part of the campaign.

The average person in Elrood sector comes from a working family heritage, and takes pride in his or her job, family, and life. While Elrood isn't as wealthy or developed as other sections of the galaxy, the people here don't desire that kind of life. They have made their choice and are happy with it, and expect other people to respect that choice. They are a friendly, trustworthy people, but they are slow to welcome newcomers to the fold.

Of course, there are many who have taken an extreme position, and the player characters may find themselves in conflict with some of these people. What follows are descriptions of some of the more common personality types.

Jealous. Due to their distance from what everyone else perceives as "the action," many Elroodians feel isolated and ignored. Many have an inferiority complex when exposed to non-Elroodians, especially those who have credits to spare and expensive equipment. They are embarrassed by their isolation and their lack of material wealth.

Superiority Complex. Other Elroodians have adopted a belligerent, defensive sense of pride in their sector. They see their isolation and lack of prosperity as qualities that have made them stronger, tougher, and smarter than the "rest of the pampered galaxy." To them, Elrood sector is their personal training ground and it has made them better beings.

Defensive. There are those who point out that some planets in the sector do have luxuries and a measure of wealth. These people are very opinionated and will aggressively correct anyone who describes Elrood as a backwater area. Sometimes, they feel physical violence is needed to "pound some sense into those ignorant non-Roods."

Shyster. The final type of personality is the "always looking for a credit" attitude. These people, tired of being able to afford only mediocre goods and service, are determined to rise above their surroundings and elevate their station. These people always seem to have some sort of "get rich quick" scheme in the works. These people are obsessed with status and the trappings of wealth. Though this personality type includes many honest Roods who want to do more than just subsist, it also includes con men, swindlers, smugglers, petty larcenists, and other unsavory types.

The Campaign's Goal

Before deciding how to start the campaign, gamemasters and players should discuss what sort of goal the characters are working for. Is the campaign supposed to introduce the characters to the Rebellion, or is this strictly a profit making venture? Expectations should be stated up front, since it will do no good for the gamemaster to concoct an elaborate "Rebels vs. the Empire" storyline, only to have the players disappointed, having hoped for a "tramp freighters" campaign.

With the overarching goals mapped out, a starting point is needed. A good place to start this sort of campaign would be on Elrood proper. Elrood comes closest to being a "typical" *Star Wars* planet, with spaceports, high technology, interesting locations, Humans, droids, and other common elements. Perhaps the characters all came to planet Elrood to seek their fortunes.

Radell Mining is the best opportunity for freelance work. If the characters do not have a vessel, Radell has several old freighters that need a *little* work, which can be lend-leased to the characters with an option to buy. Radell may ask the characters to search for new planets (which would put them on the right track to find the sector's featured unexplored planet).

For a different flavor, the characters could be in debt to a crime boss such as Lud Chud. If a character starts out with a ship, this could be the arrangement. The characters may have to work off the debt by transporting cargo to isolated or restricted ports such as Lanthrym or Derilyn. Add to this the usual hazards of Elrood travel (Imperials, pirates, and natural hazards) and typical crime boss ways of doing business ("My good man, I don't care that you were attacked by pirates — you left with a cargo and it was never delivered. Now, let's discuss a payment schedule ..."), and you have an instant campaign goal.

For an action-packed start, the characters could be on Imperial-occupied Derilyn, and they must deal with that situation, hopefully making an eventual escape.

An even more extreme situation is to have the players create their characters, but start with no equipment, ships, or weapons. Stick them on Berea as indentured miners and run them through their escape. Naturally, gamemasters may want to warn the players about this different way of starting a campaign ahead of time!

The galactic civil war is not a big topic in the sector, so it is likely that the characters know little of the war. There is an Imperial presence here and the Alliance has several small espionage cells and listening points, but that is all. Gamemasters can bring the war to the characters by having a Rebel gamemaster character arrive on Elrood, perhaps needing help and turning to the characters for aid. Maybe the Rebel is being pursued by a small contingent of Imperial forces, and the characters get accidentally caught in the crossfire.

If that is too abrupt, perhaps the Empire has imprisoned a Rebel on Berea, and some Rebel representatives hire the characters to take them to the mining planet for a rescue mission.

Running With Unluckies

Unluckies, as the slang goes, are characters who are not from Elrood Sector but are visiting, working, or stuck there. This is the best option if using already established characters.

The best gamemaster character for easing the player characters into the Elrood sector is Grakkata, the Wookiee pirate. Since the Wookiee is very unsympathetic towards the Empire, she may be good company for the characters, showing them the sites of Elrood sector. Grakkata can be a great gamemaster plot device for getting the characters out of jams that are not of their own doing. However, Grakkata has a long memory, and she will collect on any debts.

When first venturing to Elrood sector, the characters will probably first stop at Coyn, the "Gateway to Elrood Sector." As the world closest to major galactic trade routes, characters will have excellent opportunities to pick up information, establish contacts and get caught up in other peoples' problems. Coyn by itself is interesting enough as it is a world ruled by a militaristic warrior-based species.

For characters who are traders or smugglers, the most readily available opportunity for an adventure is to smuggle arms to the resistance on Derilyn or to the militia on Torina. This will pose plenty of problems since pirates enjoy plundering such cargo, and the Empire would be determined to stop any arms shipments they can find, sending the smugglers to Imperial Mining, Ltd. (IML) mining camps on Berea.

For Rebel characters, perhaps the Rebellion sent them to Coyn to recruit Coynites for the cause. Perhaps they are on a fact-finding survey of Elrood sector to determine the sentiments of its people.

A fact-finding survey would send the characters all over the sector, meeting people and visiting most of the interesting locations. Groups of Unluckies will attract attention from the natives and the Empire. The last thing the Empire wants is for Rebel spies to come to this lightly defended sector and cause trouble. Thus, every non-Rood is under suspicion of being a spy.

If the characters stay long enough, they will slowly begin to gain the trust and respect of the locals (provided, of course, that the characters act in a manner that would make them likable). If the characters prove adept at the initial tasks given to them, many offers of work will pour in.

New Discoveries

This section's last entry, the unexplored planet Kuras III, offers a whole world for exploration. Elrood is an area of space with many unexplored systems, and Kuras III is just the beginning. Kuras III offers a unique ecosystem, new forms of intelligent life and enough adventure and mystery to sustain several adventures.

However, there is no need to stop at just the one planet. There are dozens of systems that are far off the known trade routes waiting to be explored. Some of these systems may have been visited once by traders or scouts, others may have been the subject of probe flybys, and still others may never have been visited before. For complete information on running these types of campaigns, see *Galaxy Guide 8: Scouts*.

To keep things moving along, the gamemaster may want to inject a rival into these exploration adventures. For example, introduce an exploration party from IML on a world rich in minerals. Obviously, IML will want to claim the planet and will go to any lengths to keep that claim. The discovery of this planet is sufficient justification for the Empire to send one of the Imperial Star Destroyers over there to reinforce the claim.

New worlds should not overly disrupt the balance of things in Elrood Sector. Finding planets with huge natural deposits or stashes of super weapons from a long-dead species will upset play balance. If anything particularly valuable appears in Elrood Sector, there will be at least three different factions scrambling to get their share — completely changing the nature of the sector.

After the Battle of Endor

Though this product is set during the period between *Star Wars: A New Hope* and *The Empire Strikes Back,* it is easy to adapt this information to the New Republic period.

Elrood becomes a region of open conflict. Derilyn remains an Imperial stronghold and many of the other planets align with the New Republic or declare their neutrality. The Star Destroyers

Thunderflare and *Stalker* restrict their patrols to the Derilyn system and Imperial Interdicted Space. Occasionally the huge ships conduct raiding sorties in other regions of the sector. These raids are conducted either for supplies or upon receiving word of a particularly vulnerable target that is too good to pass up.

Imperial Interdicted Space is now even more aggressively patrolled, as the Sector Moff is determined to hold on to this possession on behalf of the Empire. Even though violators are still interned on Berea, many are also destroyed outright once their cargoes have been seized. The Empire is through playing games.

The rivalry between Radell Mining and Imperial Mining explodes into a corporate war. No one in Elrood Sector deals with Imperial Mining, since the Empire lacks the power to hold its captive market. Fortunately for Imperial Mining, the rest of the Empire needs its ores. Ore traffic from IML now goes *out* of Elrood sector, taking cargoes to remaining Imperial worlds. Meanwhile, Imperial Mining openly attacks Radell operations. Radell manages to survive due to constant business from the other corporations of Elrood Sector.

The New Republic wants to remove the Imperials from Derilyn. News of Imperial atrocities on Derilyn has fired up Republic worlds in nearby sectors and spurred them to action. The New Republic is looking for teams to go to Derilyn and begin a campaign of sabotage against the Empire, scouting for ideal landing sites, arms smuggling to resisters, and general nuisance raids. All of this is meant to soften up Imperial power as a prelude to a New Republic invasion. The type of people best used to conduct this harassment campaign are player characters (naturally).

In time, Elrood joins the New Republic, and becomes headquarters for New Republic operations in the Elrood sector. Coyn remains neutral, but favors the New Republic as the less dishonorable of the two factions.

Elrood Sector Overview

Elrood sector is in a backwater corner of the Metharian Nebula Territories region of the Empire. This sector has moderate wealth, and is for the most part beyond the scope of galactic events. Elrood sector has never been sufficiently profitable or rebellious to merit complete Imperial domination, nor is it a particularly tempting target for the Rebel Alliance.

The sector's isolation has discouraged large-scale investment by major galactic corporations. Instead, the sector's trade depends upon a number of small, local companies that conduct trade amongst the various worlds of the sector.

However, the sector isn't totally free of Imperial influence. To ensure compliance with Palpatine's regime, one planet, Derilyn, was placed under the yoke of Imperial martial law. When the Empire's space fleets arrived in orbit around Derilyn, few had any idea what was in store for the world. The ensuing carnage was excessive, but served as a lesson to the rest of the worlds in the sector: in quick order, the rest of Elrood sector fell into line.

History

In the days of the Old Republic, Elrood sector enjoyed better fortunes. In comparison to the Core Worlds, Elrood and Derilyn had long been minor settlements and not worthy of much attention. While the worlds featured abundant natural resources, they weren't rich enough to justify extensive investment by outside interests. The other "major" worlds in the sector, such as Coyn, Kidron, and Merisee, were slowly explored and colonized by local interests.

The residents of Elrood sector's planets, of necessity, began developing their own trade routes, including the Elrood-Derilyn Trade Route, or the "E-D Run." Elrood is at one end of the sector, and Derilyn at the other, with the other planets as stops along the route. Elrood struggled, but survived: it never achieved wealth, but never suffered economic collapse.

When the Empire ascended into dominance, Elrood sector was seen as just another piece of unremarkable booty taken from the feeble Republic. The Empire was too enamored of its more choice prizes to pay much attention to Elrood.

Still, Elrood sector was not completely ignored by the Emperor. Derilyn, the planet closest to the bulk of Imperial-controlled space, was seized by Imperial forces. The Empire installed a brutal military dictatorship and Derilyn became the main naval base for Elrood sector. As the military suspected, the subjugation of one world was enough to frighten the others into submission.

Official descriptions notwithstanding, the Elroodians began implementing a series of subtle anti-Imperial acts. The most significant thing Elrood did was to slow down trade on the E-D Run. Elrood's traders pioneered a run, called the Coyn Route, from Coyn to a nearby trade route. Now, Derilyn could safely be circumvented. Slowly and quietly, traffic to Derilyn was halted, and now Torina, last stop before Derilyn, marks the end of the Elrood-Derilyn Trade Route.

The Elrood-Derilyn Trade Route

This is a trade route first established in the heyday of the Old Republic. It takes 18 hours (at hyperdrive x1) to go from Elrood to Derilyn. Coyn, the midpoint of the run, is known as "The Gateway to Elrood sector" because it is the main connecting point with other trade routes running throughout the rest of the galaxy.

With the Imperial crackdown on Derilyn, Torina has become the last official stop on the E-D Run. This has boosted Torina's fortunes considerably as many refugees from Derilyn have settled on this once ignored world.

While, in theory, the Empire controls the entire sector, it has thus far bothered to extend full control over only one planet: Derilyn. The Empire has established a region of space encompassing the Derilyn and Berea systems, known as

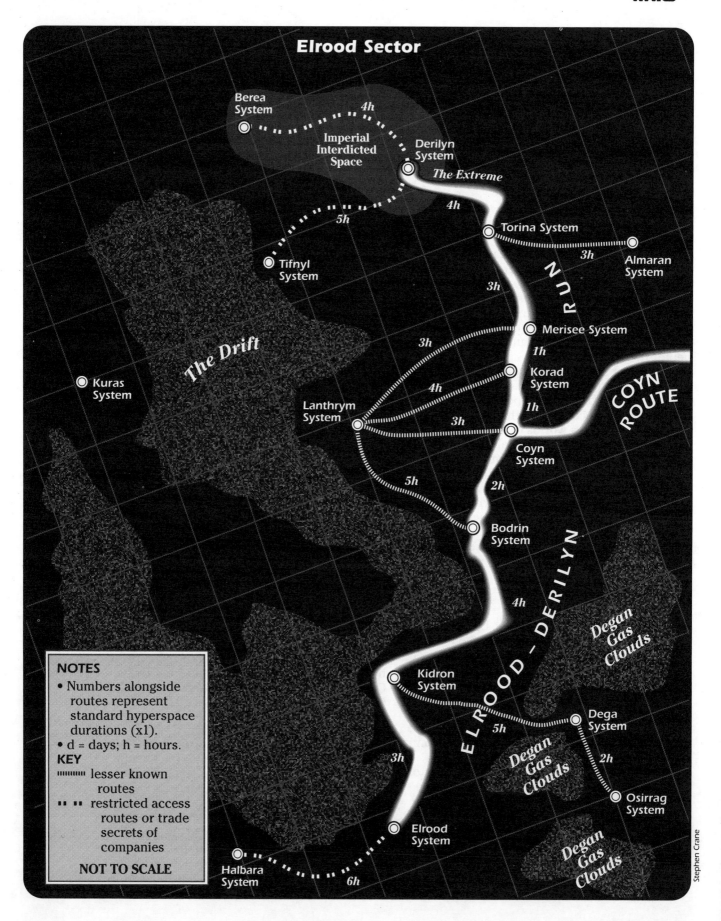

Elrood Sector

Berea System

4h

Imperial Interdicted Space

Derilyn System

The Extreme

4h

5h

Torina System

3h

Almaran System

Tifnyl System

RUN

3h

Merisee System

1h

Kuras System

The Drift

3h

Korad System

4h

1h

COYN ROUTE

Lanthrym System

3h

Coyn System

5h

2h

Bodrin System

4h

ELROOD – DERILYN

Degan Gas Clouds

Kidron System

Dega System

5h

Degan Gas Clouds

2h

3h

Osirrag System

Elrood System

Degan Gas Clouds

Halbara System

6h

NOTES
- Numbers alongside routes represent standard hyperspace durations (x1).
- d = days; h = hours.

KEY
||||||| lesser known routes

▪▪ ▪▪ restricted access routes or trade secrets of companies

NOT TO SCALE

Stephen Crane

Imperial Interdicted Space. Imperial customs ships constantly patrol Derilyn system space and the section of the trade route from Torina to Derilyn, known as "The Extreme." Local spacers warn visitors that it is extremely unlikely for a ship not to be boarded, harassed or confiscated by Imperial forces on Derilyn or in Imperial Interdicted Space. Since the risks of such a run far outweigh the benefits, trade from Torina to Derilyn has dwindled to a trickle.

For ships flying The Extreme, roll 2D: on a 2, 3 or 4 the ship is confronted by an Imperial patrol (select from the ships listed under "Imperial Forces").

The confrontations can occur either when the ship emerges from hyperspace, or when the Imperials have placed an asteroid in the hyperspace travel lane, forcing the ships to emerge into realspace, where they can be boarded and searched.

Other portions of Elrood sector are regularly patrolled, although the chances of confrontation are much lower. For ships flying anywhere else along the E-D Run, roll 3D: on a 3, one of the Imperial ships comes across the ship and the captain decides that a cargo inspection or some other form of harassment is in order.

Imperial Forces

The Empire maintains two Star Destroyers, the *Thunderflare* and the *Stalker*, and a *Bayonet*-class light cruiser called the *Rintonne's Flame*, who patrol the whole of Elrood sector.

The Empire also maintains a handful of smaller patrol ships, customs vessels, and Skipray Blastboats. There are several TIE wings. The Empire has a small armed presence on most of the worlds in Elrood sector, a full military base on Derilyn, and an obscure observation post in the Tifnyl System.

The two Star Destroyer captains have developed quite a rivalry. Captain Zed, of the *Stalker*, is a hard-nosed navy traditionalist. Captain Pryl, of the *Thunderflare*, is of a younger generation and is determined to make a name for herself. Captain Zed considers Captain Pryl to be a soft-hearted woman who is best used as a supply clerk and has no business being a combat officer. Captain Pryl thinks Captain Zed is a crude, two-dimensional buffoon with no cunning.

The two captains engage in a continual contest of one-upmanship. Each tries to catch the most smugglers, impound the most vessels, destroy the most Rebels, all in hopes that sector Moff Villis Andal will take notice. Pryl has been known to anonymously send out warnings of where Zed's ship is patrolling, in hopes of scaring away any prey for the *Stalker*. Moff Andal, far

from seeing these actions as means of achieving greater rank for either captain, sees this rivalry as a source of amusement. Every so often, Moff Andal drops a hint to Pryl or Zed about some great deed the other did, in hopes of causing the other captain to push harder.

Imperial Star Destroyers: *Stalker* and *Thunderflare*. Capital, *capital ship gunnery 4D+2, capital ship piloting 4D+1.* Maneuverability 1D, space 6, hull 7D, shields 3D. Weapons: 60 turbolaser batteries (fire control 4D, damage 5D), 60 ion cannon (fire control 2D+2, damage 3D), 10 tractor beam projectors (fire control 4D, damage 6D). Each ship also has a wing of 72 TIE starfighters.

■ Captain Akal Zed

Type: Star Destroyer Captain (of the *Stalker*)
DEXTERITY 2D
Blaster: blaster pistol 6D, brawling parry 4D, dodge 4D
KNOWLEDGE 3D
Alien species 4D, bureaucracy 4D+2, intimidation 7D, languages 4D, law enforcement 5D, planetary systems 5D, tactics: capital ships 8D
MECHANICAL 2D
Astrogation 5D, capital ship piloting 5D, communications 4D, sensors 3D, starship gunnery 4D+2
PERCEPTION 3D
Command 6D, investigation 5D
STRENGTH 2D
Brawling 7D, stamina 6D+2
TECHNICAL 2D
Droid programming 4D, security 5D
Character Points: 14
Move: 10
Equipment: Swagger stick, blaster pistol (4D), comlink

Capsule: Captain Akal Zed is a big, balding, muscular man of middle age. He has a thick neck, a bulbous nose, hard steel gray eyes, and a permanent scowl.

Raised from childhood in a family of strict discipline and military tradition, Zed has always devoted himself to the Empire and all it stands for. Zed was given his first command after distinguishing himself in the Battle of Fleyars IV, where he took command of the *Carrack*-class cruiser *Seswennan Nightcloak* when the ship's captain was fatally wounded. Eventually he earned command of the Imperial Star Destroyer *Stalker*. His first assignment aboard the *Stalker* was to suppress an uprising on Valera. While he stopped the uprising, he also lost several support vessels due to a fundamentally flawed battle plan. Imperial Command transferred him and his vessel to Elrood sector as punishment for his mistake. He desperately wants to redeem himself in the eyes of Imperial Command.

A cold, heartless disciplinarian, Zed is a fanatic for order. To him, the Empire represents order at its best. He, therefore, has complete, unquestioning loyalty to the Empire, and demands nothing less from his subordinates. His intention is to keep Elrood sector secure and be transferred to a more prestigious position.

Zed strictly enforces regulations and feels that

Mike Vilardi

terror and brutality are exceptionally effective ways to maintain order. In this way, he is a two-dimensional thinker. His opinion of Captain Tanda Pryl is very low — he sees her as spoiled, weak and incompetent, not worthy of the uniform of the Imperial Navy.

■ Captain Tanda Pryl

Type: Star Destroyer Captain (of the *Thunderflare*)
DEXTERITY 2D
Blaster 4D, dodge 5D, melee combat: knife 3D+1
KNOWLEDGE 4D
Alien species 6D+2, bureaucracy 7D, cultures 7D, intimidation 6D+2, languages 7D+2, law enforcement 7D+1, planetary systems 7D, tactics: capital ships 8D, willpower 8D
MECHANICAL 2D
Capital ship shields 4D, communications 6D+2, sensors 6D
PERCEPTION 4D
Bargain 7D, command 7D, investigation 6D+1, persuasion 7D+2, search 6D
STRENGTH 2D
TECHNICAL 4D
Computer programming/repair 6D, first aid 5D, security 6D
Special Abilities:
Force Skills: Control 4D, sense 5D
Control: Accelerate healing, control pain, remain conscious, resist stun
Sense: Life detection, life sense, sense Force
Control and sense: Projective telepathy
This character is Force-sensitive.
Force Points: 2
Dark Side Points: 5
Character Points: 14
Move: 10
Equipment: Knife (STR+1D), blaster pistol (4D), comlink

Capsule: Tanda is an attractive woman in her late 30's with brilliant cobalt blue eyes. She wears her blonde hair in a large braid down her back.

Growing up in a privileged family taught Tanda how to subtly manipulate people, while her father's influence gained her entrance to the Naval academy. However, she wasn't lacking in ability, as her meteoric rise through the ranks of the Imperial Navy showed. She is currently captain of the Imperial Star Destroyer *Thunderflare*. Tanda was assigned to Elrood sector two years ago. Her extensive readings into the Skywalker incident (at least those she had clearance for or could get access to in other ways) have convinced her that those people who exhibit great manifestations of the Force are most likely to be found in remote regions of the Empire (of course, this is simply a theory, and probably not too accurate, either). She wants to find those people so she can mold them into willing servants of the Empire.

Whereas Akal Zed is a brute, Tanda Pryl is a devious officer who can seem to be quite reasonable. Her mind is always buzzing with several different schemes and machinations. Pryl is the sort who would be willing to talk things over with characters, hopefully to trick, convince, or blackmail them into doing her bidding. She considers Zed to be a maddened rancor: plodding, clumsy and easily outsmarted. Pryl has no doubt that she could best Zed in a battle of wits.

Even though Pryl enjoys subtlety and the diplomatic approach, she is willing to use violence and torture to achieve her ends. She has a cruel streak, and has been reported to take a personal hand in torture, even enjoying the pain she inflicts on others.

Her goals are to be promoted to admiral, and to find as many beings gifted in the Force as she can, and either turn them to the dark side or eradicate them.

■ Rintonne's Flame

Craft: Sienar Fleet Systems *Bayonet*-Class
Type: Light cruiser
Scale: Capital
Length: 200 meters
Skill: Capital ship piloting: Bayonet
Crew: 120, gunners: 30, skeleton 40/+10
Crew Skill: Astrogation 5D, capital ship gunnery 4D, capital ship piloting 4D+1, capital ship shields 4D, sensors 4D+1
Passengers: 48 (troops)
Cargo Capacity: 3,500 metric tons
Consumables: 1 year
Cost: 5 million credits (new), 2.3 million (used)
Hyperdrive Multiplier: x1
Hyperdrive Backup: x10
Nav Computer: Yes
Maneuverability: 2D
Space: 8
Atmosphere: 175; 500 kmh
Hull: 4D
Shields: 2D+2
Sensors:
  Passive: 40/1D
  Scan: 80/3D
  Search: 160/4D
  Focus: 6/3D+2
Weapons:
  8 Heavy Turbolasers
    Fire Arc: 2 front, 3 left, 3 right
    Crew: 2
    Skill: Capital ship gunnery
    Fire Control: 2D
    Space Range: 3-15/35/75
    Atmosphere Range: 6-30/70/150 km
    Damage: 7D
  6 Laser Cannon
    Fire Arc: 2 front, 2 left, 2 right
    Crew: 1
    Skill: Capital ship gunnery
    Fire Control: 3D
    Space Range: 1-3/12/25
    Atmosphere Range: 2-10/30/60 km
    Damage: 2D
  2 Tractor Beam Projectors
    Fire Arc: 2 front
    Crew: 4
    Skill: Capital ship gunnery
    Fire Control: 2D
    Space Range: 1-5/15/30
    Atmosphere Range: 2-10/30/60 km
    Damage: 4D

Capsule: The *Rintonne's Flame* is an old *Bayonet*-class light cruiser that has seen better days. It is undermanned. The captain's name is Dongal Tezrin, and he is a very irritable person. The last thing he wanted was to be assigned to a do-nothing sector in a nearly obsolete ship. Thus, he is always in a bad mood, which he takes out on hapless naval crew or, more often than not, innocent ships and their crews that are halted and searched. Captain Tezrin enjoys interning vessels and taking their crews to Berea.

■ Greetbos

Craft: Sienar Fleet Systems GAT-12j Skipray
Type: Defense/Patrol Blastboat
Scale: Capital
Length: 25 meters
Skill: Starfighter piloting: Skipray Blastboat
Crew: 2 (1 can coordinate); gunners: 2, skeleton 1/+5
Crew Skill: Astrogation 4D, capital ship gunnery 5D, starfighter piloting 5D, starship gunnery 5D+1, starship shields 4D+2
Cargo Capacity: 20 metric tons
Consumables: 1 month
Cost: 285,000 credits (new), 150,000 (used)
Hyperdrive Multiplier: x2
Nav Computer: Limited to 4 jumps
Maneuverability: 1D+2 (2D+2 in atmosphere)
Space: 8
Atmosphere: 415; 1200 kmh
Hull: 2D+1
Shields: 2D
Sensors:
  Passive: 40/1D
  Scan: 80/2D
  Search: 100/3D
  Focus: 6/4D
Weapons:
  Three Medium Ion Cannons *(fire-linked)*
    Fire Arc: Front
    Crew: 1
    Skill: Capital ship gunnery
    Fire Control: 3D
    Space Range: 1-3/12/25
    Atmosphere Range: 100-300/1.2/2.5 km
    Damage: 4D
  Twin Laser Cannon Turret
    Fire Arc: Turret
    Crew: 1
    Skill: Starship gunnery
    Scale: Starfighter
    Fire Control: 1D
    Space Range: 1-3/12/25
    Atmosphere Range: 100-300/1.2/2.5 km
    Damage: 5D
  Proton Torpedo Launcher
    Fire Arc: Front
    Crew: 1 (same gunner as ion cannon)
    Skill: Starship gunnery
    Scale: Starfighter
    Fire Control: 2D
    Space Range: 1/3/7
    Atmosphere Range: 30-100/300/700
    Damage: 9D
  Concussion Missile Launcher
    Fire Arc: Front
    Crew: 1 (same gunner as ion cannon)
    Skill: Starship gunnery
    Scale: Starfighter
    Fire Control: 1D
    Space Range: 1/3/7
    Atmosphere Range: 1-50/100/250
    Damage: 6D

Capsule: The *Greetbos* is the Skipray Blastboat most likely to be encountered by the characters in their adventures. It is commanded by Lieutenant Kader Tentrata, a sullen naval officer who looks at the Star Destroyers and the *Rintonne's Flame* with sullen, resentful envy. Pity the poor pilot who is stopped by Lieutenant Tentrata, for that pilot will become a victim of his foul temperament. This

usually means getting a punishment that is far more severe than warranted. There are several other Blastboats in the sector that might be encountered as well — the gamemaster is encouraged to devise unique personalities for their crews as well.

Other Imperial Vessels

There are 12 hyperdrive equipped patrol craft assigned to Elrood sector for patrolling trade routes, as well as the defense of Derilyn system. These craft can be equipped with a "TIE Modular Hangar," which attaches to the hull of the ship and can carry a pair of TIE fighters for additional firepower.

Patrol Craft. Capital, *capital ship gunnery 4D+1, capital ship piloting 5D.* Maneuverability 2D, space 5, hull 3D+1, shields 3D. Weapons: 4 laser cannons (fire control 2D, damage 4D+2), 2 medium ion cannon (fire-linked, starfighter scale, fire control 3D, damage 4D).

There are six system patrol craft assigned exclusively to Derilyn system. They patrol the entire system looking for vessels trying to sneak through the Imperial blockade of the system. Note that these craft will only be encountered in Derilyn system as they aren't equipped with hyperdrive.

System Patrol Craft. Capital, *capital ship gunnery 4D, capital ship piloting 4D+2.* Maneuverability 2D+1, space 7, hull 3D+1, shields 3D. Weapons: 4 laser cannons (fire control 2D, damage 4D).

Aside from the TIE fighters on the Star Destroyers, Derilyn itself has an orbiting space station, the Derilyn Space Defense Platform, with two full wings of TIE/ln fighters (144 fighters).

Derilyn Space Defense Platform. See the chapter on Derilyn for game statistics on the space platform.

TIE/ln Fighters. Starfighter, *starfighter piloting 3D+1, starship gunnery 3D.* Maneuverability 2D, space 10, atmosphere 415; 1200 KMH, hull 2D. Weapons: 2 laser cannons (fire-linked, fire control 2D, damage 5D).

The Drift

The Drift is a huge stellar gas cloud located between Lanthrym and unexplored sector territory. The cloud's rather exaggerated reputation as a navigational hazard has prevented further exploration of the farthest reaches of the sector.

In truth, The Drift is a massive dust cloud with a modest number of asteroids and planetoids. However, due to the nature of the cloud, starship sensors have a very difficult time plotting a safe route through The Drift. Any ship trying to pass through The Drift would have to navigate the region at torturously slow sublight speeds, tak-

Imperial Observer's Report, Elrood sector

Lieutenant Darvis Tret, Reporting.

I have spent the last six months of my tour of duty investigating Elrood sector. All that I can say is that I am very pleased that not a single drop of Imperial blood was shed to gain this sector. This region was not one of the jewels in the Republic's crown.

Elrood sector is devoted to agriculture, mining and manufacturing, although it excels at none of them. I have found the inhabitants of the worlds to be unfailingly compliant. They are a simple folk who are ignorant about everything save that they are at the bottom of the pecking order. The region of space has been settled for thousands of years, and frankly, there's not much to show for it. The population is predominantly Human and Gamorrean, with a smattering of other galactic species, as well as several native species, including the Coynites, Orfites, Meris and Teltiors.

There are only a few worlds worthy of note. The sector capital is called Elrood (a testament to the originality of the sector's denizens), a bureaucratic world that is also the headquarters of the sector's largest corporation, Radell Mining.

Kidron is a refuge planet for those who have earned the animosity of the powerful, wealthy, or dangerous. At first, I thought that this planet might prove to be a possible nest of Rebel sympathizers. I am happy to report that Kidron's citizens are refugees from local law enforcers, bounty hunters, collection agents and gangsters. This world poses no threat.

Coyn is a planet populated by warriors who uphold a strict, archaic code of honor. They excel as weapons makers. I am delighted to report that many Coynites willingly fight for the Empire. Again, no presence is needed here.

Merisee is an agricultural planet that also boasts a rather extensive medical community. The people are peaceful and typically compliant.

Derilyn is the last major planet, and the last stop on the Elrood-Derilyn Trade Route. Of all the worlds, Derilyn is the most valuable, since it has respectable natural resources and manufacturing complexes. It is my recommendation that Derilyn be seized and occupied. This action would also have a chilling effect on those who might consider rebellion.

Establishing a naval base here would be ideal, as forces could easily patrol the rest of the sector from here. A pair of Star Destroyers will be more than enough to handle any potential trouble in the sector.

There are many systems in this sector that have not yet been explored. The Republic wisely refused to allocate further resources to an already mediocre region.

Historical Note: This report was filed shortly before the Empire seized Derilyn. Lt. Tret was promoted for his efforts on behalf of the Empire.

---

ing *years* to cross even the narrowest portion of The Drift. At this time, there are no routes going around The Drift, so that region of Elrood sector beyond The Drift (and containing the so far unknown Kuras system) remains unexplored.

The Degan Gas Clouds

There are several small clusters of gas clouds near the Dega and Osirrag systems, collectively known as the Degan Gas Clouds. While these gas clouds pose a navigational hazard, the minor trade route running from Kidron to Dega does much to alleviate the inconvenience of the clouds. However, the legends surrounding the gas clouds are worth noting: ancient spacers' legends suggest that the clouds hide several rogue planetoids which harbor great treasures abandoned by an ancient space pirate. Still other legends suggest that a group of Star Dragons (Duinuogwuin) inhabit the clouds and fiercely guard their territory. Finally, other legends suggest that the gas clouds are inhabited by a kind of "ghost ship" or "dimensional creature," both of which are purported to manifest themselves in times of great danger, either helping or attacking those who have ventured into the clouds (the legends vary). Naturally, all spacers publicly dismiss these stories as "deranged babbling of someone who's been in the void too long" … but spacers are a superstitious lot and no one has ever investigated these legends by travelling into the gas clouds.

Minor Planets And Systems

The following worlds and systems, while not "major" worlds, are of some interest and are worth noting. Gamemasters are encouraged to flesh out these worlds as needed, since they suggest a wealth of adventure possibilities.

Almaran System

Located close to Imperial Interdicted Space, Almar is a "second-class" planet even by Elrood standards. Since it isn't part of the Elrood-Derilyn Trade Route, it has a lesser volume of traffic than Elrood sector's main planets.

Almar's biggest attraction is the Almar Upside, a space station that has docking and repair facilities, as well as the standard establishments, such as shops, bars, and hotels. Built by a corporation headquartered on Derilyn, Almar Upside was going to be a resort where the wealthy people of Elrood could come to relax, play, and spend money. Of course, Elrood's hoped-for fortunes never materialized. The corporation made the best of things, and tried to keep the station going.

When the Empire moved in on Derilyn five years ago, the corporation was swallowed up. Before the Imperial forces got a chance to catalogue the corporation's holdings, the computer banks were wiped. No "official" record of ownership of the station existed. The space station was considered fully independent. Over the years, the Rebel Alliance has quietly taken control and responsibility for the station. They have converted parts of it into a surveillance and listening post, aimed at Imperial Interdicted Space.

Since the space station still receives some traffic, every effort is made to conceal the true loyalties of those who run it. To the outsider, and even to most employees, Almar Upside is simply an independent space station. All surveillance activities are hidden away in a very isolated corner of the station.

Almar, also called Almar Downside, is a tropical paradise. The planet is covered by sandy, colorful beaches, rolling orange-grass covered hills and lovely flowers. Proximity to its sun, no axial tilt, and a high amount of unique temperature-moderating pollen in the atmosphere keeps the entire planet comfortably warm year round.

A shuttle runs from Almar Upside to Almar Downside. The only starship services are provided by a small control tower and spaceport located outside the only sizable city (it has about 100,000 residents). The planet's entire population consists of immigrants from other worlds, and the main trade is tourism. Because of the world's isolated location, it is a poor one, playing host to only a few hundred thousand tourists per year. The world has many small craftsmen and traders, as well as localized agriculture, so the planet, while poor, offers a primitive but relaxing lifestyle for residents.

Berea

Berea is host to a mining colony owned by Imperial Mining, Ltd. of Derilyn, which in turn, is

under the direct control of the Empire. This world is the chief source of ore for IML.

The mine worker population is about one thousand people, plus several thousand automated mining droids. About one quarter of the workers are normal laborers; the rest come from interned freighter crews, supposedly waiting for some nebulous legal entanglements to be straightened out. Of course, they will have a long wait. All workers are regarded with suspicion since Berea's work conditions border on the criminal. Workers labor under the watchful eye of armed guards. Hired workers have marginally better quarters, as well as acceptable pay and equipment; conscripted workers labor under the most difficult of conditions.

Access to Berea is strictly controlled by IML, with only corporate ships and Imperial warships allowed into the system. All other ships entering the system are warned that they are trespassing in IML space and told to leave or face being shot down and imprisoned.

Merchants and free-traders are not allowed to land or trade on Berea; all of Berea's goods come from IML shuttles from nearby Derilyn. Berea has a small spaceport at the main mining complex. Besides the small docking facility, the complex has a small bi-state memory plastic administrative building, a storage shed for mining vehicles, an ore-loading facility, and 20 long barracks buildings (each providing shelter for 50 miners).

Climate on the planet is cool and dry. Nighttime temperatures drop below the freezing point of water, and vicious wind and hail storms are common. A common form of punishment is to force troublemakers to spend a night without shelter during one of these storms. Security is maintained by 20 private troops contracted by IML.

20 IML Guards. All stats are 2D except: *blaster: blaster pistol 4D, brawling 4D, security 3D, intimidation 5D*. Move: 10. Blaster pistol (4D), armored vest (+1D physical, +1 energy), datapad, comlink.

Adventure Hook: Characters who are careless enough to get captured by the Empire could be sold into service to IML. The characters need to engineer a breakout. However, two of the miners in their work shift are Imperial stooges, and will attempt to warn Imperial Mining about any breakouts they learn of. Since any remaining miners will be punished if a breakout occurs, they make it their business to know these sorts of things very quickly—the characters may have to fend off hundreds of angry miners.

Bodrin

A small temperate planet, Bodrin is on the Elrood-Derilyn Trade Route. The planet has a small spaceport offering clean facilities, food, repairs, and supplies.

Bodrin has a warm summer, and cold snowy winters with very high winds. During the five month winter, the citizens hunker down in their homes, all mining stops, and the planet practically closes up for the season.

The planet's economy depends on this small trade and some quarrying. Bodrin has a fine, marblized rock called bodrite that is in demand throughout the sector. The rock is used in floors and walls for elaborate palaces, expensive office complexes, and other ornate buildings of the wealthy. Because of the value of bodrite, Bodrin only has to produce about 2,000 metric tons of the rock per year to maintain its trade balance. The product is difficult to quarry, so the planet is not wealthy by any means, but it is self-supporting.

Planetary government is administered by the Elrood Quarry Corporation. Individuals may not carry weapons on Bodrin. Bodrin's police (often hired mercenaries) are heavily armed and have very little tolerance of crime — trespassing, assault, robbery, and other crimes are dealt with harshly. Bodrin is a quiet, frontier planet. The small towns are closely knit and crime is rare.

Dega

This is a medium-sized world orbiting a red sun. It is devoid of intelligent life. Dega used to be one of Radell Mining's mining worlds, but the veins played out several decades ago.

Dega: A world devastated by the ravages of corporate mining.

The ecosystem has been destroyed. Plant life is scarce, and the water, what can be found of it, is poisoned by chemical wastes. Hot winds eerily whistle through the monstrous, rusted chunks of obsolete mining equipment and smelting facilities, all judged too old and useless to incur the expense of moving them off-planet. These silent steel ghosts rise from a planet surface that bears deep scars and holes from various mining operations.

The ground under Dega's surface is honeycombed with mining tunnels. Many are now unsafe, and a minor disturbance (such as a blaster skirmish) could cause a sizable collapse.

Dega has but one use now: it is a favored site for negotiating illegal deals, exchanging contraband, hiding hostages, and the like. Dega has become a neutral meeting ground for the many gangs, bounty hunters and criminals of the sector. While there have been many minor battles and betrayals on Dega, the truce has held for most of the groups operating on Dega.

Adventure Hook: While travelling through the Elrood sector (but not on the E-D Run) the characters find a light freighter that has been holed by a small asteroid. The crew of three is dead. On one unfortunate is a small information disk which reveals that a Radell Mining executive's teenage daughter was kidnapped by six bounty hunters hired by Imperial Mining. The girl was taken from Elrood to Dega.

On this ship were the three bounty hunters who were sent to deliver the ransom demands to the girl's father. The demands are for 1,000,000 credits plus the schematics for a new mining drill that Radell is developing. The cash and the plans are to be delivered to Dega Smelting Facility #4-Z3. As the situation now stands, the girl's father knows that she is missing, but not why.

Halbara

A tropical planet with great mountain ranges, Halbara is a world rich in ores, and is the primary source of Radell's mineral wealth. Halbara's climate is hot and steamy in the spring and summer. The fall is a rainy season, while the winter is characterized by powerful monsoon-like storms.

Daytime temperatures reach about 30 degrees centigrade, with thick and uncomfortable humidity. Nighttime temperatures fall to about 15 degrees, but the humidity breaks most of the time. The world is thick with jungle growth, animals and insects (which pose a major annoyance unless using the proper repellents).

At least a dozen mines dot the planet. All operations are run from a centralized location called Halbara One. Halbara One facilities include a spaceport, an ore-loading facility, a small corporate office building, and an apartment complex for the miners.

Radell treats its miners well, with good pay and adequate safety considerations. Radell is aware of the threat of Imperial Mining, Ltd., and as a result has hired over one thousand Coynite mercenaries (see the entry on the planet Coyn) to guard its facilities. The mercenaries' chief mission is to be on the lookout for industrial sabotage. Therefore, a vessel that enters the system unannounced is suspicious. Normal procedure requires that visitors go to Radell Mining headquarters on Elrood and get an authorization code and permission to visit the mining colony.

Korad

This small dusty planet is akin to a roadside stopover that has seen better days. There is a small automated landing pad on the planet's north pole that is serviceable for repairing minor ship damage. Most ship pilots simply bypass Korad and continue on the E-D Run.

These days, Korad has one prime business: salvage. The planet was originally settled in the time of the Old Republic by a corporation called Renew, which specialized in metal reclamation and wreck salvage. Korad was used as a dumping ground for old ships, vehicles, machinery and other wastes. Many years ago, Renew went bankrupt, leaving the world independent. To this day, the world is a giant refuse yard — it is a place where just about anything can be abandoned with no questions asked (since no one is in charge of the planet). Many criminals use the planet as a good place to dump the bodies of beings who are "in the way."

Circling the planet's circumference like a natural space ring is a band of scrapped vessels, many dating back to the Old Republic. The barren surface is littered with wrecks, ranging from starfighters, to freighters, to repulsorlift vehicles, to old droids, to old landspeeders. The atmosphere is thick with the odor of leaking fluids from the wrecks, spilled chemicals and the like. Korad's atmosphere requires a breather mask.

On Korad, a character can find the remains of practically every model of vessel or planetary vehicle. Naturally, most are stripped. Finding a useful part is a Very Difficult *search* skill roll. The closest thing to a caretaker is a wheezy old public relations droid named Emtee-Seventee. MT-7T is still functional, though its programming is incomplete, as parts of its memory have been erased. The droid is left over from the days when Renew was still in business. When Renew went bankrupt, the remaining staff evacuated quickly. There was only one vessel for evacuation purposes, and there was just no room for the droid.

It is believed that several groups of scavengers and refugees have taken up residence in the

Mike Vilardi

■ One of Korad's countless yards of discarded ships...

unending piles of refuse. Several groups of Ugors frequent the area.

Lanthrym

An ice planet orbiting a yellow sun, Lanthrym is a world of people still angry about a slight that occurred centuries ago. When the Elrood-Derilyn Trade Route was assembled, Lanthrym and Coyn competed to be the third major stop on the route. When Coyn received the endorsement, the governor of Lanthrym was enraged and insulted.

Though that governor is dead, a descendant of his lives on as governor and carries on that hatred. As a result of the trade route choice, Coyn's fortunes increased while Lanthrym's declined.

The population, fed a constant stream of propaganda by the government, is sullen and resentful. Lanthrym is the only planet in the sector where Gamorreans are in the majority, and the politicians have openly suggested that Coyn was chosen because the Coynites "have chosen to cultivate good relations with their Human masters." People who come from Coyn are often assaulted and their ships vandalized.

Due to its weak economy and the desire to get even with the other worlds that have slighted them, Lanthrym has tacitly allowed criminals and smugglers to operate with minimal interference. Of late, the pirate Dorok and his men have moved into the Lanthrym system. Law enforcement officials are corrupt ("justice" goes to the one who pays the most) and the only real law hinges on a being's skill with a blaster.

Most of the buildings are underground, fed by geothermal energy. Lanthrym boasts a large number of bars, clubs, casinos, arenas for gladiator combat, hotels, and other establishments that cater to the baser interests.

Lanthrym has a thriving black market and forgery trade. Items and weapons banned or regulated in the Empire can be found here at greatly inflated prices. Those who need false identification so that they may "disappear" are well advised to come to this world as well.

Governor Alrym II is a plain-looking, spindly man. He never travels anywhere without his six hired Gamorrean guards, and two female companions, one on each arm.

Lanthrym is also the sector's leading producer of salt and other sodium products. Aside from the profits from rare sodium compounds, the mines are a perfect form of punishment for those who exceed even Lanthrym's liberal standards of behavior.

Adventure Hook: A nervous man hires the characters and their ship to take him to Lanthrym. The man owes a local crime boss a large amount of credits, and he is coming to ask for an extension. As it turns out, a gang of toughs, eager to make a name for themselves, jump the characters and try to kill them. The characters' employer dies during the fight.

The man was a friend of Governor Alrym, a fact not known by anyone until after the victim's death, when the local law enforcement officer investigating the scene (long after the gang has fled) positively identifies the victim. The local law believes that the characters are somehow responsible for the man's death. The characters' ship is impounded. The characters must somehow retrieve their ship and avoid the law while trying to establish their innocence.

Osirrag

This small planet boasts a pleasant climate of light breezes, perfumed air, and moderate temperatures. Summers are warm and calm; winters are cool with minimal snow. During the spring and summer, small delicate insects spin gossamer strands everywhere.

Osirrag boasts a small number of colonies, mostly engaged in subsistence agriculture. The world lies far off the main trade routes and seems to offer few resources, although it is a pleasant and safe world.

There is a common folktale of this planet. Off in the unsettled wilderness of the world, there is believed to be a species of sentient wind creatures. Each of these creatures is invisible to the unaided eye, but they are reputed to communicate by whistles. The legend states that one young boy, hundreds of years ago, searched out these creatures, and was welcomed by them. They learned to communicate with him, and somehow they have extended his life span for many centuries. It is believed that he is their guardian, responsible for the conduct of his people and the defense of these creatures.

Tifnyl

Tifnyl System has no habitable planets. The largest moon of the fourth planet, a gas giant, has a thin atmosphere and a primitive ecosystem.

The Empire has set up a small listening post here. A crew of 10 technicians and 10 Imperial Navy troops man the station. One of the two Imperial Star Destroyers docks here once a month to rotate crew members and drop off supplies.

The post's military value is negligible. It was established by Moff Villis Andal as a ploy to get additional credits sent to his sector from the public dole, and so far the plan has worked remarkably well.

Adventure Hook: The Alliance has found out about the existence of the listening post, and has commissioned the characters to destroy it with a commando raid. However, Moff Andal has recently been asked to again account for the post's existence thanks to an audit in the Empire's Office of Military Accounting. Moff Andal has deliberately leaked out information to the Rebels about its presence to lure the Rebellion into attacking it. Thus, the Moff can claim that the post's function is as a trap for capturing Rebels …

Torina

For years, Torina suffered the stigma of being a minor stop on a small trade run. When Derilyn was seized by the Empire, Torina became more important to sector trade. In the past few years, a major land spaceport and two orbital spaceports were built. Hotels, bars, casinos, and warehouses have sprung up to handle the new economic boom. The Torines (a near-Human race) have invested their profits in additional industry, but also have a strong aesthetic streak and have spent much on beautifying their world and maintaining the overall ecosphere.

Besides trade, Torina has a thriving electronics industry. Most consumer electronics can be found on Torina for 20 percent less than normal rates. However, they are local knockoffs, and are thus not as reliable as brand name products (for example, if using a complication on the Wild Die, a Torine product fails). One repair attempt can be tried, and it is a Moderate task. If the roll succeeds, the item resumes operation. If the roll fails, the item is permanently damaged and cannot be repaired. Once characters have learned better, they will probably seek out "brand name" electronics and find out that Torina levies a 50 percent tariff on imported electronics!

The primary corporation that manufactures these inferior products is Quality Electronics of Torina. They have offices and major retail outlets on Coyn, Lanthrym, and Elrood proper, and their products are available through independent merchants throughout the sector.

If there is one emotion that governs most Torines today, it is fear. Despite their newfound wealth, the Torines see themselves as teetering on the brink of Imperial domination. Any day now, the Torines expect to see a huge Imperial fleet arriving in-system, bent on conquering the small planet. Thus far, the only overt Imperial presence is the occasional shuttle that transports a few Imperial officers here, ostensibly for relaxation purposes.

Behind the placid images of a peaceful and prosperous world, Torina is a center of Imperial and Rebellion espionage. The world is controlled by the Empire, no matter how marginally. However, the Empire is keeping a close eye on the planet to determine if a more forceful presence is warranted. Naturally, the Rebellion is trying to quietly earn the Torines' support. The Torines must be very careful in the next few years to avoid violent retribution for "rebelliousness."

Devron Zal

Mike Vilardi

Type: Small Corporation Junior Executive
DEXTERITY 2D
Blaster: hold-out blaster 5D, dodge 5D
KNOWLEDGE 4D
Bureaucracy 6D, business 6D+2, languages 5D, planetary systems: Elrood sector 5D+2, value 6D, willpower 7D
MECHANICAL 1D
Ground vehicle operation 2D
PERCEPTION 4D
Bargain 7D, con 6D, persuasion 6D
STRENGTH 2D
TECHNICAL 2D
First aid 3D, security 3D+2
Character Points: 5
Move: 10
Equipment: Hold-out blaster (3D), comlink, datapad, recording rod, several flashy business suits, Radell Mining expense card

Capsule: Devron is a junior executive with Radell Mining. His official title is "Chief Contractor Liaison" — he is in charge of hiring temporary and contract employees. He joined Radell at an early age as a prodigy, and has rocketed to his current position. He wants to see Radell triumph over Imperial Mining.

A handsome young man with a warm handshake and an impish grin, Devron is smooth, confident, and polished. He is an extremely good dresser who uses lots of cologne and hair lotion.

Beneath his polished veneer is an accomplished, hard-nosed negotiator. He is always looking for ways to gain the upper hand in negotiations with freelancers. A man of great ambition, he wants to rise higher in the company by any means possible. If those he hires do their job well, he is warm and friendly towards them. His disdain is evident for those who fall short of his expectations.

The Unexplored Systems

Due to the backward nature of the Elrood sector and the many navigational hazards off the established travel routes, there are many unexplored systems in Elrood sector (these unexplored systems are *not* shown on the sector map on page 100). Gamemasters are encouraged to make exploration a prominent theme in Elrood sector. While there aren't any undiscovered space-faring civilizations in this area of space, there could be many information age or lower tech-level planets out there that haven't made contact, as well as countless unregistered settlements, lost cultures, alien artifacts and other elements that can be the focus of exploration adventures. For more information on this type of adventure, see *Galaxy Guide 8: Scouts.*

Radell Mining Corporation

Radell Mining Corporation (RMC) was founded on the planet Elrood centuries ago to handle the anticipated flow of mineral wealth from Elrood sector. The company has never become a major force in galactic mining, but enough revenue can be wrung from the planets so that Radell makes a respectable profit and continues to be the largest company in the sector.

Radell's main source of ore is in the Halbara system, and it treats the route from Elrood to Halbara as a vital "trade secret." Radell has holdings in several nearby sectors, but it isn't very important to the galactic economy. Locally, working for Radell is a sign of prestige.

These days, Radell is interested in hiring exploration parties to find new sources of mineral wealth in the sector. It also employs freelancers to guard ships and facilities against corporate sabotage, often perpetrated by its prime competitor, Imperial Mining. Radell pays for reasonable expenses, plus a base rate of between 75 and 300 credits per day.

If the characters seek employment through Radell, their most likely contact is Devron Zal.

Though there are dozens of such executives who hire adventurers, Devron is one of the best and he is known for being able to quickly and accurately assess recruits.

Imperial Mining, Ltd.

Founded on Derilyn a few years ago by retired Imperial naval personnel, Imperial Mining, Ltd. (IML) owes its success to the fact that the Empire forcibly persuades some customers to use IML.

IML's chief source of ore is the Berea system, a short jump from Derilyn and securely within the bounds Imperial Interdicted Space. Many Elrood citizens feel that IML is an active front for the Empire. Whispered stories of espionage and sabotage designed to promote the Empire's interests abound.

IML has a sizable cargo fleet courtesy of the Empire's navy — ships entering the Derilyn system are often boarded and searched, and many confiscated ships become the property of IML. As one might expect, many of the ship seizures are questionable (at best). Crew members aboard such ships are quickly convicted of smuggling and sent to work off their sentence as slave-miners leased to IML. Individuals are paid 25 credits a day for their labors, but IML's charges to "contract employees" for equipment, room and board comes out to 23 credits a day, so a worker can only reasonably expect to earn 736 credits "take home" pay per year.

Crime Bosses

Like most other regions of the galaxy, the criminal underworld is alive and well in Elrood sector. There are several prominent crime bosses in the sector.

These characters can have many uses in an Elrood sector campaign. Characters may encounter the bosses when they need a quick, "no questions asked" high interest loan (for guidelines on "loan sharking," see pages 27-29 of *Galaxy Guide 6: Tramp Freighters, Second Edition*). Perhaps the characters' heroics are attracting too much attention, and the crime bosses want the characters "silenced." A crime boss might anonymously help sponsor a down-and-out group of characters, only to "call in the favor" later (the favor could involve striking against a rival crimelord, or perhaps smuggling some contraband through heavy Imperial patrols).

■ Lud Chud

Type: Rakaan (Neuter) Crime Boss
DEXTERITY 2D+1
Blaster 4D, dodge 6D, pick pocket 5D, running 4D, webs 6D
KNOWLEDGE 2D+2
Bureaucracy 5D, business 6D, intimidation 7D, law enforcement 4D+1, planetary systems: Elrood sector 5D, streetwise 7D+1, value 5D

MECHANICAL 2D+1
Communications 6D
PERCEPTION 4D
Bargain 6D, command 7D, con 7D+2, gambling 6D, hide 8D, persuasion 8D, sneak 8D
STRENGTH 4D+2
Brawling 6D, climbing/jumping 8D
TECHNICAL 2D
Security 4D
Special Abilities:
Fangs: STR+1D damage
Webbing: Chud can shoot 2 webs from its abdomen every round, using its *webs* skill. Breaking out of a web is a Very Difficult *Strength* or *lifting* task. The webs retain their potency for two hours, and have a range of 3-4/8/12.
Neuter Phase: In neuter phase, Lud Chud may add +1D to *Strength* and all *Strength*-related skills, as well as increase Move by +2.
Character Points: 12
Move: 14, 12 (swimming)
Equipment: Blaster pistol (4D)

Capsule: Lud is an 80-year-old Rakaan. It has always had a talent for crime, and has settled on Torina as the premier crime boss. It was only when the Empire took over Derilyn and Torina rose in importance did Lud's criminal empire gain much worth.

Lud has influence, property, and henchmen throughout Elrood sector, but it concentrates its activities on Torina, Lanthrym, and Elrood. At these sites, it engages in loansharking, protection rackets, black marketeering, forgery, smuggling, and other unsavory activities.

Few beings have seen Lud. It allows others to circulate the misperception that it is a Humanoid male.

A cunning but lazy being, Lud sits in its lair and hatches new schemes while revelling in its power. Though it is willing to talk and negotiate, it is a clever negotiator and twists words to get people to do what it wants.

Lud eats people who do not agree with it. It keeps many victims dangling in cocoons in its lair. Lud is getting close to Transition; it is currently in neuter phase.

Boss Kaggle is Lud's biggest rival. Lud's chief ambitions are to be the absolute head of all crime in the sector, and to get rid of Kaggle.

■ Boss Kaggle

Type: Dazouri Crime Boss
Rest Form
DEXTERITY 1D
Brawling parry 1D+2, dodge 6D, melee combat 1D+1, melee parry 4D, pick pocket 7D
KNOWLEDGE 3D
Bureaucracy 6D, business 6D, cultures: Elrood sector 6D+1, intimidation 6D, languages 5D, law enforcement 5D+2, planetary systems 6D, streetwise 6D, survival 5D, value 5D, willpower 6D
MECHANICAL 1D
PERCEPTION 3D
Bargain 6D, command 6D, con 7D, forgery 5D+1, gambling 6D+2, hide 7D, persuasion 6D, sneak 6D
STRENGTH 1D
Brawling 2D, climbing/jumping 3D, melee combat 1D+1, stamina 3D
TECHNICAL 3D
Computer programming/repair 6D, droid programming 5D, droid repair 5D, security 7D

Rage Form:
DEXTERITY 5D
Brawling parry 5D+2, dodge 10D, melee combat 5D+1, melee parry 8D
KNOWLEDGE 1D
Intimidation 4D
MECHANICAL 1D
PERCEPTION 1D
STRENGTH 5D
Brawling 8D, climbing/jumping 7D, lifting 6D+2, stamina 7D
TECHNICAL 1D
Special Abilities:
Rage: When a Dazouri is wounded, badly frightened, threatened with bodily harm, successfully intimidated or infuriated, he transforms into his rage form. He can also initiate it at will, but it is a Very Difficult *Perception* task. Kaggle can prevent his rage transformation with a Heroic *Perception* task.

Dazouris and Lahsbees are closely related races: "genetic cousins" in the same way that Humans and near-Human races are closely related. Like the Lahsbees, Dazouris physically transform from one form to another. The character must allocate dice for the *rage* and *rest* forms. Dazouris also receive a bonus of +1D to *Dexterity* and *Strength* for their rage form. Dazouris retain the same skill adds, no matter their form. Dazouris in rage form may only use *brawling parry, dodge, melee combat, melee parry, intimidation, brawling, climbing/jumping* and *lifting*.
Claws: STR+2D damage (rage form only)
Teeth: STR+1D+2 damage (rage form only)
Horns: STR+1D damage (rage form only)
This character is Force-sensitive.
Force Points: 1
Dark Side Points: 4
Character Points: 14
Move: 8 (in rest form), 12 (in rage form)
Equipment: Datapad

Capsule: Boss Kaggle is a Dazouri, a species that has two forms, rest and rage. Starting out as a petty thief, he used the combination of his intelligence and his violent form to rise in the criminal underworld of his home sector.

In his normal Dazouri rest form, Boss Kaggle is a scrawny, hairless, one-meter-tall creature with spindly limbs. He has big, black saucer eyes, vestigial horns on his upper forehead, and a thin reedy voice.

In his rage form, he transforms into a 3.2-meter-tall hulking brute with shaggy black fur, huge claws and fangs, and a pair of wicked horns.

Boss Kaggle makes his home on Lanthrym, where he has a palatial home and an impressive force of bodyguards. Even though he does not truly need guards, their presence perpetuates the illusion of him being a small, fragile creature.

In his rest form, Kaggle is a shrewd, calculating little creature who appears physically helpless. He voices a distaste for violence and a dislike of pain ("Oh, please don't threaten me, gentlemen, it upsets me so! You really don't want to upset me, do you?") Everything in his manner speaks of "talking this out."

In rage form, Kaggle is a homicidal maniac that mows down anything that is standing. Usually, Kaggle's bodyguards and aides leave the room when they see that he is about to make the change. This makes many of Kaggle's soon-to-be-victims

Mike Vilardi

overconfident, feeling that they can now manipulate the small alien.

One of Kaggle's biggest objectives is to build up a large crime empire and get rid of his hated rival, Lud Chud.

Pirates

There are a couple of active pirate bands in Elrood sector. Despite their best efforts, the Imperials have been unable to eliminate or capture them, much to the chagrin of Moff Andal.

■ Grakkata
Type: Wookiee Pirate
DEXTERITY 1D
Bowcaster 4D+1, brawling parry 3D, dodge 4D, melee 2D+2, melee parry 4D
KNOWLEDGE 2D+1
Business 3D, intimidation 7D, languages 4D, planetary systems: Elrood sector 4D+2, streetwise 3D, survival 4D, value 3D, willpower 3D
MECHANICAL 1D
Astrogation 3D+1, repulsorlift operation 4D, space transports 5D, starfighter piloting 4D+2, starship gunnery 3D+1
PERCEPTION 1D
Command 2D, hide 3D, sneak 4D
STRENGTH 4D+2
Brawling 6D+2, climbing/jumping 6D, lifting 6D, stamina 5D+1
TECHNICAL 2D

Rakaans

Rakaans are large, predatory creatures from Rakaa IV, a warm jungle and forest world on the edge of the Core. The creatures are rarely encountered away from their homeworld.

Physically, Rakaans have a segmented, mottled green to dark brown body, with a bloated abdomen and ten limbs. The back eight legs work together for fast locomotion and swimming, while the front two limbs, longer and nimbler, are tool-using limbs with prehensile hands and opposable digits.

Rakaans can shoot webs to trap prey. The webs are created in a small sac on top of the abdomen, and are shot out of the top side of the abdomen segment. Normal webs can last for about two hours. Rakaans who chew on the nargk root native to their world can mix its juices with their saliva to produce a preservative adhesive that can last for many weeks without losing strength. This adhesive is used to cocoon victims for later feeding. A pair of glands inside a Rakaan's mouth produces an acidic substance that dissolves the webs.

The Rakaan "head" is mounted on a long neck. The face boasts four segmented eyes, which can move independently of each other, and a small opening that leads to the Rakaan's hearing organs. A series of pits on the head allows the Rakaan to breathe when the rest of the body is underwater.

The Rakaan mouth is located underneath the abdomen, and is equipped with a set of mandibles. A Rakaan can also breathe through its mouth. The brain is located in the center of the abdomen, along with the other major vital organs, well-cushioned from impacts and injury.

Rakaans are native to warmer climates: they go into hibernation in cold weather (below zero degrees standard). The normal Rakaan life span is about 160 standard years.

Rakaans have five life phases, which also correspond to unique sexes — child, female, neuter, male, and andro. Each Rakaan normally experiences at least three phases during its lifetime. There is no steady cycle of the life phases: on average, a Rakaan is in child phase for the first 30 years of its life, but it may

stay in this phase for as few as five or as many as 60 years. Likewise, the retention of the other sexes is highly variable. A Rakaan might retain a sex for as little as three months or for as long as 80 years. Some scientists theorize that the distribution of the sexes, and the biological change from one sex to another, called the Transition, is part of a natural rhythm that ensures that there are enough Rakaans of all sexes to perpetuate the species. Scientists have noted that in times of famine, the neuter population skyrockets, while in times of severe depopulation, such as during hive wars, the neuter population plummets, children mature quickly and the male, female and andro populations increase at a very rapid rate.

When a Rakaan is in Transition, the old sex characteristics disappear, while the new ones mature and grow, often within the span of two to three standard weeks. During this period, Rakaans become very violent and ravenously hungry.

The child phase is the earliest of all phases. The Rakaan is physically much smaller than all other phases (normally only about half to one meter tall), and it is in this phase that Rakaans learn much about survival from the more mature members of their species.

In the neuter phase, Rakaans are quite strong, but still physically small (about 1.5 to 2 meters tall). Neutral Rakaans are used as hunters, guards and warriors, as they have a very compact but dense muscle structure. Their altered metabolism allows for the very efficient use of energy, and thus their food requirements are smaller than in other phases. In times of peace, with no overriding threats, upwards of 80 percent the Rakaan population may be in neuter phase. During times of conflict, the Rakaan population is also overwhelmingly neuter. However, as soon as the conflict dies down or the population reaches a critically low number, neuters begin changing into the other sexes and begin bearing children.

In male phase, Rakaans are responsible for fertilizing the Rakaan eggs which females lay. A male Rakaan is only slightly larger than the neuter phase (about two meters tall).

In female phase, Rakaans lay eggs. After the eggs are fertilized, the female retakes the eggs into her abdomen, where they are nourished. Rakaans in female phase are largest, reaching their full height, and their abdomen normally elongates, giving them a length of up to four meters. After the eggs have been nourished for three months, the eggs are released into a nesting chamber, where the andro phase Rakaans are responsible for bringing the eggs to maturity.

The final Rakaan phase, andro, is of average size for the Rakaan species. The andro is responsible for nurturing fertilized eggs. The andro's glands produce a unique paste, released through the mouth, which must be spread over the eggs. The nourishment from the eggs feeds the young Rakaan until they are ready to hatch into child phase, three months later.

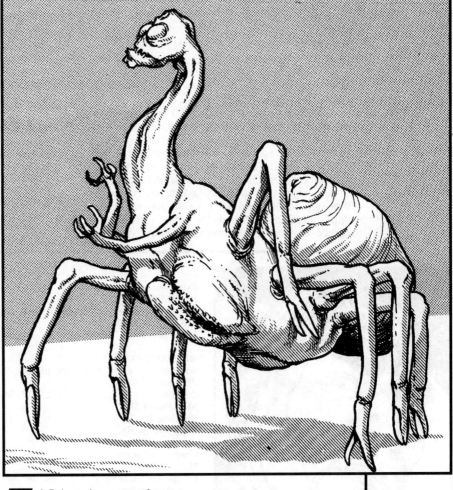

■ A Rakaan in neuter phase.

■ Rakaan
Attribute Dice: 12D
DEXTERITY 1D/4D
KNOWLEDGE 2D/4D+2
MECHANICAL 1D/3D+1
PERCEPTION 1D/5D
STRENGTH 2D+2/5D
TECHNICAL 1D/2D+1
Special Skills:
Dexterity skills:
Webs. Time to use: One round. This is the skill used to shoot the Rakaan's webs.
Special Abilities:
Fangs: Do STR+1D damage.
Webbing: Rakaans can shoot up to two webs every round; their bodies can produce three webs per standard hour (assuming the Rakaan is well fed), and the abdominal sac can hold up to 10 webs. Breaking out of the webbing is a Very Difficult *Strength* or *lifting* task. Normal webbing lasts up to two hours, although with the preservative saliva Rakaans make, a web can last for several weeks. The webs have ranges of 3–4/8/12.
Phases: Rakaans have several unique life cycle/sex phases that affect their die codes. They are child, neuter, male, female and andro.
Child: -1D to *Strength*, -2 to *Dexterity*, -3 to *Move.*
Neuter: +1D to *Strength*, +2 to *Move.*
Male: +2 to *Perception*, +1 to *Strength.*
Female: +2 to *Strength*, +2D armor to abdomen area, -1 to Move.
Andro: -3 to *Move.*
Move: 11/15 (walking), 11/14 (swimming)
Size: 1.5–3 meters tall, 2–4 meters long

Computer programming/repair 3D, droid repair 3D, repulsorlift repair 3D, starship repair 4D+1
Special Abilities:
Berserker Rage: +2D to *Strength* when in immediate danger. See page 137 of *Star Wars: The Roleplaying Game, Second Edition* and page 124 of the *Gamemaster Handbook*.
Climbing Claws: Add +2D to *climbing*.
Force Points: 2
Dark Side Points: 1
Character Points: 7
Move: 11
Equipment: Bowcaster (4D), comlink, datapad

Capsule: Grakkata is a 2.5-meter-tall Wookiee with gray shaggy hair. She keeps her equipment and bowcaster stored on harnesses crisscrossing her chest. Her eyes are a soft green color.

Grakkata has plied the space lanes of Elrood for the past three years. She has been on the run from the Empire ever since she escaped from slavery several years ago. After absconding with a light freighter originally confiscated by the Empire, Grakkata came to Elrood sector to "disappear."

Although she is a pirate, Grakkata adheres to the Wookiee code of honor. As a rule, she raids only Imperial-affiliated vessels or other pirates. Her choice of targets has made her many enemies.

Grakkata shares the Wookiee tendency toward violence, but her intimidating presence is often enough to get appropriate levels of cooperation from her victims. Aside from piracy, Grakkata is involved with smuggling, illicit passenger ferrying and gun running. She loves travelling the Extreme, as it represents a challenge.

Characters will have a strong ally in Grakkata if they make friends with her. She knows Elrood sector inside and out, and if they earn her confidence, she will provide advice and act as guide for the newcomer characters. Grakkata wants to stay alive and prosper, and see the Rebellion beat the Empire, which will enable her to return to Kashyyyk.

■ Treespirit
Craft: Ghtroc Industries class 720 freighter
Type: Modified light freighter
Scale: Starfighter
Length: 35 meters
Skill: Space transports: Ghtroc freighter
Crew: 1; 1 can coordinate
Crew Skill: see Grakkata
Passengers: 10
Cargo Capacity: 135 metric tons
Consumables: 2 months

Dorok Zalaster

Mike Vilardi

Type: Bloodthirsty Pirate
DEXTERITY 3D+2
Blaster 6D, dodge 5D, pick pocket 4D
KNOWLEDGE 3D
Alien species 4D+2, intimidation 6D+1, planetary systems: Elrood sector 6D+2, streetwise 5D
MECHANICAL 2D+2
Space transports 4D, starfighter piloting 4D+1, starship gunnery 4D, starship shields 3D
PERCEPTION 2D
Command 4D, con 3D, forgery 3D, hide 5D, sneak 5D+1
STRENGTH 3D
Brawling 5D+2
TECHNICAL 3D
Security 4D
Character Points: 9
Move: 10
Equipment: Blaster pistol (4D), two grenades (5D), blast vest (+1D physical; +1 energy), comlink

Capsule: Dorok is an older 1.75-meter-tall Human male. His hardened face indicates a hard life of crime. His bald head is covered with tattoos. A huge scar runs from the top of his head, down the left side of his face, ending at his chin. He has an evil smirk.

A criminal since he was a young pickpocket in the Corellian System, Dorok is hiding out in the Elrood sector with his band of devoted pirates.

A dirty fighter, cruel, avaricious, and opportunistic, Dorok is exactly the sort of person you don't want to meet in a dark alley. He cares little for galactic politics. Dorok steals from everyone and is not averse to killing everyone on a ship just for the sheer pleasure of it. Dorok thinks he has the gift of a witty turn of a phrase, but he is little more than a murderous bully.

Dorok is a highly successful pirate—that's all that he does well. He fancies himself a jack of all trades, but fails miserably in all other endeavors. Dorok and his men have a pirate base on the isolated world of Lanthrym. The base exists with the quiet acceptance of Lanthrym's government.

He has many spies throughout the sector, who scour cantinas, starports and other spacer haunts looking for information on ship schedules and cargoes.

Mike Vilardi

Cost: 46,750
Hyperdrive Multiplier: x2
Hyperdrive Backup: x15
Nav Computer: Yes
Maneuverability: 2D
Space: 4
Atmosphere: 280; 800 kmh
Hull: 4D
Shields: 2D
Sensors:
  Passive: 15/0D
  Scan: 30/1D
  Search: 50/3D
  Focus: 2/4D
Weapons:
  Four Laser Cannons (fire-linked)
    Fire Arc: Turret
    Crew: Pilot or co-pilot
    Skill: Starship gunnery
    Fire Control: 2D+1
    Space Range: 1-3/12/25
    Atmosphere Range: 100-300/1.2 /2.5 km
    Damage: 6D

Capsule: The *Treespirit* is a battered-looking Ghtroc freighter that Grakkata has modified substantially since she stole it several years ago. Its most noticeable feature is the color scheme: the entire ship is a soft forest green to match the color of her native Kashyyyk. What isn't readily noticeable are the four retractable laser cannon: they've been an unpleasant surprise to many careless TIE pilots.

Dorok's Pirate Fleet

Dorok has a pirate fleet consisting of *The Last Thing,* a modified customs cruiser, and eight scout ships. All were captured during various heists (the escapade leading to the capture of the Imperial Customs cruiser is Dorok's favorite tale). While the ships aren't as well maintained as they were previously, the fleet is still a danger to poorly armed private freighters.

Dorok has 34 underlings actively involved in piracy, along with his countless spies. They are all unprincipled dregs who would sell each other out, but Dorok keeps them in line because of the wealth he can offer them. If Dorok's men attack the characters, use the following stats.

Dorok's pirates. All stats are 2D except: *blaster 5D, space transports 5D, Strength 3D, brawling 4D+1.* Move: 10. Blaster pistol (4D damage).

■ The Last Thing

Craft: Seinar Fleet Systems 344 class Light Cruiser
Type: Modified Imperial Customs Light Cruiser
Scale: Starfighter
Length: 42 meters
Skill: Space transports: 344 Light Cruiser
Crew: 4, gunners: 4, skeleton 2/+10
Crew Skill: Space transports 4D, starship gunnery 4D, starship shields 3D
Passengers: 10 (troops); 6 (prisoner cells)
Cargo Capacity: 150 metric tons
Consumables: 3 months
Cost: 375,000 credits
Hyperdrive Multiplier: x2
Hyperdrive Backup: x10
Nav Computer: Yes
Maneuverability: 2D
Space: 9
Atmosphere: 400; 1,150 kmh
Hull: 5D
Shields: 2D

Sensors:
   Passive: 30/1D
   Scan: 60/2D
   Search: 90/3D
   Focus: 4/4D+1
Weapons:
   Four Laser Cannons
     Fire Arc: 2 front, 2 turret
     Crew: 1
     Skill: Starship gunnery
     Fire Control: 3D
     Space Range: 1-3/12/25
     Atmosphere Range: 100-300/1.2/2.5 km
     Damage: 5D

Capsule: *The Last Thing* is an old Imperial light cruiser captured through clever deceit and a well-executed plan. Dorok has made extensive modifications to it. The name comes from Dorok: "My ship is the last thing my victims see."

Mike Vilardi

■ Dorok's Scout Ships

Craft: Tykannin Drive *Redthorn*-class scout ship
Type: Modified scout vessel
Scale: Starfighter
Length: 24 meters
Skill: Space transports: *Redthorn*-class scout ship
Crew: 2
Crew Skill: *Space transports 5D, starship gunnery 4D+1*
Passengers: 2
Cargo Capacity: 10 metric tons
Consumables: 6 months
Cost: 55,000 credits
Hyperdrive Multiplier: x2
Hyperdrive Backup: x15
Nav Computer: Yes
Maneuverability: 1D
Space: 5
Atmosphere: 295; 850 kmh
Hull: 3D+2
Shields: 1D
Sensors:
   Passive: 30/0D
   Scan: 50/1D
   Search: 75/2D
   Focus: 5/3D
Weapons:
   One Laser Cannon
     Fire Arc: Front
     Crew: Pilot or co-pilot
     Skill: Starship gunnery
     Fire Control: 1D
     Space Range: 1-3/12/25
     Atmosphere Range: 100-300/1.2/2.5 km
     Damage: 4D

Capsule: Dorok owns eight stolen scout ships. The vessels have been modified according to Dorok's instructions.

Bounty Hunters

Elrood sector is an area that plays host to several bounty hunters. Despite the presence of a "refuge" world (Kidron), the dangers of openly hunting individuals on Kidron discourages much action on that world. Bounty hunters most commonly frequent Coyn (because it is a major crossroads in the sector) and Elrood (because it is a major trade route on the world). Aside from Grea, there are few experienced bounty hunters: those few bounty hunters who do comb the space lanes of the sector tend to be on the amateur and inexperienced side.

Grea The Orfite

Grea the Orfite is Elrood Sector's "patron bounty hunter": she is the most famous and most experienced of those who regularly operate in the sector. This wizened Orfite has "served" Elrood sector for over two decades. She has tenaciously guarded her territory, and in her years of bounty hunting, has had few failures.

A middle-aged Orfite with the characteristic large nose, Grea stands at just under 1.5 meters. She does not look like a dangerous bounty hunter —which she uses to her advantage. An Orfite scent mask is always within easy reach.

Elrood Slang

Elrood sector, much like other regions of the galaxy, has its own slang. Although each world has its own unique phrases and words, these slang terms are fairly common and well-known in most areas. While they may have fallen out of favor, or never have been very popular, most people will know and understand these phrases.

Almosters: Residents of Lanthrym, which almost won a coveted spot on the E-D Run. **Warning:** Lanthrymers do not like to be reminded of this. Using this phrase around them is likely to provoke a fight.

Blackheads: Imperial officers. Named for the black caps they wear.

Businessman: A smuggler.

Chirps: Any droid that communicates through electronic languages of beeps and whistles and cannot speak Basic.

Dreamers: The Rebel Alliance. While the Elroodians would love to see the Empire fall, they think the Alliance is a pipe dream.

Drift, The: A huge cloud of gas that spans much of the sector. It is reputed to be extremely dangerous to navigate and there are no known hyperspace routes through the region.

E-D Run: Nickname for the Elrood-Derilyn Trade Route.

Extreme, The: The section of the E-D Run that is under Imperial control, running from just beyond Torina to Derilyn. So named due to the belief that anyone travelling the run from Derilyn to Torina is extremely unlikely to make the run without being boarded or harassed by the Empire.

Finally Made His (Her) Fortune: The person died. Normally used as biting sarcasm.

Flying Rocks: Ore carriers.

Flying Triangles: Imperial Star Destroyers.

Gate, The: Coyn, the closest planet to the rest of the galaxy.

Gnats: Also "Swarm of Gnats." TIE fighters.

Grunts: Gamorreans. Derisive term.

Guest: Someone taking refuge on Kidron.

Helping the Emperor: Someone who has been seized by the Empire and forced to work in the mines of Imperial Mining.

His Imperial Travesty: The Emperor.

Krilhead: A stupid person. Named for the unintelligent bovine creatures that act as the chief source of meat for the sector.

Link, The: The informal sector-wide network of gossippers that passes unofficial secrets and rumors that the mainstream media will not touch.

Proties: Short for protocol droids, this is a derisive term for anything (or anyone) that is perceived as useless.

Race the Run: Go from one end of the E-D Run to the other.

Race the Run Adrift: Same as above, but the pilot actually made it to Derilyn.

Rock Chewers: Miners.

Roods: Anyone born or having lived most of their life in the sector.

Rulebook: Also "Law Book." A blaster. Describes the many beings who must take the law into their own hands, and enforce it at blaster point.

Run, The: Nickname for the Elrood-Derilyn Trade Route.

Self Service: Pirates. In essence, they help themselves to others' ships and the cargoes within.

Shags: Wookiees. Generally used affectionately, but can be derisive.

Shoot the Stars: Engage hyperdrive.

Stopshort: The planet Torina, which is the last planet before Derilyn. Torina is one stop short of the end of the Run.

Taken Up Mining: Someone who tried to complete the E-D Run, but was caught by the Empire.

Ticktils: Bilars and any other "cute" species. A pronunciation of TCTL, which stands for "Too Cute To Live."

Toz: The chief grain found on Merisee, which has been transplanted to many of the other worlds in Elrood sector. It is used in breads, mushes, flour, and brewed into utoz, a popular alcoholic beverage.

Tozzed: Drunk.

Tracers: Bounty hunters.

Unluckies: Term for people who are not from Elrood sector but now find themselves there.

Utoz: A very popular drink brewed from fermented toz grain.

Utozz: A brand of Utoz, created by the Utozz Prime Brewery Corporation, the largest and oldest brewery on Merisee.

Wet-dock: As opposed to dry-dock, where ships are repaired, a wet-dock is a bar.

What's the Trouble?: How much does this cost? What is the price?

White Wonders: Stormtroopers. Derisive term.

Grea was born on Kidron. She left her home planet as soon as she was able. Her years as a drifter yielded impressive results: she won a small ship from a gambler and picked up her military skills while ferrying a group of mercenaries around the nearby Methall'has sector.

Grea is ruthless and amoral, but pragmatic and honest. Once she is hired to find someone, nothing can shift her focus. While she will consider any task, regardless of the moral implications, she is true to her word and will not lie to a client. Her objective is simple: to make as many credits as possible.

Like all Orfites, Grea can use her highly developed sense of smell to track people, determine what sorts of things were in a room (provided those things give off any sort of scent), and even fight in total darkness unhindered. For tracking her quarry, Grea relies on a combination of a network of informants plus her keen senses.

The Neverquit

Grea's ship, the *Neverquit,* is a small, custom-built vessel from the Coyn Shipyards. It is the only one of its kind, though the schematics exist to build more. The vessel looks like a dagger, with the engines set into the "handle." It has a belly-mounted laser cannon turret. The entire vessel is black. The appearance of the *Neverquit* has become a harbinger of bad luck to local spacers. "*Neverquit's* nearby, someone's gonna die" is the litany often repeated when the ship is sighted.

■ Grea The Orfite

Type: Orfite Bounty Hunter
DEXTERITY 3D
Blaster 5D+2, blaster: heavy blaster pistol 8D, blaster: repeating blaster 7D, brawling parry 5D+2, dodge 8D+1, firearms 7D+1, melee combat 5D+2, melee parry 5D, pick pocket 4D+1, thrown weapons 4D+2
KNOWLEDGE 3D
Alien species 6D, bureaucracy 5D, intimidation 7D+2, languages 5D+2, law enforcement 4D+1, planetary systems 4D, streetwise 5D, streetwise: Elrood sector 7D, survival 6D, value 5D, willpower 7D
MECHANICAL 2D
Astrogation 4D, communications 3D, ground vehicle operation 4D+2, repulsorlift operation 3D+1, sensors 3D, space transports 6D+1, starship gunnery 4D+2
PERCEPTION 4D
Bargain 6D, command 5D, con 7D, gambling 4D+2, hide 5D+1, investigation 6D, persuasion 6D+1, search 9D+1, sneak 6D
STRENGTH 4D
Brawling 8D, stamina 6D
TECHNICAL 2D
Blaster repair 3D, computer programming/repair 4D, first aid 4D+1, security 6D, space transports repair 4D+1, starship weapon repair 3D+2
Special Abilities:
Olfactory Sense: Orfites add +2D to *search* when tracking someone by scent or when otherwise using their sense of smell. They can operate in darkness without any penalties. Due to poor eyesight, they suffer -2D to *search, Perception* and related combat skills when they cannot use scent; they also suffer a -2D penalty for targets over five meters away. See Orfites under the entry for Kidron.
Character Points: 13
Move: 12
Equipment: E-web repeating blaster (8D), heavy blaster pistol (5D), blast vest (+1D against physical attacks, +1 against energy), comlink, datapad, medpac, breath mask, Orfite scent mask, Orfite power harness

Elrood

Elrood

Type: Terrestrial plains
Temperature: Temperate
Atmosphere: Type I (breathable)
Hydrosphere: Moderate
Gravity: Standard
Terrain: Urban, plains
Length of Day: 28 standard hours
Length of Year: 364 local days
Sapient Species: Humans
Starport: 4 Imperial class, 1 private Imperial class, 8 standard class
Population: 6 billion
Planet Function: Sector capital, manufacturing, trade
Government: Representative democracy
Tech Level: Space
Major Exports: Starships, refined metals and ores, processed alloys
Major Imports: Electronics, foodstuffs
System: Elrood
Star: Elrad (yellow)
Orbital Bodies:

Name	Planet Type	Moons
Trinka	searing rock	0
Acatal	barren rock	0
Elrood	temperate plains	2
Akana	barren rock	1
Thrang	gas giant	7
Tufar	ice ball	0

World Summary

Elrood serves a triple role in its sector: capital, major manufacturing complex and trade center. The world is comfortable, with a pleasant climate and large landmasses within habitable zones. Due to its status as sector capital, Elrood is a busy world, bustling with starships and aliens from many species.

The planet supports several immense urban megaplexes, and large factories dot the landscape. Elrood is home to the largest free ore refineries in the sector (Derilyn has similar facilities, but its status as an Imperial occupied world prevent easy access to these plants). Most of the ore is brought here from mining worlds throughout the sector. Elrood's chief exports are refined metals, which find their way into buildings, starships, and processed alloys.

System Datafile

Elrood system, star: Elrad, yellow sun. Six planets in system—third planet, Elrood, can support life. Others can support artificial colonies. Elrood is the main system planet.

Elrood is the capital of Elrood Sector. Heavy ship traffic ahead. Please turn ship's comm to channel XTX984, local planetary spaceport control channel, for landing instructions.

ATTENTION TRAVELERS: This is Elrood Space Central. Welcome to Elrood. Please turn to channel XTX984 for instructions.

Elrood has two moons: Sharene and Lodos, named after a prominent husband and wife who were with the first colonists many thousands of years ago. Both moons figure prominently in local culture and folklore.

System Summary

The Elrood system is located on the edge of the sector. Elrad, the system's sun, is a common, main sequence yellow star. Elrood is the system's third planet.

Trinka, the closest planet to the sun, is a harsh, hot rock, and seems to lack any commercial potential, although there is a small Elroodian scientific outpost on this world.

The second planet, Acatal, is another barren world, though it has a thin atmosphere (type II). There is a small mining facility here, owned by Radell Mining.

Akana is the fourth planet. It is an unremarkable world with a trace atmosphere and almost no moisture. Aside from a few microbes embedded in the rocks, the world is barren. Akana could be terraformed, but it is an unnecessary expense at this time. Akana has a small, sealed artist's colony, a place of isolation where people can go to think in peace and solitude. The colony is

World Map of Elrood

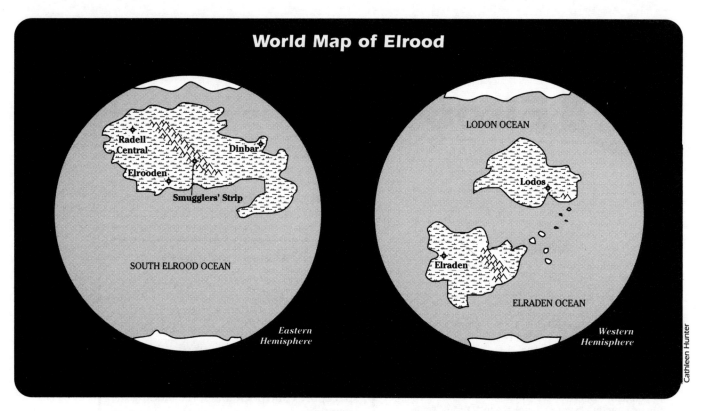

Radell
Central
Dinbar
Elrooden
Smugglers' Strip
SOUTH ELROOD OCEAN
Eastern Hemisphere

LODON OCEAN
Lodos
Elraden
ELRADEN OCEAN
Western Hemisphere

Cathleen Hunter

subsidized by Elrood's government. Akana's only moon, Akanala, is a brilliant orb in the night sky and a source of inspirations for poems and stories. Akanala's brilliance is due to rich deposits of sparkling quartz, which causes the entire surface to glisten. "Akanala is the diamond in Akana's sky" has to be the oldest, most overwrought cliché among the writers of Elrood, but it is nonetheless true.

The largest planet in the Elrood system is the gas giant Thrang. From Elrood, it appears as a small, bright green globe the size of a man's thumbnail in Elrood's night sky.

Tufar is the last planet in the system, and is little more than a frozen ball of ice and methane. The grimmest feature of the planet is an abandoned listening post established when the system was first settled. After the incident that destroyed the station, the world took on a mystique of misfortune, and thus has been ignored since. The life support failed when a small meteor breached the airtight prefabricated structure. The six unfortunates who manned the station were flash-frozen at their posts and their corpses remain there to this day.

Landing Procedures

Whenever a ship approaches the system and switches to channel XTX984, the following procedure occurs. Because of the very orderly nature

of the Elroodian bureaucracy, the same procedure is always used:

"This is Elrood Starport Command. Incoming vessel, please identify yourself, and your intentions. Use standard protocol, please."

Once identification and intentions are established, and the ESC sensors confirm the transponder code, they run a brief check to make sure that the ship is not listed in Elrood's records as wanted or stolen. Elrood is not directly tied into the Imperial databases, but it periodically receives updates when an Imperial patrol enters the system. As a result, minor offenses may not show up, but if the ship is wanted by the Empire for a major class one or class two infraction (as explained on pages 45–47 of *Galaxy Guide 6: Tramp Freighters, Second Edition,* or pages 21-22 of *Galaxy Guide 7: Mos Eisley)* the offense will almost certainly show up on their computer records.

If the ship checks out on Elrood's records, a scan of the ship's engine performance is made, and it is given permission to land. Any variances at all from operating norms will result in the ship being required to have repairs done while on Elrood. Normally, most starports will overlook a few minor violations, but Elrood strictly enforces Imperial standards. The characters may be quite surprised to find that they have many hours of work ahead of them or will have to pay out several hundred or thousand credits to get their vessel up to snuff. Of course, this procedure benefits the local shipwrights as well, but Elrood Starport Command is *not* corrupt and isn't doing this for personal gain — they are this strict because … that's what the rules are, that's why. Characters who are disgruntled by this turn of events can't simply decide to leave — this is clearly resisting law enforcement officials, which is a class three infraction.

"Permission granted, (vessel name). When you land, please observe all standard decontamination procedures. If needed, a decon team will be sent to your vessel to ensure compliance. We will need to see your shipping manifest and cross-verify it with your actual cargo. You will be required to show us your valid pilot's license and ship's ownership files."

If the ESC has found any anomaly with the ship drives, they will be mentioned now. If requested, ESC will provide the names and Elrood Planetary Communication Net (EPCoN) numbers of recommended starshipwrights. ESC will also mention anything else that they feel may be wrong with the ship, such as an uninspired name, potential modifications (to increase safety), procedures for securing and procuring cargoes on Elrood, the EPCoN numbers for the Elrood Department of Visitor Relations, Department of Tourism, and Department of Interstellar Trade.

"Land at (name of starport and specific bay). Download code XP-445-T78Y, which is being transmitted now, into your ship's computer upon coming within 50 kilometers of your starport destination. When activated, you will be linked with our navigation beacon and automated landing system. Safe landing, and enjoy your stay."

The ship will receive a sophisticated computer code, which when loaded into the ship's navigation system, links it into Elrood's fully automated navigation and landing system. This system takes all ships under the control of Elrood's computer routing system, and ensures a safe landing. Manual landings are prohibited on Elrood, and any character insisting on doing the piloting himself will receive a 300 credit fine.

If the ship or the crew is wanted for any serious infractions, or some other major problem has been discovered, several armed guards will be

Mike Vilardi

waiting at the landing bay to inform them of the problem, or in extreme cases, arrest them.

Elrood Starport Command's security teams are immaculately dressed and thoroughly professional soldiers. They are dressed in spotless white uniforms (including white blast vests). However, these men and women are more than hired muscle — they are also public relations officials for the starport. In essence, they provide law enforcement, but they are also responsible for providing information, lending assistance, and they must be polite, helpful and charming at all times. Intimidation is not part of their training, although their sheer physical presence is intimidating enough, if need be.

ESC Security Team. All stats are 2D except: *blaster 6D, cultures 4D+1, law enforcement 6D, brawling 5D, security 5D.* Move: 10. Blaster pistol (4D), armored vest (+1D to physical, +1 energy), datapad, and comlinks.

If the characters decide to flee Elrood, engage in combat with other ships in Elrood space or do something to require their apprehension, they will have to face one or more *Prosperity*-class light cruisers.

■ Elrood Prosperity Cruisers

Craft: Elrood StarYards Ltd. *Prosperity*-class Customs Cruiser
Type: Light cruiser
Scale: Capital
Length: 300 meters
Skill: Capital ship piloting: *Prosperity*-class light cruiser
Crew: 100, gunners: 24, skeleton 35/+15
Crew Skill: Astrogation 4D, capital ship gunnery 4D, capital ship piloting 4D, capital ship shields 4D, sensors 5D
Passengers: 40
Cargo Capacity: 2,500 metric tons
Consumables: 6 weeks
Cost: 12 million (new), 7 million (used)
Hyperdrive Multiplier: x1
Hyperdrive Backup: x16
Nav Computer: Yes
Maneuverability: 3D
Space: 9
Atmosphere: 400; 1150 kmh
Hull: 4D
Shields: 2D

Mike Vilardi

Sensors:
Passive: 50/1D
Scan: 90/2D
Search: 200/3D
Focus: 10/4D
Weapons:
6 Heavy Turbolasers
Fire Arc: 3 front, 1 left, 1 right, 1 back
Crew: 2
Scale: Starfighter
Skill: Starship gunnery
Fire Control: 2D+2
Space Range: 3-15/35/75
Atmosphere Range: 6-30/70/150 km
Damage: 4D
2 Tractor Beam Projectors
Fire Arc: 2 front
Crew: 6
Skill: Capital ship gunnery
Fire Control: 1D
Space Range: 1-5/15/30
Atmosphere Range: 2-10/30/60 km
Damage: 4D

Capsule: The *Prosperity*-class Customs Cruisers, built by Elrood StarYards, Ltd., are popular amongst the worlds of the sector. While not exceptional combat vehicles and incapable of holding their own against Imperial fleet vessels, they are more than adequate for customs inspections, pirate actions and other common planetary defense activities. Elrood itself has two dozen Prosperities, with one assigned specifically to each starport and the rest assigned to patrol and outer orbit customs inspections.

Elrood Starports

The starport most likely to be used by the characters will be Elrooden Starport. There are four Imperial class starports on Elrood, located in the megaplexes of Elrooden, Dinbar, Elraden and Lodos. A fifth Imperial class starport, Radell Central, is strictly for Radell Mining's ore carriers. There are eight standard class ports to serve smaller cities. All Imperial class starports are assigned a *Prosperity*-class cruiser and several cloud cars. Because Elrood is a peaceful world, there is no need for extensive defenses, and thus there are no weapon emplacements around these areas.

Elrood is a world that prides itself on appearances, and this naturally extends to its starports. The starports are an antiseptic white, and are kept spotless. There are no transients, drunks, con men, beggars, or other riffraff here, and there are always plenty of security guards around eager to lend assistance and enforce the law. The air is filtered, purified and mixed with perfumes for added comfort. There are countless protocol droids (for translation as well as information) and valet droids to carry bags and luggage, all of them polished to reflective brilliance.

Typical Debarkation Procedure

Once a vessel lands at its designated bay, a security squad approaches the vehicle with a customs official and a medical droid. First, the

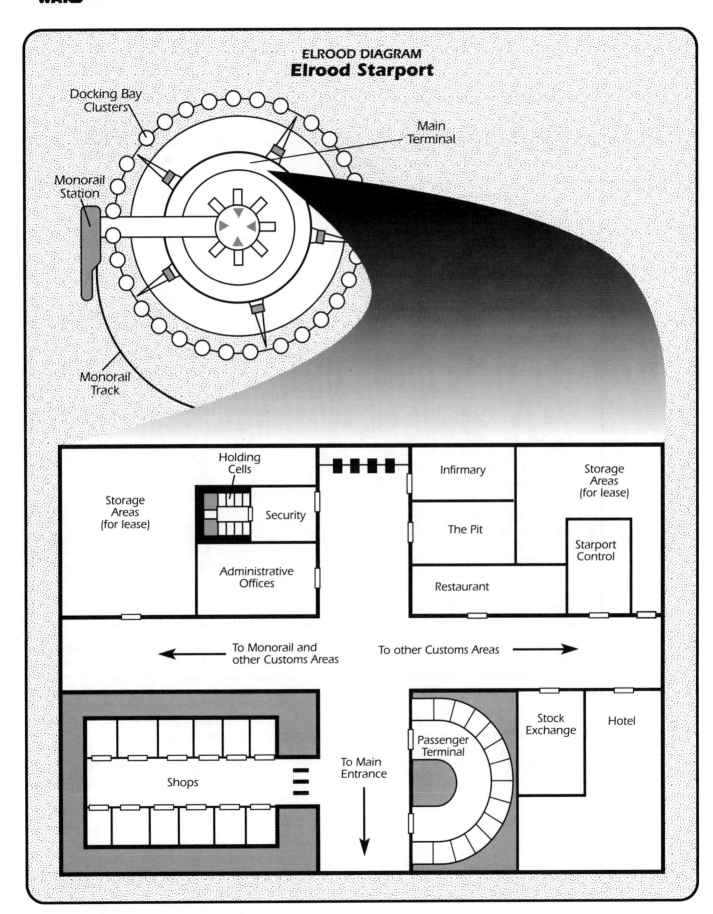

ELROOD DIAGRAM
Elrood Starport

Docking Bay Clusters

Main Terminal

Monorail Station

Monorail Track

Holding Cells

Storage Areas (for lease)

Security

Administrative Offices

Infirmary

The Pit

Restaurant

Storage Areas (for lease)

Starport Control

To Monorail and other Customs Areas

To other Customs Areas

Shops

To Main Entrance

Passenger Terminal

Stock Exchange

Hotel

Elrood Starport Main Regulations

• Basic landing fee is 10 credits per 10 meters of ship length. This includes decontamination fees. Berthing is 10% of the docking fee per day.

• Port customs fees are 1% of value (based on Elrood Customs standard assessments) of cargo to be delivered or to be picked up.

• A fine of 20% of Elrood Customs standard assessments will be assessed on additional or missing cargoes when compared to the ship's manifest.

• Ships must register with Elrood Starport Command prior to departure. A departure time and flight path will be assigned. In the event of a ship missing its departure time, the ship's captain must file for a new departure assignment.

• Ships are expressly forbidden to discharge weaponry within Elrood System. Violation of this will result in fines and imprisonment.

• Visitation fee is 5 credits per sapient (no fee for droids).

• The following cargoes are contraband. Carrying them will result in seizure of cargo plus a fine of 40% of the cargo's value. Failure to pay this fine will result in the impounding of the offender's ship.

Cargoes:
Weapons (special permits must be purchased before travelling to Elrood)
Armor
Unregulated ores (special permits must be purchased before travelling to Elrood, with the fee being 3% of the Elrood Customs standard assessment value)

Animal species not indigenous to Elrood
Spice
Illegal or unregistered substances (special permits for prescription substances must be purchased before travelling to Elrood, with the fee being 5% of the Elrood Customs standard assessment value)

Elrood Laws And Customs

• The official language of Elrood, like that of the Empire, is Basic.

• All ranged weapons are illegal on Elrood. No bladed weapon may exceed a length of 10 centimeters. Permits are required to carry any weapons — all permits must be acquired through Elrood Starport Permits Office (for visitors; residents must go through a different office) for a cost of 25 credits per local week (eight days). Any carried weapons must be prominently displayed.

• Armor is prohibited on Elrood.

• Nonsapient creatures must be either kept secured on board ship or restrained on a leash.

• All droids must be fitted with restraining bolts.

• Elrood has very strict standards of conduct and behavior, and stiff penalties for violation of these laws. Off-worlders are advised to ask law enforcement officers for clarification of Elrood's legal system. Violent behavior, smuggling, and sales of regulated items are serious offenses on this world.

medical droid checks all crew members for diseases and parasitic infections. The crew is given a series of painless immunization injections to protect against any potentially dangerous diseases on Elrood.

A small transponder, encoded with the user's unique cellular structure, is painlessly inserted under the skin on the back of each person's hand. The transponder identifies the person and certifies that the being has passed all immigrations and customs requirements. It will break down into harmless component substances after a month, so there is no need to have it removed. All Elroodian law enforcement officials carry datapads which are equipped with scanners that can determine an individual's identity within a few seconds.

Meanwhile, decontamination droids survey

the ship's exterior and interior, eliminating any dangerous organisms. After the crew has been decontaminated and inoculated, the customs officer checks the ship's cargo manifest against the contents of cargo hold. The customs official then assesses docking fees and tariffs, which must be paid immediately.

Spaceport Features

The spaceport features a monorail station that moves the characters to Elrooden proper in a matter of a few minutes. Fare is one credit.

For those who wish to travel Elrood sector in luxury, the Elrooden Starport is the embark and debark point for Transsector Lines Ltd., a company that runs passenger ships from Elrood to Torina. Ships leave at midday every other day, and also stop at Coyn and Merisee. Each passenger vessel carries 150 passengers. Fare one way is 250 credits for standard passage, 1,000 for luxury passage.

For cargo traders and independent haulers, a location of prime importance within the spaceport is an establishment called "The Pit." Despite its unpromising name, it is a bar and restaurant where independent cargo haulers, contractors, traders and others come to do business and exchange stories. Unlike many other taverns, the Pit has a relaxed and professional atmosphere, and like the rest of Elrood, it is a calm and orderly place. There is a five credit cover charge to enter.

Inside, the Pit has a huge, sunken conversation pit (there are no seats in the conversation pit). Above the pit, at floor level, are a number of booths where business can be conducted in private. The booth seats are programmed to conform to the anatomy and comfort of the occupant. Along the walls are data panels showing ship arrivals or departures, and available cargoes.

The conversation pit is usually bustling with pilots and shipping agents. Pilots try to outbid each other to carry cargo, while the shipping agents try to hunt for the best bargains. The conversations are often lively.

Characters can get a job hauling freight if they hustle enough cargo merchants over the course of a few hours. Make *bargain, business* or *persuasion* skill checks to see how well they do.

The Pit's main barkeep is Travis Chaz. Chaz has been here for about 30 years and has "seen it all."

■ Travis Chaz
Type: Wizened Bartender
DEXTERITY 2D+2
Blaster 5D, brawling parry 5D, dodge 7D, melee combat 6D, melee parry 5D
KNOWLEDGE 4D
Alien species 6D, bureaucracy: Elrood 7D, intimidation 6D, languages 7D, planetary systems: Elrood 7D+2, streetwise 5D+2, value 7D, willpower 6D
MECHANICAL 3D+1
Astrogation 4D+2, space transports 5D+1, starship shields 4D+1, starship gunnery 4D+2
PERCEPTION 3D
Bargain 5D, gambling 5D, persuasion 6D+2, sneak 5D
STRENGTH 3D
Brawling 7D
TECHNICAL 2D
First aid 4D
Character Points: 8
Move: 10
Equipment: Blaster carbine (5D, hidden under bar).

Capsule: Chaz is a burly man in his mid-60's, though he has the health of a man 20 years younger. His hair is white as snow. He has several scars on his arms and face, and he walks with a slight limp.

Everyone in the Pit at one time or another speculates about Chaz's past, mostly because Chaz won't say anything about it. Some say he was a Jedi Knight or a former Republic Senator, while still others

suggest he was a pirate or bounty hunter.

Chaz is a no-nonsense, quietly friendly man. His vocabulary is quite extensive, betraying a high degree of intelligence that belies his profession.

Chaz knows about the illegal landing field, which customs officials are easily fooled, how to get black market goods, and which employers are the most honest. If he likes someone, he will quietly take care of them by pointing out less reliable prospective employers or employees.

Chaz also knows a lot about the whereabouts of different personalities that haunt the Elrood Sector. This information he does not give out easily.

Smugglers' Strip

Despite strict regulations on the part of Elrood's government, the smuggling trade is alive and well on Elrood. All incoming ships are brought down into the atmosphere over the mountains on the northern continent (roughly in the middle of the triangle formed by Dinbar, Elrooden and Radell Central), where they are instructed to travel at a 10,000 meter flight ceiling. However, sensor readings do not cover the entire region, so for a substantial portion of the journey to any of these cities, ships are unobserved.

Several years ago, the enterprising crime cartel of Lud Chud built a small, isolated landing station deep in one of the mountain valleys. Now known as "Smugglers' Strip," this area is about 1,500 kilometers northeast of Elrooden. The actual facility itself is a simple level patch of ground with several memory-plastic "temporary" shelters on the mountainside — to the casual eye, this could be a homestead or small farm. Instead, below ground level, there are vast underground storehouses for keeping contraband weapons, spice, medicines and any other materials that are smuggled onto Elrood (many items are smuggled in simply to avoid the tariffs). The area around the facility has carefully placed sensor bafflers to disguise the presence of the underground hangars and any trace emissions left from the comings and goings of starships.

Smugglers' Strip is a smooth operation — a ship landing can be unloaded of contraband, be refueled and be back on its flight plan within the span of a few minutes. With careful high speed flying, a ship can arrive at a starport on schedule so that the automated flight system or flight controllers have no idea that the ship even stopped.

The field itself always has half a dozen mob musclemen, and usually a more "refined" representative of the mob, who provides payment and otherwise ensures that deals are completed. Landspeeders are available to bring cargo into the cities, where it is sold on the black market.

Lud Chud realizes that Elrood Space Central is very efficient. He is very careful about doing

Mike Vilardi

business at the strip. Only a few ships per month are allowed to land here. As a result, black market prices are five times higher than standard cost.

Finding a black market dealer is a Very Difficult *streetwise* task, and takes two hours per attempt. Among the likeliest locations is Elrooden proper and the Pit.

In order to get in on the smugglers' scam, the characters must first prove themselves trustworthy to Lud Chud or one of his subordinates. Normally, a crew is also expected to pay a 500 credit "sign-on" fee to be brought into the organization, and from then on the crew must follow Lud Chud's orders or risk his wrath.

Average Mob Muscle. All stats are 2D except: *blaster: blaster rifle 6D, melee combat 5D, brawling 6D, streetwise 5D*. Move: 10. Blaster rifle (5D), vibroblade (STR+3D), comlink, landspeeder (one speeder per four mobsters).

Elrooden

Elrooden is the capital city of the planet Elrood. A huge, sprawling megalopolis, Elrooden and vicinity is home to 100 million. Elrooden has never had a centralized plan, so the city has sprawled out over countless square kilometers in an odd mixture of residences, businesses, and factories. Clusters of huge buildings tower overhead, creating artificial canyons below, where private residences, multi-story residences and small businesses crowd for space. Many of the buildings have underground levels, and there is an elaborate underground repulsor rail transportation network linking major portions of the city. Above ground, the city has the monorail network, which has several main lines (including the link to the starport) as well as countless minor lines for commuters and casual travelers. There is a major repulsor highway network for personal vehicles, as well as several airspeederways, which are patrolled by cloud cars and marked by computer-monitored navigation buoys.

Radell Mining Corporation Building

This building, the tallest on Elrood, resembles a needle, with a wide base tapering to a point. With the stylized symbol of Radell Mining on its northern face, there is no doubt that this is Radell's corporate headquarters. Near the center of the city, the building is unusual in that it is surrounded by a large park (privately owned by Radell but open to the public). The building has a grand entranceway, with a wide set of polished white bodrite stairs over ten meters tall. The building has a large elevated and covered walkway (nearly 300 meters long) that connects to the major monorail station across the boulevard

that seals off the park.

Radell is an ever-present facet of life on Elrood (for which the local people are thankful, since it has enabled them to maintain a decent standard of living). Whenever on Elrood, the characters will notice the Radell logo and the company colors, navy blue and tan, everywhere. This is particularly true within the Radell complex, where the logo and colors are prominently displayed on walls, on uniforms and just about anywhere else that can be imagined.

The building itself contains offices, meeting rooms and accommodations for travelers, guests and freelance workers in the temporary employ of Radell. When characters are supposed to report directly to Radell headquarters, they come here. Radell has its own security forces to patrol the building and the grounds.

Radell Security Guards. All stats are 2D except: *blaster 4D, dodge 4D+2, command 4D, Strength 3D+2*. Move: 10. Blaster pistol (4D+2), blast vest (+1 energy, +1D physical), blast helmet (+1 energy, +1D physical).

Elrood Bazaar

The Elrood Bazaar is not only the largest marketplace on Elrood, it is the largest in the whole sector. Within the confines of the bazaar, tourists find an endless array of shops (large and small), offering every imaginable (but legal) product — starships, droids, language disks, holograms, clothing, souvenirs, furniture — almost anything can be found here.

While Elrood Bazaar is far from the most largest facility of its type in the galaxy, it is nonetheless impressive to tourists who travel from throughout the sector to visit here. Aside from the endless array of shops and services, the bazaar contains restaurants for every income level, the Elrood Sector Stock Exchange, landspeeder rental and retail locations, a cultural and entertainment park with rides, virtual simulations and hologram experiences, and large traditional picnic parks. Aside from conspicuous consumption, the bazaar's choices are so diverse that it is as much recreational facility as shopping area.

The facility is huge — the Grand Plaza, or Daya, is over three kilometers across. Between the Daya and the ring of permanent shops surrounding the area, called the Perma, there are literally a million different businesses. The bazaar has both a monorail station and immense underground parking facilities (the main speederway linking the starport and the capital city passes near the bazaar).

The entire bazaar is open day and night, year round (although many of the smaller businesses shut down for the night). The Daya features

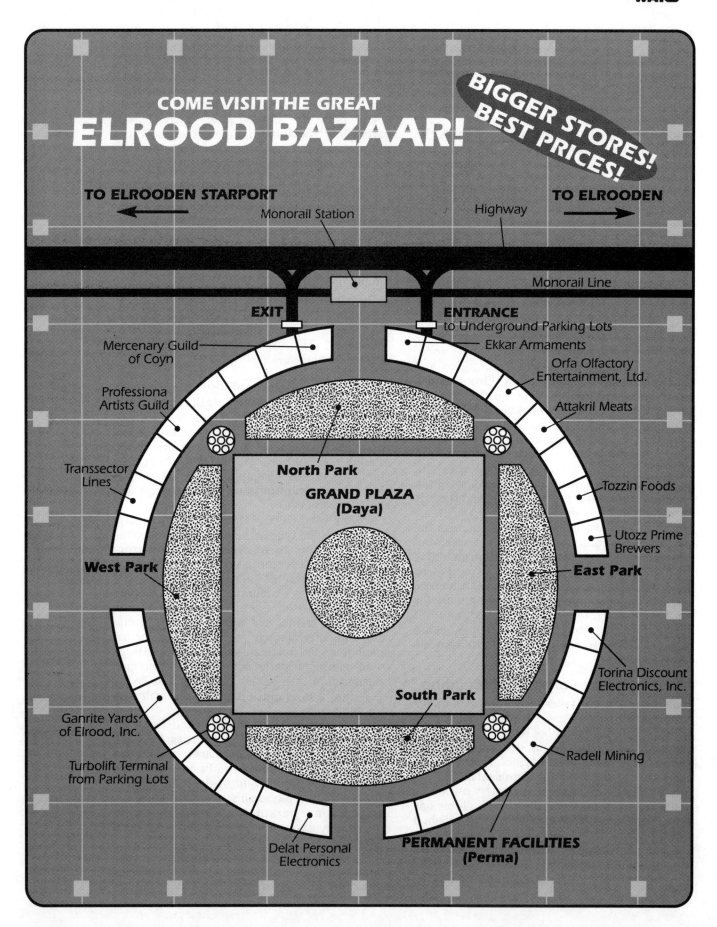

COME VISIT THE GREAT
ELROOD BAZAAR!

BIGGER STORES!
BEST PRICES!

TO ELROODEN STARPORT ←

TO ELROODEN →

Monorail Station

Highway

Monorail Line

EXIT

ENTRANCE
to Underground Parking Lots

Mercenary Guild of Coyn

Ekkar Armaments

Orfa Olfactory Entertainment, Ltd.

Professiona Artists Guild

Attakril Meats

North Park

GRAND PLAZA (Daya)

Tozzin Foods

Transsector Lines

Utozz Prime Brewers

West Park

East Park

South Park

Torina Discount Electronics, Inc.

Ganrite Yards of Elrood, Inc.

Turbolift Terminal from Parking Lots

Radell Mining

Delat Personal Electronics

PERMANENT FACILITIES (Perma)

oddities, prepared food, small items, live entertainment, and unusual bargains. During the day, the Grand Plaza is choked with crowds buying, selling, and haggling for their choice of goods. The Perma's stores are generally much larger and feature the more upscale and exclusive goods: vehicle, droid and starship dealers dominate much of this area.

Many of the companies found in the Elrood Sector have branch offices in the bazaar, ranging from large, retail stores to one room offices with only a representative and computer.

Of course, the Elrood Bazaar isn't as clean and wholesome as the local government would prefer. While there are many undercover agents who scour the area looking for black market dealers and pick pockets, these elements are a fact of life. Characters who want illegal goods should make a Difficult *streetwise* check (roleplay these scenes out). At night, characters may find themselves jostled, and their wallets lifted. There are a very small number of actual assaults and armed robberies — certainly not enough to give people pause about going out at night. Like Radell and the Starport, Elrood Bazaar has its own private security teams.

Elrood Bazaar Security Guards. All stats are 2D except: *blaster 3D+1, dodge 4D, languages 3D+1, Strength 3D+2.* Move: 10. Hold-out blaster (3D+2), blast vest (+1 energy, +1D physical), comlink, datapad.

Here is a listing of some of the more prominent companies in the bazaar:

Radell Mining: The largest mining interest in the sector, Radell sells refined ores and metals. It also produces some finished goods. This office is more of a showcase for Radell's contributions to Elrood society (a public relations exercise), while showing off some of the novel and famous projects in which Radell metals and ores have been used. Major contractors sometimes approach Radell through this office.

Delat Personal Electronics: A small Elrood company, Delat makes consumer goods such as chronometers, datapads, location transponders, comlinks, droid restraining bolts and holographic projectors.

Ganrite Yards of Elrood, Inc.: A small starship manufacturing company based on Elrood, Ganrite's product line consists of "clones" of other companies' established designs. Their most common vessels are small freighters and personal transport craft, and their most popular model is the Ganrite Bratillia light freighter, which is basically a knock-off of the venerable SoroSuub StarMite light freighter.

Transsector Lines: Transsector's corporate headquarters are in Dinbar, and this small transport line serves all of Elrood Sector, with infrequent trips to nearby sectors. Transsector is the most reliable line in the sector and also the oldest (in fact, Transsector's founder was one of the navigators who helped plot the Elrood-Derilyn Trade Route). Prices and service are modest, and reservations can normally be made within six hours of departure.

Professiona Artists Guild: The guild has a small booth area in the Daya, where the most popular and critically acclaimed works of guild members are on display. There are several sand casting sculptures, holographic paintings and interactive mood chambers, but the most famous (and popular) display is "The Lovers' Dilemma," a mixed media mood chamber and holographic painting by Walls, a brilliant but temperamental artist whose works are widely sought. The name "Professiona" was selected as a way of suggesting an exotic and cultured image. For those who are interested in studying with the masters, literature and holos on the various programs at the Akana colony are available.

Mercenary Guild of Coyn: The Coynite mercenaries are famous throughout the sector for their competence and skill. Those who need the services of the mercenaries may inquire about contracts at this location, although anyone who goes through here will be scrutinized by Elrood's government. Anyone who wants illegal services performed is likely to be arrested by Elroodian security officers.

Ekkar Armaments: The prime business for Ekkar is the sale of short-bladed knives (since these are the only weapons that may be legally possessed on Elrood). Characters without weapon permits must also complete an application for a permit, since a weapon may not be sold without one. Characters may also purchase any kind of legal weapon here for delivery on Coyn, Ekkar's corporate headquarters.

Orfa Olfactory Entertainment, Ltd.: Orfa's trade is the relatively untapped field of olfactory entertainment. Of course, scent is the primary sense for the Orfites of Kidron, but this company has finally branched into olfactory products for Humans and other species. At this time, Orfa's products are a hot novelty item, and they are quite popular among the trend-setting youth of Elrood.

Attakril Meats: This Kidron-based company sells meats in bulk quantities to restaurants and chain grocery stores, as well as choice cuts of meats for individuals. Attakril has made an effort to produce food packages for every budget, and buying directly from the company means big

Mike Vilardi

savings for the consumer.

Tozzin Foods: Like Attakril, Merisee-based Tozzin Foods sells to restaurants, grocery stores and individuals. Their products include a wide range of bread and grain products, unique vegetable products and pastries.

Utozz Prime Breweries: Makers of the ever-popular (or at least common) Utozz, this company sells to major markets and private consumers through this location.

Torina Discount Electronics, Inc.: Torina Discount Electronics, Inc. is smaller than Quality Electronics of Torina, but it produces much higher quality products. In fact, Torina Discount is widely regarded as a competitive local brand, and many Elrood Sector residents will purchase the company's products, despite a higher price, over quality products of companies from other regions of the galaxy. Torina's prime focus is home consumer goods such as holographic projectors, entertainment centers, simple home computers and kitchen appliances.

History

The planet Elrood was colonized by the Old Republic thousands of years ago. The first settlers found a world rich in basic natural resources — plenty of flora and fauna, a breathable atmosphere, good water, rich soils for crops, and some mineral deposits for mining and construc-

tion. The name Elrood was chosen to recognize the senator who had fought for the funding for this colonization effort.

Slowly, settlements blossomed into towns and cities, while more and more colony ships arrived over the centuries. Elrood had little to offer the machines of industry. However, for those who wanted a simple life of hard work and a decent place to raise a family, the world was ideal.

As Elrood's population grew, so did its power and prestige. Eventually, a colony was established on Derilyn, marking the first trade route in this region. In short order, the Coynites, Orfites, Meris and Teltiors were discovered, and diplomatic relations were established with these worlds. In time, the E-D Run was pioneered and Elrood became a sector capital, with full acceptance in the Republic.

Elrood, always keenly aware of its Republic heritage, was a staunch supporter of the old order. When Palpatine took power, many were swept up in the emotions and promises of Palpatine and hoped for the best. However, Elrood changed little. The increased taxes were a burden, but life went on much as it had for centuries before.

Now, Elrood is a world compliant in the hands of the Empire. Many of the people, especially those in industry, are dissatisfied with the Empire, as it has favored the huge galaxy-spanning corporations over smaller, regional companies such as Radell Mining. However, the Elroodians are a pragmatic lot, and see the Rebel Alliance as a dangerous entity — a bunch of foolhardy revolutionaries who lack the ability to govern and cannot foresee the consequences of their actions.

Elrood keeps a nervous eye on Derilyn, ever fearful that the Empire may decide to crack down on Elrood and impose martial law. Elrood has several shipyards capable of producing military vessels, which may someday be in service to the Rebel Alliance.

Moon Days

Elrood's culture has several days of special significance tied to the phases of the two moons, Sharene and Lodos. The myth of Sharene and Lodos is tied into the folklore of the planet. Sharene and Lodos were original colonists, first married under the twin moons of Elrood. In time, the phases of the moons came to be associated with these two lovers, mirroring their lives: ever changing, always turbulent, yet no matter what happened, the two were together always. As many of the Elroodians are poets and romantics at heart, they have built this myth over thousands of years.

The Lovers' Embrace: Moons within one hand span of each other. During these times, Elroodian couples exchange little gifts and give each other love poems and stories. Couples take vacation time to be together, romance blossoms and marriages during these phases are traditional. This happens on three occasions per year, but the periods of lovers being together last for several days at a time.

The Lovers' Conflict: The moons are on opposite sides of the sky. Whether it is biological, psychological or some other unknown factor, it is known that violent crimes on Elrood are at their peak during these times.

Akana and Its Moon

Akana is the fourth planet, a desolate rock with an unbreathable atmosphere. The Professiona Artists Guild exists on this barren world, and is a frequent retreat for many of Elrood's artists. Elrood has long-maintained an artistic tradition, and many young and talented writers, artists, musicians and sculptors are tutored by masters.

A small passenger ship makes the Elrood to Akana run once a week, at a cost of 20 credits one way. Staying at the Akana retreat costs 10 credits a day, but compared to the cost of more traditional training at galactic universities, the colony is a bargain. While this has never occurred, this colony would be an excellent location for a Jedi to train and meditate in peace.

Whenever Akana's moon, Akanala, reaches its full phase, the artist colony throws a wild party, with much revelry, romance, and displaying, reading or performance of everyone's work.

■ Crix Griff

Type: Slippery Con Man
DEXTERITY 2D
Blaster 4D, dodge 4D+1, pick pocket 5D+1
KNOWLEDGE 4D
Alien species 5D+2, cultures 6D, languages 4D+2, streetwise 6D+1
MECHANICAL 2D+1
Repulsorlift operation 2D+2
PERCEPTION 4D
Bargain 5D, con 6D+1, disguise 6D, forgery 5D+2, gambling 4D+2, persuasion 5D+1
STRENGTH 3D+2
TECHNICAL 2D
Security 4D
Character Points: 7
Move: 10
Equipment: Hold-out blaster (3D+2), 800 credits, electronic lock-picker (+1D to *security*)

Capsule: Crix Griff is a slippery con man who has walked the shadows of Elrood's rather rigid society for many years. The fact that he is still loose on the streets is a testament to his inventiveness and subtlety. Griff is a Human of medium build, with thinning brown hair. He is a thoroughly nondescript man, which he uses to great advantage. He also uses a great many number of disguises, and can alter his appearance with ease.

Griff can be found either in the Elrooden Starport or at the Elrood Bazaar, searching out easy marks for his con games. He takes any number of disguises, from the poor working man to the elegant, well-to-do tourist. He finds some way to make acquaintances with individuals who fit his needs, and simply and subtly learns about their background: home world, reason for visiting Elrood, favorite hobbies and other things that help identify a person. Then, he springs his trap.

Sometimes, he simply fleeces these people of credits after befriending them. More often, though, he sets people up to take a fall for other criminals. Boss Kaggle or one of the other criminals will contact Crix, explaining that they need "fall men" for a mission that they are undertaking. The fall men will find themselves accused of the crime, and eventually, enough damaging evidence will be discovered to have them blamed for the crime. Crix will sometimes make sure that damaging "evidence" will end up in the characters' possession (actually, cleverly duplicated items of evidence, or sometimes Crix will be able to get items from the actual scene of the crime and plant it on the characters). In other cases, Crix will take the information he has learned about the characters and carefully feed it to "witnesses" to the crime and officials who are investigating the crime. Crix is so smooth that people forget that they learned this information from the con man and simply associate this information with the characters. Between the evidence and the testimony of the witnesses, the characters end up with lengthy jail terms while the true perpetrators get away with the crime.

Adventure Idea

Radell Mining hires the characters and their ship to take a Radell junior executive to Torina, with a one day stopover at Coyn. The executive, a young man named Tevrin Dol, is an intense, materialistic, success-oriented, wealth-obsessed, obnoxious, high-energy individual — in other words, snide and arrogant. Tevrin is being sent to Coyn to negotiate with other corporate representatives over trade agreements — Radell will import more materials from other regional companies, and they will, in turn, take more refined ores from Radell for industrial use elsewhere in the galaxy. After that, Tevrin has to go to Torina and meet with local Radell executives and evaluate operations on that world. He is then supposed to return to Elrood with sensitive data detailing investments, production quotas, and profit and loss figures.

On the characters' ship, Tevrin wants luxury accommodations, and valet service. He will expect to have one character as his personal attendant for the trip. Unfortunately, Imperial Mining has caught wind of the trip, and hires some independent spies to tail Dol and report on his activities. These spies have orders to intercept the vessel before it returns to Elrood. Imperial Mining wants the data, and has asked the pirates to get the information as quietly as possible — although that may mean a "random" murder or two of Dol's "body guards" (the characters) to disguise their infiltration of the ship.

Adventure Idea

A prospective employer wishes to talk with the characters at the Pit. The employer goes to great length to shield his face. While the employer will not reveal this information, his story is that he is a Rebel agent on Elrood to make contact with a secret Rebel intelligence cell. The agent's transport off Elrood has been unavoidably detained and he must reach Coyn within the next 20 hours to reach his transport out of the sector.

Of course, this won't be a smooth mission — the characters encounter a huge drunken alien pilot who confuses them for an enemy and promptly begins a brawl in the Pit. There is also a small group of local Imperial spies looking for the agent.

Finally, a bounty hunter knows the agent's identity and intends to capture him and turn him over to the Empire for whatever reward is being offered. If the hunter discovers that the characters are hooked up with the agent, he will break into their vessel and plant some contraband, then anonymously notify Elrood customs. When the contraband is found, the ship is grounded until the matter can be sorted out. Now that the characters are stuck on the planet, the bounty hunter can nab the Rebel agent and bring him to Derilyn.

3333333

Coyn

Coyn

Type: Terrestrial forest
Temperature: Temperate
Atmosphere: Type I (breathable)
Hydrosphere: Moderate
Gravity: Standard
Terrain: Forest, plains, mountains, marshes
Length of Day: 20 standard hours
Length of Year: 380 local days
Sapient Species: Coynites (N)
Starport: 5 stellar class
Population: 800 million
Planet Function: Homeworld, trade
Government: Feudal garrison-state
Tech Level: Space
Major Exports: Lumber, weaponry, mercenaries
Major Imports: Foodstuffs, high tech, metals

System: Coyn
Star Name: Coynek (orange star)
Orbital Bodies:

Name	Planet Type	Moons
D'Skar	searing rock	0
Coyn	terrestrial forest	1
Sat'Skar	barren rock	0
Ba'Har	gas giant	5
Tro'Har	ice ball	0

World Summary

Coyn ("land of conflict and blood") is a relatively flat, temperate planet covered with large tracts of woodland. Coyn has regular seasons, including a hot summer and a moist and cool winter. The poles are cold, with moderate ice caps. The equatorial regions are warm and humid.

System Datafile

Coyn system, star: Coynek, orange star. Five planets in system—second planet, Coyn, is inhabited. Coyn is a major trade crossroads system in Elrood Sector.

From the Coyn Bureau of Tourism:

You are approaching the planet Coyn, Gateway of Elrood Sector, and homeworld of the proud and noble Coynite people.

Coyn is famous for its weaponry and is also home to the Mercenary Guild of Coyn, which boasts the mightiest warriors of this world. Our mercenary activities are famous throughout the galaxy.

As our guests, you are expected to honor and obey the En'Tra'Sol, the King-Law. It is a legal system that has provided for our needs for thousands of years, and it is the standard of conduct by which *all* are judged.

As you approach our world, keep in mind the following things:

• We are a warrior culture and value honor, valor, and loyalty. Cowardice and weakness are despised.

• A weapon drawn must be used for a warrior to retain honor.

• Warriors who have shown bravery in combat are respected, kindred spirits.

• Never touch a Coynite with your bare hands unless that person has granted permission. This is a punishable crime.

• Hollow threats, failure to defend oneself, falsely preparing one's weapon for combat, deception, thievery and dishonesty are punishable crimes. One who displays these traits or acts in such a manner is branded af'harl, or "cowardly deceiver." af'harl are "unseeable" in the eyes of the Coynites, and have no legal rights. They may be enslaved, beaten, murdered or dealt with in any way that a Coynite citizen sees fit. af'harl who have been enslaved are property of that Coynite's estate and thus are protected by and answerable to that Coynite. Coynites are responsible for the actions of their af'harl.

• Allowing an opponent to surrender in combat is only permissible if that opponent swears tracc'sorr, or fealty.

Enjoy your stay.

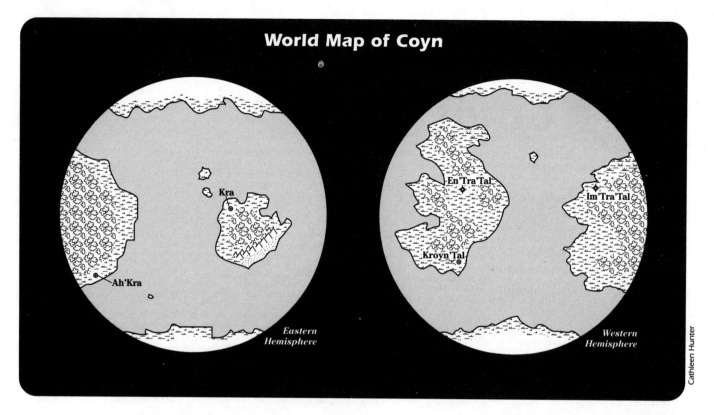

World Map of Coyn

Kra · Ah'Kra · Eastern Hemisphere · En'Tra'Tal · Im'Tra'Tal · Kroyn'Tal · Western Hemisphere — Cathleen Hunter

Coyn is ruled by a militaristic sovereignty. The absolute ruler is the En'Tra ("King-Master"), whose formal title is En'Tra'Sol'Tais'Tra ("King-Master of Law, Land and Cities".) The En'Tra, in turn, parcels out land to various noble families, called En'Tra'Ag'Tra ("King-Master's highest-servants").

Most of the nobility comes from families with a lasting martial tradition — the Coynites are a species of warriors and thus respect and follow those who prove themselves formidable warriors. This system has lasted for thousands of years. The capital is in the city of En'Tra'Tal, or "King-City."

The world bustles with trade, as it is the first world that most ships visit upon entering Elrood Sector. However, the rather brutal warrior culture makes the world a dangerous place — experienced spacers are normally very careful when dealing with the Coynites and their unique perceptions of justice.

System Summary

Coynek ("light of land of conflict and blood") is an orange star that gives the skies of Coyn a pink and orange cast. D'Skar ("dagger"), the planet closest to the sun, is a small, nightmarish planet with frequent earth tremors and volcanic activity.

Sat'Skar ("sword") is a "sister planet" to Coyn, with a comparable mass. The world is extremely hot (due to increased levels of "greenhouse gases") with a type III atmosphere. The only life forms are primitive fungi, bacteria and microbes.

Ba'Har ("battle blade") is a multi-colored gas giant with five moons. Ba'Har has a small band of rings, the remains of a moon torn apart by gravitational stresses thousands of years ago.

Tro'Har ("farthest blade") is the outermost planet in the system and is an inhospitable ice ball. The Coynites have placed an automated navigational beacon here to direct incoming traffic.

Gateway to Elrood Sector

Coyn is the crossroads of the E-D Run and the Coyn Route, the route leading to other major trade routes in the galaxy. Since the occupation of Derilyn, the Coyn Route has become the major passageway to other sections of the galaxy, and thus Coyn is called the "Gateway to Elrood Sector."

Coyn's starports, both orbiting and planetary, are popular stop-offs for fueling and supplies prior to leaving the sector. Ships coming into the sector often stop here because of the many cargo storage facilities. Often, galactic freighters simply dump their cargoes here. Then, regional cargo lines pick up the cargo and deliver it to the other worlds along the E-D Run.

Of course, there is much more than trade going through Coyn. Elrood's backwater status is an invitation to those who want to disappear for a while. Accordingly, many bounty hunters (Grea included) and Imperial officials frequent Coyn. Violence is a major problem in the spaceports, due largely to the Coynites' system of law.

Coyn Starports

To handle the great volume of traffic passing through the system, Coyn has five stellar class starports. The prime starport is Skraj'Tais, "Skyland." It is an orbiting space station capable of hosting hundreds of ships at a time. It is similar in design to Kwenn Space Station and is the major starport for those who have no business on Coyn itself.

The other four stellar class starports are on the surface of the planet. They are En'Tra'Tais ("Kingland"), Im'Tra'Tais ("Princeland"), Ah'Kra'Tais ("Common-craftersland"), and Kroyn'Tais, "Warriorland." There is also a one standard class starport, Kra'Tais ("Craftersland"), which is a common destination for those purchasing goods from Coyn. Each of these starports is within major cities: En'Tra'Tal, Im'Tra'Tal, Ah'Kra, Kroyn'Tal and Kra.

Characters may be sent to any of the starports, although if they make it clear that they are just passing through, they will almost certainly dock at Skraj'Tais. The main Imperial base on Coyn is at Kroyn'Tais, although there is a minimal presence in the system.

The starports are similar in design, but En'Tra'Tais starport is the largest. The city of Ah'Kra has excellent medical, repair and resupply services. Im'Tra'Tais is the most luxurious starport. Each starport has two *Prosperity*-class defense ships, purchased from Elrood.

Visiting ships are hailed by the Coyn'Skraj'Har ("Coyn-sky-blade," or Coyn's space fleet). The new arrival must declare what cargo is carried, intended business and requested length of stay. If the ship is here to pick up a specific cargo, this will be verified. Berthing fees are 50 credits a day, regardless of the starport.

One good thing about Coynite starports is that once a ship berths, the Coynites take it upon themselves to be fully responsible for the ship's security. Starport security patrols the pads, making sure that no ship is broken into.

Starport Security Guards. *Dexterity 3D, blaster: blaster pistol 5D, Knowledge 1D, Mechanical 1D, Perception 3D, Strength 3D, brawling 5D, Technical 1D.* Move: 12. Blaster rifle (5D), coyn'skar (STR+2D), blast vest (+1D physical, +1 energy).

Coynites

The Coynites are a tall, heavily muscled species of bipeds. Their bodies are covered with a fine golden, white or black to brown fur, and their heads are crowned with a shaggy mane.

They are natural born warriors with a highly disciplined code of warfare. A Coynite is rarely seen without armor and a weapon. These proud warriors are ready to die at any time, and indeed would rather die than be branded af'harl.

Coynites could conceivably live up to 250 standard years, but their warrior culture results in an average life span of a mere 53 years. Coynites reach physical maturity in their early twenties.

Mike Vilardi

Coynite children are born in var'sairk (capitalized when referring to noble families; means "birth-group" or litter) of two to six children, and all children of a litter are of the same sex.

Coynite appearance and conduct are tied to a rigid social code, the En'Tra'Sol. The length of a Coynite's mane is directly related to social status — the more respected and successful a warrior, the longer the mane and the more intricate the braids of that mane. The type of braid used is also an indication of the Coynite's family and the Ag'Tra (ruling noble) that the Coynite swears loyalty to.

■ Coynites

Attribute Dice: 13D
DEXTERITY 2D/5D
KNOWLEDGE 1D/3D+2
MECHANICAL 1D/4D
PERCEPTION 1D/4D+2
STRENGTH 2D/5D+1
TECHNICAL 1D/3D
Special Skills:
Mechanical skills:
Beast riding: tris. All Coynites raised in traditional Coynite society have this *beast riding* specialization. Beginning Coynite player characters must allocate a minimum of 1D to this skill.
Special Abilities:
Sneak: Coynites get +1D when using *sneak.*
Claws: Coynites have sharp claws that do STR+1D+2 damage and add +1D to their *brawling* skill.
Intimidation: Coynites gain a +1D when using *intimidation* due to their fearsome presence.
Story Factors:
Honor: To a Coynite, honor is life. The strict code of the Coynite law, the En'Tra'Sol, must always be followed. Any Coynite who fails to follow this law will be branded af'harl ("cowardly deceiver") and loses all rights in Coynite society. Other Coynites will feel obligated to maintain the honor of their species and will hunt down this Coynite. Because an af'harl has no standing, he or she may be murdered, enslaved or otherwise mistreated in any way that other Coynites see fit.
Ferocity: The Coynites have a deserved reputation for ferocity (hence their bonus to *intimidation*).
Move: 11/15
Size: 2.0–3.0 meters tall

Coynite Society

The Coynites have a militaristic, feudal society. Warfare and aggression are considered essential to Coyn society.

The planet is ruled by King Im'Toral XV and Queen, Em'Tora VIII. Below them are the 29 Ag'Tra ("Nobles"), heads of the noble families of the world. Each noble family runs a Sarrh'Tais ("law-land"), so that the entire world is under control of the Ag'Tra, who are loyal to the king.

Each Ag'Tra has at least 58 Kroyn, elite warriors of exceptional honor and status. Each Ag'Tra sends one Kroyn to serve as the En'Tra's bodyguard for one year. Thus, the En'Tra always has 30 Kroyn as a personal elite guard (one from each noble's holdings and one from the king's own

family or territory).

The vast majority of noble families were so appointed thousands of years ago, although every few centuries, a new family will be added to the noble bloodlines by the En'Tra's decree. It is possible that a family may have its noble status stripped by decree of the En'Tra, but this has never happened. This is probably due to the likelihood that the dishonored family would attempt to unite disgruntled factions and lead a revolution — very few En'tras have felt secure enough in their power that they would risk a full-scale civil war.

Coynites value bravery, loyalty, honesty, and duty. Coynites save displays of affection for their own families in private surroundings.

Curses in the Coynite language include zee'tah (fear), mora'ga (weakness), kzah (poison), fa'tar (peace), and the worst of all: af'harl (cowardly deceiver).

There are several greetings used in Coynite society, including "Sat'skars Kabar'Rattar" ("Swords together, blunted in friendship"), "Sat'skars Kabar'Ba" ("Swords together, joined in battle"), a challenge to battle or a warning that animosity exists and great care should be taken or a challenge to combat will be made, "Sat'skars Fas'Tawws'Rattar ("Swords ended in honor and friendship," which means all conflicts have been satisfactorily resolved, thus we are friends) and "Sat'skars Fas'Ba" ("Swords ended in battle," meaning that there remain unresolved differences that will not be forgotten).

Coynites value long hair, since in their culture long hair is a sign of great combat ability and honor. Aliens with long hair or shaggy coats (such as Wookiees) are treated with respect. Beings who are bald (or hairless) are shunned as deformed beings.

Jedi Knights are a source of fascination to the Coynites. On one hand, there is little doubt that the Jedi are formidable warriors with a code. However, Jedi are not supposed to simply rush into fights or provoke them; peaceful methods of resolving a conflict are preferred, and violence is a last resort. This code mystifies the Coynites, but they greatly respect their abilities and their adherence to their own strict code.

Coynite names are more than "mere" words — they are stories. By literally translating the meaning of the phrases, it is often possible to know the history of an item, or a person, or a location. The longer a name, the more honored a being is or more noble his family. However, Coynites seldom use their full names except when first establishing who has higher standing, such as upon first meeting. As a concession to off-world customs, Coynites will allow aliens to use shortened versions of names, but only if the alien confers the appropriate level of respect upon the Coynite. To deride an object of great importance or be disrespectful is an unforgivable offense.

When all syllables of a Coynite name are capitalized, it means that the object, place or person is worthy of great respect. All things associated with the En'Tra are always capitalized. Likewise, proper names are capitalized. Some phrases or names are *never* capitalized — this indicates a relationship with af'harl ("cowardly deceivers").

When creating gamemaster characters, these traditions should be remembered. Many Coynite warriors of noble birth have very long names, which might be translated as "Trel'tak, honorable warrior who defeated a noble of higher standing, of Clan Muls'rak, leaders of the War of Unification."

The En'Tra'Sol (King-Law)

Many thousands of years ago, the Coynites were divided into numerous warring clans. This, combined with their rapid technological development, resulted in a species that not only fought well, but excelled in weapon design and manufacture.

Eventually, one Coynite clan learned how to manufacture biological weapons. Whether the action was accidental or intentional is not known, but a dangerous toxin was eventually released. The microbe spread across Coyn, uncontrolled. The toxin was passed by physical contact — anything as simple as a touch of hands could spread the deadly organism. The plague killed over half of the planet's population.

Toral, chief of the strongest clan, realized that the Coynite species was heading towards extinction. He began a series of reforms with his allies and eventually succeeded in not only banishing biological weapons, but also instituted a code of law for the warrior society. Toral's leadership and wisdom united the warring clans under one law (the En'Tra'Sol) and one leader. During this time, the Coynites established the tradition of no personal contact without express permission first. The effect of the biological toxin was so pronounced that the ban on contact became part of the En'Tra'Sol.

Under this law, clan infighting was not eliminated, but the scale of the conflict was greatly reduced. Toral's son, Arl'Toral managed to bring peace to the planet. Arl'Toral channeled his people's natural aggressiveness into a rigid code of conduct by revising the En'Tra'Sol.

Shortly thereafter, settlers from Elrood first discovered Coyn. During these exchanges with the strangers from space, Arl'Toral realized that the best way to ensure peace on Coyn was to channel these aggressive energies to other pursuits. In short order, the first Coynite mercenary units were formed.

Mike Vilardi

What follows is a summary of the En'Tra'Sol.

• A Coynite's sratt ("word" or "promise") is his life. All speech, action and story are sratt; once given, it is eternally binding. One who breaks sratt may be branded af'harl.

• Combat is the natural order of life. Conflicts and disagreements must be settled openly in combat.

• An unsheathed or drawn weapon must be used. If a weapon is drawn in anger, it must be used. To not respond to a challenge, or to challenge or threaten idly is to be branded af'harl.

• It is forbidden to show mercy in combat. It eliminates the honor of victory in combat and removes the honor of he who is shown mercy, making them af'harl. Combat is to the death unless one swears tracc'sorr ("submission and blood-loyalty" or "fealty") to the other, in which case they become part of that Coynite's family. At the beginning and end of each combat, all survivors must acknowledge and salute the opponent's honor.

• af'tah ("deception") or harl'tah ("cowardice") are unforgivable sins. Use of kzah ("poison") is deception and cowardice. Challenging the injured or weak to combat is cowardice and is unforgivable. Those who deceive or show cowardice are branded af'harl.

• One must unquestioningly obey all to whom he has sworn tracc'sorr. All superior clan members, Ag'Tra and En'Tra are to be obeyed without reluctance or hesitation. Not to do this is to be branded af'harl.

• One may only break tracc'sorr by publicly declaring fas'tracc'sorr, or "end of submission and blood-loyalty." Superior clan members, nobles and, of course, the En'Tra, may challenge anyone doing this to combat.

• Pain, sadness, guilt, regret, reluctance, or fear are emotions of af'harl and may not be expressed without losing all honor.

• It is forbidden to touch another without first receiving permission. The penalty for this is death.

• af'harl are no longer Coynites. af'harl have no rights, no property, no meaning. They are to be murdered, enslaved, or dealt with as any Coynites see fit. A Coynite may take responsibility for af'harl, but all actions of that af'harl are that Coynite's responsibility.

The Assembly of the Ag'Tra

There are 29 Ag'Tra (nobles) who answer directly to the En'Tra. Of these 29, nine are sympathetic to the Empire, five are sympathetic to the Rebellion, and the remaining 15 are neutral. While subterfuges and behind the scenes skulking are not a permissible part of Coyn life, nobles are permitted to indulge in a little political wrangling, and some of this involves setting up unfavorable circumstances for rival nobles, or even large battles with lopsided odds. Even so, if any hard evidence of such behind the scenes planning comes to light, the noble will be branded af'harl. In an extreme case, the entire noble family may be branded af'harl, in which case a new family from within that territory will be selected to be the new noble bloodline.

Unique Coynite Items

These items are available to off-worlders. Ekkar Arms of Coyn is the chief manufacturer and seller of these items. These weapons are hand-crafted by individual weapons' masters, which explains their cost.

■ Coyn'skar

Model: Ekkar arms coyn'skar
Type: Coynite bladed pole
Skill: Melee combat
Cost: 400
Availability: 3
Difficulty: Moderate (blade), Very Difficult (disarm with hook)
Damage: STR+2D (blade), STR+2 (hook)

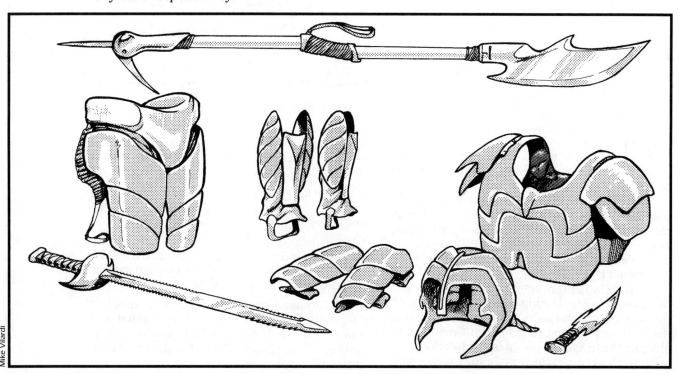

Mike Vilardi

■ Top: coyn'skar. Middle: Coynite battle armor. Bottom left: sat'skar. Bottom right: d'skar.

Capsule: The coyn'skar is a pole weapon with a lengthy, sharp blade on one end and a hook at the base. The shaft is tooled in such a way as to offer maximum grip. The hook can be used to trip or disarm an opponent.

■ Sat'skar

Model: Ekkar Arms sat'skar
Type: Coynite sword
Skill: Melee combat
Cost: 700
Availability: 3
Difficulty: Difficult
Damage: STR+3D+1

Capsule: A Coynite sword, it must be used with both hands (if swung one-handed, damage is only STR+1D and the difficulty increases to Very Difficult). The blade has grooves in it that cause terrible wounds.

■ D'skar

Model: Ekkar Arms d'skar
Type: Coynite dagger
Skill: Melee combat
Cost: 150
Availability: 3
Difficulty: Moderate
Damage: STR+1D+1

Capsule: A Coynite dagger, this is the most common weapon among Coynites. These weapons are known for their fine craftsmanship and deadly blades.

■ Coynite Battle Armor

Model: Ekkar Arms Coynite battle armor
Type: Coynite personal battle armor
Cost: 3,000
Availability: 3
Game Notes: Adds +2D protection from all physical and energy attacks. All *Dexterity* skills are penalized -1D.

Capsule: This bulky yet functional suit includes a helmet and is made from the stands of walt'sor plants, found only on Coyn. Despite the suit's rather humble origins, it provides excellent protection against physical and energy attacks.

Coynite Companies

Ekkar Arms: This is Coyn's chief manufacturer of arms and armor. Whether it is Coynite native weaponry or blaster rifles, thermal detonators and vibro-axes, Ekkar's products are of the highest quality. As a result, all of Ekkar's merchandise costs 10 percent more than average prices. However, in return, weapons such as blasters are easier to repair (one level of difficulty lower) and can withstand more punishment (consider +1D over normal body).

Mercenary Guild of Coyn: This is the main Coynite mercenary organization, and it is officially affiliated with the En'Tra. Each noble family is required to contribute a specific number of soldiers for mercenary service, and individuals are allowed to join at their discretion. The Mercenary Guild of Coyn hires out its services to all legal organizations seeking military forces for legal activities. In other words, the mercenary guild may hire out soldiers to serve for the Empire, or to serve for a corporation, but the guild will not hire out soldiers to the Rebel Alliance. As Coyn is within the Empire, it will not risk a full invasion by the Empire — a hopeless fight isn't honorable.

Warriors always have the option of rejecting mercenary missions, but no warrior has ever used this option, since it would result in lost honor. All warriors have sworn to defend Coyn and Coyn's interests in the event of attack.

Guild entry free is 100 credits and annual dues are 50 credits. The Guild gets 15 percent of the mercenary's pay. Weapons and armor can be purchased from the guild at a 10 percent discount.

The Mercenary Guild is a venerable, trustworthy operation with a reputation above reproach. Mercenaries who violate their contracts, flee from a battle, turn on their employer, or otherwise commit treason or show cowardice are branded af'harl. In some cases, such as desertion, the guild will send other mercs to hunt down and execute the coward. The Mercenary Guild has offices on Elrood, Torina, Derilyn, and Lanthrym.

Average Coynite Mercenary. *Dexterity 3D+2, blaster 5D, brawling parry 4D, melee combat 5D, Knowledge 1D, survival 4D, Mechanical 1D, Perception 2D, Strength 5D+1, brawling 6D+2, Technical 1D.* Move: 10. Character Points: 3. Blaster rifle (5D), Coynite battle armor (+2D to all attacks), coyn'skar STR+2D (blade), STR+2 (hook).

Rols'Kus ("Arena of the Games")

The Rols'Kus ("arena of the games") is a 250,000-seat amphitheater located in the capital, En'Tra'Tal. It is the site of the immensely popular kus'nar gladiatorial games of the Coynites. Since Coynites view these combats as sport, they are not to the death unless the loser is unwilling to submit to his opponent. Of course, most combats do last until one of the recipients receives a very serious injury, so most "cultured" beings view these combats as barbaric.

There are games every night, and during holidays, day-long contests and championships are held. As a rule, off-worlders are not usually featured in these combats. Coynites view participation in these games as an honor, and many young warriors focus their dreams on being named Tawws'Kroyn, "Most Honorable Champion Warrior."

Most of the contests are brawling or melee combats, though there is a target shooting contest for archaic guns, blasters, and bows. Each game is played in a series of elimination rounds. The arena itself is climate controlled and equipped

Mike Vilardi

Mike Vilardi

Zal Tuag Th'Trar, Junior Zal'Tra

Type: Security Force Member
DEXTERITY 4D
Blaster 5D, brawling parry 6D+1, dodge 5D, melee combat 6D, melee parry 6D
KNOWLEDGE 2D+2
Alien species: Humans 4D, cultures 7D, intimidation 4D+2, survival 5D, willpower 5D+2
MECHANICAL 2D
Beast riding: tris 6D
PERCEPTION 4D+1
Command 5D+1, persuasion 5D+1, search 6D+2
STRENGTH 5D
Brawling 7D+1
TECHNICAL 1D
First aid 2D, security 2D
Special Abilities:
Sneak: +1D to *sneak*.
Claws: STR+1D+2 damage, +1D to *brawling*.
Intimidation: +1D to *intimidation*.
Character Points: 8
Move: 12
Equipment: Sat'skar (STR+3D+1), blaster pistol (4D), Coynite armor (+2D to all attacks, -1D to all *Dexterity* actions)

Capsule: Zal Tuag Th'Trar is a 2.7-meter-tall robust youth of pure white coloring and a deep dark brown mane that he wears in an elaborately braided ponytail down his spine. A member of the Th'Trar clan, his father is a noble who is quietly sympathetic to the Rebels. Zal has chosen to acquaint himself with off-worlders who stand out from the normal rabble, learn their ways, and report the findings back to his father. Since Zal is young, he is not yet ingrained in the ways of his people, and thus is a bit more flexible around non-Coynites, although he is characteristically self-righteous about his heritage. He is cocky, and enjoys pointing out how superior Coynite culture is over others. Young Zal is an enthusiastic warrior, an outgoing sort, who has a great natural curiosity about off-worlders. Despite this, he is a friendly sort, and the perfect guide for characters.

Mike Vilardi

Zal Afreg Kt'Aya, Junior Zal'Tra

Type: Security Force Member
DEXTERITY 5D
Blaster 6D+1, brawling parry 6D+1, dodge 6D+1, melee combat 7D+2, melee parry 6D+2
KNOWLEDGE 2D+2
Intimidation 5D, survival 5D, willpower 4D
MECHANICAL 2D
Beast riding: tris 6D
PERCEPTION 3D
Command 5D, hide 5D, search 6D, sneak 7D
STRENGTH 5D+1
Brawling 7D+2
TECHNICAL 1D
First aid 2D+1, security 3D
Special Abilities:
Sneak: +1D to *sneak*.
Claws: STR+1D+2 damage, +1D to *brawling*.
Intimidation: +1D to *intimidation*.
Character Points: 6
Move: 11
Equipment: Sat'skar (STR+3D+1), blaster pistol (4D), Coynite armor (+2D to all attacks, -1D to all *Dexterity* actions)

Capsule: Zal Afreg is a 2.8-meter-tall Coynite, with soft gray fur and a black and white streaked mane in two ponytails. Despite his soft color, Afreg is a muscular, towering specimen with steel blue eyes.

Zal Afreg is of the Kt'Aya clan, whose head noble favors neutrality in the galactic civil war. Zal Afreg is the favored son of the oldest Var'Sairk. Zal Afreg is Zal Tuag's chief rival, as opposed to enemy, though he comes dangerously close to being one. Arrogant, smug, and somewhat of a bully, Afreg adheres to the En'Tra'Sol code so strictly that he has learned how to bend it just enough to torment others and get away with it. He lacks personal honor, but this has yet to be revealed.

Mike Vilardi

Tamaron Pol

Type: Con Artist
DEXTERITY 2D
Blaster 3D, dodge 4D+1, melee parry 3D+2, pick pocket 6D+2, running 2D+1
KNOWLEDGE 2D
Alien species: Coynites 7D, bureaucracy 2D+1, languages 3D+1, streetwise 4D+2, value 2D+1
MECHANICAL 2D
Beast riding 3D, hover vehicle operation 4D
PERCEPTION 2D
Bargain 4D+1, con 5D+2, forgery 2D+2, gambling 3D, hide 3D+2, persuasion 3D+1, search 4D, sneak 3D+2
STRENGTH 2D
Climbing/jumping 3D+1
TECHNICAL 2D
Computer programming/repair 3D, droid programming 2D+2, security 3D+1
Character Points: 8
Move: 10
Equipment: Hold-out blaster (3D), comlink, glow rod, recording wand, dice, cards, other gambling implements

Capsule: Tamaron is a Human in his late 20s. He wears a "lost-puppy" look on his face. He has sandy brown hair with a cowlick, which makes him look younger than he is. Tamaron was born on Lanthrym, and left as a teenager to serve on a freighter, lying about his age to get work. He has since settled on Coyn, where he enjoys the sport of dodging Coynite security forces.

Having been born on the frigid iceball known as Lanthrym, Tamaron has sworn not only never to be cold and poor again, but also not to do an honest day's hard work in his life. Tamaron is not a cocky, swaggering con man. On the contrary, he appears to be just the sort of person others would take advantage of, and here is where his genius lies. Beings see Tamaron and feel they have nothing to fear, and grow overconfident. Tamaron then proceeds to bilk them of their savings.

Tamaron has found that the busier Coynite spaceports have many innocent dupes who have just arrived from outside Elrood Sector. Usually, he represents himself as a guide to the planet or the sector, and will offer to show people around for a respectable fee.

Although Tamaron is not above a little flirting with females, he has no interest in even a superficial relationship. To him, first he must make his fortune, then he will think of other things, such as women. Tamaron abhors violence and would rather run than fight.

with a holo projection system so that each patron has a perfect view of the action.

Arquas'Tais ("Land of Fallen Ones of Valor")

Located outside the capital, this is a vast cemetery. An honor guard of four Coynites in full battle regalia always watches over the field.

Here are buried all Coynites who have fallen in battle. Additionally, members of other species who have fought for Coyn or died in service to the Mercenary Guild are buried here.

Noted Personalities

Listed above and on the previous page are descriptions of some of the more interesting Coynites characters might encounter.

Creatures of Coyn

■ Tris

Type: Domesticated riding animal
DEXTERITY 4D
Running 5D
KNOWLEDGE 0D
Intimidation 5D
PERCEPTION 3D
Search: tracking 5D
STRENGTH 5D
Stamina 7D
Special Abilities:
Hooves: Do STR+1D damage
Teeth: Do STR+2D damage
Move: 16
Size: 2.0 meters tall at the shoulder, up to 3.5 meters long
Scale: Creature
Orneriness: 5D+1 (1D for Coynite soulrider)

Capsule: The tris is a huge, dun-colored, muscular, six-legged steed favored by the Coynites. From childhood, each Coynite is taught how to ride a single young tris, which becomes the Coynite's companion. The Coynite who rides the tris is called its kars'asruul ("soulrider"). From this point on, Coynite and tris are bonded spiritually.

Most tris have a mane, and it is grown and braided to match that of its owner. Many Coynites also decorate their tris with painted runes telling of the rider's accomplishments. Tris are intelligent, ferocious, and headstrong. They are very difficult to ride, except by its kars'asruul.

Tris are carnivores, as evidenced by their fangs. These huge teeth, coupled with the shaggy manes and blood red pupil-less eyes, make for a very fearsome appearance.

Breaking a tris takes six months and is a Heroic *beast riding* task. The task can be spread out over two years, requiring two Moderate *beast riding* tasks. The trouble is worth it, for the result is a loyal, bonded mount, more friend and companion than pet or beast of burden.

■ Tangak

Type: Carnivorous predator
DEXTERITY 4D
Dodge 6D
KNOWLEDGE 0D
Intimidation 6D
PERCEPTION 3D
Hide 6D, sneak 5D
STRENGTH 5D
Brawling 7D, lifting 6D, stamina 7D
Special Abilities:
Claws: Do STR+3D damage
Teeth: Do STR+2D damage
Camouflage: Tangaks can effectively blend in with their surroundings. Tangaks gain a +2D bonus to their *sneak* dice if the terrain has buildings, trees and bushes, or large piles of rock to hide near.
Move: 13
Size: 3.0–3.5 meters tall
Scale: Creature

Capsule: Tangaks are huge, shaggy, bipedal predators. These crafty carnivores are the worst enemy (and thus the favorite hunting sport) of the Coynites. While lacking true intelligence, they are cunning and dangerous; in fact, some tangaks use elaborate traps to capture prey. Despite their huge bulk, these beasts can move very quietly and surprise their prey. This, coupled with their camouflage ability, makes them very dangerous to hunt.

The favored food of tangaks is tris. Considering that tris are fearsome animals in their own right, a fight between a tris and a tangak is a terrible thing to behold. Though tangaks shun cities as a rule, some of the older and more confident tangaks will creep into cities at night and stalk Coynite prey through the artificial canyons made by the tall buildings.

Adventure Idea

While at the starport, the characters' ship is broken into. A young Coynite, who was responsible for the characters' ship's security, will be branded af'harl due to loss of honor; the youngster is so distraught that he will commit suicide rather than be branded af'harl. The only way this can be halted is if the property is recovered or the perpetrator is caught.

Naturally, the characters' sense of morality should motivate them to prevent this. The young Coynite will accompany the characters. He will be a good source of information about Coyn, and is the perfect way to teach the characters the customs of Coyn.

The thief, a Coynite of great skill, is hiding in Im'Tra'Tal, where he is trying to fence the stolen

Mike Vilardi

goods. The thief will be in a rough section of the city, backed up by his larcenous friends. Of course, if the characters can find evidence proving that the Coynite is a thief, he will be branded af'harl, many other Coynites will join up to capture and execute or enslave him.

Adventure Idea

The characters are invited to an Ag'Tra's mansion for a party and to spend the weekend. Perhaps this is due to their connections — this is easy to justify if the characters include a New Republic bureaucrat, well-connected gambler or arrogant noble. They learn that an Imperial delegation is also here. The delegation's mission is to secure weapons and a platoon of Coynite mercenaries.

There is opportunity here to show how rough and tumble a Coynite party can be, as well as giving the characters a chance to actually *talk* to an Imperial representative rather than just shooting her (the shooting part comes later). This is an excellent opportunity to show the Imperial mindset. From an Imperial's perspective, the Empire is perfectly justifiable, bringing order to the galaxy and holding together a society that was just a few steps from slipping into anarchy and warfare.

The characters must discredit the delegation. Of course, the Imperials will not be pleased at this and will take vengeance once the characters have left Coyn.

Kidron

Kidron

Type: Tropical jungle
Temperature: Hot
Atmosphere: Type II (breath mask suggested)
Hydrosphere: Moist
Gravity: Light
Terrain: Jungle, mountains
Length of Day: 20 standard hours
Length of Year: 276 local days
Sapient Species: Human, Gamorreans, Orfite (N), various aliens
Starport: Standard class
Population: 20 million

Planet Function: Homeworld, refuge, trade
Government: Anarchist council
Tech Level: Space
Major Exports: Kril meat, exotic plants, Orfite scent-based tech
Major Imports: High tech
System: Kidron
Star: Kidros (orange giant)
Orbital Bodies:

Name	Planet Type	Moons
Tue	searing rock	0
Kidron	tropical jungle	4
Kuantar	gas giant	22
Alvor	gas giant	13
Spoi	ice ball	0

System Datafile

Kidron system, star: Kidros, orange giant. Five planets in system—second planet, Kidron, is Orfite homeworld. Kidron is a refuge world whose primary industry is agriculture.

From a story related by Captain Rars Lefken, tramp freighter captain …

"… you know, I've been to a lot of strange worlds. Planets with flying lizards; worlds where the locals were half-plant and went into hibernation every night; planets where the local beasties make rancors look about as dangerous as Bilars … but Kidron is a *strange* world.

"You see, it's set up by refugees, for refugees. Everyone is here because they're hiding from someone else. People have about as much individual freedom as you could expect to find on a world. No customs, no import tariffs, no regulations. Near as I could tell, no laws either. Weapons everywhere, spice liquor addicts, hucksters. You want something that's illegal, Kidron's the place to go.

"Still, there is a code of behavior there. You try to cause trouble and they pull together like sand fleas on a bantha. Slavers are dead men since everyone there is *running* from people like that. Goes double for bounty hunters. Don't attack someone, or everyone'll jump in to 'straighten things out.'

"One time I saw a bounty hunter — young kid and in way over his head — try to grab a local. The locals just pulled their blasters and fired. Must have taken fifty blaster bolts before he hit the ground. Poof! Instant *disintegration.* Wasn't pretty.

"Watch your step, play nice and *don't* try to remove someone without their permission and you'll be fine."

World Summary

Kidron is a hot, jungle-covered planet close to its sun, with a thin atmosphere. Kidros' light makes the skies of Kidron glow a bright orange, and the world is blessed with spectacular sunsets and sunrises. While habitable, Kidron is far from comfortable or hospitable. However, thanks to the generosity of the native Orfites, Kidron is a refuge world for the dregs of the galaxy who would like to be forgotten.

Kidron, at first glance, appears to be little more than a settlement of outlaws and cutthroats. It is much more. It is a world where those who have a history of trouble — whether its source be crime bosses, corporations or even the Empire — can disappear and begin new lives. No questions are asked and no facts are volunteered, but as long as people abide by the few laws of this new world, they will have no problems. These people are called "guests" by the native Orfites, who have little understanding of the larger galactic culture but feel that people who are willing to abide by their rules have a right to live in peace. Most of the guests live in the High City of Refuge, although there are some other very small settlements on the world.

The Orfites are a people with a simple culture. They have generously shared their world with people that most of the galaxy considers beneath notice, and that generousity has been returned with warm friendship and profound respect. While

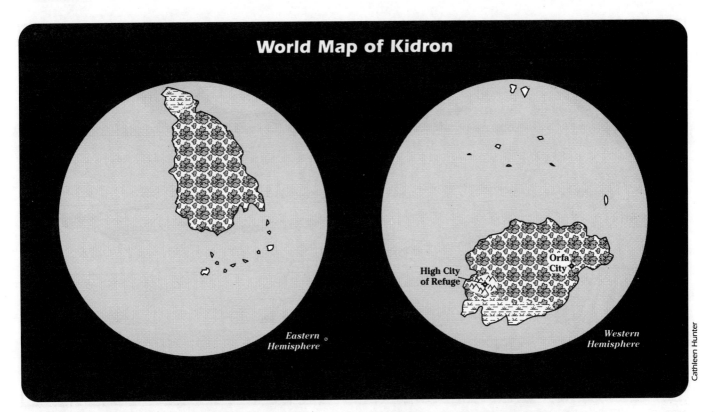

World Map of Kidron

Eastern Hemisphere

High City of Refuge

Orfa City

Western Hemisphere

Cathleen Hunter

most of the Orfite sahhs ("tribes") have ignored high technology, some have adapted to the larger culture of the galaxy. Some enterprising Orfites developed the unusual olfactory masks, which are popular among Orfites and other species.

Kidron sustains itself by selling kril meat to other worlds in Elrood Sector. The meat is a staple in diets around the sector. While kril farming has spread to most of the other worlds, Kidron remains the most plentiful and inexpensive source of the meat.

System Summary

Kidros is an orange giant. Tue is a small, insignificant rock of molten lava, considered to be of no commercial worth. Kuantar and Alvor are a pair of gas giants, both a bright violet color. Kuantar has a series of rings that is sometimes visible in Kidron's night sky. Spoi, the outermost planet, is a small ice ball that has been ignored by the residents of Kidron.

Orfites

The Orfites are a humanoid species with a stocky build. Due to Kidron's thin atmosphere, they have large lungs. Orfites have wide noses with large nostrils and frilled olfactory lobes. Their skin has an orangish cast, with fine reddish hair on their heads. To non-Orfites, the only distinguishing characteristic between the two sexes is that females have thick eyebrows.

Due to their stocky build and their planet's low

Kidron's Light Gravity

Kidron is a light gravity world. Characters accustomed to standard gravity should apply the following modifiers:

-1D to all *Dexterity*-related actions until the character has spent one standard month on the world. After one month, a character's reflexes will have adjusted to the lighter gravity.

+1D+2 to *lifting, climbing,* and *jumping.* This effect lasts for six standard months, after which the character's muscles will have lost strength to the point where the bonus is lost. This bonus may be kept if the character actively exerts himself and lifts heavy weights on a regular basis.

+2 to Move for a period of one standard year.

gravity, most Orfites must wear a power harness to give them increased strength when they go to standard gravity worlds.

Orfite society revolves around the sense of smell, their most powerful sense. Orfites produce powerful pheromones, and each Orfite's scent is distinctive in much the same way that physical appearance is distinctive among Humans.

Orfites have a peaceful and flexible society; the Orfites have reached a consensus on indi-

Mike Vilardi

The High City of Refuge

vidual freedom and responsibility to society. Hospitable and pleasure-seeking are the two best descriptions of the Orfites as a whole. They are generous, eager to share and they expect others to share with them.

The Orfites have a simple social structure. Each Orfite sahh (tribe) has control over a vast tract of jungle. Plentiful food and water and little need for advanced technology ensures that more complex organization is unnecessary. Within a sahh, each member has immense freedom of choice and action. The Orfites have a simple legal code: before using the possessions of another or using their land, ask their permission. Naturally, theft, assault and murder are crimes. Punishment takes the form of permanently scarring the offending Orfite's face and then banishing them from the sahh, forcing them to venture to an unclaimed area. Other sahhs will not take in a scarred Orfite. The Orfites lack the aggressive instinct of other species, and warfare has never occurred between sahhs.

Trade between sahhs and individuals is normally simple barter. Since there is very little technology on the world, a fully regulated economy is also unnecessary.

The mainstay of the Orfite diet is kril meat. All individuals are responsible for raising their own krils, although individuals and sahhs share with those who, through misfortune, lack enough food. Within a sahh, each person normally has a spe-

cial role, besides the herding of krils. Some are sahh healers, many are weavers and cloth makers, some are storytellers, and many are tool makers. There are no selected leaders — all tribe members vote on all matters, and only with a clear majority are new actions or endeavors undertaken. If the sahh cannot agree on a new course of action, the sahh simply maintains the traditional ways with no change of action. Sahhs always have a common meeting area; the frequency of meetings depends on the needs of the sahh. Family units of Orfites build their own homes somewhere in the territory claimed by the sahh; any disputes are settled by vote of the entire sahh.

Orfites are a free and open people. Those who strongly disagree with their sahh's decisions are free to leave at any time. Often, groups of disgruntled Orfites will get together and form new sahhs, settling on some of the great expanses of untended and unclaimed wilderness.

Since the "guests" (refugees) first came many years ago, some Orfites were very curious about what was beyond their world. The sahh to first greet the guests welcomed these people with gifts and sharing of stories. A greedy, corrupt senator had falsely accused four people of crimes against the Republic, and they chose to flee to Kidron, hoping for asylum.

At the time, a meeting of all sahhs was called (this was only the third such meeting of all Orfites in their recorded history, dating back over five millennia). After much debate, all agreed to welcome the guests and allow them to settle on an unclaimed area. After all, the Orfites had been granted a wonderful world, and they could never use it all. It was their duty to share their bounty with those who needed it. The first village eventually grew into the High City of Refuge. Since that time, peace has reigned: the Orfites continue to welcome new visitors and the city's residents have respected the traditions and ways of the Orfites.

Over the centuries, many Orfites have been drawn to this new and strange culture. Fascinated by the technology, some established Orfa City, a city that mixes traditional Orfite ways and high technology. In that time, the Orfites have developed the Orfite scent masks and power harnesses, giving Kidron a unique technology. To ensure smooth relations between all Orfite sahhs, the High City, Orfa City and any other groups which might venture to the world (such as the Empire), the Orfites established the Council of Gordek (explained below). There have been no conflicts between the traditional and the technological Orfites — they respect and accept each others' differing views, and large expanses of unclaimed territory haven't "forced" either Orfa City or the High City of Refuge to expand into the lands of the sahhs.

■ Orfites

Attribute Dice: 12D
DEXTERITY 1D/3D
KNOWLEDGE 2D/4D+2
MECHANICAL 1D/4D
PERCEPTION 2D/5D+1
STRENGTH 1D/2D+1
TECHNICAL 1D/3D
Special Abilities:
Olfactory Sense: Orfites have a well-developed sense of smell. Add +2D to *search* when tracking someone by scent or when otherwise using their sense of smell. They can operate in darkness without any penalties. Due to poor eyesight, they suffer -2D to *search*, *Perception* and related combat skills when they cannot use scent. They also

suffer a -2D penalty when attacking targets over five meters away.
Light Gravity: Orfites are native to Kidron, a light gravity world. When on standard gravity worlds, reduce their *Move* by -3. Without a power harness on such worlds, reduce their *Strength* and *Dexterity* by -1D (minimum of +2; they can still roll, hoping to get a "Wild Die" result).
Move: 11/14
Size: 1.0–2.0 meters

Council of Gordek

The Council of Gordek is an official representative for the Orfites. The council has four members, chosen by vote from among all the sahhs. These Orfites are chosen for their ability to listen and interpret the intentions of others, and their purity of thought. Councillors are retained until a sahh declares that a new vote should be held for the council.

The councillors are charged with listening to disputes between sahhs. They cannot mediate

Four is the Number

Four is a sacred number in Orfite society, considered to be a bringer of good luck. Kidron has four moons, each Orfite has four lungs, and the first guests were a group of four travelers. People who travel in groups of four, or who have a ship that has the number four in its name, are considered lucky, and are fawned over. They are given special benefits by Orfites in the hopes that this luck will rub off — they receive price discounts, better services, preferred seats at restaurants and small gifts.

conflicts, although through their observations they can often suggest compromises that both sides will find acceptable. They also mediate any conflicts between the High City of Refuge, Orfa City and any other parties. Their final and most important duty is that of diplomatic representative. Whenever dignitaries from other worlds venture to Kidron, the councillors must greet, entertain and negotiate with these people.

The Gordek knows of a dangerous secret. They have scout reports indicating that the two largest moons, Primor and Segual, are loaded with valuable ores. These reports were filed two centuries ago. Any mining company that learned of this would probably take the moons for their own use, and in all likelihood, the idyllic Orfite lifestyle would end. The Gordek has no intention of letting anyone know of the ore. The Gordek would, with some reluctance, even kill to keep the secret from leaking out.

Relations with the Empire

Kidron is a world that is insignificant to the Empire. The Empire considers the Orfites little more than uncivilized savages. The High City of Refuge is beneath its notice. Only through the grace of the Empire is this world allowed to live in peace.

The Gordek realizes that this is the case, and the councillors go out of their way to ensure that their world remains unexceptional and easily forgettable.

The Empire has allowed the High City of Refuge to remain a neutral location out of convenience. If ever it turned out that there was something worth taking or someone worth capturing, the illusion of freedom would dissipate under the heels of Imperial occupation troops.

Orfa City

Orfa City is the only major Orfite city on the planet. Established by those Orfites interested in the wondrous technology brought by the first guests, the city has grown to a population of over three million beings. The main industry is scent mask manufacturing. The masks are quite popular with Orfites and have become a popular recreational device for non-Orfites.

Orfa City has several other important industries, not the least of which includes maintaining the kril meat export business. While each sahh normally trades with other sahhs for goods, they receive regular credits from their off-world customers. Several large accounting firms keep track of payments and sahh funds — the sahh often uses these credits to purchase equipment or goods that cannot be made from the natural resources of Kidron. However, most sahhs have chosen to forgo reliance on technology, so these

purchases are infrequent. In fact, most of the credits earned by sale of kril meat is sitting in accounts collecting interest.

Though off-worlders and guests are allowed to visit and even live here, the population is overwhelmingly Orfite. The Gordek and the Orfa Olfactory Corporation are here. The city has a major starport, as well as the kril slaughter houses.

Orfite Equipment

■ Orfite Scent Masks

Model: Orfa Olfactory Corporation Scent Mask
Type: Recreational olfactory scent mask
Cost: 200 credits (400 credits off Kidron)
Availability: 2

Capsule: With scent as their primary sense, Orfite entertainment runs in that direction, too. The biggest selling item is the Orfite Scent Mask.

The apparatus consists of a breath mask connected by a tube to a small belt unit. The belt unit holds about half a liter of water. A small tablet is inserted into the unit. The belt unit creates a mist that travels up the tube and into the breath mask.

There are several different scent tablets available: "Kidron Flowerbed," "Kidron Jungle Morning After a Rainstorm," "Goodscent," "Suppertime," and "Seabreeze" are the most popular. There are also intoxicant tablets that can be used. These come in many varieties and degrees of potency.

In recent times, these devices have become a trendy recreational device among other species in Elrood Sector. Orfa Olfactory Corporation has produced many new scent tablets for specific species. Scent tablets are five credits apiece, while intoxicant tablets are ten credits each. At this time, the scent masks are completely unregulated, although the existence of intoxicant tablets may lead to the masks being regulated by the Imperial bureaucracy.

■ Orfite Power Harnesses

Model: Orfa Toolco Power Harness
Type: Strength enhancer
Cost: 800 credits
Availability: 3
Game Notes: Negates penalties for Orfites on standard gravity worlds.

Capsule: These harnesses enable the Orfites, who are used to the low gravity of Kidron, to act freely and without penalty on standard gravity worlds. The harnesses are lightweight units with mini servo machines built into the joints. Although the harnesses attach to the back, waist, shoulders and thighs, the harness is small enough not to be obvious under normal clothing. The servos aren't very powerful, and provide no enhancement in light gravity, nor can they be modified to give bonuses.

Kidron System Defense (KSD)

Kidron has long been responsible for its own defense. To address that, the High City Council formed the Kidron System Defense, or KSD. The forces include a Corellian Corvette (the KSD flag-

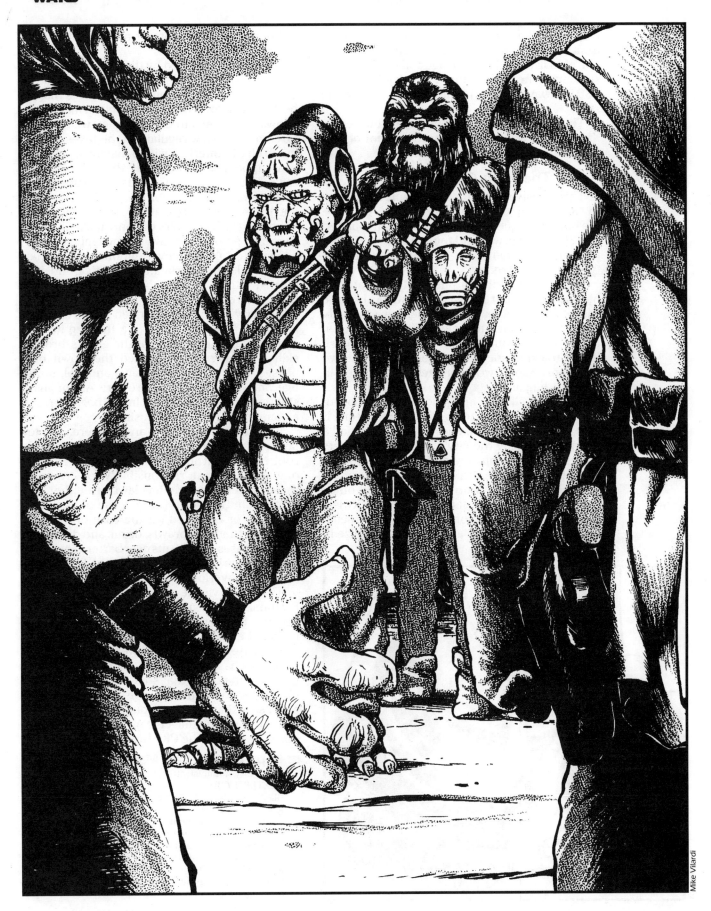

Mike Vilardi

ship), four *Prosperity*-class defense ships bought from Elrood shipyards, three system patrol craft, one old TIE (bought as salvage and refurbished), six refurbished Z-95s and a Skipray Blastboat. KSD is always looking for new guests to crew the ships.

The overwhelming percentage of crewmen on KSD vessels are guests (only 10 percent of KSD forces are Orfite).

The High City of Refuge

This massive metropolis (its name shortened to "Refuge" by the population within) is where the bulk of the guests live. The city is surrounded by a 30 meter tall wall and topped by a reinforced transparisteel dome that holds in a breathable type I atmosphere.

The gravity is still light, and the temperature is blisteringly hot, but at least the guests can breathe easily. A set of four gated airlocks are the only means of entrance to Refuge. Each airlock entrance has a mounted ion cannon for defense from attacking starships. There is a primitive spaceport about two kilometers away, deep in Kidron's jungle.

Refuge itself is a hodgepodge collection of buildings of varying size, age, and architecture. It is as if each sentient species in the galaxy had a hand in designing the city's layout. The streets are winding and confusing, and filled with crowds. Since there is no centralized planning, residential buildings, bars, stores, factories and office buildings all share the same blocks; the city is a mis-matched collection of buildings, with no definable neighborhoods or areas. Bars specialize in

krilliz, a drink made from fermented kril milk. It's an acquired taste.

The city is governed by the City High Council, which has fifteen beings selected by general election. The council genuinely believes that the best type of government is the government that allows its citizens to do what they wish. Therefore, there are few regulations, no taxes and not much else to interfere with behavior — any level of weaponry is permissible, there are no laws regulating spice, liquors and other substances, and there are no prohibitions against gambling and other behaviors that are traditionally regulated. Council members not only make the laws; they also enforce the law. Council members are allowed to take whatever actions they feel are warranted to bring criminals to justice, and often entrust citizen militias to assist them in situations where additional firepower is necessary.

The city's economy is driven by the export of kril meat. The city also has a thriving internal economy because many of the guests brought skills with them and opened their own businesses. Free enterprise is alive and well in Refuge, and shops of all sorts are here. Although the standard Imperial credit is in use here, barter is a common way of doing business.

Incredibly, crime rates are low here. The few laws pertain to the rights of individual citizens — robbery, assault and murder are illegal. Since no one wants to take responsibility for criminals, those who violate the few laws are either banished from the world (in the case of assault or robbery) or executed (in the case of murder). Certainly there are brawls, drunk and disorderly conduct cases, arguments over barter value, petty theft, and price gouging, but most of these offenses are overlooked or not even illegal.

The most visible resident of Refuge is Kep Fortuna, the city manager hired by the City High Council. Kep is responsible for overseeing funding for the laws and programs instituted by the Council. He also has veto power over any laws or programs passed — this position was given this power in the belief that someone removed from direct election would be more likely to do what is necessary than do what would be popular. However, the city manager can be removed from office by vote of the City High Council.

Mike Vilardi

■ Kep Fortuna, City Manager
Type: City Administrator/Mobster
DEXTERITY 3D
Blaster 5D, dodge 6D, melee parry 5D+2
KNOWLEDGE 4D
Alien species 9D, bureaucracy: Kidron 8D+1, business 8D, cultures 8D+1, intimidation 8D, languages 9D+1, law enforcement 8D, planetary systems 8D, streetwise 11D+2, survival 8D+2, value 9D, willpower 9D
MECHANICAL 2D+1
Beast riding 4D, ground vehicle operation 4D, hover vehicle operation 5D, repulsorlift operation 3D

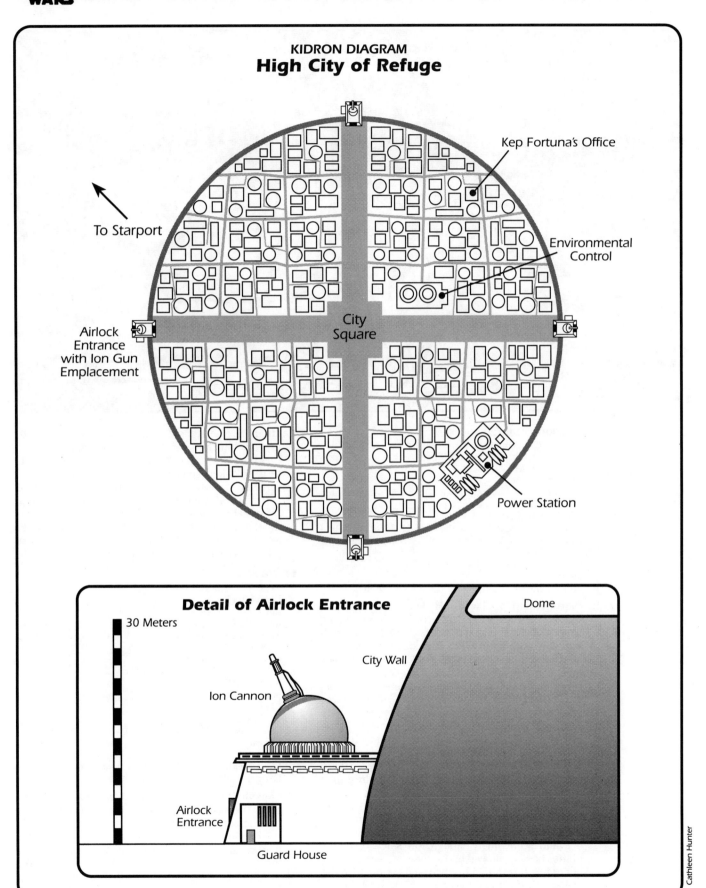

KIDRON DIAGRAM
High City of Refuge

To Starport

Kep Fortuna's Office

Environmental Control

City Square

Airlock Entrance with Ion Gun Emplacement

Power Station

Detail of Airlock Entrance

30 Meters

Dome

City Wall

Ion Cannon

Airlock Entrance

Guard House

Cathleen Hunter

Mike Vilardi

PERCEPTION 4D+2
Bargain 9D+1, command 9D, con 8D+1, gambling 7D, hide 7D, persuasion 9D+1, sneak 7D
STRENGTH 2D+2
TECHNICAL 1D+1
Computer programming/repair 3D+1, droid programming 2D+2, first aid 2D, security 4D
Special Abilities:
Tentacles: Twi'leks can use their head tails for communication. See page 137 of *Star Wars: The Roleplaying Game, Second Edition.*
Character Points: 12
Move: 10
Equipment: Blaster pistol (4D), datapad, comlink

Capsule: Kep is a Twi'lek. He keeps his head tails draped over his shoulders. Kep is hiding from Jabba the Hutt. It appears that Kep was visiting a distant relation, Bib Fortuna, at Jabba's palace. Somehow, a few small trinkets from Jabba's inventory accidentally found their way into Kep's robe pockets. Kep has long since sold the items, and eventually ended up on Kidron, where he was able to bribe his way into being selected as city manager. While Kep has tried to keep order in the city and maintain good relations with the Orfites, he has also sold his power to a local crime boss, Staarn. So far, Kep has managed to keep Staarn happy without revealing his affiliation to the public at large.

Kep is a sneaky, ambitious fellow who is always looking for ways to turn adversity to advantage. He is a coward and would rather talk or con his way out of a jam. Interestingly enough, Kep's new responsibilities have mellowed him somewhat, so that he is not only interested in his own welfare, but also the welfare of Refuge and the guests. Thus, while he will

still con, cajole, manipulate, blackmail, and bribe, he does it with the best interests of Refuge in mind.

At the worst, guests warily tolerate him. At best, he is well liked, since Kep is a very good administrator. Kep "advises" people on the best courses of action, and his advice most always turns out to be remarkably sound. This is because Kep has manipulated Refuge events enough so that while people are free to do what they want, it is in their best interests to do things his way.

■ Staarn

Type: Bothan Crime Lord
DEXTERITY 3D
Blaster 5D, dodge 4D+1
KNOWLEDGE 2D+2
Alien species 5D+2, bureaucracy 4D+1, business 4D+2, cultures 5D, languages 4D+1, streetwise 6D+2
MECHANICAL 2D+1
Astrogation 3D+2, space transports 3D+2
PERCEPTION 4D+1
Bargain 7D, con 6D+2, forgery 5D, gambling 6D+1
STRENGTH 2D+2
TECHNICAL 3D
Computer programming/repair 5D+1
Character Points: 8
Move: 10
Equipment: Blaster pistol (4D), elegant robes and Bothan business suit, comlink, datapad

Capsule: Staarn is a Bothan crime boss who has spent the past two decades on Kidron. Ousted from his society shortly after going through his clan's rite of adulthood, Staarn took up a life of crime. To him, organized crime wasn't much of a stretch from the usual Bothan in-fighting and maneuvering. He has built up a small ring of confidence tricksters and specializes in illegal, high-interest loans. He disdains dealing with slaving and spice smuggling, viewing such activities as crude and unrefined. Staarn enjoys being the center of attention: his spacious townhouse is known for its wild parties. He can often be seen about Refuge, flaunting his wealth through his rich clothes and expensive speeders. It is common knowledge that Staarn is a criminal, but most of the people of Refuge view him as harmless: you'd have to be a fool to take out a loan from him. Most of Staarn's business comes from off-world. Staarn, being a practical being, is more than willing to arrange creative solutions to defaulters. Rather than physical harm, he will often ask a "simple favor," such as retrieving vital information on secret business dealings, special computer codes to military or business complexes, or other bits of priceless help. Of course, Staarn has been able to use this information to generate a personal fortune.

Creatures

■ Kril

Type: Domesticated food animal
DEXTERITY 1D
PERCEPTION 1D
STRENGTH 1D
Lifting 3D, climbing 4D
Special Abilities:
Hooves: Do STR+2 damage
Horn: Do STR+1D+1 damage
Move: 7
Size: 1.5 meters tall at the shoulder, up to 2.5 meters long
Scale: Creature
Orneriness: 2D

Capsule: Krils are the most plentiful form of livestock on Kidron. The creatures are large, climbing herd herbivores perfectly suited to the jungle environment and light gravity of the world. Krils have a single horn on their foreheads, and large, wide saucer eyes. Many Humans find the krils to be "adorable," something that puzzles the Orfites.

Krils are not particularly intelligent, and are easy prey for Kidron's predators; they reproduce quickly enough that the species survived. The Orfites domesticated them thousands of years ago, breeding them into larger creatures with more meat. Krils are calm animals, but can be spooked into stampeding with an Easy *intimidation* roll.

Krils emit a braying call when angry, and a soft humming when they are content. The humming is pleasing to Humans, which only serves to make the krils more adorable, in their opinion.

■ Jammer

Type: Wild predator
DEXTERITY 2D
Dodge 4D, flight 4D+2
PERCEPTION 3D
Hide 6D, sneak 8D
STRENGTH 2D
Brawling 6D, stamina 7D
Special Abilities:
Flight: Jammers can fly using the *flight* skill.
Tentacles: Do STR+1D damage
Teeth: Do STR+2D damage
Scent Sacs: Scent clouds effectively blind Orfites and krils, both who use smell as a primary sense. When caught in a five meter diameter scent cloud, the Orfites and krils suffer -2D to all actions using vision or smell.
Move: 6 (walking), 12 (flying)
Size: 2.0 to 3.0 meters long, average wingspan 3.0 meters

Capsule: Jammers are manta-ray like creatures that live in the jungles of Kidron. They use a combination of air sacs and their "wings" to keep aloft. They are ferocious predators who can emit a horrendous stench cloud five meters in diameter that "jams" the olfactory senses of the Orfites and the krils, their traditional prey. Non-Orfites who have no breathing apparatus must make a Very Difficult *Strength* roll or be nauseous and unable to move for 1D+1 rounds.

Adventure Idea

A criminal (possibly a henchman of Lud Chud or Boss Kaggle that the characters met when dealing with one of those bosses) wishes to hire them to take her to Kidron for refuge. She claims to be tired of the dangerous life of organized crime.

While this is true to an extent, she is also hiding a datachip that details the crime boss' dealings with the Empire. She had hoped to sell the information, but all her attempts have gone awry.

The crime boss, unhappy with this betrayal, hires a bounty hunter to catch the thief. Of course, she expects this. The Empire, equally unhappy, sends some undercover Imperial Security Bureau (ISB) agents to retrieve the chip; she does *not* know about this. The characters find themselves tailed and endangered as they travel throughout Kidron.

Merisee

Merisee

Type: Agricultural plains
Temperature: Temperate
Atmosphere: Type I (breathable)
Hydrosphere: Moderate
Gravity: Standard
Terrain: Plains
Length of Day: 24 standard hours
Length of Year: 315 local days
Sapient Species: Meris (N), Teltiors (N)
Starport: 3 standard class
Population: 310 million
Planet Function: Agriculture, homeworld
Government: Participatory democracy
Tech Level: Space
Major Exports: Grain, alcoholic beverages, pharmaceuticals
Major Imports: High tech
System: Meris
Star: Maris (yellow)
Orbital Bodies:

Name	Planet Type	Moons
Meris I	searing rock	0
Meris II	steaming jungle	0
Meris III	steaming jungle	1
Merisee	terrestrial	2
Meris V	barren wasteland	2
Meris VI	frigid wasteland	0

World Summary

Merisee is a temperate planet, with a mild, consistent climate and plenty of fertile land. Merisee has two moons, Tola and Meriso. The world is homeworld to two closely related races of aliens, the Meris and Teltiors, and Merisee has become a major agricultural producer for Elrood Sector. The world is a paradise in many ways, with a prosperous economy, an enlightened government and a high standard of living with much personal freedom. However, there is a darker side to Merisee — the Loag, a special order of assassins, with a long, though obscure history, who inhabit this world.

System Summary

Maris is a yellow star, the source of life in Meris system. The first two planets are searing and undeveloped. Meris II is home to primitive, heat-resistant life forms — some corporations have investigated the possibility of genetically engineering these bacteria to produce molecules that can be incorporated into heat shielding. At this point, experimental results have been promising, but the process is expensive.

Meris III's rich natural environment has led to the development of many unique life forms; one plant has proven to be a particularly effective treatment for Taren plague and related viruses. There are several harvesting colonies on the planet, with pharmaceutical refinement factories on Merisee.

Meris V is a chilly, barren wasteland. There are some as yet undiscovered ore deposits. Meris VI is a frigid planet swept by constant ice storms. Meris VI has a breathable type II atmosphere in warmer seasons; in winter, the air is too cold to be safe without a heating mask filter.

Starports

Merisee has three primary starports: Merisee Prime, Merisee Agra, and Merisee Dispatch. Merisee Prime and Merisee Dispatch are both located outside the capital city of Caronath.

Merisee Prime is the largest port on the world,

System Datafile

Meris system, star: Maris, yellow sun. Six planets in system. Merisee, fourth planet in system, is the agricultural center of Elrood sector.

Upon entering Meris system, the characters' ship will receive the following broadcast …

"Welcome to Merisee, 'Breadbasket of Elrood Sector.' We hope your stay here is pleasant. If your arrival has been previously scheduled, please turn to frequency J-33-567-Y32 for further instructions. If you have a medical emergency, please tune to frequency J-45-411-K77, and notify the duty officer in charge. An emergency team will be waiting for you when you land. If you have other business to declare or need further instructions, turn to override channel 47, where a traffic controller will assist you."

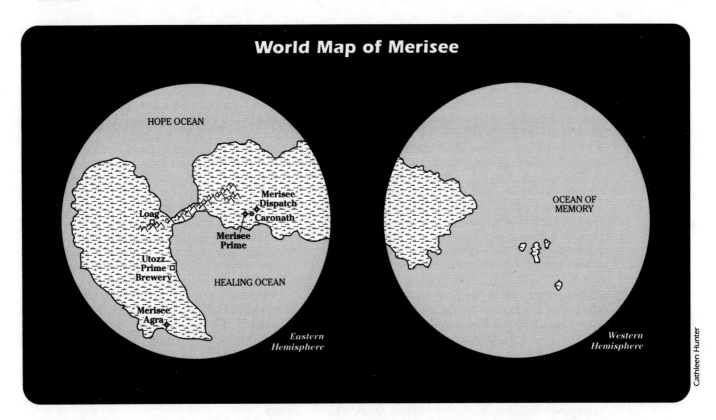

World Map of Merisee

HOPE OCEAN

Loag

Merisee Dispatch
Caronath

Merisee Prime

Utozz Prime Brewery

HEALING OCEAN

Merisee Agra

Eastern Hemisphere

OCEAN OF MEMORY

Western Hemisphere

Cathleen Hunter

and is primarily for passengers, business travelers and small and moderate cargo vessels. Merisee Dispatch is a passenger facility and also provides direct access to the medical facilities in the city.

Merisee Agra is a cargo port, where toz grains, Utozz, and various pharmaceuticals are shipped in bulk. For those major vessels capable of planetary landing, there are appropriate facilities. However since many bulk transports aren't capable of planetfall, a large portion of the port's traffic includes surface-to-orbit transports.

History

To understand the Merisee of today, it is important to understand the history of the world. Merisee is the homeworld of a humanoid alien species with two distinct races, the Meris and the Teltiors.

For millennia, both races remained ignorant of each other. The world's two major continents were separated by a vast ocean that was constantly disturbed by devastating storms. The storms were so fierce that even the coasts of the continents were dangerous to live on — it was not uncommon for flood waters to reach over 100 kilometers inland (the majority of Merisee's land is plains just barely above sea level). This prevented long-range exploration, so while the two races both developed technology, sea travel was virtually unknown.

This changed thousands of years ago. Inexplicably, violent volcanic eruptions and seismic

shifts wrenched the planet. Weather patterns shifted and temperatures changed just enough to change the air streams. The oceans calmed and a land bridge connecting both continents emerged. This period is referred to as "the Joining," and preceded a period of bloody warfare that would hang like a shadow over Merisee for a thousand years.

First contact between the Teltiors and the Meris was violent. The two races had completely conflicting philosophies and attitudes, and struggle seemed inevitable for neither side considered compromise possible. The first two or three centuries saw sporadic warfare and abortive colonization attempts on the other race's continent. Eventually, the conflict escalated into full-scale warfare. Over the next seven centuries, billions died, as the rich farmlands were devastated by radiation and biological weapons. However, due to the need to survive, the Meris and Teltiors developed very advanced medical techniques.

As the world faced final devastation, and with both populations on the brink of extinction, the races made a peace. Reluctantly, they put aside their differences and began working on restoring their world. Fortunately, a planet is a hardy thing and the world slowly rebounded from the centuries of abuse. As new generations were born and raised in a tradition of cooperation, hate became distrust, and then rivalry, and then, in time, friendship.

While the world was still reeling from the

effects of a thousand years of war, and the populations were still small, there was hope. The Old Republic discovered the planet and in quick time, Merisee joined. At first, the Republic lent assistance by loaning countless decon droids, who sped up the repair of Merisee's fragile ecosphere. In a few centuries, Merisee had gone from being a world dependent upon the Republic to one that was providing food, medicine and other valuable goods to other member worlds.

The warlike factions of Meris and Teltiors, unable to tolerate the idea of peace, retreated into the mountains. Ironically, both groups' hatred of each other drove them together. These two violent factions realized that the days as warlords were past. However, there were others off-world who would pay handsomely for those who savored killing. Both groups united into a single group called the Loag, a mixture of the Meri and Teltior words for warrior. They perfected their arts of combat and assassination and became a secret cult of hired killers.

As the cult grew, however, the Loag became overconfident. They wanted the population of Merisee to bend to their will. The Loag began an escalating campaign of terror and sabotage; they instigated incidents between the two races. The general populace learned to fear the name Loag. However, the Loag did not count on the intervention of the Jedi.

A half dozen Jedi Knights, aware of the pattern of hired killings coming from the Merisee area, resolved to end the terror. A year later, the Loag was scattered and broken, the cult's power stripped away. It was presumed that the Loag was destroyed, but that was not so. Many Loag assassins faked their deaths and sought seclusion and secrecy.

A grateful population venerated the Jedi Knights, who lost three of their number in the campaign. The remaining three left Merisee.

Quietly, the Loag was rebuilt. This time, the assassins selected only those who would be bound by the rigid tradition of secrecy. The organization flourished again, but this time with a greater veil of secrecy. Even today, the average Merisee native says that the Loag cult was long ago destroyed. It is unknown if the Loag will ever seek power on Merisee again.

Caronath

Caronath is the capital city of Merisee, with a population just over five million. As the only major city on the planet, is it home to many of Merisee's corporations. It is the most common destination for off-world business travelers, as well as the center of Merisee's impressive medical facilities.

The Meris and Teltiors are a hard working people and not given to wild celebrations. Caronath is a quiet city, with few social clubs or taverns. The few ones here do a very brisk business. If there is someone from off-planet on Merisee, he will be very easy to find, since there are not many places to look. The most popular Merisee social spots are the Utoz Houses.

Caronath does offer a large number of public parks, many of which have "thinking gardens." For a small fee (averaging five credits per hour), a person can rent a small, closed off area of a park. They will have this area all to themselves for solitude and contemplation. Of course, these gardens can be used for less noble purposes — it is known that meetings of shameful lovers or contracts for Loag assassins have been arranged within the seclusion of these gardens.

There are also many counselors near the parks or who have businesses in the city proper. These counselors offer advice and listen to the problems of others. This tradition was established as part of Merisee's medical tradition, the people here believing that healing is a physical and mental process. However, this tradition is popular with those who simply want privacy and advice.

■ Meris

Attribute Dice: 12D
DEXTERITY 3D+2/6D
KNOWLEDGE 1D/4D
MECHANICAL 1D/4D
PERCEPTION 1D/4D
STRENGTH 2D/4D
TECHNICAL 2D/4D
Special Skills:
Knowledge skills:
Weather Prediction. Time to use: one minute. This skill allows Meris to accurately predict weather on Merisee and similar worlds. This is a Moderate task on planets with climate conditions similar to Merisee. The task's difficulty increases the more the planet's climate differs from Merisee's. The prediction is effective for four hours; the difficulty increases if the Meri wants to predict over a longer period of time.
Agriculture. Time to use: five minutes. Agriculture enables the user to know when and where to best plant crops, how to keep the crops alive, how to rid them of pests, and how to best harvest and store them.
Special Abilities:
Skill Bonus: Meris can choose to focus on *one* of the following skills: *agriculture, first aid* or *medicine.* They receive a bonus of +2D to the skill, and advancing that skill costs half the normal amount of skill points.
Stealth: Meris gain a +2D when using *sneak.*
Move: 10/12
Size: 1.5–2.2 meters

Capsule: The Meris are a tall humanoid race with dark blue skin. They are very similar to their fellow Teltiors; distinguishing characteristics include a pronounced eyebrow ridge, a conical ridge on the top of the head, webbed hands with an opposable thumb and opposable end finger, inward spiralling cartilage leading to the ear canal and several thick folds of skin around the neck. Meris move with a fluid grace, and have amazing coordination.

While once a true race of warriors, the Meris have learned how to peacefully coexist with the Teltiors. Many Meris have applied their intelligence to farming and healing, but there are many others who have gone into varied fields, such as starship engineering, business, soldiering and numerous other common occupations.

The Meris are a friendly people, but they will not blindly trust those who haven't proven themselves worthy of trust. Like most other species, Meris have a wide range of personalities and behaviors — some are extremely peaceful, while others are quick to anger and fight. The Meris are a hardworking people, many of whom spend time in quiet contemplation or playing mental exercise games like holochess.

■ Teltiors

Attribute Dice: 12D
DEXTERITY 3D/5D+2
KNOWLEDGE 1D+1/4D+2
MECHANICAL 1D+1/4D+1
PERCEPTION 1D/4D
STRENGTH 2D/4D
TECHNICAL 1D+2/4D
Special Abilities:
Skill Bonus: Teltiors may choose to concentrate in one of the following skills: *agriculture, bargain, con, first aid* or *medicine*. They receive a +1D bonus, and can advance that single skill at half the normal skill point cost.
Stealth: Teltiors gain a +1D+2 bonus when using *sneak*.
Manual Dexterity: Teltiors receive +1D whenever doing something requiring complicated finger work because their fingers are so flexible.
Move: 10/12
Size: 1.5–2.2 meters

Capsule: The Teltiors are a tall humanoid race, closely related to the Meris. They have pale blue to dark blue or black skin. They lack the Meris' pronounced conical ridges, eyebrow ridge and folds of neck skin. They have a much more prominent vestigial tail and three fingered hands. The three fingers have highly flexible joints, giving the Teltiors much greater manual dexterity than many other species. Teltiors traditionally wear their hair in long ponytails down the back, although many females often shave their heads.

The Teltiors have shown a greater willingness to spread from their homeworld, and many have found great success as traders and merchants. Although the Teltiors don't like to publicly speak of this, there are also many quite successful Teltior con men, including the infamous Ceezva, who managed to bluff her way into a high stakes sabacc game with only 500 credits to her name. She managed to win the entire Unnipar system from Archduke Monlo of the Dentamma Nebula.

The Loag

The Loag, the group of assassins once thought eliminated, have returned to Merisee. Their actions, while hidden from the commoners of Merisee, have far-reaching effects around the planet. The Loag has a secret citadel carved from a hollowed out dormant volcano near the land bridge.

■ The races of Merisee: a Meri (left) and a Teltior (right).

It is extremely difficult to make contact with the Loag. If their presence was ever publicly revealed, Merisee's government or the Empire would take actions to eliminate them. The Loag cult accepts contracts from many sources — crime lords, disgruntled governments, even Imperial officers and dignitaries with someone to silence. The Loag cult has many loyal informants throughout the galaxy who contact those who would hire Loag assassins. There have been some cases of informants who attempted to betray the Loag — they all ended up dead at the hands of Loag assassins, so even informants cannot tell when they are being spied upon. Assassination fees are high (the lowest known fee was 5,000 credits), but the Loag is known for being able to fulfill its contracts.

There is a power struggle going on within the Loag. The largest faction wants to make sure that the Loag remains anonymous, aware of the legacy of the past and convinced that it is too early to make a move for power. They want to conduct all the business they can, mostly off-world, and help defend their best interests.

The smaller faction, which currently comprises about five percent of the Loag but also boasts some very charismatic leaders, wants to become more visible and exert power and influence over Merisee affairs. If they believe that the Loag is being threatened in any way, they will take matters into their own hands. They are convinced that the Empire wouldn't crack down on this bid for power *if* the group made it clear that they would be loyal to the Empire and the sector Moff, who clearly despises Merisee's virtually invisible and ineffectual governor, Branff Miro.

■ Typical Loag Assassin

Type: Assassin
DEXTERITY 4D
Blaster 7D, brawling parry 6D, dodge 8D, grenade 7D, melee combat 7D, melee parry 6D, missile weapons 7D, pick pocket 6D, running 8D, thrown weapons 6D
KNOWLEDGE 3D
Alien species 4D, cultures: Elrood Sector 5D, intimidation 7D, languages 4D, law enforcement: Elrood Sector 5D, planetary systems: Elrood Sector 3D+2, streetwise 4D, survival 6D, willpower 6D
MECHANICAL 2D
Beast riding 5D, communications 4D, ground vehicle operation 5D, hover vehicle operation 5D, repulsorlift operation 5D, swoop operation 4D
PERCEPTION 3D
Command 6D, con 7D, hide 7D, persuasion 5D, search 6D, sneak 8D
STRENGTH 4D
Brawling 7D, climbing/jumping 6D, stamina 6D, swimming 6D
TECHNICAL 2D
Blaster repair 4D, computer programming/repair 4D, demolitions 5D, first aid 5D, security 5D
Force Points: Varies, typically 0–5
Dark Side Points: Varies, typically 0–5
Character Points: Varies, typically 3–15
Move: 10
Equipment: Blaster pistol (4D), Merisee curved dagger (STR+1D, 3D for poison for five rounds), zolall poison vial, camouflage clothing (+1D to *sneak* in darkness), comlink, molecular climbing spikes (+2D to *climbing*).

Capsule: A Loag assassin is usually dressed in slate-gray camouflage clothing (complete with hood), with his items in small packs located conveniently all over his body.

Loag assassins smear their Merisee curved daggers with zolall venom. One application is good for four hits or two hours. The average vial has enough for ten applications.

The Cult of Those Who Redeem
After the Jedi defeated the Loag, many Meris and Teltiors began worshipping them and their

Mike Vilardi

code. They formed the Cult of Those Who Redeem, and they are commonly called the Cult by Merisee residents. This organization has taken on quasi-mystic status on the planet.

Prospective members must go through an exhaustive schedule of tests to join, and those within the organization must swear to keep their affiliation secret.

Members of the Cult swear to try to uphold the Jedi Code to the best of their ability. They also attempt to unlock the secrets of the Force, but this is less important than maintaining the purity of spirit and thought necessary to be a Jedi. Many of Merisee's most popular and influential personalities are members of the this cult. They act in a variety of ways to preserve peace, protect the weak and innocent, and improve the quality of life on their world. Some take direct action, acting as vigilantes, while others work within the government or business to support enlightened government policies or provide help and assistance to those who need it.

The Cult must remain secret so as not to trigger a "cleansing" by the Empire. Since Emperor Palpatine realized that the greatest threat to his rule was the Jedi Knights, he cannot allow a cult worshipping their ideals and spreading their myths to exist. Any Jedi who visits Merisee will attract the attention of the Cult, sparking what would surely be an interesting encounter.

Merisee Grand Medical Facility

Located in the heart of Caronath, the Merisee Grand Medical Facility is a series of several buildings dedicated to the healing arts. While prices are expensive (about double the normal charge of medical treatment), the care is better (reduce any difficulties by one level) and quicker (cut healing times to two-thirds normal).

The Grand Medical Facility is staffed with the Elrood Sector's finest doctors, nurses, specialists, technicians, and medical droids. There is even a staff of droid programmers who will reprogram and recalibrate medical droids for off-worlders.

Merisee Asylum

This is a special facility adjoining the Grand Medical Facility. Special containment cells have had to be built to accommodate the vast assortment of beings who pass through here.

This is a likely place to find victims whose minds have been tampered with by someone using the dark side of the Force, aside from the common causes of mental illness. Some important clues about the whereabouts of such people can be found by talking to the victims, although it may take several hours or even days to gain any useful information.

Utozz Prime Brewery

This is a huge corporation with headquarters on Merisee. UPB is the biggest brewer of Utozz, the brand name for a fermented malt beverage made

Utoz is an acquired taste ...

Mike Vilardi

from the toz grain; it is widely popular throughout the sector. The second largest Utoz brewer is Merisee Smooth.

UPB employs many people as transport pilots. They have had some problems with hijacked shipments of the popular brew, so there is the possibility that they might employ characters are guards.

Intoxication is a very real possibility with Utoz. Every mug requires a *stamina* roll to prevent the imbiber from getting drunk. The first *stamina* difficulty is Easy. The difficulty increases by one level per mug drank; the difficulty decreases one level per hour that passes without another Utoz.

Collective Farms

Because of the expense of modern farming, Merisee's most common agreement is the collective farm. This arrangement allows for the most efficient use of droid machinery and other equipment. An average collective farm is a self-contained community numbering between 24 and 120 people. The farm has a council (one member per eight people) that sees to the day to day operation of the community. A group called the Agra Alliance (with one alderman from each region of the planet) sets prices, controls production, and tries to ensure fair treatment for all farmers. The collective farms grow toz grain in great amounts, as well as raise several types of animals for food.

Creatures of Merisee

■ Zolall

Type: Nocturnal predator
DEXTERITY 2D
Dodge 4D
PERCEPTION 2D
Hide 4D, search 6D, sneak 5D
STRENGTH 5D
Brawling 7D, climbing/jumping 6D+1, lifting 7D, stamina 6D+1, swimming 6D
Special Abilities:
Tail: Does STR+1D constricting damage each round. Victim must make successful opposed *Strength* roll to break free.
Teeth: Do STR+2D damage, plus 4D for poison for two rounds.
Move: 9 (walking), 15 (flying)
Size: 1.7 meters long (plus an additional 2-meter tail), 3.5-meter wingspan
Scale: Creature

Capsule: The zolall is a hairless, slippery, smooth-skinned creature with a long tail and floppy triangular wings. It keeps itself aloft by air sacs located in its abdomen.

The zolall is a nocturnal hunter that haunts the wild areas of Merisee. It is a vicious, daring predator that will attack herd animals and people alike. If a victim is struck by the zolall's tail, he is wrapped tight in its coils. He can do no other action beside attempting to break free.

The Loag assassins prize the zolall for their poison sacs, located under the creature's tongue. Zolalls can be trained as watch animals, although they are never completely trustworthy. Merisee medical experts also value zolall venom, for, in a modified form, it can be used as an anesthetic.

Pharmaceuticals

The planet Meris III is an important source of exotic plants that are used for pharmaceutical purposes. A small harvesting station and landing field, manned by two dozen Merisee natives, oversees harvesting.

The chief drug company is Merisee Prime Pharmaceutical, headquartered in Caronath. The company's biggest concerns are pirates who hijack the processed shipments, or illegal harvesters who try to harvest the plants and take them to some other planets for processing.

Adventure Idea

The characters are hired by Merisee Prime Pharmaceutical to guard a valuable shipment of antivenin from Merisee to Coyn. Unfortunately, some pirates have caught wind of the shipment, and will make two tries to get the shipment.

The first attempt will be right before the characters leave Merisee Prime Starport. Essentially, the first attempt is a land based skirmish. The second will be in space, where the pirate ships attempt to disable and board the characters' ship.

Adventure Idea

A Cult member, who happens to work as a chemist for Merisee Pharmaceutical, is trying to develop a serum that gives the wearer Force-like powers. Of course, the serum will not work, but this is not known.

Several radical Loag, Imperial agents, and criminal elements will want the formula for their own use.

The Cult member may be misguided, but he is no fool. He hires the characters to be his bodyguards, though he refuses to tell them what he is working on. The characters will have to fend off attacks from the various elements, while trying to ascertain what it is the chemist is working on.

Derilyn

Derilyn

Type: Occupied urban police-state
Temperature: Temperate
Atmosphere: Type I (breathable)
Hydrosphere: Moderate
Gravity: Standard
Terrain: Urban, plains, forest, mountains, desert
Length of Day: 27 standard hours
Length of Year: 350 local days
Sapient Species: Coynites, Gamorreans, Humans, Meris, Teltiors
Starport: 2 Imperial class, 2 stellar class
Population: 2 billion
Planet Function: Trade, manufacturing
Government: Imperial governor police state
Tech Level: Space
Major Exports: High tech
Major Imports: Raw materials
System: Derilyn
Star: Deril (medium yellow)
Orbital Bodies:

Name	Planet Type	Moons
Dar	searing rock	0
Alorthas	searing rock	0
Kalis	jungle	1
Takornan	jungle	2
Derilyn	terrestrial	1
Fahul	barren rock	2
Sotipe	gas giant	14
Serrata	gas giant	5
Belorphyn	ice ball	0

World Summary

Derilyn is a planet under the boot of the Empire, brutally conquered by Imperial forces 10 years ago. Derilyn boasts a variety of terrains, including deserts, mountains, swamps, plains, woodlands, and arctic zones. Its orbit and axial tilt give it seasons with a hot summer (20° to 30°) and a cold winter (-10° to 10°).

Derilyn serves as the Empire's base for Elrood sector operations. System space around the planet is known as "Imperial Interdicted Space." The world is held under police state conditions: all civil rights are suspended, citizens may be arrested upon suspicion of treason (without any proof), and all penalties for offenses (proven or suspected) are the province of the commanding regional military officer. Commerce is strictly supervised and citizens live in constant fear of being hauled away by Imperial forces.

System Summary

The Deril system has a medium yellow star. The two planets closest to the star are uninhabitable. Dar and Alorthas are small, thin-atmosphere, sun-scorched worlds of no real economic value. Kalis is a harsh world with a thick, boiling atmosphere. There is no life on the world. Takornan is a jungle world with a type III (breath mask required) atmosphere. The exotic fauna and the considerable mineral deposits make it a prime target for Imperial exploitation.

Fahul is an airless, lifeless world. The Empire is considering building a slave prison on the world, as there are some valuable ore deposits buried deep in the planet's crust.

Sotipe and Serrata are gas giants. Serrata is a near-star, its mass falling just below the necessary level to make the transition. In the sky of Derilyn, Serrata is a reddish disk as wide as the length of a man's index finger.

Belorphyn is an inhospitable ice ball with an oblong orbit (due to Serrata's influence): for a portion of its "year," it actually is closer to Deril than Serrata.

System Datafile

Derilyn system, star: Deril, medium yellow star. Nine planets in system, Derilyn is inhabited. This world is under Imperial martial law.

From the Corellian Merchants' Guild:
WARNING! Derilyn is a restricted system under martial law. Imperial blockades zealously enforce trade restrictions — violators or suspected violators are likely to end up as slaves for the Imperial Mining Corporation. Proceed at your own risk.

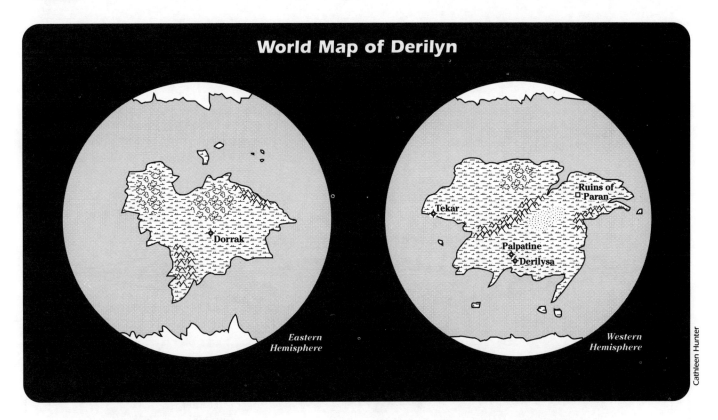

World Map of Derilyn

Dorrak

Eastern Hemisphere

Tekar

Ruins of Paran

Palpatine

Derilysa

Western Hemisphere

Cathleen Hunter

Approaching Derilyn

Characters wishing to travel to Derilyn are *strongly* advised to obtain a Derilyn Travel Waiver before going to the system. This permit may be obtained from any Imperial Navy office within the sector (there are offices in Elrood's and Coyn's major starports). The permit costs 100 credits. To get a permit, the ship's captain must provide a complete list of cargo, ship's weaponry, crew members and passengers, destination port, business to be conducted on Derilyn, customers' names on Derilyn, and projected arrival time. Characters may try to forge permits as described on page 84 of *Star Wars: The Roleplaying Game, Second Edition.* A new permit must be acquired for each trip to Derilyn.

While the permit won't necessarily grant the vessel permission to enter the system, it means the local patrol ships are much less likely to confiscate the vessel and enslave the crew members for violating the Imperial blockade of the system. Additionally, upon applying for a permit, most ships are searched by Imperial customs inspectors, and naturally, most ships are boarded and searched upon entering Derilyn system.

The contingent of Imperial forces in the system is charged with preventing all unauthorized ships from landing anywhere in the system. If a ship refuses to submit for customs inspections, the Imperials have standing orders to disable or destroy the ship. These extreme orders have had the

desired effect: few ships attempt to enter the system, and those that are caught entering illegally normally submit to inspection in short order. The characters are most likely to encounter one of the Skipray Blastboats, patrol ships, or customs vessels (normally paired with TIE fighters for additional firepower). For complete game statistics and information, see "Elrood Sector Overview."

Ships that are searched while still in space are directed to their appointed port; a small number of ships with permits are waved through without being searched. If a ship isn't scheduled for arrival in Derilyn, it will be directed to the Derilyn Space Defense Platform, an orbiting space station and defense platform.

If a searched vessel bears any contraband or people who are specifically wanted by the Empire, the ship will be seized and the crew taken to work in the mines of Berea. The customs official that the characters will most likely run into is a man named Velgar Borf.

■ Derilyn Space Defense Platform

Craft: Modified Rendili StarDrive Space Platform
Type: Orbiting Space Defense Platform
Scale: Capital
Length: 4,225 meters
Crew: 8,750, gunners: 320, skeleton 2,560/+10
Crew Skill: Capital ship gunnery 5D, capital ship shields 5D, communication 4D+2, sensors 5D+2, starship gunnery 5D
Passengers: 10,400, 4,500 (troops), 1,000 (prisoners)
Cargo Capacity: 15 million metric tons (including sealed dry docks)

Derilyn Space Defense Platform

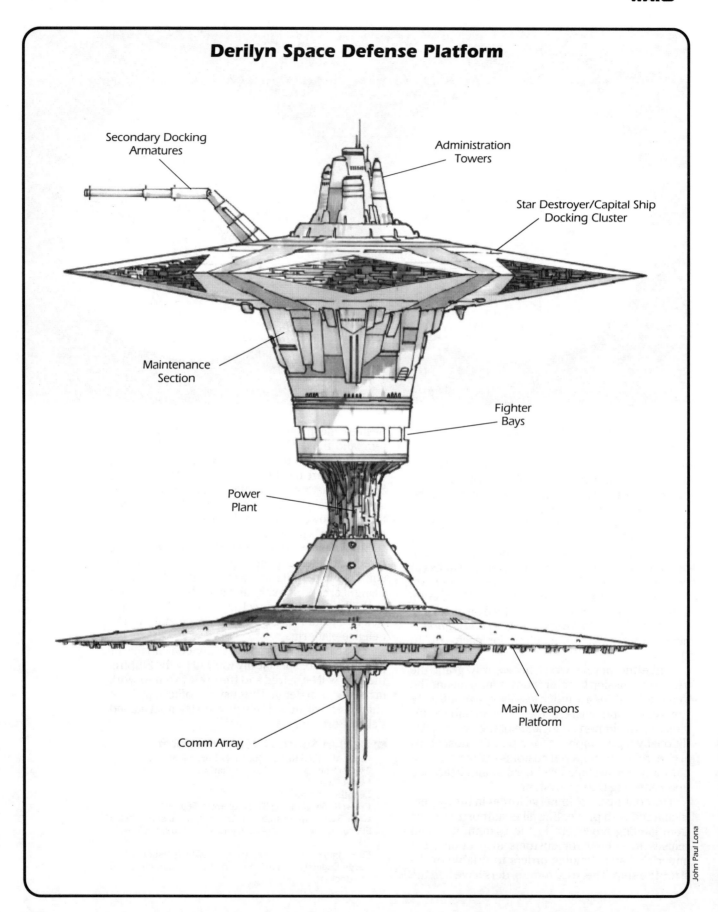

Secondary Docking
Armatures

Administration
Towers

Star Destroyer/Capital Ship
Docking Cluster

Maintenance
Section

Fighter
Bays

Power
Plant

Main Weapons
Platform

Comm Array

John Paul Lona

Velgar Borf

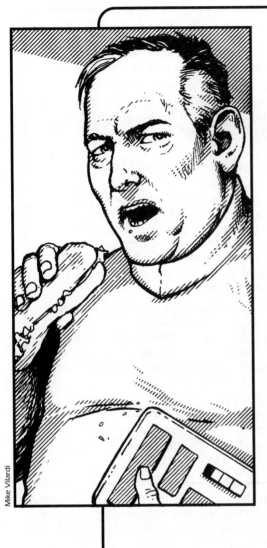

Mike Vilardi

Type: Corrupt Customs Official
DEXTERITY 2D
Blaster 4D+2, dodge 5D+1
KNOWLEDGE 3D
Bureaucracy: Imperial customs 7D+1, languages 5D, law enforcement: Imperial customs 6D+2, planetary systems: Derilyn 5D+2, streetwise 6D+1, value 7D+2, willpower 3D+2
MECHANICAL 3D
Communications 5D, sensors 7D, space transports 6D, starfighter piloting 4D, starship shields 5D, swoop operation 4D
PERCEPTION 4D
Bargain 8D, command: Derilyn customs forces 7D, con 8D+1, forgery 6D, hide 7D, investigation 7D+1, persuasion 8D, search 8D+2, sneak 7D+2
STRENGTH 2D
TECHNICAL 4D
Computer programming/repair 8D+1, droid programming 7D, first aid 6D, security 8D+1, space transports repair 6D, starfighter repair 5D+1
Character Points: 8
Move: 10
Equipment: Blaster pistol (4D), comlink, datapad, glow rod, detection equipment (+1D to *search*), toolbelt

Capsule: Velgar is a slightly overweight middle-aged Human with unruly black hair. He wears the uniform of an Imperial Naval customs officer, but the uniform is often a bit rumpled or stained. It is a wonder that Velgar got as far he did. Joining Imperial Naval Officers School as a result of family connections, Velgar proceeded to behave in a thoroughly substandard fashion. His personal grooming habits and indifferent attitude created the image of a very poor officer. Velgar, however, has a knack for finding things and getting information, and this talent enabled him to crack the infamous Red Nalroni smuggling ring.

This got him a promotion he ill deserved. Eventually, after several years of thoroughly unspectacular duty, the Empire transferred him to Derilyn. The slovenly appearance of Lt. Borf is partially an act … partially. He truly doesn't care about his appearance, but he exaggerates it because it keeps strangers off guard. Borf is an excellent customs officer, but he is apathetic. He is also a good mechanic, which enables him to find hiding places for smuggled goods.

Velgar is bribable, but this must be done out of sight of the troops. Since there are other customs officers, Velgar has thus far managed to convincingly divert any blame on them. Lt. Borf will not take any foolish chances; he does not want to jeopardize a good thing, and he cannot risk others finding out about his largess.

Consumables: 5 years
Cost: Not available for sale
Space: Immobile; orbits Derilyn, but may not alter course
Hull: 7D+2
Shields: 5D+2
Sensors:
   Passive: 150/1D
   Scan: 300/2D
   Search: 600/3D
   Focus: 20/5D+2
Weapons:
  80 Turbolaser Batteries
   Fire Arc: 20 front, 20 left, 20 right, 20 back
   Crew: 3
   Skill: Capital ship gunnery
   Fire Control: 4D
   Space Range: 3-15/35/75
   Atmosphere Range: 6-12/75/150 km
   Damage: 5D
  40 Double Turbolaser Cannon
   Fire Arc: 10 front, 10 left, 10 right, 10 back
   Crew: 2
   Scale: Starfighter

   Skill: Starship gunnery
   Fire Control: 2D+2
   Space Range: 3-10/30/60
   Atmosphere Range: 300-1/3/6 km
   Damage: 5D+2

Capsule: In high orbit around Derilyn, the Derilyn Space Defense Platform is an impressive guardian against unauthorized intrusion. Aside from its weaponry, the space station has two full wings of TIE fighters, plus whatever patrol vessels happen to be docked there at the time. The platform serves as the central communication and transportation station for Imperial military forces on Derilyn, and by extension, Elrood Sector. This is an Imperial space fortress at its worst, capable of handling sustained attacks with ease.

History

Before the fall of the Old Republic, Derilyn was a planet much like Elrood. It had a mix of agricul-

A People in Chains

By order of General Hul, the following laws are in effect until further notice:

• Curfew extends from sundown to sunrise. All citizens must be in their residence or acquire an appropriate permit from a local Imperial Office of Occupation and Law. Violation is punishable by imprisonment or transfer to the smelting factories.

• Treason in word or deed is punishable by imprisonment or transfer to the smelting factories.

• Food will be rationed as indicated in earlier proclamations. Hoarding food is punishable by forced labor on Berea.

• Participating in illegal or unauthorized trade is punishable by death.

• Trespassing on Imperial installations is punishable by death.

• All citizens must have their ID card with them at all times. All visitors must have their ID card displayed at all times. Failure to do so is punishable by forced labor on Berea.

• Hindering Imperial forces is punishable by hard labor, imprisonment or death, depending upon the severity of the offense.

• Vessels which land or take off without permission will be captured and impounded. Surviving crew members will be sent to Berea.

• Possession of a weapon is punishable by transfer to the smelting factories. Members of the Imperial armed forces have final discretion in determining what constitutes a weapon.

• Sheltering subversives is punishable by death.

• Membership in a subversive group and/or participating in subversive activities (sabotage, espionage, assaulting Imperial personnel, contributing to or aiding in the distribution of unauthorized publications or broadcasts) is punishable by death, and the death of all family members.

• Citizens are required to report any subversive activity to the local security office. Accurate reports will be rewarded with extra food and privileges. Failure to report such activity is regarded as willful tolerance of treason and is punishable by death.

Remember! Obedience to the Empire means freedom! Subversive activity means punishment for all! Report subversives immediately! Obey the Emperor! Obey the law! It is there for YOUR protection!

---

ture, manufacturing, and natural resource extraction, and was the terminus of the Elrood to Derilyn Run, making Derilyn a jewel in the rather modest crown of Elrood sector.

Then came the Empire. Derilyn's population was outraged by Palaptine's power grab. The late Senator Wuxod from Derilyn made his planet's opinions abundantly clear; he disappeared. Some in Imperial City whispered that Palpatine's security forces were behind this. Derilyn's outrage grew — and the Empire acted.

The Derilytes did not realize just how strong the Empire was, or to what lengths Palpatine would go to enforce order. On the first day of Fifthmonth, Derilyn found out firsthand.

A huge invasion force, consisting of six Imperial Star Destroyers, several wings of TIE fighters, and a full sector army, smashed down on the vocal, but unprepared, planet.

The city of Paran, Derilyn's third largest city and birthplace of Senator Wuxod, was annihilated by the concentrated gunfire of the orbiting Star Destroyers. TIE bombers deliberately bombed the helpless civilian shelters.

Rather than surrender, the Derilytes fought on, hardened by the horror of the attack. Despite the outrage, the valor, and the sacrifice, the Empire rolled over the Derilytes with the speed and ease of a rancor stepping on a drunken Jawa. The planet was secured in three days; the struggle is known as the Sixty Hour War by the Derilytes.

With Derilyn's armed forces disarmed, the Empire established a permanent presence. For the next several months, the rest of the sector experienced what is now called the Time of Panic. During this time, the citizens of the rest of Elrood Sector braced themselves for the worst, anticipating that the Empire, having secured Derilyn, would enslave the rest of the sector. For reasons unknown to all but the Empire, this never happened.

The Empire got what it wanted — a proud world subjugated and utterly humiliated. Palpatine knew that the other worlds were watching Derilyn closely. With this world defeated, the others would submit to the Empire. To this day, it has remained so: the other worlds of Elrood Sector are ever fearful that they will share the same fate as Derilyn.

Derilyn Today

Martial law is in effect over the entire planet. Derilyn's Martial Governor is General Afren Hul of

Mike Vilardi

the Imperial Army. The people, sullen, bitter and devoid of hope, live a difficult life. All goods are rationed, strict curfews are in effect, and working conditions are brutal. Only when the Derilytes get behind the closed doors of their homes do their emotional natures come forward. In some ways, Derilyn is just as dead as if the Imperial fleet had destroyed the planet.

Most Derilytes share some common emotional characteristics: they are extremely stubborn, forthright, and especially enamored of fighting against impossible odds. There is no stigma to surrendering, but it takes some time for the average Derilyte to realize that a given situation requires surrender; on the other hand, surrender normally means that one will live to fight another time. Derilytes have never been known to make friends easily, but when they do, they are fiercely loyal. As a result of the invasion, many Derilytes have also become suspicious people.

The Imperial Presence

The Imperial occupation force is the equivalent of a Sector Army (see page 97 of the *Imperial Sourcebook*). There is a total of 1,180,309 personnel, including 774,576 troops (officially; actual numbers can vary based on distribution of forces around the sector, attrition, training, rotation and other factors). There are over 66,000 repulsorcraft here, as well as nearly 14,000 heavy repulsor tanks. There are also three full wings of TIE fighters, split among traditional TIE/ln combat models, TIE bomb-

ers and TIE/rc ships (modified to conduct detailed observation of communication bandwidths, movement of civilians and otherwise provide detailed intelligence). These fighters are at separate bases in Dorrak, Derilysa and Tekar. While the forces may seem excessive, bear in mind that part of the Empire's strategy is to maintain enough troops to frighten the rest of the sector into submission — the forces here are more than up to the task.

There are four major military bases on the world, in addition to countless minor bases and outposts for observation and occupation of the planet. The largest of these is Base Derilysa, located on the outskirts of the capital city. The next largest is on the outskirts of Tekar, the city most likely to be visited by off-worlders who have business here. The final two major bases are in Dorrak and Palpatine.

There are considerable tensions between the Navy pilots and the Imperial Army occupation forces (one reason why the TIE fighters were not assigned to the standard bases). The commanders of the Star Destroyers do not like General Hul, who they feel is not giving them enough credit in his reports to the Empire. Hul, in turn, does not like Lieutenant Borf, the head customs officer, and feels that the Navy is not doing its part in keeping out smugglers and pirates.

■ Sector Moff Villis Andal

Type: Imperial Bureaucrat
DEXTERITY 2D
Archaic guns: Kiliean bolt gun 5D, dodge 4D+1, running 3D+2

General Afren Hul

Type: Tyrannical Military Governor
DEXTERITY 3D
Blaster 5D, dodge 6D, grenade 4D, melee combat 5D+2, melee parry 5D
KNOWLEDGE 4D
Alien species 7D, bureaucracy: Imperial 8D, intimidation 8D, law enforcement 8D, planetary systems: Derilyn 7D+1, streetwise 6D+2, tactics: ground forces 9D, tactics: army operations 11D, willpower 9D
MECHANICAL 2D
Communications 4D, ground vehicle operation 4D, hover vehicle operation 5D, repulsorlift operation 4D+1, sensors 3D+2, walker operation 5D
PERCEPTION 4D
Command: Imperial troops 9D+1, investigation 6D, persuasion 6D, search 6D
STRENGTH 3D
Brawling 4D+2, stamina 5D+1
TECHNICAL 2D
Blaster repair 4D, computer programming/repair 5D, first aid 4D, security 5D+2, walker repair 4D
Force Points: 2
Dark Side Points: 2
Character Points: 12
Move: 10
Equipment: Blaster pistol (4D), command baton, comlink

Mike Vilardi

Capsule: General Afren Hul is the Imperial governor of Derilyn. He has taken up residence in the Government Palace in Derilysa, the capital city. He has a permanent honor guard of 24 stormtroopers and 12 Coynite mercenaries.

General Hul, a man in his early 50's, dresses in a very sharp, spit and polish military style. He is bald, and has bushy eyebrows that are so thick they appear to be one solid, unbroken brow. His eyes are steel gray, with a penetrating gaze. Hul is burly, and hasn't softened during his time behind a desk.

General Hul worked his way up through the officer ranks, and distinguished himself just enough to be promoted but not enough to get a plum assignment. He spent his share of time in combat, and is very savvy about firefights, ambushes, and guerrilla warfare.

A no-nonsense, rigid, unyielding man, General Hul is a firm believer in iron discipline. Very much a fanatically loyal servant of the Empire, he believes that there are no civilians and no off-limits targets in war. He believes in total victory. As a military governor, he has been ruthlessly efficient in keeping the peace. A cruel, sadistic man, Hul enjoys disciplining the people of Derilyn. ("So you don't know the location of the resistance cell? Oh, don't worry, I shall not kill you. I mean, if you don't know, well, that's hardly *your* fault, correct? Your husband and children, on the other hand … oh, what is that? You remember? Well, how fortunate! That ensures you and your family will remain together." (After the Rebel has given her testimony, Hul turns to the nearest Imperial officer.) "Kill her and her family. I hate breaking up a happy home."

Hul has an intense hatred of aliens and droids, the latter he uses for target practice whenever he sees one. As governor, he can afford that luxury, and has been known to personally execute anyone who would "debate" the matter with him.

KNOWLEDGE 4D
Bureaucracy 7D, cultures 6D+1, intimidation 5D, languages 5D+2, law enforcement 6D, planetary systems 5D+1
MECHANICAL 2D
Astrogation 5D, beast riding 5D, space transports 4D+2
PERCEPTION 4D
Command 5D+2, persuasion 6D
STRENGTH 2D+2
TECHNICAL 3D+1
Computer programming/repair 4D, droid programming 4D+1
Force Points: 4
Dark Side Points: 5
Character Points: 9
Move: 9
Equipment: Cape, walking stick, pocket computer with comm up-link to space yacht, several changes of fine clothes, personal medallions and jewelry.

Capsule: Sector Moff Villis Andal is a young man from a well-connected Atrisian noble family. He spent most of his youth in the manner of noble families: studying the delicate arts of Kiliean bolt gun marksmanship and riding his loirbnigg, an eight legged reptillian steed native to the reserve world of Frisal. His most notable accomplishment was winning a pair of local championships in high-gravity sprint running.

As he grew older, he moved on to a prestigious military prep academy, his mother intent on seeing him become a valued officer or diplomat. While he lacked the drive for honors, he finished well enough to be accepted into the Imperial Diplomatic Corps. In return for an undisclosed favor to an Imperial senator (rumors abound that the favor involved a sub-

Mike Vilardi

stantial shift of credits, as well as the destruction of evidence involving bribe taking), Andal was promoted to Assistant to Elrood Sector's Moff. When that Moff died during a routine space accident, Andal was appointed to Elrood Sector Moff.

Andal is a man secure in his job, and security breeds laziness and sloth. Andal has established his sector home on Derilyn, taking up residence in the newly constructed Moff's Palace. It lies as the northern end of the Park of Peace, an open park stretching three kilometers through Derilysa. General Hul's Government Palace is at the other end of the park, which is built over the remains of Derilyn's government buildings, leveled in the initial assault on the planet.

Andal spends most of his time travelling around the galaxy in his personal space yacht, the *Andal's Dream,* going big game hunting with his well-to-do friends from the academy and, oh yes, maintaining order in Elrood Sector. He takes minimal interest in his job, leaving that task to General Hul, who thoroughly enjoys such duties. He also enjoys playing *his* two Star Destroyer captains off each other — everyone so ambitious, and so obsequious; yes, this is the life for him.

Friends of Paran (The Resistance)

The resistance on Derilyn is small and fragile. Unfortunately, General Hul has been all too efficient in his campaign against insurgents. Current active resistance members number only about 420, although there are countless sympathizers too fearful to take action.

The Friends of Paran, named after the destroyed city of Paran, operate in small cells, very similar to Rebel resistance cells. A central headquarters for the resistance operates in the ruins of Paran itself. Paran had extensive tunnels for the repulsor trains that provided mass transit; these tunnels now serve as the Resistance's base. The Empire knows nothing of the existence of the tunnels.

As a rule, only a few dozen resistance members stay in Paran. They serve as defense and counselors to Wuxod, the grandson of the late Senator Wuxod and head of the resistance.

Melodia Fharn

The resistance member the characters will most likely run into is a woman named Melodia Fharn. She is one of the most effective resistance field personnel and is based in a Tekar cell, where she has convenient access to off-world travelers.

Contacting the Resistance

Contacting the Friends of Paran is easier than one would think. There are not many non-Imperial ships that come into the system. Any visiting vessels are closely watched by resistance members, their crews tailed through the city and their business ascertained. The visitors' behavior will be watched and evaluated — those who appear to be opposed to the Empire are contacted. If the cells see a Jedi Knight using her powers, they will report back to their cell leader, who will pass the

Melodia Fharn

Type: Resistance Fighter
DEXTERITY 3D
Blaster 6D+2, dodge 4D, grenade 5D+2, vehicle blasters 5D+1
KNOWLEDGE 4D
Languages 6D, law enforcement 6D+1, planetary systems: Derilyn 5D+2, streetwise 7D, survival 8D, willpower 8D+1
MECHANICAL 3D
Beast riding 4D+1, ground vehicle operation 4D, hover vehicle operation 4D+1, starship gunnery 4D
PERCEPTION 4D
Bargain 6D, command: Derilyn resistance forces 7D+1, con 5D, forgery 6D+1, hide 8D, persuasion 6D, search 7D, sneak 5D+1
STRENGTH 2D
TECHNICAL 2D
Armor repair 4D, blaster repair 4D+1, demolition 6D, first aid 5D+2, ground vehicle repair 5D, security 4D+1
This character is Force-sensitive.
Force Points: 2
Dark Side Points: 3
Character Points: 6
Move: 9
Equipment: Blaster rifle (5D), blaster pistol (4D), 4 grenades (5D damage), comlink, armor vest (+1D physical, +1 energy), glow rod, datapad, medpac.

Mike Vilardi

Capsule: Melodia Fharn is an aging woman, with long gray hair that she keeps in a bun. Her soft blue eyes reveal a strong sense of compassion. Melodia was a nurse and counselor in the city of Tekar before the war. Married and with one son, Melodia's life was a good one. Then came the invasion. Melodia's husband, who was visiting the city of Paran, died, leaving Melodia to take care of their son. The years passed, her son grew up and married, and had two kids. Two years ago, her son and his wife, both of them resistance members, were killed. Melodia decided to fight back and take care of her grandchildren, now aged 12 and 10. She feels it is better to repel the Empire than to allow her grandchildren to suffer under tyrannical rule.

On the outside, Melodia projects the image of a sweet, grandmotherly old lady. Indeed, she is rather soft-spoken and is reluctant to speak up or use her influence to force unpopular agendas. But when she is on duty, the fires of independence burn in her eyes and she is transformed into a cool commando who has the advantage of her years of wisdom. She is also a good deal more bloodthirsty than most would suspect — "Yes, dears, I had to ventilate that stormtrooper's head before he got a bead on you. Now, that nasty man's gone, so rest a spell and have a nice cup of tea."

Melodia's companions nicknamed her "granmera" (a Derilyn term of affection for "grandmother"), because she dotes on them and takes care of them all.

news onto central headquarters, which will then make contact with the Jedi in a few hours (of course, by then, the Jedi is likely to become a fugitive from Derilyn's police state government). It is a Very Difficult *streetwise* task to find the underground.

The Friends of Paran are always looking for food, medicines, weapons, armor, electronics, or anything else that can aid their fight. Also, some resistance members have to be smuggled off planet because they are wanted by the Empire.

Average Friend of Paran. All stats are 2D except: *blaster: blaster pistol 5D, grenade 4D, streetwise 6D, hide 5D, search 5D, sneak 6D, brawling 4D.* Move: 10. Blaster pistol (4D), grenades (5D), armor vests (+1D to physical, +2 to energy).

Derilysa

This is the capital city of Derilyn, though not the largest city. The city is a place of opulence, filled with expensive eateries, amusement centers, museums, and shops. This city has been rebuilt by the Imperials, and the sheer amount of credits invested here indicates that the Imperials aren't planning on leaving any time soon. The facilities are primarily for the use of the Imperials and visiting dignitaries and businessmen (on the rare occasion that Moff Andal *is* present, he insists on holding endless parties and celebrations). When there are no important visitors, local residents may take advantage, although prices are outrageous, far beyond the means of most working people.

Though theoretically anyone can visit Derilysa, those who are not directly associated with the

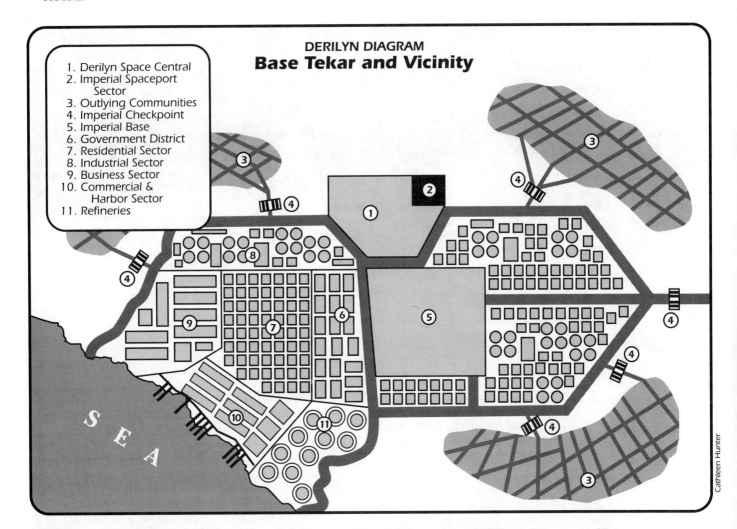

DERILYN DIAGRAM
Base Tekar and Vicinity

1. Derilyn Space Central
2. Imperial Spaceport Sector
3. Outlying Communities
4. Imperial Checkpoint
5. Imperial Base
6. Government District
7. Residential Sector
8. Industrial Sector
9. Business Sector
10. Commercial & Harbor Sector
11. Refineries

Cathleen Hunter

Empire or invited by Moff Andal or General Hul are viewed with suspicion. It is not uncommon for squads of stormtroopers to follow, question and arrest suspicious looking people (anyone who is not wealthy is immediately considered suspicious). It should be noted that because of the harsh recriminations for suspicious activities, locals will not talk to visiting spacers and aliens unless *absolutely* necessary. Even then, Derilyn residents are as perfunctory as possible (to the point of being extremely rude) to not arouse suspicion.

Tekar

The largest city on the planet, Tekar is a sprawling megalopolis. The city sports the largest starport on the planet, Derilyn Space Central, which includes the Imperial Spaceport Sector, where the area's 36 TIE fighters are stationed. Because the city was a center of resistance activities after the initial invasion, the city has faced harsher treatment throughout the Imperial occupation. Checkpoints are at the edge of the city, where IDs are rigorously checked. Checkpoints are also at several key locations throughout the city.

Imperial Occupation Soldiers. All stats are 2D except: *Dexterity 3D, blaster 4D+2, dodge 5D, intimidation 4D+2, Mechanical 1D, command 4D, Strength 3D, Technical 1D.* Move: 10. Blaster rifle (5D), grenade (5D), blast armor (+2D physical, +1D energy).

The Imperial presence in the city is highly visible: it isn't unusual for all midday traffic to be brought to a halt by a parade of soldiers and repulsortanks. Likewise, violence and sedition are even less likely to be tolerated here than in other cities. Most of the ordinary citizens are forced to slave for Imperial corporations that have set up factories on this world: the majority of goods are heavy industry equipment and droids. Each company has a large imported quality control staff to ensure that goods aren't being deliberately sabotaged, and the penalty for sabotage is death or deportation to the mines of Berea. The entire city has a constant pall of air pollution and dreariness hanging over it — a combination of real weather and the despair of a beaten people.

Mike Vilardi

Imperial Mining, Ltd. and the Berea Connection

IML is located in the capital city of Derilysa. The company was formed and is run by retired Imperial officers and low-level officials who still wanted a hand in helping the Empire while lining their own pockets. The Empire gladly gave them a corporate charter and began coercing systems to purchase ore from IML.

Imperial Mining's headquarters is a large, beautiful skyscraper, the tallest building in the city. The company is run by a board of directors. IML does not hire freelance adventurers to do tasks for them.

Although the company is inefficient and smaller than Radell Mining, IML makes a hefty profit due to their low labor costs. Of course, their labor consists mostly of interned crews of freighters (read: slaves), being detained for an indefinite period of time. IML's merchant fleet consists of these interned crews' vessels.

Once every two weeks, a huge container ship arrives from Berea, bearing the rich ores that IML refines and sells. On the return ship, the vessel is stocked with survival supplies for the mining colony. It also has a life support capsule for carrying new miners and guards.

The Ruins of Paran

The city of Paran had a population of 512,000 people. Less than 3,000 remained after the Imperial bombardment and siege, and most of them died from radiation or the effects of biological warheads used in the shelling.

Today, the city is a ruin, with nothing but the skeletal plassteel frames of burnt-out buildings and great heaps of charred rubble. The only inhabitants are the few outcasts who have somehow managed to survive in this hellish place, or those who would rather risk the dangers of a destroyed city than slave under the Empire. Many dangerous predators from Derilyn's wilderness have taken up residence in the ruins of the city.

Locating the entrance to the underground areas where the Friends of Paran are holed up takes two hours of searching and is a Very Difficult *search* task. The rubble, most of it lightly irradiated, provides an excellent cloak from sensors. It is more likely that the resistance will spot the characters long before they find an entrance and confront them. The resistance members are quite suspicious, and may require the characters to prove their intentions or face execution as Imperial spies. The resistance has not much to lose here, and they have no reason to suspect that someone may want to help them; they view their survival as a grand and noble struggle against the galaxy itself.

Adventure Idea

Use this idea only if the gamemaster wants to keep the characters on Derilyn for a while. The Rebellion hires the characters to run weapons to the resistance on Derilyn. Melodia's name is given as a contact, and she will meet the characters at the Tekar starport.

Once on the planet, the Empire suspends all outbound flights, apparently due to some Friends of Paran activity. The characters must now do their best to survive and help the resistance while not getting caught.

Adventure Idea

While on Derilyn, the resistance learns that two of their number have been impressed as miners. They will be taken off-planet to Berea the following day. The characters are asked to mount a rescue mission.

Adventure Idea

The Friends of Paran need a message hand delivered to their resistance cells on Berea. The characters are asked to go, which means volunteering for work with Imperial Mining. Of course, getting back may be a problem, since the minimum term time is three months.

Adventure Idea

A particular Friends of Paran cell, known for its extremism, has hatched a plan to bomb the Imperial Mining, Ltd. corporate building. The head of the resistance asks the characters to interfere, emphasizing that this attack would kill hundreds of innocent Derilyn citizens and have almost no effect on the Empire. It would trigger a crackdown with no beneficial effect.

He begs the characters to neutralize the cell (and hopefully not kill them) and remove the bomb. Even an anonymous tip is not good enough. IML, and by logical extension the Empire, cannot and must not know that the bomb ever existed. The cell has already planted the bomb in the lobby of the headquarters.

Kuras III

Kuras III

Type: Unexplored hostile terrestrial
Temperature: Temperate (verging on cool)
Atmosphere: Type II (breath mask suggested)
Hydrosphere: Dry
Gravity: Standard
Terrain: Volcanic mountains, canyons, cave networks, shallow inland seas
Length of Day: 18 standard hours
Length of Year: 400 local days
Sapient Species: Aganof (N), Pulras (N)
Starport: None
Population: 65,000 Aganof, 58,000 Pulras
Planet Function: Homeworld, exploration
Government: Tribal
Tech Level: Stone
System: Kuras
Star: Kuras (white dwarf)
Orbital Bodies:

Name	Planet Type	Moons
Kuras I	temperate rock	0
Kuras II	temperate desert	2
Kuras III	unexplored hostile terrestrial	1
Kuras Asteroid Belt		
Kuras IV	frozen rock	0

World Summary

Kuras III lies in the unexplored Kuras system, on the edge of Elrood Sector. The world has never been visited by representatives of the Empire, and all the available evidence indicates that the world has never been visited by off-worlders.

System Datafile

Kuras system, star: Kuras, single white dwarf star.

No other information available at this time. Likelihood of habitable planets is low.

Explore at your own risk. Standard rewards for exploration and navigational coordinates are being offered, as per Imperial Survey Corps docufile XPLR-45.934.R.E.25-0003.245.

The world is young and quite hostile to Human life. The foul smelling atmosphere is thick with volcanic ash and dangerous microbes — long term, unprotected exposure (for six standard months or longer) is likely to result in potentially lethal respiratory infections.

The world's surface is volcanically active, and is covered with steep mountains and deep canyons. The world is quite dry, with no oceans. There are a small number of lakes in craters, depressions and at the bottoms of the deepest canyons. Kuras III's interior is honeycombed with caverns, the result of the continuous volcanic activity. Because of shifting tectonics, only a few sections of the planet's surface are presently plagued with active volcanoes — many regions of the planet are inactive and stable for the time being.

Kuras III's entire ecosphere is hazardous to Human life. The world is rich in heavy metals and poisons that are difficult to filter out of foodstuffs, and most standing water is similarly polluted. As one might expect, the native life forms are adapted to each other, but they are nonetheless quite dangerous to many of the galaxy's other life forms.

System Summary

Little is known of the Kuras system. The white dwarf star was named Kuras millennia ago by the Coynites, who could observe it in the constellation Kezz'Sreik'Kuras, "Predator Beast of the Dusk."

The system was one of several systems scheduled to be observed by Republic probe droids, but the senator sponsoring the follow-up exploration lacked the political backing to force this appropriation through the Senate, and thus the system (and many others) remained unvisited.

As a whole, the system has little to offer the galactic economy. Kuras I is a lifeless rock with a trace atmosphere. Kuras II is a barren, desert planet with an unbreathable atmosphere and two small moons. Kuras III is the world of prime interest, yet would require intensive terraforming

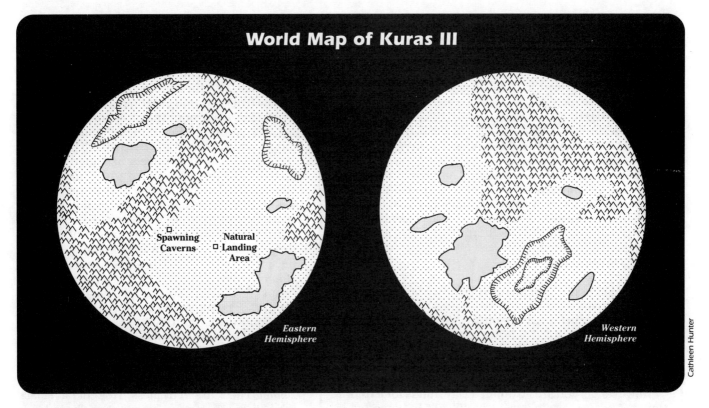

World Map of Kuras III

Spawning Caverns

Natural Landing Area

Eastern Hemisphere

Western Hemisphere

Cathleen Hunter

to be made habitable. The Kuras Asteroid Belt is a thick band of rock, metals and ice that hampers navigation into the inner portions of the system; it does have rich potential for mining. Kuras IV is a captured planet, covered with barren rock and a light frosting of frozen water and methane crystals.

Kuras Asteroid Belt

The Kuras Asteroid Belt, lying between Kuras III and Kuras IV, was responsible for the destruction of the Old Republic probe that first investigated the system. To this day, it is a major navigational hazard within the system.

In order for a ship to get past the belt, the pilot must make three Difficult piloting rolls (the specific skill depends upon the type of ship being flown). This represents the eight hours of real time it will take to cross the belt. This area of space is so cluttered with debris that it is virtually impossible to plot a hyperspace course that will bring the ship out near Kuras (suggested difficulty of Heroic +10); ships will usually have to fly through the belt.

If a pilot brings his ship to a standstill while within the belt, the pilot must make a Moderate piloting roll to avoid being hit by an asteroid for every four hours in the belt.

Failure of a piloting roll means that an asteroid has hit the ship. To determine the damage (in starfighter scale), find the number of points by which the pilot missed the roll on the chart below.

Roll Missed By:	Asteroid Size	Damage
1–2	Tiny	1D
3–5	Small	2D
6–8	Medium	3D
9–11	Medium	4D
12–14	Large	7D
15+	Very Large	3D
		(capital scale)

Ironically, the asteroid belt is also the system's richest feature, since many of the asteroids are rich in ores. For characters to successfully find valuable asteroids, they need ten minutes to complete a scan and a Moderate *sensors* total.

A Hostile World

Kuras III, by Human standards, is a dreary, overcast world. The dim light of its star and continual plumes of volcanic dust make the world perpetually overcast and hazy. The temperature is generally cool, ranging from zero to fifteen degrees standard. However, the ever-present addition of hot volcanic ash to the atmosphere, mixed with the cool lower layers of the atmosphere, creates dangerous and stiflingly hot wind storms, which often sweep the world's surface. Aside from the dramatic temperature changes, the storms often hurl huge rocks through the air and uproot what little vegetation there is. Because of these, most forms of life on Kuras make their homes in the caverns and sheltered valleys of the world.

An Unknown World...

To: The Senate Committee on New World Discovery and Exploration
From: Bryn Shal, Head Scientist, Project: Wayfarer, Republic Scout Service
Dear Senators:

Remote probe ZeX555-TR349 was destroyed in route from Elrood sector to Cegul sector, while surveying previously unexplored systems.

It is proposed that a secondary automated probe, or better yet, a manned mission, be sent to Elrood and Cegul to complete the survey. With the number of sapient species native to the region, this area of space seems to be a rich spawning ground for new life forms. Further investigation seems warranted.

End Transmission

To: Bryn Shal, Head Scientist, Project: Wayfarer, Republic Scout Service
From: The Senate Committee on New World Discovery and Exploration
Sir:

Your findings are noted and have been taken into consideration by the committee.

However, as you are no doubt aware, funds for exploration and survey are increasingly difficult to come by. In light of this constraint, there are many more promising areas than this one in a backwater corner of the galaxy. At this time, further exploration of Elrood and Cegul sectors is unwarranted.

Approval of replacement of destroyed probe will await final recommendation by Republic Scout Service, Department of Remote Exploration.

End Transmission

Historical Footnote: The first report was but one of thousands of similar reports that were filed and forgotten. To this day, no further exploration of the Kuras system was sponsored.

The largest bodies of water on the planet are the small inland and extremely deep seas with a high concentration of minerals and salts. Because of the much cooler temperatures associated with the seas, they are often the site of extremely violent heat storms. The seas are home to a variety of marine life, much of it predatory and dangerous. Because of Kuras III's hostile nature, most life forms are resistant to poisons and toxins, and many have tough armor to resist claws and bites. Like the land life forms, marine life is poisonous to Humans and similar life forms.

There are also many pools and ponds at the bottom of the canyons. They are less likely to contain the largest, most dangerous marine life forms, but there are still many formidable creatures to be found in the murky depths.

Dangers of an Unknown World

An Easy *sensors* roll will reveal that the atmosphere is type II and the characters should wear breath masks. If they choose not to, the first thing they will notice upon entering the atmosphere is a putrid, organic odor that is almost overpowering. The atmosphere irritates the inside of the mouth and nose, and leaves a bad aftertaste, like rotting vegetables. For every half hour of unprotected exposure, characters are required to resist the detrimental effects of the atmosphere, which is an Easy *stamina* task. Failing the task reduces the character's *Strength* and *stamina* by -1D. If a character loses 2D or more, all other skills drop by 2D and the character's Move is halved because the character is so weakened that he cannot concentrate. If the character's *Strength* drops to 0D, the character falls unconscious for 1D days. The *Strength* and *stamina* return after two hours of rest with plenty of safe (for example, purified or non-Kuras) fluids.

Kuras' water is also thick with contaminants and harmful bacteria. Any character who drinks this water (even a handful) must make a Moderate *stamina* check to avoid illness. If the character fails the roll by one to five points, the character is paralyzed with stomach cramps. If the character fails the roll by six or more points, the character passes out for 1D hours and will become feverish. If the character fails a second *stamina* check, the contaminants kill the character.

Simply boiling the water will *not* make it safe. Any water must pass through a complete filtration system (such as those found in survival kits and ship purification systems) to be safe to drink.

Kuras III's plants are just as dangerous: a meal of berries or vegetables will have the same detrimental effects as drinking the water. Eating one meal requires a Difficult *stamina* check. Unlike the water, the flora and fauna cannot be detoxified for Human consumption, due to the presence of numerous native toxins that are an important part of the planet's ecosphere.

Standard starship sensors can detect the bad air and water, but unless the characters have sensors to scan the food, they will be unaware that it is harmful. Characters who make Easy *survival* rolls are able to guess that the water, plants and animals are dangerous to consume. Gamemasters can give a few hints ("the plant tastes bitter") but should not go out of their way to warn players of the dangers of Kuras III (unless, of course, one of the characters is a scout and should know better or has an extremely high *survival* skill).

Mike Vilardi

Landing on Kuras III

There are no starports on Kuras III, but there are a few flat plains areas that can substitute as a landing field. There is one particularly large strip that is ideal. Its immense size and the contrast to the otherwise rugged terrain of Kuras III makes the landing site visible from orbit. Landing on the strip should be a Very Easy task, unless the ship is caught in one of the heat storms, which would increase the difficulty to Moderate (or perhaps Heroic if the storm was fierce enough).

Upon disembarking from their ship, the characters should be overwhelmed by the desolate world around them. Peaks rise several kilometers into the air, and the ground around them is rough, torn by volcanic activity and blasted by the immense wind storms. This is a world that should show nature in its most volatile form.

The Value of Kuras III

If a party of characters manages to do a survey of the planet, which would take several days, they will find a modest amount of mineral deposits: kiiral (a component of kiirium) and metarr (one of the base components of carbon-metar) are found here in great quantities. While the world isn't rich, there is certainly enough here that a small mining company might be interested in the world.

Otherwise, the world's commercial value is limited. It would require massive terraforming to

be made habitable, there is no agricultural potential and the world has minimal resources.

However, in time, the characters will learn that Kuras III offers more than danger. They are not alone …

Alien Species

Kuras III is home to two unique alien species: the Aganof and the Pulras. When the characters meet the following two species, certain things must be kept in mind by the gamemaster. These races are *alien*. They have never encountered the galaxy at large and they are very unusual life forms.

Gamemasters should look at the characters through their "eyes." What will it matter if the characters point their weapons and threaten the creatures? Since the creatures have never seen a blaster, how do they know that these newcomers (the characters) aren't simply offering them some new type of food? Since the Aganof depend on touch and have no sense of sight, consider how they will approach the situation — they may come forward with delicate caution, but want to touch the characters to determine their shape and size. On the other hand, characters who extend a hand of friendship could also be misinterpreted. The natives could be thinking, "Why is that odd creature extending a pseudopod at me? Does it mean to attack me?"

Both of the sapient species are relatively peaceful. It is up to the characters to convince them of that they are also peaceful.

Aganof

The Aganof are a large, androgynous animal species. They have approximately one dozen small appendages for movement (the exact number various with the individual), with several touch sensitive pairs of appendages running along their bodies. Their backs have heat dissipating flaps and olfactory sensors on large flexible stalks. The flaps are also coated with a digestive acid that is used to break down foods; small mouths are nestled underneath the flaps. Each end of the body contains a long, jointed limb that ends in a shelled claw.

This species lives, works, and breeds in the damp, cool caves of Kuras III. The Aganof must live in these caves, since only these locations provide enough moisture for them to survive (they absorb moisture through all of their appendages). They feed on vegetation, insects and a large variety of small herbivores. Aganof reproduce in their cool, dark caves of their world — they have both male and female characteristics and lay fertilized eggs.

The Aganof have only the senses of taste, smell and touch (which is their primary sense). The Aganof method of communication is by a combination of creating vibrations with the shelled claw. The vibrations are modified with a special organ within the claw called the "sender." The sender codes the vibrations into a sort of language that other Aganof can understand.

Nearby Aganof can detect the vibrations and decipher their meaning (actual distance depends on many factors, including soil composition and competing vibrations). Like speech, this communication can be perceived by all who are within reception distance.

Aganof language is icon-based: recipients get pictures in their minds instead of words. Thus, if an Aganof wanted to ask if a character was an "alien" who came from outer space, the character would get a picture of himself, falling to the ground (Aganof cannot conceive of the sky), plus the feeling that the pictures were interrogative.

The Aganof are an intelligent species, with a society and a culture. All the Aganof born in the same cave are essentially a tribal unit. The eldest Aganof is the adviser of the cave-fellows, and thus his opinion is given more weight than any others in the cave-unit. The Aganof tribes peacefully co-exist with each other, with inter-tribal meetings quite common (their purpose being to share stories, trade knowledge and exchange tribe members for mating purposes). The Aganof have stories, songs, and even a form of art involving the arranging of the dead and decomposing bodies of their departed fellows.

A favorite Aganof pastime is having philosophical debates and intellectual arguments. Among the issues debated are what lies above "the ground" (since their limited senses cannot detect very much about their world around them; the concept of space is completely alien to them).

Aganof are tranquil, calm and friendly sorts. Their society is a peaceful one, and there is not even a word in their vocabulary for "war." They understand defense against predators, but not

Mike Vilardi

organized aggression and murder of other intelligent creatures. Conflict among members of their own species is almost unknown.

The Aganof would have a very difficult time grasping the concept of the Rebellion against the Empire. Both the concepts of outer space and warfare would have to be explained to them. Even if the Empire came to their world and enslaved them, they would have a difficult time distinguishing between the Empire and those who would fight it, possibly meaning that the Aganof would learn to fear and even attack all Humans and aliens from beyond their world …

■ Aganof

Attribute Dice: 11D
DEXTERITY 1D/2D
KNOWLEDGE 1D/4D
MECHANICAL 1D/2D
PERCEPTION 1D/4D+2
STRENGTH 1D/3D
TECHNICAL 1D/3D
Special Skills:
Perception skills:
Vibration Detection: Aganof use this skill to detect ground vibrations and determine the proximity of creatures and beings around them. The difficulty depends on the distance and type of vibration:

Light vibration (such as made by a small creature)	Difficult
Moderate vibration (such as made by a creature 20–100 kilograms)	Easy
Heavy vibration (such as made by a much larger creature)	Very Easy

Modified by soil:

Loose soil that easily carries vibration	-5 or more
Packed soil or material that absorbs vibration	0
Soils or materials that absorb virtually all vibration	+5 or more

Distance:

0–2 meters	0
3–10 meters	+5 to difficulty
11–30 meters	+10 to difficulty
31+ meters	+15 or more to difficulty

They can also detect air variations, such as temperature change, movement, and so forth, and thus can sometimes detect approaching flying creatures, or even sense incoming projectiles and dodge them.

Aganof can also use their hard shells and this skill for "speech" through ground vibrations, as naturally as Humans use their mouths and sense of hearing for speech.
Special Abilities:
Blindness: Aganof cannot "see" in the way that Humans can; they cannot hear in the traditional sense, but they can detect intense air vibrations. Their prime external sense is touch and a sensitivity to ground vibrations. By judging the intensity and frequency of vibrations, in combination with the type of surface they are standing on, they can detect creatures near them.
Claw: Causes STR+1D+2 damage.
Move: 4/6
Size: 1.3–2.5 meters tall, 1.5–3.5 meters long

The Spawning Caverns

This is a series of caverns with rotting subterranean fungi lining a dirt-covered floor. This is the sacred spot where the Aganof reproduce. Characters attempting to negotiate the treacherous passageways down are faced with two Difficult *climbing* tasks. Failure on either one results in the character falling for 3D damage.

These caverns are the only place where the Aganof will make an honest attempt at defending their property. Clumsy Aganof will attempt to ram invaders with their bulk.

The Pulra

The second sentient species of Kuras III is the Pulra, an amorphous life form that roams the surface of the planet. Pulras are brownish, green or black, gelatinous and shape-changing creatures.

They have no sensory organs. They have a highly flexible body structure, allowing them to assume a countless variety of forms. This is the evolution of a sophisticated attack and defense form: they can use this ability to change color and shape to hide from predators or lay traps for their prey. They are omnivores, eating plants and small animals.

Pulras, while most commonly about 50 cubic centimeters, can reach sizes upwards of 150 liters. These creatures can also manipulate their genetic code so that several Pulras can form one entity, called a "bind."

Pulras' prime sense is a form of sonar: they broadcast ultrasonic signals, and then determine their surroundings around them based on the echo of the signals.

Pulras live in large colonies, normally having from two dozen to over one hundred members. Because of their social nature, all Pulras are able to grasp the concept of teamwork and cooperation. They react more favorably to other groups of beings, as this serves as a common frame of reference.

For reproduction, an individual Pulra simply starts retaining food energy to nourish a new Pulra growing within its body; it appears to be a form of fission. Pulras don't fully understand what triggers the growth of a new Pulra, but they suspect that it is due to natural biochemical fluctuations.

Pulras, while not perfectly harmonious, generally get along with each other peacefully. All disputes are normally settled by the colony as a whole. There are few inter-tribal conflicts, but when they do occur, they are quite brutal. The Pulras are curious about the Aganof; they know they are intelligent, but have had no luck establishing effective communications with them.

Their biochameleon process can work on other sentients: a Pulra can create the form of any appendage, and within certain bounds, they can replicate the functions of certain mechanisms. For example, a Pulra could replicate an arm and attach itself to a Human to serve as a bionetic replacement. However, they couldn't replace someone's eye because the structure, function and interaction with the body is simply too complex.

Due to the clarity of their thoughts, Pulras would have little difficulty in grasping concepts such as space travel. They can easily piece together the theory that if they are on a planet orbiting a star, then other stars must also have planets, and those planets must have life on them, and some of those life forms may have created means to leave their world. Pulras have no interest in space travel or technology. The Pulras call their world "Host."

■ Pulra

Attribute Dice: 6D
DEXTERITY 1D/3D
KNOWLEDGE 1D/3D

Mike Vilardi

MECHANICAL 1D/2D
PERCEPTION 1D/3D
STRENGTH 1D/2D
TECHNICAL 1D/3D
Special Abilities:
Added Strength: Pulra can grow to enormous sizes and can gain many more *Strength* dice as a result.
Amorphous: Pulras can change their shape. This process takes a few minutes. They can form appendages for combat (doing STR+1D damage), or other forms for a variety of tasks (such as turning into a wheel to roll down a hill).
Bind: Several Pulras can join shape to create a larger creature. Use the "Combined Action Bonus Table" on page 69 of *Star Wars: The Roleplaying Game, Second Edition* to determine the bonus for Pulras joining.
Echo Location: Pulras sense the outside world by sonar echo location at ultrasonic frequencies.
Move: 2/5
Size: 20 cubic centimeters to 150 liters

Flora and Fauna of Kuras III

Bear in mind that the names given to these creatures and plants are names that could be given by the characters. Since the two alien species lack language in the traditional sense, the characters are likely to be the ones to name these items.

Metalwood

Metalwoods are huge trees that grow to a height of 30-40 meters. Their leaves are a metallic gray and their trunks are smooth, dark gray, like sheet metal. These odd trees grow only where there are ore deposits underground. The trees' roots actually go deep into the planet's crust, and tap the ores for sustenance. With the energy from the white dwarf's rays, the trees refine the ore and make it into layers which are used as bark.

Waterfungi

These mushroom-like fungi grow in pools of shallow water. They live by absorbing nutrients found in the ground water: clean water is then released by the fungi as a waste product.

A Moderate *survival* task will show that the water flowing past the waterfungi is clearer and cleaner. It only stays clean for a few minutes before thoroughly mixing with the rest of the dangerous (to characters) water.

Infectious Moss

This sickly fuzzy moss is a disgusting swirl of green, gray, and tan. This moss clings to living tissue and multiplies quickly. Characters who touch the moss with exposed flesh must make a Moderate *stamina* roll or be infected with the moss. Once on the characters' skin, the moss will begin to feed off the characters' natural body minerals. Each day, the character must make a Difficult *stamina* roll or lose 1D of *Strength*. Once the character is down to 0D, he dies from the infection. Curing the infestation is a Difficult *medicine* task, or a Heroic *first aid* task. Only one attempt of each skill can be

Mike Vilardi

done per day per infected victim. The Aganof actually savor the moss as a delicacy and will eat it off a character if given permission.

■ Hairy Savages

Type: Violent anthropoid species
DEXTERITY 5D
Brawling parry 6D, dodge 6D+1, melee combat 7D, melee parry 6D+2, running 5D, thrown weapons: rocks 6D+1
PERCEPTION 2D
Hide 4D, search: track 5D+1, sneak 6D
STRENGTH 5D
Brawling 7D, climbing/jumping 7D, lifting 6D+2, stamina 6D+2, swimming 6D+1
Move: 10 (walking), 12 (travelling through trees)
Size: 1.7–2.2 meters tall
Equipment: Throwing rocks (STR+1D), stone knives (STR+1D), sharpened sticks (STR+2D)

Capsule: These large anthropoids are savage predators and possess rudimentary intelligence. They can formulate simple tactics and use primitive tools. The savages are foul-tempered brutes, who, though they hunt to survive, still seem to take an unusual amount of pleasure in inflicting pain on their quarry. The creatures live in the trees, plants and caves of Kuras III, and feed on both the Pulra and Aganof. They will attack any characters who visit the world.

■ Wild

Type: Dangerous grazing animal
DEXTERITY 4D
Dodge 6D+2, running 8D+1
PERCEPTION 3D
Hide 6D+2, sneak 6D+1
STRENGTH 2D
Brawling 4D, stamina 4D
Special Abilities:
Fangs: Do STR+1D damage.

Newborn: Newborn wilds get +2D to *Strength, brawling* and *stamina.*
Move: 13
Size: 1.5 meters tall at the shoulder, up to 2.5 meters long

Capsule: Wilds are another creature named by the Aganof and the Pulras. Adult wilds are calm herbivores that graze on the plants and fungi of Kuras III. The creatures get their name "wilds" due to the birth process. The wilds have three genders. The male and female each deposit their genetic codes to the third sex, called the carrier. The young gestate in the carrier's womb. At the time of birth, the litter of eight to twelve young goes into a frenzy and the newborns burst their way out. The newborns then consume the carrier, allowing them to survive for an extended period without having to graze and travel. For the first few months of life, the sexless newborns are in a feeding frenzy — they will attack any creature. They consume immense quantities of food, and rapidly grow to adulthood. Upon reaching adulthood, the wilds take on their sex characteristics and become calm, grazing herbivores.

■ Quicker

Type: Flying omnivore
DEXTERITY 4D
Dodge 6D, flight 6D
PERCEPTION 4D
Search 7D
STRENGTH 4D
Brawling 6D+1, lifting 7D, stamina 6D
Special Abilities:
Beak: Does STR+1D damage
Talons: Do STR+2D damage
Move: 14 (flying)
Size: 2.0 meters long, 4.5-meter wingspan

Mike Vilardi

Capsule: The quicker is a flying species so named by the Pulras (it moves quicker than any other life form they have sensed). The quicker is an omnivore who inhabits the high mountains of Kuras III, but tends to come down to the lowlands to find food. Most quickers are nocturnal and their eyes glimmer a sinister green as they fly at night.

Adventure Idea

This is the typical marooned setting. Coming through the asteroid belt, the characters' ship is damaged, requiring an emergency landing.

After landing, they must explore their immediate surroundings, repair the ship, and get supplies in order to stay alive.

Adventure Idea

An Imperial Scout vessel is tracked leaving the secret base on Tifnyl and heading in the direction of the Kuras III system. The Empire is sending a ship to the unexplored planet. The Rebellion sends the characters after the ship, and instructs them to tail the ship but not to reveal their presence until after the scout ship reaches its destination.

The Imperial ship will land on Kuras III and begin preliminary sensor sweeps. The Pulras and Aganof will be spotted. There is a possible three way confrontation in store here between the characters, the Empire, and the natives of Kuras III.

Adventure Idea

Radell Mining Corp. hires the characters to look for new ore deposits, and orders them to go to Kuras system. Imperial Mining, Ltd., however, always keen to stay ahead of the competition, will send out some mercenaries of its own. The mercenaries have been instructed to kill any explorers from other companies and to find new ore deposits.

Adventure Idea

While lying over at Lanthrym, the party encounters a grizzled prospector and his small scout ship. The man has apparently stumbled on a new discovery, an asteroid belt with a few large asteroids, laden with mineable ores.

He wants to go back there, but cannot find anyone who is willing to listen to him. He has the coordinates on his nav computer, ready to go.

If the characters take an interest in the man, then other people will follow their lead. Many people on Lanthrym will not show interest in something until someone else shows interest first. Once someone shows interest, they rationalize, that "someone" must know something the rest of the people on Lanthrym do not know. Thus, everyone will now want to get involved.

Crime bosses, mining companies, and the Empire will seek to get involved in this affair. It is even possible that the old prospector is killed, and asks the characters to carry on for his sake.

Adventure Idea

An Imperial vessel, preferably a freighter or even a small troop carrier, broadcasts a distress call. They are in the Kuras system, where they hit an asteroid while going through the field. The ship managed a crash-landing on Kuras III, but they need spare parts for repairs.

The twist is, the distress signal is garbled, with some words missing. Thus, the characters have no idea that this is an Imperial ship. Since the vessel is broadcasting the distress call on all bands and not just Imperial frequencies, there is no evidence to link the ship with the Empire.

There is lots of opportunity for combat as well as exploration. A suggested twist is for the Imperial crew to have already made first contact with the native species, but, failing to realize that the two species are sentient, opened fire on the so-called horrible creatures.

This fact can be divulged to the players or withheld. If withheld, it will mean that when either the Aganof or the Pulras meet the characters, the species may assume the characters are also hostile.

Imperial opposition should consist of a crew of six, and possibly a dozen stormtroopers. And, of course, the Empire may have picked up the signal and sent its own rescue ship.

Adventure Idea

A band of pirates (possibly Dorok's men, Laerron Woern's pirates from *Wanted by Cracken,* or Thalassian slavers from *Galaxy Guide 9: Fragments from the Rim*) has discovered Kuras III and decided to establish a base of operations on the distant world. They selected Kuras III because it is unknown: a perfect secret base location. They have also discovered the native species of the world and enslaved them. The pirates force the sentients to perform hard labor for them, and upon discovering the Pulras' shape-shifting abilities, have begun selling them.

The characters happen upon the pirate camp when they either follow a pirate ship to the system, are contracted for a delivery to a pirate ship in open space and the ship brings them to Kuras, or the characters are captured by the pirates and brought here as more slave labor. If enslaved, the characters might even learn that some Imperial soldiers or citizens have been enslaved, and this gives the characters an opportunity to work closely with some Imperials — a chance to recognize the humanity of the Imperials or possibly sway the Imperials to the side of the Rebellion. The characters have a perfect opportunity to incite a slave revolt and teach the natives that not all off-worlders are evil.

Algara II

Algara

Type: Temperate plains
Temperature: Temperate
Atmosphere: Type I (breathable)
Hydrosphere: Moderate
Gravity: Standard
Terrain: Forest, plains, mountains, urban
Length of Day: 24 standard hours
Length of Year: 360 local days
Sapient Species: Humans, Xan (N)
Starport: 1 Imperial
Population: 1 billion
Planet Function: Homeworld, tourism
Government: Self-perpetuating bureaucracy
Tech Level: Space
Major Exports: Precious minerals, weapons, intoxicants
Major Imports: Manufactured goods, luxury items
System: Algaran
Star: Algar (yellow)
Orbital Bodies:

Name	Planet Type	Moons
Kerilt	steaming jungle	1
Algara II	terrestrial	4
Tonder	volcanic	1
Krizzin	barren rock	0
Algara V	gas giant	14
Algara VI	gas giant	0

System Datafile

Algaran system, star: Algar, yellow sun. Six planets in system, four can sustain life in some fashion. Algara II, otherwise known as Algara, main system planet.

Algara is a bustling planet, especially the capital city of Algarine, site of the starport. Many hard to find goods and services may be purchased in Algarine. Algara is a member in good standing of the New Republic.

TRAVELLER'S ADVISORY: Algara is governed by a huge and complex bureaucracy. Be prepared to answer a number of questions and pay out a significant sum in credits. Those whose business concerns stretch the limits of legality may wish to avoid Algar.

"During your visit to our fair planet, won't you consider spending some of your time and credits at the Club Prosperine, Algara's most exclusive resort? It has everything an off-world guest would ever want! Stop by today!"

(The preceding message was paid for by the Algara Bureau of Tourism, the Algara Board of Interstellar Promotions, and the Algara Board of Off-Worlder Affairs.)

World Summary

The planet Algara is located in a star system well away from Imperial space. As the Algaran government supports the New Republic, this distance has proven to be a boon to the population. Algara boasts three continents, the main one being Kreesis. This continent features the planetary capital, Algarine.

Algara's major industries include mining, weapons manufacturing, and the distilling of liquor. Several large, well-known corporations have branch offices here. Algara depends on a heavy volume of business to stay healthy.

All of those credits that Algarians earn in industry go toward importing luxury items as well as manufactured goods. A free-trader can earn a healthy income by dealing with the Algarians, provided he has infinite patience, for the local bureaucracy is notoriously labyrinthian.

Algarian society is constructed around a rigid class structure, which has led to the formation of a pro-Imperial resistance group among the disenfranchised.

System Summary

The Algaran system is located well within the New Republic's sphere of influence. Its yellow star, Algar, boasts no unusual features.

The first planet, Kerilt, contains a breathable atmosphere and is suitable for habitation. The dense jungles and stiflingly high humidity make it a daunting place nonetheless. Actual colonization has not yet begun.

Algara II, also known as Algara, is the main planet in the system.

Tonder, the third planet, is an unstable volcanic world. Scientists speculate that once it cools down (expected to occur sometime in the next 3,000 years), it could be a viable colony world. There is currently a struggle between the Algarian Bureau

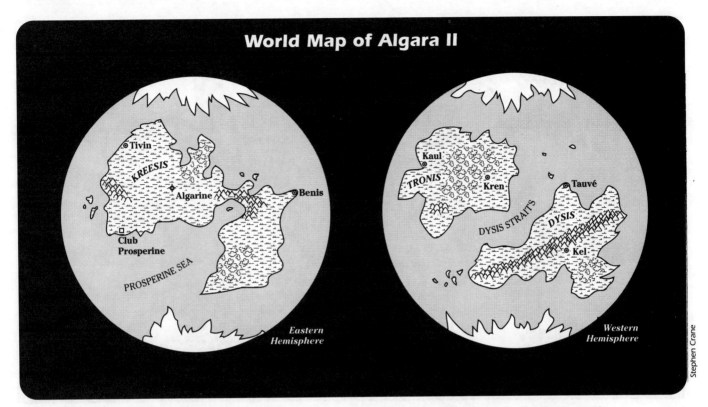

World Map of Algara II

Tivin · KREESIS · Algarine · Benis · Club Prosperine · PROSPERINE SEA · *Eastern Hemisphere*

Kaul · TRONIS · Kren · Tauvé · DYSIS STRAITS · DYSIS · Kel · *Western Hemisphere*

Stephen Crane

of Planetary Colonization and the Bureau of Volcanoes over which has jurisdiction on Tonder.

Krizzin, the fourth planet, is barren rock with an atmosphere, though remote probes have discovered the existence of underground mineral deposits. Algara V and VI, a gas giant and an ice ball respectively, are considered useless.

Algara

The planet Algara has normal seasonal variations. Springs are wet and windy, summers hot and humid, and winters are cold, with significant amounts of snowfall. Summer temperatures reach 25 degrees Centigrade at their zenith, while winter temperatures can drop as low as 15 degrees below zero.

Algara has four moons, all of them home to lunar settlements managed exclusively by Algarians. The satellites are, from largest to smallest, Tallakron, Radeon, Omakaton, and Kevron. Tallakron has a military outpost, Radeon and Omakaton have mines, and Kevron has an astronomical research station.

Algara was settled by Humans hundreds of years ago. The Algarians have standard Human statistics and no special abilities.

Algarian Society

The words "nightmare bureaucracy" immediately spring to the minds of most free-traders when the planet Algara is mentioned. Algara has rules, regulations, and forms governing every conceivable thing and activity on the planet.

The following paragraphs describe the typical routine that most off-worlders have to go through in order to set foot on Algara, no matter their intent:

1. The ship enters the Algara system and is notified that it must remain in orbit until a customs officer can board and inspect it. In the meantime, the pilot must fill out an Off-Worlder Visitation Intent data disk, which requires the following information: names and planet of origin of all crew, name and type of ship, where ship was registered, last planet visited, current cargo manifest, and intentions while on Algara. Of course, there is a 10 credit filing fee. While the pilot is filling this disk out, the customs officer and four troopers come aboard and inspect the ship for contraband.

2. Upon successful completion of search, the customs officer takes the O.V.I.D.D. from the pilot, scans it, then gives the pilot an Inspection Clear chip, which certifies that the ship is authorized to land. There is a five credit filing fee.

3. Once the ship lands, the harbormaster asks the pilot to initialize a Ship Damage Waiver disk, which absolves the starport of any responsibility for any damage the ship might sustain while docked.

4. Leaving the starport docking area, the characters move into the personal customs area, where they must fill out a Weaponry Declaration disk. These data disks must list each weapon that each character has. Proof of licensing must be furnished, or the weapon is confiscated.

Mike Vilardi

5. Once the WDD is filled out, the characters must purchase a Native Weaponry License for 10 credits. This permits them to carry weapons while on Algara.

6. Having done all this, characters interested in trading must file for a Domestic Business Permit, which allows them to buy and sell items in bulk. Cost of the permit is five percent of the total value of the goods to be imported or exported.

7. Finally, regardless of why they came to Algara, they must pay a 25-credit Visitor's Tax, and are then given their Algarian Visitor Identification chip.

8. Of course, if the characters are bringing droids onto the planet, they must file for an Immigrant droid chip for each, specifying model, make, and what skills and attachments it has. Each IDC costs five credits, and the droid is given a small bolt marker which classifies it as a legal visitor to the planet.

Algarian Social Structure

Algarian society is divided into several sharply defined classes. The upper classes get the best services, prices, seats on transportation, etc. Marriages between members of different classes are forbidden, and all Algarians and Xan must wear badges identifying their rank in the society. Members of the lower classes are required by law to defer to their "betters."

The Algarian social classes, in order, are:

The Gentry: Wealthy landowners, corporation owners — the rich and powerful.

The Bureaucracy: Upper middle-class Algarians who manage government agencies. The Bureaucracy works closely with the Gentry in setting Algarian policy.

The Intelligentsia: People of means who serve as scholars, professors, scientists, doctors.

The Belligerency: Members of the military, regardless of rank.

The Prosperines: Business executives, and people who work in non-physical occupations (computer programmers, bank tellers, customs officers)

The Talents: Skilled laborers, regardless of profession.

The Domestics: The servant class, employed by members of the Gentry, Bureaucracy, Intelligentsia, Belligerency and Prosperines.

The Drones: Unskilled laborers, grunt workers, regardless of profession.

The Mechanicals: All droids.

The Flotsam: Beggars, the insane, and the unemployed.

Xan are not allowed to ascend beyond the level of Talent. The vast majority are Talents, Drones and Domestics.

The Xan

The Xan are native to Algara. They are hairless, slender humanoids with large, bulbous heads. Their height averages between 1.5 and 1.75 meters. Skin coloration ranges from pale green, to yellow to pink. Their eyes have no irises, and are big, round pools of black. Xan faces do not show emotion, as they lack the proper muscles for expression.

The only pronounced difference between Xan physiology and that of normal Humans is their vulnerability to cold. The Xan cannot tolerate temperatures below one degree Centigrade. When the temperature ranges between zero and minus ten degrees Centigrade, Xan fall into a deep sleep. If the temperature goes below minus ten degrees, the Xan die. As a result, most Xan live in the equatorial regions of Algara.

Like most sentients in the galaxy, the Xan are emotional beings. Their code of behavior is very simple: do good to others, fight when your life is threatened, and do not let your actions harm innocents.

Life expectancy among the Xan is roughly 80 years. Xan births are single-offspring, and a female Xan can give birth between the ages of 20 and 50. Unfortunately, the Algarians strictly regulate the number of children Xan women can bear. Centuries of Algarian domination has resulted in the virtual extinction of the Xan culture. What little remains must be practiced in secret, in small private gatherings. Unfortunately, most Xan have never heard the history of their people. Instead, they are fed the Algarian version of events, which speaks of Xan atrocities against the peace-loving Humans.

Most Xan can speak Basic as well as their own native sign language. A small percentage of the Algarians are also trained in the Xan language, to guard against any attempts at conspiracy among the lower classes.

The Human colonists' advanced technology allowed them to quickly dominate the Xan, a condition that has prevailed for 400 years. The vast majority of Xan are classified as Drones, doing unskilled, menial work.

Their status as second-class citizens has turned the Xan into a sullen race. They do the work required of them, no more, no less, and waste no time in complaining about their lot. They do, however, nurse a secret sympathy for the Empire. Most believe that the freedom the New Republic gives each planetary government to conduct its affairs in its own way is tantamount to a seal of approval for Algarian oppression. The Xan do not believe that their lives could be worse under Imperial rule, and believe the Empire might force the Algarians into awarding the Xan equal status.

The Xan are forbidden by Algarian law to travel into space. The Algarians do not want their image to be tarnished in any way by Xan accusations.

■ Xan

Attribute Dice: 12D
Attribute Minimum/Maximums:
DEXTERITY 2D/4D
KNOWLEDGE 2D/4D
MECHANICAL 2D/4D
PERCEPTION 2D/4D
STRENGTH 2D/4D
TECHNICAL 2D/4D
Special Abilities:
Cold Vulnerability: Xan cannot tolerate temperatures below one degree celsius. Between zero and -10 degress, Xan fall into a deep sleep, and temperatures below -10 celsius kill Xan.
Move: 6/8
Size: 1.5–1.75 meters tall

Algarine

Algarine is the sprawling capital city of the planet, and home to one of the most complex bureaucracies in the galaxy. A monorail line connects Algarine with the other major cities on the continent, Tivin and Benis, as well as to Club Prosperine.

Algarine is home to 20 million beings, plus an additional one million visitors from off-world. It is a bustling city with well-stocked shops, crowded entertainment centers, humming factories, and traffic-clogged streets. It is a city in motion.

It is difficult to point to one single Algarian as the head of the planetary government. Each as-

Xan

Rob Caswell

pect of life has its own bureau. All of these bureaus in turn are overseen by the Bureau of Revenue, which collects taxes and tariffs and allocates them as the need arises, within pre-set limits. The Bureau of Revenue may sound like it enjoys a certain amount of autonomy, but it is actually composed of one member from each of the other Bureaus, all of which still have authority over their representative.

A number of corporations have branches in Algarine, including Algar Mining (a frequent target of sabotage by the Imperial Resistance); Feduch Importers, believed by the New Republic to be a front for a lucrative smuggling and slaver operation; Prosperine Entertainment and Distilleries, operators of Club Prosperine; and Kexeerian Blasters Technology.

Algarian Law

Algarian law is enforced by on-planet security forces as well as a small space fleet, based in Algarine. The fleet is composed of a military configuration Corellian corvette named the *Bureaucrat's Triumph*, and a dozen Z-95 Headhunter starfighters.

Captured smugglers and pirates have their cargoes and ships seized, and a fine of 10,000 credits levied against them.

Off-worlders who fail to correct proper data are fined 10 times the amount of the standard fee, or 100 credits if the diskwork did not require a paid fee. Second offenses double the fees. Third offenses triple the fees. A fourth offense leads to the character being banned from Algara.

Club Prosperine

The largest resort on Algara, Club Prosperine charges 500 credits per night, meals included. Here, Algarians and off-worlders alike may rest, play, eat, and sleep to their hearts' content. There are sports facilities, casinos, cabarets, electronic games of amusement, several fine restaurants and cantinas, and even a service that matches up single visitors with each other, based on gender, interests, and species.

Everything in the Club Prosperine screams the word "luxury." Guests are waited on hand and foot. Exotic foods and drinks from all over the galaxy can be found here.

The grounds of the Club Prosperine are surrounded by a power fence to keep out, as the club's owner calls them, "undesirables." Droids are prohibited from entering the Club.

The Club Prosperine is owned and run by Dellin Sorth, a smarmy, fawning, weasel of a man from the Prosperine social class. He also serves as CEO of Prosperine Entertainment and Distilleries.

The Imperial Resistance

With cells located in the cities of Algarine, Tivin, Kaul, and Tauve, the Imperial Resistance is well-entrenched on Algara. Currently, the Resistance numbers 69,000 members, of which 40,000 are Xan and 29,000 are Algarians. The vast majority of the Resistance members hold normal jobs based upon their various social classifications. The Resistance is made up mostly of Talents,

Mike Vilardi

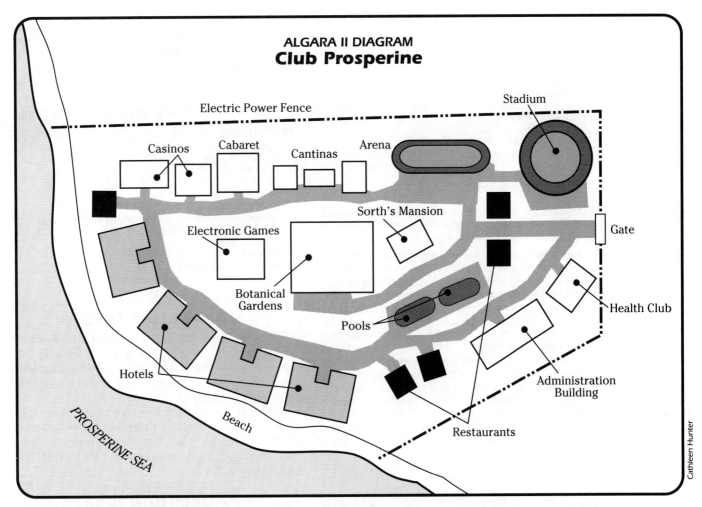

ALGARA II DIAGRAM
Club Prosperine

Electric Power Fence

Casinos · Cabaret · Cantinas · Arena · Stadium

Sorth's Mansion

Electronic Games

Botanical Gardens

Pools

Hotels

Beach

PROSPERINE SEA

Gate

Health Club

Administration Building

Restaurants

Cathleen Hunter

Drones, Domestics and some Flotsam.

Both Human and Xan Resistance members participate in attacks on symbols of the existing system. The Resistance goes out of its way not to injure innocents, meaning anyone who is not a Bureaucrat or a Belligerent. Targets of sabotage have included the robotic-driven industrial plants, the monorail to Club Prosperine, and military installations.

The Resistance often sends pirate broadcasts out to the populace, encouraging them to rise up and revolt. Unflattering anti-Bureaucratic graffiti finds its way on to prominent walls in the starport, for all off-worlders to see.

Cells of Resistance members meet in secret locations in their respective cities. A city may have up to 50 cells — Algarine has 220. Most of the time, the members of one cell do not know the others, for the sake of security.

The Algarian Bureaucracy has labelled the Resistance "pro-Imperial terrorists," and to a great extent, this description is apt. But the simple truth is that the Resistance has the right idea about the problems on Algara, but are looking to the wrong side for help. The government, mean-

while, is backing the right side, but for all the wrong reasons. The Algarians have embraced the New Republic because it lets them run the planet the way they want to. Despite the fact that their Bureaucracy crushes the people into a state of near-helplessness, they are intelligent enough to know that if the Empire moved in, the social structure would crumble, and all their privileges would be lost.

Both the Imperials and the New Republic remain unaware of the existence of the Imperial Resistance on Algara.

The Imperial Resistance is run by an ex-Belligerent, Onstruk Don, who has grown weary of the class system on Alagara. Angered by the way the Xan were treated, he made an effort to win their trust and has trained many of them to the point where they are a marginally effective guerilla force. (The Bureaucracy's official announcement was that Don was kidnapped by the Resistance and is being held hostage.)

■ Onstruk Don, Leader of the Imperial Resistance
Type: Human Revolutionary
DEXTERITY 3D

Blaster 6D, blaster: blaster rifle 5D, dodge 6D, melee combat 7D
KNOWLEDGE 3D
Scholar: Algaran history 8D, streetwise 9D, value 7D+2
MECHANICAL 3D
Repulsorlift operation 7D+1
PERCEPTION 3D
Bargain 6D+1, command 9D, hide 6D, search 7D, sneak 8D
STRENGTH 3D
Stamina 4D
TECHNICAL 3D
Computer programming/repair 4D, demolition 8D, droid programming 3D+2, droid repair 4D+1, first aid 5D, security 7D
Character Points: 10
Move: 10
Equipment: Blaster pistol (4D), comlink, vibro-blade (STR+1D+2), medpac, pocket computer, explosive charges (5D), standard detonators, glow rod

Capsule: Onstruk Don was a Belligerent, enlisting as an officer and rising through the ranks to achieve the rank of colonel. He grew disgusted with the rigid social system and the injustice the Xan had to suffer through, and thus he arraned his own disappearance. He contacted the scattered and disorganized Resistance, and eventually brought them together into an effective unit.

Don is a man of compassion with a hunger for justice. He is a brilliant tactician and an expert in demolitions. His hatred of the Bureaucracy and passion for change on Algara have blinded him to the true evil of the Empire.

He is a solidly-built man with silver hair and a few wrinkles. His eyes are icy blue and his jaw is square and firm.

Dhislugs

Dhislugs are huge, slimy creatures with twin antennae on their heads (which serve as primary sensor organs). They have eyes, but they are virtually useless. Their sole other "facial" feature is a toothless maw. Dhislugs can grow to a length of four meters, although most are in the three meter range.

Dhislugs enjoy damp, dark areas. They congregate in colonies of up to 10 in the sewers and waste disposal pits of Algarine and other cities. They emerge only at night, using acid secretions to melt their way through gratings. They will rarely venture far from these openings, crushing the first prey they spot and dragging it down for a feast. The Bureaucrats have blamed the damaged sewer accesses on everything from natural erosion to terrorist activity by the Imperial Resistance. Algara's urban areas, specifically their underground waste disposal systems, have become home to the dhislugs. Thus far, its victims have primarily been Xan living in poorer areas, limiting the amount of attention the problem receives. However, a Bureau of Algaran Gastropod Mollusk Research has been formed to study the problem.

Dhislugs need to feed at least once a week to remain healthy. They are strict meat-eaters, but not picky, attacking almost any creature that wanders by. They attack by wrapping themselves around their prey and either crushing it to death or burning it with the acid they secrete from special glands. While not armored, a dhislug body's natural resilience does provide some protection against physical (non-energy) weapons.

■ Dhislugs
Type: Predatory Slug
DEXTERITY 3D
PERCEPTION 2D
Sneak 3D
STRENGTH 5D
Special Abilities:
Armor: +1D to *Strength* against physical attacks
Constriction Attack: STR+2D damage
Acid: 5D damage
Move: 3
Size: Up to 3 meters long
Scale: Creature

Adventure Idea

The New Republic hires the characters to run some data to Algara II. This simple hook gets the characters to the planet. The New Republic will warn the characters to make sure that their diskwork is in order.

At some point after the characters' ship has landed but before they disembark, the Imperial Resistance, which has found out about the data shipment, will raid the vessel and try to steal the information.

Adventure Idea

The characters are supposed to meet a fellow off-worlder New Republic representative at the New Republic Cantina in Algarine. As the characters approach the cantina, their contact staggers out of an ally and collapses at their feet, dead.

The characters only have a few minutes to search his body before the police arrive and, of course, the characters will have to answer lots of questions if they are found by the body.

The victim died of a vibro-blade wound. There is nothing on his person except his Visitor Identification chip, which indicates that he was staying at the Club Prosperine and that he owned a droid.

When they arrive at the club and check out his room, they find a group of Xan and Humans going through the room, searching for something. What has happened is that the New Republic representative has been conducting his own investigation and has discovered the true nature of the situation on this planet. He recorded it all on his 3P0 protocol droid. The Imperial Resistance thought he was a spy and had him killed. They are now searching his room for the data he gathered, believing it to be incriminating evidence against their movement.

The droid, in the meantime, has taken the monorail back to the Algarine starport, awaiting the passenger ship that the agent had booked passage on in order to leave the planet.

The ideal outcome of this adventure is the characters' finding out the true nature of the Resistance, while not getting killed by them, as well as avoiding arrest for the agent's murder.

 # Atraken

Atraken

Type: Desolate Wasteland
Temperature: Cool
Atmosphere: Type III (breath mask required)
Hydrosphere: Arid
Gravity: Standard
Terrain: Wasteland
Length of Day: 20 standard hours
Length of Year: 304 local days
System: Kattellyn
Star: Kattellyn (yellow)
Orbital Bodies:

Name	Planet Type	Moons
Kronas	desolate searing rock	0
Atraken	desolate wasteland	3
Trilos	barren mining satellite	

World Summary

The planet Atraken is the primary world of this system. Atraken is a wasteland, ravaged by the Clone Wars to the point of irreparable ecological disaster. The planet has been totally written off the world logs as a place for visitors to travel and trade.

However, what the overwhelming majority of the galaxy is unaware of is that a small segment of the Atraken population escaped the conflict and fled by ship to Trilos, one of the three moons of Atraken.

Now miners and colonists dwell in pressurized shelters above and below ground. Most of

System Datafile

Kattellyn system, star: Kattellyn, yellow sun. Two planets, Kronas and Atraken. Atrakenite mining colony on Trilos, primary Atrakenite moon.

ALERT: RESTRICTED SYSTEM! The population of the planet Atraken was decimated during the Clone Wars. There is no one left on the planet to trade or interact with. Possible hazards include biochemical weaponry residue, unexploded ammunition, and other sustained environmental hazards. This system is dead and off-limits to all personnel.

the ores they mine are processed on the planetoid itself and used to expand the colony. In essence, it is a self-sustaining world.

Standing water is found in underground springs, and massive hydroponic and fungal gardens provide nutrients.

The Atrakenites have, in the last few years, begun making salvage runs back to their home world.

System Summary

The yellow star Kattellyn has only two planets in its system — sadly, both are dead. Kronas is a ball of searing rock that orbits much too close to the sun to ever sustain even the tiniest shred of life. Atraken is a bombed-out husk, a poisoned legacy of the Clone Wars.

Atraken has three moons, Trilos, Doulos, and Mrykos. Only Trilos is capable of sustaining life of any kind, and it is here that an Atrakenite mining colony was set up several years before the Clone Wars erupted. Atrakenite refugees made their way here and have bolstered the population to its current level.

The Kattellyn system is on a well-travelled trade route, but the disaster of Atraken is common knowledge to most spacefarers. Knowing the details of the catastrophe is an Easy *planetary systems* task. Those traders who have, largely by accident, discovered the Atraken settlements on Trilos have seen their tales dismissed as fantasy in other parts of the galaxy.

Atrakenite Society

This is a survivor-based society, a society built on a sadness that has not yet gone away. This, combined with the stark and gloomy setting of Trilos, makes for a somber people that seem to have little time for leisure or laughter.

The Atrakenites are a stubborn lot, and they have chosen as one people to stay in their system and try to honor the memory of their dead by rebuilding their society. In a way, it is a form of

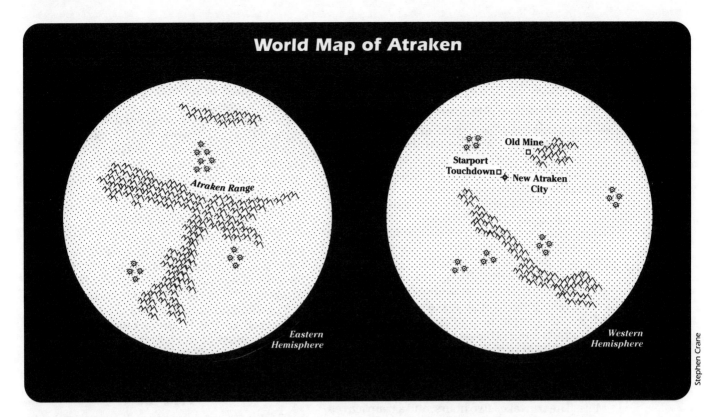

World Map of Atraken

Atraken Range

Eastern Hemisphere

Old Mine

Starport Touchdown

New Atraken City

Western Hemisphere

Stephen Crane

penance. Many of the refugees are still suffering from survivor's guilt.

There is only one distinction made in Atrakenite society, that which exists between the descendants of the miners and the descendants of the original refugees. Neither group has dominance over the other, and marriages and the like are certainly permitted between the two. The Atrakenites maintain the largely ceremonial division simply as a way to remember their heritage and to keep their history alive.

The professional organization called the Atrakenite Guild of Miners runs the day-to-day affairs of the planetoid. When the refugees first came to Trilos, it made sense that the miners were the ones to set up a functioning government, since it was they who knew the planetoid well. The organization is headed by an eight-member Mining Council, which consists of the descendants of six mining families and two refugee families.

The destruction of their planet has given the Atrakenites a strong streak of non-violence. They have become outright pacifists and will not attack another creature unless their lives are directly threatened and there is no other alternative available. Some of the traders who have landed on Trilos and spoken about the Empire-New Republic conflict have been surprised by the Atrakenite reaction. The Atrakenites do not want anything to do with either side. They do not

care who runs the galaxy as long as they can be left in peace and allowed to rebuild their own shattered lives.

Starport Touchdown

This is a limited services starport, formerly used as the main starport in the pre-Clone War days. Now, it lies mostly unused. Most of the spacecraft used to evacuate Atrakenite survivors have been disassembled, and only two craft remain.

The two surviving craft are light freighters, the *Atraken Hope* and the *Atraken Memory*. Only the *Atraken Memory* still functions, while the *Atraken Hope* is now used for spare parts to keep the freighter working. Unfortunately, the *Atraken Memory* is currently under repair.

One interesting bit of salvage from post-Clone War days that drifted into the system was the battered hulk of an X-wing fighter, obviously battle-damaged as a result of a run-in with Imperial forces. Though the pilot was dead, the R2 droid still functioned. Using their resourcefulness, and dumping the memory banks of the R2, the Atrakenites have managed to build other R2 units.

The X-wing now sits on the runway of the starport, unable to be completely repaired due to the lack of certain key parts. The Atrakenites are willing to trade it for needed goods, but the value of what is offered must equal at least half of the price of an X-wing.

In order to repair the X-wing, the characters need to purchase spare parts found only at stellar class starports and costing 50,000 credits. Once this is achieved, repairing the ship takes two weeks and is a Difficult task.

New Atraken City

The word "city" is a slight misnomer, as the population of New Atraken hardly qualifies the site for such a classification. It is located half a kilometer below the lunar surface and connected by access paths to the starport.

It was, at one time, a tiny community, populated by miners and their families. Once the refugees from Atraken arrived, the little mining village had to be expanded to fit everyone. Current population stands at 40,000.

The city has two cantinas, the Last Resort and the Downside. There are no hotels, casinos, or restaurants here. The cantinas are the only places where the people of Atraken/Trilos can go to rest, drink, and exchange news.

The citizens of New Atraken City live in modular apartments grouped together in building configurations.

The city is connected by a subway to the Old Mine. The trip takes two hours, and a train leaves every hour on the hour. The subtrans is double-tracked, so that trains going back and forth present no problem. There are no other stops on the route.

Current Mines

The Atrakenites have begun new mines. Each one is set in one of the big craters in the planetoid's western hemisphere. Travel to these mines is accomplished using pressurized landspeeders and ore barges.

Each mine has a pressurized dome with sleeping facilities for 180 workers. The mines are very productive, and there are even plans for expanding the subtrans to reach each of them, once enough raw material has been mined, refined, and made ready to use.

The Old Mine

Located one kilometer below the surface, this huge cavern (10 kilometers long by six kilometers wide) was the first mine established by Atraken. It has since been played out, and now houses the Atrakenites' manufacturing equipment.

The Old Mine also hosts a community now, composed of the laborers charged with constructing most of the goods. Current Old Mine population is 10,000. The community has one cantina, also called the "Old Mine."

The Ee

The Ee are a species of small worms native to Trilos, not more than six centimeters in length. Ee coloration is grey or tan, with a darkened area marking the location of their heads. The moon Trilos is infested with Ee, who enjoy burrowing

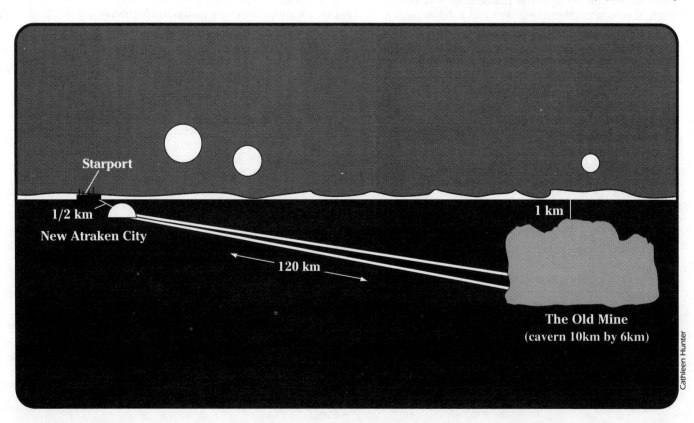

through the rock and eating very small amounts of minerals and fungus. The cold, harsh conditions of space do not bother the Ee, and they are able to exist with very little oxygen.

Ee have tactile, olfactory, and audio nerve endings all over their bodies serving as sensory organs. The head contains one optical organ that allows sight. Their tiny mouths have a sharply defined taste organ, so that the burrowing Ee may be able to tell what sort of mineral it is burrowing through. Some Ee have even become connoisseurs of particular minerals.

The Ee have two unusual abilities. The first is that their digestive system allows them to ingest several different types of mineral and rock, and produce alloys. These substances are used in the construction of Ee equipment (see below). Also, when an Ee eats into a vein of metal ore, it refines the metal to its purest form, since what it is really consuming from the ore are the impurities. The Ee then take the threads of pure ore and, using their mental powers, weave and weld the metals into functioning devices. Most of these devices are powered by solar power, collected by micropanels on Trilos' surface and stored in micropowercells, all of which are formed by the Ee manufacturing process. The Ee have also found that ingesting certain chemicals allows them to produce different substances from the minerals they take in, but they are forced to rely on the unwitting Atrakenites to provide the needed solutions.

One of the most unusual things about the Ee is their mental prowess. The species is quite intelligent and has developed a number of powers of the mind to enable them to rise to a level of civilization unheard of for most invertebrates.

Each Ee has male and female characteristics, and reproduces by laying 1D eggs. The incubation period is a time-consuming, random affair, with the young taking 2D months to form. Average Ee life expectancy is 20 years.

Ee Society

The Ee are individuals but have a linked group mind, and consequently the issue of government is a simple one. Each Ee puts its thoughts into the problem, and the course of action which results is an amalgam of all the ideas submitted. Despite this potentially confusing system, the Ee manage to get things accomplished.

Ee dwellings consist of hives made of cone-shaped rock formations, found on the moon's surface as well as in underground caves.

Ee society is divided into the following categories, based on occupation:

Purifiers: Those Ee especially adept at processing ore into pure elemental form.

Weavers: Ee who show talent in taking the processed materials and forming them into the

machinery needed.

Thinkers: Ee who have a knack for theories, principles, and such.

Mindbenders: Ee who have especially strong mental talents.

Bulwarks: Ee whose primary duties involve the protection of the race.

None of these castes is considered superior to any other, but exist only to make the best use of every Ee's talent.

The Ee have no spoken language. They do possess an icongraphic alphabet, which uses symbols to represent words and ideas, but this system is only rarely used. Most of the time, the Ee rely on their telepathic power to communicate with each other.

The Atrakenites have not discovered the true nature of the Ee.

As for the Ee, they have been watching the Atrakenites very closely, reading their minds, and observing their behavior. The Ee feel pity for the Atrakenites, who have lost their home planet. The little creatures are waiting for the group mind to finally decide when the time is right for contact. Many Ee feel that this will be soon.

Until then, special measures are taken to ensure that the Atrakenites never learn of the Ee civilization. Ee iconography is never done in a

Mike Vilardi

place where the Atrakenites are known to pass by or frequent. The minds of traders who stop at Trilos are manipulated by the Ee so that their tales of the planet are so fantastic as to not be believed.

The Ee have learned of the existence of the Empire-New Republic civil war. The Ee came to the conclusion, rather quickly, that the Empire is the prime offender. The Ee also feel that if the Empire were to find out about this mining facility, it would move in, brutally taking everything it wished and turning it into an Imperial production facility. This is another reason why they feel it necessary to remain hidden, although many of the species are bothered by toying with alien memories.

Ee are small and fragile, but have great knowledge. Combined with their mental abilities, they can accomplish much despite their physical limitations. They have a marked distaste for physical confrontation, firmly believing in discretion and secrecy.

Ee are known for their arrogance: they are intolerant of beings not as intelligent as them or not structured like them ("Yes, yes, I know you are not a segmented-bodied, telepathic invertebrate. I guess we cannot all be perfect!"). They have little patience when it comes to explaining difficult procedures or complex concepts.

They are natural explorers and have mapped most of Trilos; given the chance, most Ee would love to explore the larger galaxy.

■ Ee

Attribute Dice: 6D
Attribute Minimum/Maximums:
DEXTERITY 0D
KNOWLEDGE 2D/4D
MECHANICAL 0D/1D+2
PERCEPTION 2D/4D
STRENGTH 0D/+2
TECHNICAL 1D/4D
Special Skills:
Unrelated skills (not tied to any attribute):
Physical skills. Time to use: One round to several hours, depending upon power. This is one of the three Ee mental abilities used for the mental powers outlined below.
Mental skills. Time to use: One round to several hours, depending upon power. This is one of the three Ee mental abilities used for the mental powers outlined below.
Environmental skills. Time to use: One round to several hours, depending upon power. This is one of the three Ee mental abilities used for the mental powers outlined below.
Special Abilities:
Mental Abilities: Ee have mental abilities which some might attribute to Force-sensitivity (although there is no proof of this notion). They have three skills governing these abilities: *physical skills, mental skills,* and *environmental skills.* Ee who possess the skills start at 2D and can increase the skill at double the normal Character Point cost.
No Physical Manipulation: Ee have very little ability to physically manipulate items or tools. They must rely on their mental abilities.
Story Factors:
Unknown: The settlers on Trilos are unaware of the existence of the Ee.
Move: 3/5 (burrowing or crawling)
Size: 1–6.5 centimeters
Note: Ee should not be player characters

Ee Mental Powers

All Ee are adept at at least one type of mental power, be it physical skills, environmental skills, or mental skills. One Ee in 10 is adept at two categories, and one Ee in 100 is adept at all three.

Ee begin with 2D in these skills, but may increase their skills. Effective range of all powers, unless otherwise stated, is five meters.

Physical Skills

Cell Burst: Disrupts the cells in organic or inorganic matter, causing 4D damage. Difficulty is Easy for organic matter and Moderate for inorganic matter.

Healing: Completely removes an injury. Difficulty: Very Easy for wounded victims, Easy for incapacitated ones, and Difficult for mortally wounded ones. **Note:** These difficulties are DOUBLED when the target is non-Ee.

Pliability: Causes any substance to become flexible. Difficulty: Easy to Heroic, depending upon innate flexibility of material.

Telekinesis: Though Ee telekinesis is different than the Force power of the same name, for simplicity's sake, the same description can be used for both. Ee difficulty numbers of telekinesis are two levels higher than those of the Force power.

Teleportation: Ee with this power can teleport objects which weigh no more than one kilogram. The object can be teleported one meter per three points rolled (round down). For example, if a 15 is rolled, an Ee can teleport an object up to five meters. If the power user attempts to teleport himself, difficulty is Difficult. Standard difficulty: Moderate.

Environmental Skills

Light: This power must be centered on an object weighing no more than one kilogram. The object must be within 10 meters of the Ee. When used successfully, a globe of light 10 meters in diameter is created. The object can be moved and the light globe will move with it. Difficulty: Very Easy.

Null Gravity: An Ee interference field disrupts the gravity in a two-meter radius. Anyone caught in it, floats upward until the Ee ceases using the power. The Ee must be on the perimeter of the radius, and the null gravity area cannot be moved. Difficulty: Difficult.

Power Drain: Drains all power out of a battery or other charge-holding device. Difficulty: Moderate.

Raise/Lower Temperature: Affects a 20-meter diameter circle. Difficulty is Very Easy for a five-degree Centigrade change, Easy for a 10-degree change, Moderate for a 15-degree change, etc.

Mental Skills

Group Mind: Enables all Ee to communicate with each other. All involved Ee must be within 30 meters of each other (Ee normally form a "chain" to keep in contact). Difficulty: Very Easy.

Memory Alteration: Rearranges the memory patterns of the victim. The Ee's power roll must exceed the victim's *Perception* roll. Ee use this power to change the memories of aliens, so that they tell outlandish, and easily dismissed, stories about Trilos.

Mindlink: Allows two-way mental communication, even if recipient has no mental powers. Difficulty: Difficult.

Projective Telepathy: This is somewhat similar to the Force power, with the difficulty Easy, or Moderate if the target is in an extremely emotional state.

Sensory Overload: Causes the target to experience a huge influx of sight, sound, taste, hearing, and touch stimuli, causing him to pass out. Difficulty based on victim's *Perception*: 1D–2D: Very Easy; 3D–4D: Easy; 5D–6D: Moderate; 7D+: Difficult.

The effects of *memory alteration*, *cell burst*, *power drain* and *healing* remain even after the power is no longer being used.

Whenever an Ee uses a mental power, it must rest for twice the amount of time spent performing that action. The maximum amount of time an Ee can spend using a mental power is one hour.

Ee Technology

The Ee have developed and continue to manufacture the following items: solar panels, intruder sensors, motion sensitive alarms, lighting panels, fortifications for their dwellings and supports for tunnels

All of this machinery is, of course, to scale with the Ee race and of no use to the average visitor.

The World of Atraken

The once-beautiful planet of Atraken now stands as a monument to mindless destruction. Opposing forces in the Clone Wars made it their battlefield, destroying each other, the planet's environment, and over 90 percent of the native population.

Nowadays, Atraken's oceans, those that have not been boiled away, are huge bodies of poisonous water. Most plant life has been blasted away, and almost all animal life is gone. The very air is poisonous, carrying either the remains of chemical weapons or virulent strains left over from germ warfare. The only life form that remains are large, burrowing insects called "diehards" that have adapted to eating the poisons of Atraken.

All that stands now are the shattered remains of Atraken's cities and a carpet of debris, the last bits of evidence that a thriving civilization once existed here.

Exploring Atraken

The only legitimate reason for exploring Atraken is for purposes of salvage. In order to survive for any length of time on that blasted planet, full protection space suits will be needed. Even these, however, are not enough — the howling winds of Atraken, laced with corrosive chemicals, will slowly cause a suit to lose its structural integrity, eating away at the non-metal parts.

In game terms, consider the suit to have a *Strength* of 5D for purposes of protection from the hostile environment of Atraken. For each hour spent on Atraken, a cumulative 1D is rolled against the suit. As soon as a wound result is scored, the suit has lost integrity, and the character is vulnerable.

Once a suit is compromised, the character is attacked by a cumulative 2D damage for every 10 minutes of exposure.

Visibility on most parts of the planet is down to 20 meters. Dust and other pollutants in the atmosphere obscure sunlight. Daytime temperature hovers at about two degrees Celsius, while nighttime temperatures dip to minus ten degrees Celsius.

Atraken Events

For every half hour spent on Atraken, roll 2D and consult the "Atraken Hazards Table" to see what peril, if any, the characters encounter.

Storms last for 6D minutes. It is possible to have overlapping conditions.

Searching for Salvage

Characters exploring Atraken may attempt to salvage materials. Each character may attempt to find salvage once per hour. For each character attempting such an action, roll 2D and consult the "Salvage Table" for the results.

■ Cidwen

Type: Aggressive avian
DEXTERITY 5D
PERCEPTION 4D
STRENGTH 1D+1
Special Abilities:
Beak: STR+2D damage
Claws: STR+2D+2 damage (works out as 3D+3 damage)
Move: 30 (flying), 22 (gliding)
Size: 0.5 meters long, 1-meter wingspan
Scale: Creature

Capsule: Cidwens are ebon-hued birds with sharp beaks and vicious claws. They nest in ruins throughout Atraken. Their keen eyes allow them to spot diehard activity from a distance, at which point they take to the air and snatch up the offending insects.

Though cidwen are capable of flight, they often glide when stalking prey to reduce the noise they make. Cidwens have been known to attack Humans and other species, especially if their nests are disturbed, but they will often only fight until the offending being has been driven off.

Mike Vilardi

■ Diehards

Type: Hardy insects
DEXTERITY 5D
PERCEPTION 1D
STRENGTH 4D
Special Abilities:
Mandibles: STR+2D damage
Armor: +2D to resist damage from energy attacks
Move: 24 (flying)
Size: 0.5 meters long
Scale: Creature

Capsule: Diehards are immense insects which have survived the catastrophe on Atraken through simple resilience. The diehards have survived, even thrived, despite the plagues, the radiation and the devastating ecological changes of this world. Diehards are especially resistant to energy weapons, so primitive slug-throwers are the preferred means of stopping these savage attackers.

Diehards are not very intelligent, relying on instinct. For attacks, they use simple swarms (although their swarms normally have only four or five members). Once a diehard hits a target, it digs into the victim with its mandibles (pulling a diehard off someone requires an opposed *Strength* total).

Adventure Idea

This should be the first adventure set in the Kattelyn system.

The characters spot a Corellian stock light freighter adrift in space. It does not answer any hails. If the characters board it (gamemasters can use the interior blueprint of the *Millennium Falcon* found on pages 22–23 of the *Star Wars Sourcebook, Second Edition*), they will find that the crew of four is dead.

The ship appears to be ruined, as if vandals tore into it with vibro-axes. None of the systems save the computer and the environmental control still work, and even these will go in 1D hours.

This is what happened: The freighter *Lucky Bantha* discovered the Kattelyn star system. The crew stopped off at Trilos, exchanged some small goods and pleasantries, then, against the advice of the Atrakenites, went to check the ruined planet of Atraken for salvage.

Unfortunately, the crew did two things wrong. First of all, their space suits were of cheap quality, and easily compromised. This led to their catching radiation sickness, which eventually caused their deaths. Secondly, they *did* find some salvage, unaware that a small nest of diehards was included with it.

When the crew brought the salvage into their cargo hold, the diehards left the salvage and began eating away at the ship itself. Of course, the crew was already dead of radiation poisoning by the time the diehards had managed any significant damage.

The names of the ship and crew, their last port-of-call and its coordinates, their next planned destination, their activities on Atraken, and their final entry, are all on the ship's computer. It is a Moderate *computer programming/repair* task to obtain each of the above listed bits of information out of the computer.

Atraken Hazards Table

Roll	Encounter
2–5	No encounter.
6–7	Massive dust storm. Visibility cut to five meters. -1D to all *Perception* and *Dexterity*-related skills.
8	Ground collapses underneath character's feet. Roll for falling damage. Total distance fallen equals 3D.
9	Characters come upon a fairly intact building.
10	Electrical storm prevents communication and sensor operation.
11	Characters encounter 1D diehards.
12	High radiation area. All characters hit by 4D of radiation damage, regardless of protection.

Salvage Table

Roll	Result
2–6	Nothing.
7–8	Useful spare parts for droids.
9	Useful spare parts for spaceships.
10	One random piece of broken equipment, gamemaster's choice*.
11	One random broken weapon, GM choice*.
12	A broken landspeeder**.

*Recommend that only two such items be found by any one party of characters. Can be repaired, Very Difficult task.

** Recommend that only one such item be found by any one party of characters, and only once. Can be repaired, Very Difficult task.

The dead crew members, incidentally, are still irradiated. Unless the bodies are jettisoned, the characters will suffer 3D of radiation per hour spent in the *Lucky Bantha*.

Adventure Idea

Once on Trilos and acquainted with the natives, the characters are asked to investigate some odd goings-on in the Old Mine. Large amounts of chemicals used in manufacturing are missing, and all evidence points to the theft being an inside job.

This curious event is the work of a few ambitious Ee, who are defying their group mind and using their powers to get the Atrakenites to produce large quantities of chemicals for their use. They alter the memories of the Atrakenites so that they do not recall mixing the solutions.

There are a few small Ee tracks in the dust, which can be found with a Very Difficult *Perception* task. The tracks lead to a cone, which is the entryway down into a five meter wide cavern, where the Ee have a small communities.

The Ee will not wish to be revealed to the Atrakenites. It will be rather interesting to see how the characters react to telepathic worms who are living refineries.

Adventure Idea

While the characters are on another planet, they are approached by a somber-looking elderly couple. They offer to pay the characters 50,000 credits to fly them to the Kattelyn system.

The old couple know of the fate which befell Atraken. They are the children of two refugee families who fled the planet before the war broke out. Now, in their declining years, the old couple wish to go back and see their homeworld one last time before they die.

The couple are unaware of the existence of the Trilos colony. The characters are unaware that the couple are New Republic sympathizers who are being followed by Imperial agents. A confrontation on Atraken between the Imperials and the characters may be called for.

For gamemasters and players who like happy endings, add the following wrinkle: the old couple doesn't know it, but they have relatives still alive on the mining colony.

Adventure Idea

In the realm of the truly off-beat, an Ee approaches the party in a cantina (perhaps after the party has drunk a bit too much), and asks them to take it to the moon Trilos in the Kattelynn system. For payment, the Ee can give the characters 5,000 credits worth of pure metals, but can only pay this price once it gets back to Trilos.

It seems that a free-trader who visited Trilos wound up with an Ee in his spacesuit. The curious Ee wanted to see "what was out there," but has seen enough.

What could make this adventure even more. unusual is having a horde of half-drunk aliens who love worms as a delicacy, or for putting in their drinks, notice the Ee talking to the characters. The drunken aliens will give chase to the characters, demanding the worm. Of course, the aliens have their own ship (or ships), too.

Carosi XII

Carosi

Type: Terraformed world
Temperature: Cool
Atmosphere: Type I (breathable)
Hydrosphere: Moderate
Gravity: Light
Terrain: Galciers, mountains
Length of Day: 30 standard hours
Length of Year: 400 local days
Sapient Species: Carosites
Starport: 1 standard
Population: 2 million
Planet Function: Homeworld, medical services
Government: Democracy
Tech Level: Space
Major Exports: Prosthetics, cybernetics
Major Imports: Manufactured goods, food, luxury items
System: Carosus
Star: Carosi (red giant)
Orbital Bodies:

Name	Planet Type	Moons
Carosi VI	searing rock	0
Carosi VII	desolate swamp	1
Carosi VIII	jungle	2
Carosi IX	gas giant	6
Carosi X	gas giant	10
Carosi XI	gas giant	15
Carosi XII	cool terrestrial	1

World Summary

There are very few planets that have openly supported first the Rebel Alliance and now the New Republic; Carosi XII is one of them. Located far from the Imperial Core, but close to an important free-trader route, the arctic planet is visited by many who seek healing of the mind or body. Carosi XII is a safe haven for free-traders and New Republic agents alike, thanks to a Republic base established close to the sole Carosite city.

The topography of Carosi XII is made up mostly of mountains, stretches of open, frigid plains, and gigantic glaciers. The sole sea, the Avuae, provides a terrestrial haven for the Carosites. The only city on the planet, Newlife Point, is located on the shores of the Avuae.

The planet still has some latent volcanic activity, the most popular manifestation of this being the hot springs located south of Newlife Point. The springs are known for their soothing properties and are used to accelerate healing.

The Carosites are the only intelligent species native to Carosi XII. There are a few species of marine life and wildlife, but nothing of any great note.

System Summary

The Carosus system has undergone some dramatic changes in the recent past. Three hundred years ago, the sun, Carosi, an orange star, reached the point where it had consumed most of its hydrogen and began an unusually rapid expansion. Carosite astronomers predicted that the sun would soon turn into a red giant, devouring most of the inner planets.

The first five planets in the system were destroyed. Carosi IV, the Carosite home planet, was swallowed up by the sun. Carosi V, a prime candidate for colonization, was also destroyed. Carosi VI, a planet with potential for terraforming, is now the closest planet to the sun, and consequently has had any life-giving potential burned away. Carosi VII and VIII have rapidly turned into stiflingly hot greenhouses only suitable for colonization at some later date, and Carosi IX, X, and XI are useless gas giants. Only Carosi XII, once a frozen ice ball and now improved to merely

---

System Datafile

Note: Update files to indicate new system status. Carosi is no longer an orange star, but is now a red giant. Please adjust star maps and navigational computations accordingly.

Carosus star system, star: Carosi, red giant. Formerly 12 planets in system, has been reduced to seven planets due to solar expansion. Old numerical reckoning retained; closest planet to sun is Carosi VI.

Carosi XII, New Republic planet. Primary function: Medical care and prosthetics. NOTE: If emergency medical care is required, comm Carosi XII starport on standard broadcast bandwidths. An emergency trauma team will be standing by.

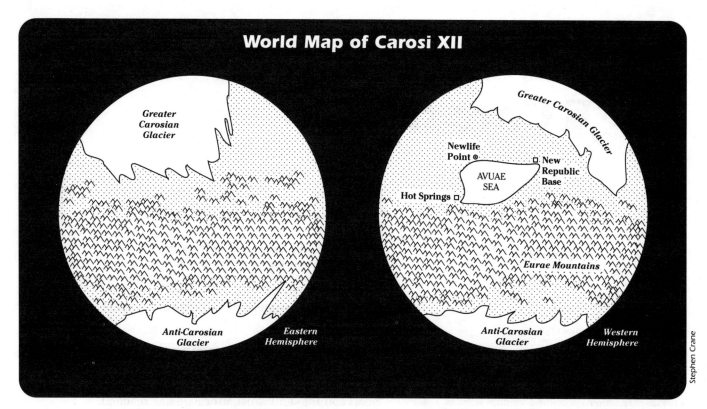

World Map of Carosi XII

Greater Carosian Glacier

Anti-Carosian Glacier

Eastern Hemisphere

Greater Carosian Glacier

Newlife Point ◉

AVUAE SEA

Hot Springs □

□ New Republic Base

Eurae Mountains

Anti-Carosian Glacier

Western Hemisphere

Stephen Crane

"cool" status, has a habitable environment.

It was Carosi XII that the scientists spent decades terraforming in anticipation of colonization. The results have paid off, though the work is not yet complete. As a result, Carosi has a great need for scientists and other specialists interested in building a world.

Carosites

The Carosites are a bipedal species, one and a half meters tall and quite thin, with unusually long necks. Their faces have long snouts, small dark eyes, and a fine layer of fur. This fur covers their bodies as well, and keeps them warm. Their senses are extremely acute, and their hands are very nimble and well coordinated.

Carosites have a life expectancy of 120 standard years. The Carosite reproductive cycle is a very fleeting thing. Carosites can only have young twice in their lifetime. Each birth produces a litter of one to six young. This accounts for the Carosite's intense respect for life, since they have so few opportunities for renewal. It was this respect for life that helped the Carosites develop their amazing medical talents, from which the entire galaxy now benefits.

The only social unit in Carosite society is the family, consisting of an adult male, adult female, young, and any family member that is too old to take care of itself.

Carosites are a gentle, beneficent species with a talent for healing and invention. Carosites are also hopeless optimists.

Tradition and ritual are very important to the Carosites. The destruction of their home planet has served to strengthen their resolve to remember and venerate the past.

Verbal or written promises are regarded as completely binding by Carosites, and they extend that courtesy to off-worlders, expecting visitors to the planet to reciprocate. Thus, Carosites are frequently disappointed by what they perceive as the dishonor prevalent among some other species.

Though Carosites are more devoted to healing a body than harming it, they will vigorously fight to defend their homes, families, and planet. If a Carosite's convalescing patients are being threatened, the Carosites on hand go into a berserk "life-saving fanaticism" state. This enables a Carosite to add 2D to their *Strength* dice for as long as the patient is endangered.

Although the Carosites have the ability to engage in space exploration, they have chosen instead to devote their time, energy, resources, and intelligence to perfecting the medical arts. They use the *Sudden Restoration*, a Carosite space vessel that functions as a hospital ship, to spread their talents to needy systems. The *Restoration* travels the galaxy, bringing free medical care to all in need. The *Restoration* has also visited New Republic and neutral worlds in the aftermath of battles and administered care to the civilians. (In general, the vessel avoids Imperial space, given the Empire's long-standing policy of discrimination against non-Humans.)

Since the ship aids anyone in need, the *Restoration* is generally safe from any attack. Many pirates and free-traders would take it upon themselves to hunt down anyone who harmed the *Restoration* or its crew.

A little known "side business" of the Carosites is their programming of medical droids. Technicians on Carosi can "squeeze" the maximum performance out of medical droids. Increasing a medical droid's existing programming while on Carosi XII takes half the standard number of credits.

The Carosites also enjoy teaching medicine, and have set up a school. Famous doctors, surgeons, scientists, and other medical personnel come to Carosi XII to either study or teach.

Carosi Society and History

The Carosites as a people are still trying to find their bearings after the massive emigration to Carosi XII. The evacuation took a total of 20 years, meaning that the Carosites landed on their new home roughly 200 years ago. Though the Carosites venerate and continue to observe their old customs and traditions, there is a fragment of Carosite society that is pushing for new traditions to go with their new home. This is a source of heated debate among the population.

The other bone of contention has been provided by a small but vocal segment of Carosites who call themselves "The Preventers." They feel that their people must take aggressive action against the weakened Empire, so that no more lives will be lost to the galactic conflict. The arguments on this subject are loud, emotional affairs.

Once every 10 years, the Carosites elect one of their number to serve as the ultimate planetary authority. This leader is advised by a group of 11 counsellors, chosen from the 11 most prominent families.

Medical metaphors are very common in the

Carosites

Rob Caswell

Carosite language. Things such as the state of the New Republic, the state of the planet, or a business deal are described in medical terms. For instance, a business deal that has taken some bad turns but may still be salvaged would be described as follows: "The business is ailing, but may be healed with proper treatment."

The Carosites are loyal to the New Republic, but events often lead them to treat Imperials or Imperial sympathizers. The Carosites regard every life as sacred and every private thought inviolate. The Carosites would never try to interrogate, brainwash, or otherwise attempt to remove information from the minds of their patients.

■ Carosites

Attribute Dice: 12D
Attribute Minimum/Maximums:
DEXTERITY 2D/4D
KNOWLEDGE 2D/4D+2
MECHANICAL 1D/3D
PERCEPTION 2D/4D+2
STRENGTH 1D+2/4D
TECHNICAL 2D/5D

Mike Vilardi

would like to learn more about it.

There has never been a Carosite Jedi. Carosites are not interested so much in becoming Jedi or in learning everything there is to know about the Force. They merely wish to study the power so they may channel it into new ways of healing. This is not so unusual, since there are Carosites who are still engaged in trying to adapt blaster technology to healing.

Medical Care

All things considered, the promise of excellent medical care is still the thing which attracts people to Carosi XII. The Carosites charge their patients an amount commensurate with their ability to pay. Full expenses run upwards of 500 credits per day, although poor patients will be charged considerably less.

A tricky area is the realm of prosthetics and cybernetics. Prosthetics are units used to replace damaged or lost limbs and organs. These units do not improve upon what was lost, they merely replace it with an artificial replica that can perform its function adequately. Carosites refuse to install cybernetic *enhancements*, however.

The Carosites have also made significant strides in the cataloguing and treatment of many kinds of mental illnesses. Their sanitariums are clean, well-lit places where healing, not incarceration, is emphasized.

Newlife Point

Newlife Point is the only city on Carosi XII. It was built on the landing site of the first refugee ships. There is still much left to build, so the city is still in development. Much of the skyline is dotted with the skeletal frames of buildings under construction.

The Newlife Point starport is located in the northwestern section of the city, close to the major hospitals, asylums, and cybernetics fitting centers.

There are a few aspects of Newlife Point which off-worlders regard as negatives. By far, the worst

Special Abilities:
Medical Aptitude: Carosites automatically have a *first aid* skill of 5D; they may not add additional skill dice to this at the time of character creation, but this is a "free skill."
Protectiveness: Carosites are incredibly protective of young, patients and other helpless beings. They gain +2D to their *brawling* skill and damage in combat when acting to protect the helpless.
Move: 7/11
Size: 1.3–1.7 meters tall

Carosites and the Force

The existence of the Force is not disputed by the Carosites. They believe it exists, and they of these is considered to be the pathetically small number of bars extant. It appears that the Carosites are not enamored with alcohol and the effects it has, both long- and short-term, on the physiologies of many beings. As a result, establishments that serve liquor are kept to a minimum, and the liquor itself is taxed heavily. In all fairness, it needs to be mentioned that the revenue generated goes towards the continued improvement of medical facilities most likely to be used by off-worlders.

The other aspect of Newlife Point that fails to impress visitors is the constant stream of dietary advice given to restaurant patrons by the waiters, cooks, doormen, busboys, and passersby. "Eat right and live right," is the most popular phrase heard in restaurants. Some visitors to Carosi XII claim the Carosite doting is worse than the excessive fretting done by some protocol droids.

Hot Springs

Located inside a beautiful crystalline cave are several huge pools of mineral-laced warmed water. The water is heated by underground volcanic activity.

The mineral content and the high temperature combine to produce a relaxing and very healthy bath. Soaking in the hot springs for two hours allows an injured character to make one extra natural healing roll per day.

There are always six Carosite attendants on duty to help visitors. The Hot Springs are connected to Newlife Point by an underground transrail system. Some people enjoy taking pleasure boats from Newlife Point to Hot Springs. The springs are located a short two kilometer walk from the Avuae coast.

New Republic Outpost

The current Carosite leader, Omo Taj, has given the New Republic permission to construct an outpost on Carosi XII. The outpost is built into the side of a mountain near northern shore of the Avuae Sea. Its location is not disclosed to off-worlders, and its secret is guarded most jealously.

Gamemasters can use the floorplans for the Tierfon Rebel Outpost, found on pages 112-116 of the *Star Wars Sourcebook, Second Edition*.

The outpost complement is:

Personnel

Pilots	28
Ground Troops	54
Officers	14
X-wing ground crew	32
Y-wing ground crew	32
Technicians	24
General Staff	24
Intelligence Personnel	10

Vehicles

Airspeeders	5
Landspeeders	2
Speeder Bikes	4
X-Wing starfighters	8
Y-Wing starfighters	8
Shuttles	4

The outpost commander is Balderik Rajana, an idealistic young man who has been fighting the Empire for as long as he can remember. He maintains good relations with the Carosites.

The Avuae

The Avuae is a small sea and the only aboveground body of water on Carosi XII. The Avuae is teeming with marine life, which serves as a source of protein for the Carosites. The water is extremely cold, but due to its high mineral content, it never freezes over.

Many Carosites enjoy a refreshing dip in the icy water of the Avuae. The Carosites claim that the water has healing properties, and that all creatures can benefit from a good soak in the ocean. Of course, Carosites have fur to keep them warm.

■ Rinacats

Type: Mountain predator
DEXTERITY 3D
PERCEPTION 5D
STRENGTH 3D
Special Abilities:
Claws: STR+1D damage
Teeth: STR+2D damage
Move: 15
Size: 2 meters long
Scale: Creature

Capsule: The most dangerous creature on Carosi XII is the rinacat, a mountain-dwelling predator renowned for its ability to tirelessly track prey for weeks. Rinacats have been known to traverse continents to bring down particularly desired prey. Rinacats can also survive for up to a month without water.

The preferred method of attack is to find a ledge and leap down on unsuspecting targets; while the target is stunned by the attack, the rinacat will use its sharp claws and teeth to inflict a killing blow. They primarily prey on teshek and other herd animals. However, when wounded, sick or otherwise weakened, they have been known to venture down from the mountains in search of easier prey, such as Carosites. Rinacats hunt alone.

The Sudden Restoration

This huge hospital ship was named the *Sudden Restoration* only after it had already been in active service for a year. Many of its patients marvelled at "the ship which appeared suddenly in our system, and quickly began healing the sick and restoring

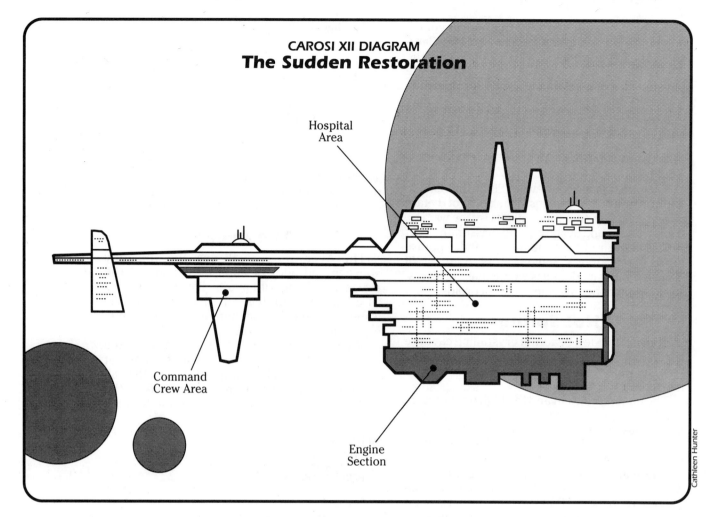

CAROSI XII DIAGRAM
The Sudden Restoration

Hospital
Area

Command
Crew Area

Engine
Section

Cathleen Hunter

the injured." The name stuck. There is talk among the Carosites of constructing more such vessels.

In a compromise with New Republic leaders, the *Sudden Restoration* has added a pair of X-wing fighter escorts, although the *Restoration's* command crew has been extremely reluctant to use them.

■ Sudden Restoration

Craft: Modified Kuat Drive Yards' Class C Frigate
Type: Modified Class C Frigate
Scale: Capital
Length: 330 meters
Skill: Capital ship piloting: C Frigate
Crew: 220, skeleton: 140/+10
Crew Skill: Capital ship piloting 3D
Passengers: 380 (medical personnel)
Cargo Capacity: 2,000 metric tons
Consumables: 1 year
Cost: Not available for sale
Hyperdrive Multiplier: x2
Hyperdrive Backup: x15
Nav Computer: Yes
Maneuverability: 1D
Space: 4
Atmosphere: 280; 800 kmh
Hull: 2D

Shields: 1D
Sensors:
  Passive: 30/0D
  Scan: 60/1D
  Search: 120/1D+2
  Focus: 4/3D

Adventure Idea

Rinacat attacks in the vicinity of the New Republic outpost have been occurring more and more frequently, claiming the lives of a number of sentries and throwing operations into disarray. Belief that it was one sick animal doing all the killings was dispelled when three rinacats were seen in the area.

The characters are hired to hunt down the offending creatures. Once in the mountains, they discover that an Imperial spy has discovered the location of the outpost and has trained rinacats to stage guerilla attacks. Both the spy and his man-eaters will have to be eliminated to ensure the security of the base.

Mike Vilardi

Adventure Idea

New Republic soldiers being treated on the *Sudden Restoration* have begun dying, all from apparently "natural causes." The characters are asked to go undercover on the ship and discover the truth.

Once there, they find to their shock that one of the Carosite physicians has been blackmailed by the Empire into acting as their agent. The New Republic soldiers are not dead, merely comatose — their coffins, shot off into space, are being recovered by an Imperial vessel and then the Republic soldiers are revived for interrogation.

Adventure Idea

The characters are hired by the Republic to go to Carosi XII and pick up some medical supplies. The supplies are to be delivered to a star system that is being blockaded by the Empire.

Once the characters arrive, they find that their mission has changed somewhat. Not only are they supposed to deliver the supplies to the planet in question, but they are also to pick up a famous surgeon wanted by the Empire, and bring him back to Carosi, without bringing the Empire along for the ride!

After the characters manage to get by the Imperial blockade and on to the planet, the characters learn that the surgeon has already been captured by the Empire, and is on a small, temporary base that the Empire has set up on the planet's moon. A rescue is called for.

To all this, the gamemaster must add the imperative that the Empire must not follow the characters back to the Carosi system lest the Empire decide to subjugate the system.

Adventure Idea

While in space, the characters receive a distress call from the *Sudden Restoration*. Apparently, someone does not respect its non-combatant nature and is attacking the vessel

Arriving at the scene, the characters find a heavily armed Corellian freighter attacking the huge ship. When the characters arrive, the ship will break off its attack and flee. The *Sudden Restoration*, bound for Carosi XII, will ask that the characters escort the hospital ship to its system.

Unknown to both vessels, the marauding freighter follows the ships to Carosi XII. The freighter is owned by a half-crazy bounty hunter/ professional killer. An Imperial official that crossed a crime boss is currently recovering on the *Restoration*. The crime boss has hired the bounty hunter to kill the official. The bounty hunter and his crew of four miscreants do not care about the hospital ship or the innocent patients on-board. They are single-mindedly focusing on killing the official.

Once the *Sudden Restoration* arrives in-system, the Imperial official is transferred to the Carosi Alpha Hospital. The bounty hunter lands several hours later and begins his search for the official by going to countless public places and trying to bribe, bully or trick anyone he can find for information.

The characters may wind up running afoul of the bounty hunter and his crew. The gamemaster must decide how successful the bounty hunter is in finding out the correct location of the target.

It is very possible that the Carosites may wish to hire the characters to serve as security for the sick official, a truly ironic twist. If this happens, the climactic scene is the successful infiltration of Alpha by the bounty hunter, ending in a battle between the hunter and his gang and the characters.

Adventure Idea

A variation of the previous, idea, a frail, sick old woman hires the characters to take her to Carosi. Unknown to them, she is a highly-placed Imperial official. Still, she bears them no ill will, for she is dying, and she only wants a less painful place to die, and the facilities on Carosi XII are ideal.

Unfortunately, a group of free-traders who are allied with the New Republic are tailing her, and will attack the characters' ship. These worthless traders are using their connections as members of the New Republic in order to do what they please.

When the characters get the old woman to Carosi XII, the free-traders will pursue and hunt them down, convinced that the characters are "Imperial stooges." They have their heart so set on committing violence that they will not stop to ask questions.

The perfect ending to this adventure would be to give the characters the opportunity to turn the free-traders in at the nearest New Republic outpost (which of course, happens to be on Carosi XII). There will be a reward for the characters for removing this blot from the Republic's reputation, plus the undying enmity of the free-traders who were thrown out. The characters may very well end up making enemies for life!

Ergeshui

Ergeshui

Type: Terrestrial swamp
Temperature: Hot
Atmosphere: Type III (breath mask required)
Hydrosphere: Moist
Gravity: Heavy
Terrain: Swamp
Length of Day: 40 standard hours
Length of Year: 380 local days
Sapient Species: Ergesh (N)
Starport: 1 limited services
Population: 800,000
Planet Function: Homeworld, biotech products
Government: Alliance of Ergesh clans and Republic representatives
Tech Level: Space
Major Exports: Biotech products, fertilizer, alcohol, textiles
Major Imports: Electronics, manufactured goods
System: Agash
Star: Agash (red giant)
Orbital Bodies:

Name	Planet Type	Moons
Ergeshui	terrestrial swamp	2

World Summary

Ergeshui, the only world in the Agash system, is a huge planet with high gravity and oppressive humidity. The rays of the red sun give an eerie crimson cast to the landscape.

Two moons circle Ergeshui. This makes for colossal tidal changes, where entire sections of the two small continents are flooded, then exposed. Due to these raging tides, there are few permanent islands exposed on the world's surface

The atmosphere on Ergeshui is composed mostly of nitrogen and carbon dioxide, and Humans on the planet must use breathing devices.

The planet is known for its plant-based products and by-products, especially fertilizer, alcoholic beverages, and textiles. In addition, the Ergesh, the dominant species on the planet, specialize in organic machines, most of them "grown" in the area called the Industrial Swampfields.

System Summary

Ergeshui is the only planet in the Agash system. Ergeshui has two moons, Magresh and Sagresh, which cause dramatic tidal changes on the planet.

The Agash system is fairly free from Imperial intervention. New Republic vessels make routine stopovers. Many free-traders put aside their revulsion at Ergesh aesthetics in order to trade for the much-prized Ergesh rum.

Ergeshui

This giant planet has two small continents. The main continent is called Ersheg, and the lesser one is named Queesh. There are few permanent islands due to the harsh tides.

The atmosphere on Ergeshui is thick and hot. On most days, thick clouds cover the skies. Despite this heavy cover, enough red sunlight filters through to give the landscape an eerie reddish cast. The temperature remains at a consistent 30 degrees Centigrade year round, day and night. Many off-worlders have remarked that the planet is like one huge greenhouse.

The most interesting natural phenomenon to be found on Ergesui are the tidal flats. Due to the prescence of the moons, there are huge variations in the tide. When the tide is out, the continents almost double in size. When the tide comes in, the exposed land is flooded. The Ergesh find this pleasant, especially since, despite their bulk and weight,

---

System Datafile

Agash system, star: Agash, red giant star. One planet only, Ergeshui. Reasonably free of Imperial influence, strong New Republic ally. Strong demand for electronics, manufactured goods. Limited service starport located adjacent to Outworlder City.

TRAVELLER'S ADVISORY: Ergeshui has a Type III atmosphere. Most species, including Humans, require breathing apparatus to survive for any length of time on the planet's surface.

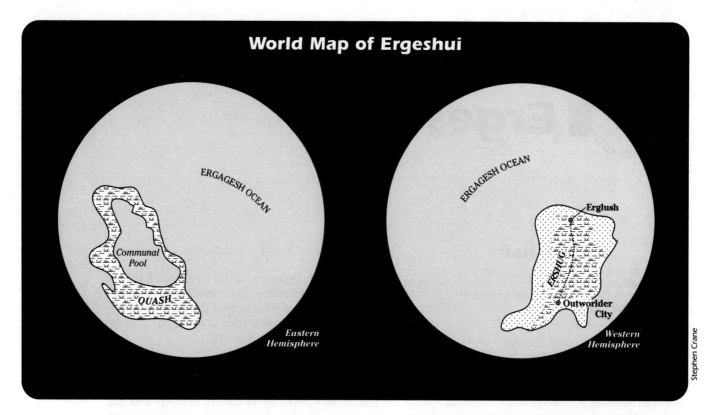

World Map of Ergeshui

ERGAGESH OCEAN

Communal Pool

QUASH

Eastern Hemisphere

ERGAGESH OCEAN

Erglush

EKSHUG

Outworlder City

Western Hemisphere

Stephen Crane

they can float. Most off-worlders find it dangerous, since the tides come roaring in at 60 kilometers per hour. The roar of the travelling water is deafening.

Any character caught in a tidal wave takes 4D of damage and must make a Difficult *swimming* check each round. Failing the check inflicts an additional 2D of damage to the character, plus a cumulative -1 penalty to additional *swimming* checks. If the character fails three checks in a row, he has drowned.

The seas of Ergeshui are composed of water, salt, and other chemical compounds. The seas are not polluted — quite the contrary, The Ergesh have taken special care to ensure they live in harmony with their environment.

Ergeshui soil is one of the planet's best-kept secrets. This soil is so laced with nutrients and minerals that it can grow and support plant life from most places in the galaxy. The Ergesh do not export this soil, as they feel that this would deplete the planet, and perhaps even pose a threat to their society.

Feeling Gravity's Pull

Characters adventuring on Ergeshui suffer a -1D penalty to all *Strength* and *Dexterity*-related actions (except for resisting damage). Characters must make one Moderate *stamina* check per round of heavy exertion. Characters who fail this check must double the amount of time they take to complete the task, or suffer a -3D penalty to all *Dexterity* and *Strength*-related actions (except resisting damage in combat).

In addition, whenever a character suffers damage from collisions or falling, an extra 2D are added to the damage.

Note that these rules are not used when characters are in Outworlder City, as it has artificially moderated standard gravity.

The Ergesh

The average Ergesh stands two meters tall and resembles a rounded heap of moving plant matter. Their bodies are covered with drooping, slimy appendages that range from two centimeters to three meters in length, and from one millimeter to five centimeters in width. Ergesh coloration is a blend of green, brown, and grey. The younger Ergesh have more green, the elders more brown. A strong smell of ammonia and rotting vegetation follows an Ergesh wherever it goes. Ergesh have a life expectancy of 200 years.

Due to their physiology, Ergesh can breathe underwater, though they do prefer "dry" land. Their thick, wet skin also acts as a strong protective layer against all manner of weapons.

Ergesh communicate using sound-based speech. Their voices sound like thick mud coming to a rapid boil. In fact, many Ergesh, especially those that deal most with Outworlders, speak Basic, though it sounds as if the speaker is talking underwater. Their grasp of Basic is good, though due to how they perceive and understand the world around them, they often omit personal pronouns (I, me) and articles (a, the).

Most small words in the Ergesh tongue are represented by vocal inflections.

Ergesh do not have faces in the accepted sense of the word. A number of the smaller tentacles are actually opticstalks, the Ergesh equivalent of eyes, while others are sensitive to sound waves.

Through the course of the average Ergesh day, a member of the species may pick up many potentially harmful microorganisms. In order to cleanse themselves, they consume kaloob, a popular refreshment among the Ergesh. Kaloob causes every gland and organ in an Ergesh body to produce excess amounts of fluids and secretions, which cleanses the body and refreshes the drinker. Note that while kaloob can be used by other species as a detoxifier and antibiotic, it produces some rather awful side effects.

If a non-Ergesh drinks kaloob, every gland, organ, and system begins to function in overdrive. Tears, sweat, and any other bodily secretion begins pouring out of their respective ducts. After 10 minutes of this, a crippling nausea strikes the victim for 20 minutes. After these tribulations, all dangerous toxins and chemicals have been purged from their systems.

Ergesh cannot get intoxicated, drugged, or poisoned by most substances. Their immune systems break down such substances quickly, then the natural secretions carry out the harmful or waste elements.

Ergesh reproduce by a special ritual. Two Ergesh each produce a seed which has their respective genetic codes. Both seeds are planted together in a special swamp called the Shoolbloorp, or "Land of Beginnings." In 20 Ergeshui days, a young Ergesh grows up from the ground, self-aware and ready to join society. Being asexual beings, Ergesh have no concept of gender. Each Ergesh may produce one seed every two Ergeshui years.

In terms of personality, Ergesh are boisterous, curious, and rather naive. They are social beings, greatly prizing friends and "family." Despite their fearsome appearance, they are not violent. Unfortunately, Ergesh have yet to become accustomed to all of the diverse species of the galaxy. To Ergesh, Humans are the "unfathomable alien species." Still, if a Human makes an effort to get to know the Ergesh species, he may find that he has made friends for life. References to gender, figures of speech, and the condition known as "dry" are lost on the Ergesh.

Ergesh personal names are long affairs, with many odd bubbling noises included. The Ergesh tolerate being given nicknames by off-worlders that they are dealing with.

Once per year, there comes a day when both moons are aligned in a certain way, with devastating effect upon the Ergesh. During this period, the Ergesh act irrational, violent, even insane. It is almost as if the Ergesh are intoxicated. This day is called the "Bad Water Pull," and all offworlders are encouraged to stay clear of the native population until the effects cease.

Ergesh definitely believe in the Force. They have heard tales of the Jedi, and are rather anxious to meet one. Since practically everything on Ergeshui is alive, the Ergesh feel that the Force is especially strong on their world.

When an Ergesh gets angry, it quakes and begins to make a sound something like gargling. They are poor combatants, with their most effective attack simply trampling over their opponents. Due to their massive bulk (an adult Ergesh weighs half a metric ton), this crude tactic is extremely effective against foes Human-sized and smaller. The major drawback of this attack is that the Ergesh must be close to his opponent to begin with, as they are not swift enough to catch a fleeing foe.

Ergesh are divided into clans, which have formed a federation that rules the planet. The eldest Ergesh from each clan is part of the governing body. This government meets monthly in the Communal Pool. The Ergesh federation keeps in regular contact with the leaders of the New Republic.

Ergesh are not hesitant about travelling into space. They wear special belts that not only produce a nitrogen field that allows them to breathe, but also retains the vast majority of their moisture. The Ergesh travel in living spaceships (see below).

When embarking on potentially dangerous expeditions, Ergesh wear a harness that holds a series of containers. In each container sits a small plant bud that produces an electrical current. When hurled at a dry opponent, the plant's current discharges and causes injury (4D damage dispersed by insulated armor). Each bud can only be used once, and an Ergesh normally carries 24 buds. Ergesh are gentle, intelligent and curious, especially about the manners and technology of offworlders. In some respects they are fearless, although much of this stems from their innocence.

Being a species which evolved in swamps, the Ergesh consider large amounts of fluid to be "natural." They prefer areas with lots of water — so much so that many other species find this everpresent liquid uncomfortable. There is no term for "dry" in their language, but there is a term for "not wet," which is used as a curse.

Concepts like manners and privacy are alien to the Ergesh; calling them "outspoken" would be an understatement. They prize life and detest that which acts against life in all its forms.

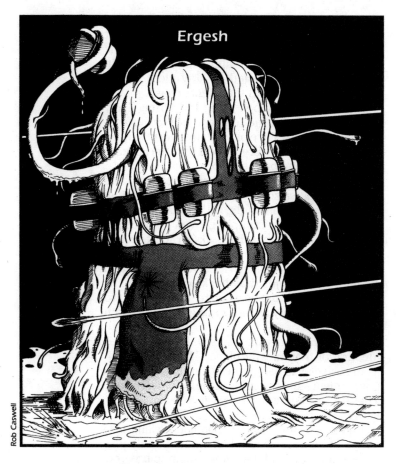

Ergesh

Rob Caswell

■ Ergesh

Attribute Dice: 12D
Attribute Minimum/Maximums:
DEXTERITY 1D/3D+2
KNOWLEDGE 2D/4D+2
MECHANICAL 2D/4D
PERCEPTION 2D+2/4D+2
STRENGTH 2D/4D
TECHNICAL 2D/4D
Special Abilities:
Body Armor: +2D to physical, +1D to energy
Move: 6/10
Size: 1.5–2.1 meters

Ergesh Society

In their dealings with each other, Ergesh are honest and fair. Theirs is a society with no classes, no discrimination, no wants. There is no crime among the Ergesh. Property is a communal thing, to be shared each according to his own need.

This utopian situation quickly breaks down when off-worlders are placed into the equation. Ergesh are often taken advantage of by unscrupulous off-worlders, but fortunately, there are usually New Republic agents around to undo the damage, or more travelled Ergesh able to come to the aid of their naive kinfolk.

Ergesh do not use money, but instead rely on a barter system. The only place credits are used (or even accepted) is Outworlder City.

Ergesh Techology

Ergesh machinery is a fusion of plant matter and manufactured materials. This equipment cannot be deprived of moisture for more than one standard hour, or it ceases to function properly. The Ergesh have their own versions of comlinks, hand computers, and an odd device known as a sensory intensifer, which serves the Ergesh in the same way that macrobinoculars serve Humans.

The Ergesh Starjumper

The Starjumper is an organic vessel, resembling a huge brown cylinder 30 meters wide, with long green tentacles trailing from the hull. The Starjumpers are biologically-engineered creatures, not life-forms native to Ergeshui. The tentacles act as navigational, fire control, and communications appendages for the ship-creature. This versatile vessel is able to make planetary landings.

All Starjumpers are sentient, thinking creatures whose huge bulks can survive the harsh rigors of space. In fact, the Ergesh and the Starjumpers share a symbiotic relationship. The ship derives sustenance from the Ergesh's bodies, and the Ergesh get to where they are going. Most Starjumpers have unique personalities, and are treated by the Ergesh as trusted friends or clan members.

Starjumpers have the ability to self-repair battle damage. Consider the ship to be a character, and allow it natural healing rolls, except that it may only perform this action (and no other) once every three hours.

The interior of a Starjumper is covered in a layer of muck. The Ergesh control the ship by touching their tentacles to certain areas of the ship, which causes particular systems to activate.

Ships cannot reproduce. Instead, they are "grown" in the tidal flats. It takes six months to "grow" a Starjumper.

Starjumpers are useful for exploration and trade, but are too fragile to be used as blockade-runners or fighting ships. Unfortunately, the ships are useless to Humans and their associated species as only an Ergesh can manipulate the controls.

In addition, the Starjumpers have a nasty tendency to be quite argumentative. They dislike combat, and even show a marked reluctance to visit certain planets where they have had bad experiences.

■ Starjumper

Craft: Ergesh Starjumper
Type: Customized biological vessel
Scale: Starfighter
Length: 200 meters
Skill: Space transports
Crew: 50, gunners: 5, skeleton: 30/+10

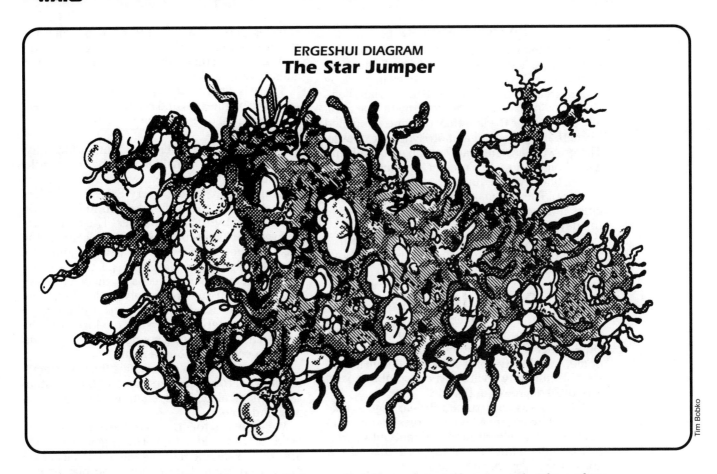

ERGESHUI DIAGRAM
The Star Jumper

Tim Bobko

Crew Skill: Space transports 4D, starship gunnery 4D+1
Passengers: 30
Cargo Capacity: 400 metric tons
Consumables: 6 months
Cost: Not available for sale
Hyperdrive Multiplier: x6
Hyperdrive Backup: x22
Nav Computer: Yes
Maneuverability: 1D
Space: 2
Atmosphere: 225; 650 kmh
Hull: 3D
Shields: 2D
Sensors:
   Passive: 30/1D
   Scan: 40/2D
   Search: 50/2D+2
   Focus: 4/3D
Weapons:
  Electrical Beam
   Fire Arc: Front
   Crew: 5
   Skill: Starship gunnery
   Fire Control: 2D+2
   Space Range: 1-3/7/10
   Atmosphere Range: 100-300/700/1 km
   Damage: 5D

Erglush

The capital city of Ergeshui is Erglush, located on the continent of Ersheg. In fact, Erglush is one of the few cities on the planet.

Buildings average 40 meters in height, and are composed of mud and other organic matter. The two favorite architectural designs are tall columns or squat pyramids, with no doors but plenty of window openings.

Buildings of Ergesh design are either solitary living creatures or an amalgam of symbiotic life forms. No doors are needed because the buildings know who they belong to. Each Ergesh has a specific tentacle/stalk configuration unique in the same way as human fingerprints, and Ergesh buildings can tell members of the species apart. Ergesh buildings have ramps instead of stairs — indeed, stairs are unheard of, and there is no such word in the native language.

Off-worlders are permitted to visit Erglush, but the vast majority prefer Outworlder City, which is connected to Erglush by the Living Monorail.

Erglush is also home to the Industrial Swampfields, located on the outskirts where the tidal flats begin. These huge fields are used to grow the organic machines that power Ergesh society. One entire section is devoted to the growing of Starjumper organic spaceships. The Industrial Swampfields produce products around the clock, and are constantly manned by over 2,000 Ergesh workers and farmers.

The Living Monorail

This transportation system consists of two huge vines, each stretching from Erglush to Outworlder City. Both vines are fixed in place by root systems, which also serve to nourish them. On each vine is a bean-shaped growth that actually slides along the length of the vine, propelled by methane gases and a photosynthetic charge. The growths are the "cars" of the monorail, and each holds up to 40 Ergesh (for counting purposes, one Ergesh equals two Human-sized passengers). The cars make the run between the two cities in four hours. Thus, every fourth hour of the day, a car leaves both cities.

Passage on the Monorail is free. The trip is non-stop. The cars are living entities that move by instinct.

Outworlder City

This area is also called Dry Ground, Safe At Last, Sanity, and, in the Ergesh tongue, Oorlglush. Outworlder City is protected by a transparent dome, and climate-controlled to maintain a comfortable humidity level and a constant temperature of 20 degrees Centigrade.

The city was constructed 30 years ago to take care of off-worlders who visit Ergeshui and cannot tolerate the climate and the land. Outworlder City is built on huge metal supports that raise it above the soggy terrain.

The starport, such as it is, is located just outside the dome, where a mechanical monorail shuttles people back and forth. Expanding the starport is the next thing on the Ergesh agenda.

At any given time, Outworlder City has 50,000 aliens living, working, playing, and resting within it. There is a permanent staff of 5,000 aliens who work the businesses and run the services. There is a perpetual quest for more workers, and the pay is good.

Very few Ergesh ever enter Outworlder City, as most of them consider it to be too sterile. Plasticrete sidewalks, metal walkways, and stairs are things that almost every Ergesh considers offensive. Still, there is an Ergesh Relations Office, staffed by 10 of the natives. The building is an Ergeshui living construct and is located at the base of the dome, where it can tap into the "healthy" soil of the planet just past the shield.

The New Republic keeps a small embassy staffed with 30 Humans in Outworlder City. They have the necessary equipment to communicate with ships entering the system or close to it. The head of the embassy is a young man named Arvin Tadle, a competent bureaucrat.

Outworlder City also contains the usual facilities so vital to spacefarers, such as bars, restaurants, medical facilities, equipment shops, casinos, and hotels.

Weaponry is tough to purchase on Ergeshui, even in Outworlder City. The Ergesh weapons are not for sale, and the only weapons that can be purchased are melee weapons and blaster pistols. One needs a license for the latter.

Mike Vilardi

Several galactic corporations have offices in the City, especially those that aspire to purchase harvesting rights to some of Ergeshui's flora. Unfortunately, not all of these companies have the best interests of the Ergesh in mind.

The Communal Pool

Located on the smaller continent of Quesh, this is a great, miry swamp pool with especially heavy vegetation. The swamp is flooded with the Ergesh equivalent of water, four meters deep. Several odd columns of plant life, arranged in a geometric pattern, mark this spot. The Pool is the Ergesh equivalent of a governmental meeting hall. Every month, the heads of all of the clans gather at the Communal Pool for a continuous 40 hour meeting, in which all planetary business is conducted.

There are 80 clans, each with about 10,000 members. Each clan leader, the eldest Ergesh in the group, brings one Ergesh as an aide and ceremonial security guard.

Travelling From Ersheg to Quesh

Intercontinental travel is achieved by huge airships, much like dirigibles. The air sac is made up of giant plant spores attached to each other. A gondola made of hardened mud and plant matter is attached to the underside of the air sac. The gondola can hold 20 Ergesh, the Human equivalent, or a combination of the two.

The airships run from Erglush to the Communal Pool. The trip takes 20 hours, with one airship departing each point every 20 hours. Intercontinental travel is not in heavy demand. Only when the clan leaders get together is there heavy air traffic, as extra airships are added to handle the increased demand.

Creatures of Ergeshui

Swamp Skimmer (Garalalesh)

"Swamp skimmers" are one of the more dangerous hazards of Ergeshui. They swim silently through the muck and waters of the swamps waiting for unwary beings to pass by. They are immense reptilian creatures with immense mouths. They try to swallow prey whole (they need to beat the difficulty number by 10 or more points to do this).

■ **Swamp Skimmer**
Type: Swamp predator
DEXTERITY 5D
PERCEPTION 2D
Sneak 5D
STRENGTH 6D
Special Abilities:

Armor: +2D physical, +1D energy
Bite: Strength damage, but if attack succeeds by 10 or more points, prey is swallowed whole
Move: 14 (swimming)
Size: Up to 3 meters long
Scale: Creature

Muckworms (Garool)

Muckworms are the deadly enemies of Ergesh as they are one of the few creatures on the planet that pose a threat to the aliens. They are vicious predators that hunt in groups of three to eight creatures; they are home in water and on land. Once they have successfully bitten a target, they will drain fluids from the target, causing an additional 2D damage every round they do so.

■ **Muckworms**
Type: Carnivorous worms
DEXTERITY 3D
PERCEPTION 2D
STRENGTH 6D
Special Abilities:
Bite: Only causes 4D damage, but causes 2D damage every additional round by draining fluids. After a muckworm has clamped onto a victim, the victim must make a successful opposed *Strength* roll to pull the muckworm free.
Move: 19 (crawling and swimming)
Size: Up to 2 meters long
Scale: Creature

Nemats

Nemats are flying insects known for the shrill nature of their buzz and their agonizingly painful sting. They generally prey on small swamp creatures, but swarms of up to 100 insects have been known to attack Ergesh and aliens.

■ **Nemat**
Type: Insects
DEXTERITY 6D
PERCEPTION 1D
STRENGTH 1D
Special Abilities:
Bite: STR+1D damage
Move: 9 (flying)
Size: 25 centimeters long, 50 centimeter wingspan
Scale: Creature

Adventure Idea

Imperial agents have been smuggled into the swamps of Ergesh, with orders to carry out a deadly research project: an effort to breed a larger, more vicious version of the nemat. It is believed that a swarm of such creatures would be sufficient to drive away the Humans staffing the New Republic's embassy and leave the planet wide open for Imperial takeover (after, of course, the bugs were eradicated by aerial spraying).

Such a scheme, if successful, could result in the enslavement of the Ergesh and the destruction of their fragile ecosystem. The characters must find a way to stop the Imperial scientists before their experiment goes too far.

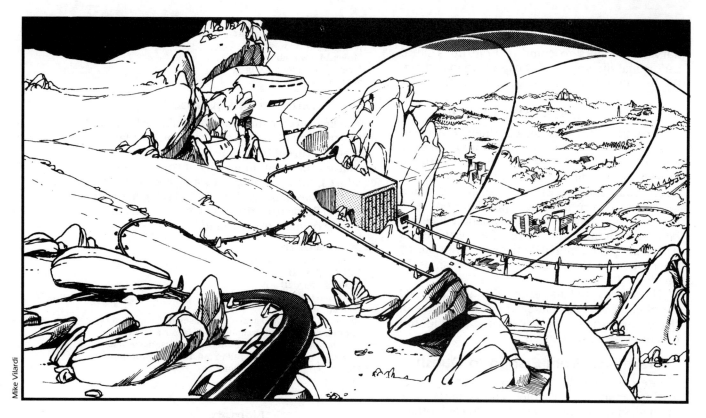

Mike Vilardi

Adventure Idea

A team of mercenaries has recently arrived on Ergesh. Their plan: steal the secrets of the Starjumper, along with a few Ergesh, and deliver the vessel to a wealthy "collector" who wants to add the ship as an oddity in his private holdings.

It is up to the characters to stop the mercs before they succeed in escaping off-planet with their captives.

Adventure Idea

Large portions of the population of Erglush are being ravaged by a mysterious disease that causes their bodies to dehydrate, inevitably bringing death. Ergesh scientists have discovered that the only possible cure lies in the genetic structure of the muckworm, necessitating the characters' travelling into the swamp to capture some of the creatures.

Unfortunately, not everyone wants them to be successful. A traitorous Ergush, in the employ of the Imperials, pursues them, sabotaging their equipment and attempting to leave them at the mercy of the swamp.

Adventure Idea

The New Republic embassy tracked something that crashed on the continent of Ersheg, but they are not sure what it was. Due to its trajectory, they do not believe it was a natural object. Impact point is near the halfway mark of the Living Monorail. The party is asked to investigate. A monorail plant car will be conditioned to stop at the halfway point for the characters, and another will be by four hours later to pick them up. The ride from Outworlder City to the halfway point takes two hours.

The object in question is a TIE fighter from the Star Destroyer *Dark Nebula*, the latter on a raid mission. The fighter was disabled and forced to make a crash landing on Ergeshui. The crash site is an hour's march from the monorail dropoff point.

The pilot is still alive and is effecting repairs to his craft and its distress beacon. He is desperately trying to call in help from his squadron comrades. The pilot will fix his distress beacon in a few hours. Help will arrive in the form of TIE fighters, a few hours after the call goes out.

If the pilot is captured alive, it is possible for the characters to get information out of him about the Star Destroyer's planned raid on a neighboring star system under New Republic control, to take place two days from now.

If the characters approach the New Republic embassy with this information, they will be informed that there are no Republic ships in the area, and their communications equipment does not have the range to reach past the system. The New Republic will suggest that the characters try to outrun the Destroyer and reach the system to warn them.

Adventure Idea

Loprana Soil-Enrichers is a corporation with branch offices on many planets, some Imperial, some New Republic, some neutral. Loprana has an office in Outworlder City, and it is a representative from that office that calls the characters in order to hire them.

The executives from Loprana want a team to investigate the Industrial Swampfields and take holo footage of the operations. Note that the executive will attempt to recruit the characters almost as soon as they land. Loprana wants to get a group of off-worlders who have not yet had much exposure to the Ergesh, so the corporation can feed the visitors propaganda about the Ergesh, as well as passing themselves off as the characters' best allies on the planet.

The New Republic embassy has their eyes on Loprana, since they know how unscrupulous that particular corporation is. They will assign four agents to tail the party. Once the agents see the party taking shots of the Swampfields, they will confront them and attempt an arrest, bringing along several Ergesh to make the whole procedure official.

The characters will have to convince the agents that they were unaware of Loprana's duplicity. In order to clear their names, the characters may have to be part of a sting operation to nab Loprana's executives in the act. This will be highly dangerous, since it is common knowledge that Loprana has hired muscle to keep their offices safe and their informants honest.

Adventure Idea

An Imperial plot is afoot to destroy the clan heads when they meet at the Communal Pool. The Empire has hired a bounty hunter and provided him with a specially engineered poison which can overwhelm even the amazing Ergesh immune system. The bounty hunter has a gang of five outlaws.

The bounty hunter arrives at the Outworlder City starport in his light freighter and begins asking the right people questions about Ergesh habits. The bounty hunter has three airspeeders to help him and his men to get around, and to carry the poison.

Adventure Idea

An Imperial sympathizer was discovered in Outworlder City and has escaped. He stole a landspeeder and roared off to the north. The characters are hired by the New Republic to bring him back. They are provided with a landspeeder.

The sympathizer is following the Living Monorail trail north to the city of Erglush. Since he is a recent arrival on the planet, he is unaware of what the capital city holds. Once he arrives at Erglush, he will realize his mistake and continue north, unaware that he is riding on a tidal flat that will soon be flooded.

Among suggested hazards/encounters for the characters are: swamp skimmers, Ergesh parties out for a stroll, and tidal shifts. As an extra wrinkle, the sympathizer could have friends lurking in the tidal flats with a light freighter. He is supposed to rendezvous with them so that they may get him off the planet.

Fyodos

Fyodos

Type: Temperate Forest
Temperature: Temperate
Atmosphere: Type I (breathable)
Hydrosphere: Moderate
Gravity: Standard
Terrain: Forest, grasslands, mountains
Length of Day: 20 standard hours
Length of Year: 360 local days
Sapient Species: Humans, Galidyns (N)
Starport: Landing field
Population: 200,000
Planet Function: Homeworld
Government: Tribal
Tech Level: Feudal
Major Exports: None
Major Imports: None
System: Tatrang
Star: Tatran (red giant)
Orbital Bodies:

Name	Planet Type	Moons
Tatrang I	desolate searing rock	0
Tatrang II	desolate searing rock	0
Tatrang III	poisonous jungle	3
Fyodos	temperate forest	3
Tatrang V	desolate mountainous	2
Tatrang VI	gas giant	23
Tatrang VII	gas giant	11
Tatrang VIII	asteroid belt	0

World Summary

Fyodos is a world of faded glory, a retrograde culture that has toppled from the apex of high technology into the dark abyss of barbarism and technophobia. The people of Fyodos are a proud, strong people, adhering to a strict warrior code and tribal customs.

The Fyodoi hatred of technology stems from a devastating war called the "Great Cleansing." Their great cities lie in ruins, many with technological artifacts hidden within them, but such areas are strictly taboo.

Fyodos has three moons, Lifemoon, Deathmoon and Warmoon. The latter is home to an old, abandoned pre-Cleansing base.

The planet and its system were mapped by the Empire, but the planet was judged to be too troublesome for purposes of base construction. Fyodos' location has no strategic value, nor is it on a major trade route. The Empire did not even bother naming the planet nor its moons. Only the star was given a name to facilitate mapping. The term "backwater" planet has shown up on every Imperial scouting report for Fyodos. The massive asteroid belt on the outer limits of the system is a navigational hazard.

System Summary

Tatrang IV, otherwise known as Fyodos, is the only habitable planet in the Tatrang system. It has three moons, their real names lost in the Great Cleansing, and they are now called Lifemoon, Deathmoon and Warmoon. The people of Fyodos, centered on the continent of Tharak, are barbaric and superstitious.

On Deathmoon and in the mountains of Tharak on Fyodos, twin energy pulses go off at eight-hour intervals. These are the automated beacon systems of the two remaining bases in the Fyodos system.

Tatrang I-III are commercially worthless. Tatrang V has rich ore deposits never touched by the ancient Fyodoi. Tatrang VI and VII are ringed gas giants with little economic value. The asteroid belt surrounding the system contains trace minerals. The largest asteroid is big enough to hold a small scout base.

Getting Into the System

The asteroid belt around the Tatrang system is a treacherous navigational hazard. In order for a

System Datafile

Tatrang system, star: Tatrang, red star. One terrestrial planet, Fyodos. Imperial astrocatalog designation Tatrang IV. Low-tech retrograde-Human population, no known strategic resources. Mapping and exploration of planet incomplete. No known Imperial installations to date. No known political inclination.

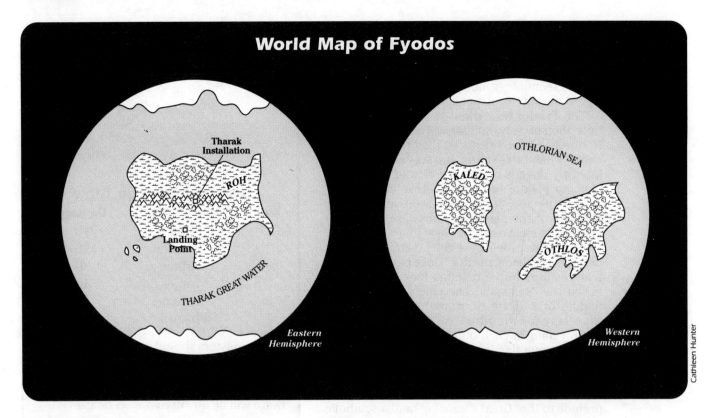

World Map of Fyodos

Tharak Installation

ROH

Landing Point

THARAK GREAT WATER

Eastern Hemisphere

OTHLORIAN SEA

KALED

OTHLOS

Western Hemisphere

Cathleen Hunter

ship to get through, an appropriate piloting roll must be made. The number of these rolls required, as well as the difficulty of the task, is determined by the speed of the vessel as it travels through the belt. The slower the ship goes, the easier it is to avoid asteroids and other debris. The gamemaster should ask the pilot's player how fast he intends to go.

It is also possible for a ship to come to a complete stop while in the belt. For every five minutes spent "on station" in the belt, the pilot must make a Moderate piloting roll.

Failing a piloting roll while passing through the asteroid field means an asteroid has hit the ship. Roll 1D and consult the Asteroid Damage Table to determine exact damage. All damage listings are for starfighter scale. If the pilot fails the piloting roll by more than 10, add a +1 to the Asteroid Damage Table roll.

Fyodos

The planet Fyodos has three major continents, Roh, Kaled and Othlos, along with several scattered islands. Only Roh contains any remnant of the humanoid race known as the Fyodoi.

Kaled and Othlos are overgrown into huge wildernesses, dominated by vast forests. Forests are also a frequent feature on Roh, but the presence of the Fyodoi has created a demand for wood for houses, fuel and such, leading to the clearing of more and more land.

Average temperature on Fydos is 20 degrees Centigrade in the daytime and five degrees at night. These temperatures run 20 percent higher in summer months and 20 percent lower in winter months.

In terms of fauna, Fyodos is a haven for predators, grazers, scavengers and birds.

Faded Glory

Centuries ago, the planet Fyodos was home to a technologically advanced culture. The Fyodoi had a thriving space program, having explored their own moons and their nearest neighboring world, Tatrang V.

The three continents of Fyodos were each populated by a race of Humans of similar technological level but widely disparate philosophical beliefs. Though they sometimes cooperated, relationships between the various groups could best be described as strained.

Tensions eventually reached such a point that war broke out between the three lands. The battles escalated until weapons of mass destruction were brought to bear — so thorough was the devastation that the war came to be known as the "Great Cleansing." The cities and entire populations of Kaled and Othlos were wiped out and the third continent, Roh, suffered 90 percent casualties. Its cities, too, suffered grievous damage.

Survivors made a point of avoiding the ruined cities, fearful that they might somehow still harbor enemies capable of strikes. Instead, the refugees wadered off and began living on what little uncontaminated land remained.

Years turned to decades, and then to centuries. The people regressed, coming to shun technology, which was seen as the cause of the Cleansing. It became taboo to approach or touch any form of technology more complex than that produced during the planet's medieval period.

The Fyodoi now dwell in stone and thatch huts, their society built around a tribal structure. Nature has slowly restored the other two continents to habitable status, and they are now populated by dozens of species of wildlife. The remaining Fyodoi have no interest in travelling across the sea, and in fact the overwhelming majority of the people are unaware that other continents even exist.

Each tribe is led by a chief, with the largest extant group being the Roh. Once per season, the tribal leaders gather together for a sacred ritual called the "summat." The chiefs gather in the middle of a circle of straw huts constructed especially for the ritual. All of the chiefs then begin yelling at each other, spouting gibberish, and continue this for four hours. At the end of that time, the chiefs rise up and set all but one of the huts aflame.

What the chiefs are doing is reenacting the prelude to the "Great Cleansing" and a symbolic version of the war itself. After this is done, the chiefs have a great feast, and talk about tribal concerns.

Every tribe also has a shaman. The title of shaman is hereditary. Each shaman teaches his son the secrets of the tribe. The greatest tribal secret is the fact that each tribe settled around a pre-Cleansing supply dump. As the people fled the great cities, they found refuge in shelters that contained food, equipment and weaponry. The only supplies now left are hundreds of thousands of rounds of slugthrower ammunition. Slugthrowing weapons are the only pieces of advanced equipment the Fyodoi are allowed to carry by tribal law, a special dispensation made so that the tribes could defend themselves from predators (in essence, the shamans are ammunition supply officers).

Once every six months, the shaman of the Roh tribe makes a solitary pilgrimage to the still-functioning Tharak military installation. There he utters incantations and presses certain buttons and levers in a sequence handed down through the generations. What the shaman is actually doing is resetting a pre-Cleansing "doomsday weapon" with a six-month time cycle. Were the countdown allowed to reach zero, the thrice-daily energy pulse sent to Deathmoon would be cut off, triggering the launching sequence for literally hundreds of atomic missiles, which would impact around the planet, almost certainly completely poisoning the world.

Visitors to Fyodos are most likely to encoun-

Asteroid Field Travel Table

Speed	Difficulty
1–2	Very Easy
3	Easy
4	Moderate
5–6	Difficult
7*	Very Difficult

Asteroid Damage Table

Roll	Asteroid Size	Damage
1	Tiny	1D
2	Small	2D
3–4	Medium	3D
5	Large	4D
6	Very Large	7D
7	Shipwreck*	8D

*Gamemasters should determine the exact nature of the wreck, including how much of the ship in still intact and whether or not any cargo is salvageable. In all likelihood, there will be no survivors on board.

ter the Roh tribe, led by Kalor. He has a wife, Alyak, and two sons, Dubeh and Meerak. The Roh shaman is named Tseeach. In a pouch on his belt is a high-tech device, a receiver which emits a high-pitched hum if the silent alarm at the Tharak installation should be tripped. Tseeah's son, Erloi, is in training to become shaman someday.

Tseeah's hut is always guarded by a Fyodoi warrior. Within are old technical manuals, detailing the repair and maintenance of electronic equipment and slugthrowers.

Average Fyodoi. *Dexterity 3D, brawling parry 4D, dodge 5D, firearms 3D+2, melee combat 7D, melee parry 6D, missile weapons 5D, Knowledge 2D, survival 5D, Mechanical 2D, beast riding 4D+1, Perception 1D, bargain 2D, hide 5D, sneak 2D, sneak 5D, Strength 3D, brawling 7D, climbing/ jumping 5D, lifting 6D, stamina 7D, swimming 6D, Technical 1D.* Move: 10. Slugthrower (3D+1), spear (STR+1D+1), knife (STR+1D).

Fyodoi usually hunt in groups of five. The average Fyodoi is loud, boisterous, narrow-minded, stubborn and a born warrior. They are friendly to those who show them friendship and formidable enemies to any who dare attack them.

It is ironic that the Fyodoi blame technology for their demise, when it is quite clear to even the most casual observer that the Fyodoi tendency to launch themselves enthusiastically into combat is in large part to blame for their plight. Their racial memories are apparently strong, however — though it is

Mike Vilardi

permitted for tribe members to fight amongst themselves given sufficient provocation, war with other tribes is expressly forbidden.

Landing Point

The remains of a starport, with nothing more than a single runway extant, lies 14 kilometers north of the Roh village. An underground transponder still broadcasts a signal intermittently. Any ship which approaches the planet will pick up the signal, which is a variant of the accepted landing field signal. Any vessel's nav systems can be used to determine the source of the signal.

The landing point is always patrolled by 2D Fyodoi, who are unaware of its significance, but post guards as one of many timeless traditional ceremonies.

Fyodoi Customs/Trade

Fyodoi are expert hunters and blacksmiths. They are usually clad in armor made of hides and tanned leather and they carry spears, bows and arrows, daggers, swords and slugthrower pistols.

The various tribes enjoy trading with each other. Any off-worlders who arrive (courtesy of the landing point) will find the Fyodoi to be enthusiastic traders. They particularly covet intoxicants and will always be willing to trade for such substances. Trades involving weapons or ammunition must be conducted with the shaman. While the average Fyodoi understands how to load, aim and fire a slugthrower, they all believe that the shaman makes the "magic metal

stingers" by some holy ritual.

In point of fact, a precious few off-worlders have landed on Fyodos and conducted trade with the planet's residents. However, the traders' accounts of a planet with huge, flying lizards (the Galidyn) and men chasing them with primitive swords have been dismissed as tall tales.

Justice among the Fyodoi, for crimes such as breaking taboos, stealing, etc. is trial by combat, usually a sword duel over a fiery pit. Occasionally, offenders are tossed into caverns inhabited by carnivorous beasts.

Taboos include going to a technology spot, entering a shaman's home unbidden, offering to the Fyodoi or using in their presence any sort of advanced technology (except slugthrower firearms). Things which cause offense but are not considered taboo include talking about the benefits of high-tech equipment or openly displaying such artifacts.

The sight of aliens does not bother the Fyodoi, though if the alien is reptilian in appearance, there may be some initial suspicion of his intentions (due to the Galidyns). Droids are regarded as demons and will be attacked immediately, as will any who accompany them (no doubt thralls of the creature).

The Fyodoi cannot comprehend the concept of a huge galactic war. They will not choose sides, New Republic or Imperial. Rather, the Fyodoi wish to be left alone so they can hunt, fish, make weapons and kill Galidyn.

Fyodoi written language can be considered obscure for purposes of comprehension.

The Force and the Fyodoi

If any character uses the Force in front of a Fyodoi, the tribesman will consider the character to be some sort of deity. While this may seem amusing at first, it will turn deadly serious when the tribe insists on keeping the deity in their camp forever. And they are just as willing to worship a dead deity as a live one.

The Moons of Fyodos

The three moons, Lifemoon, Deathmoon and Warmoon, all go through normal lunar cycles. According to the Fyodoi, battles are best fought when Warmoon is full. This includes hunting the Galidyn. When Deathmoon is full, superstitious fear grips the tribes (this can be explained, in part, by the fact that, when full, this particular satellite resembles the withered face of a corpse.) A full Lifemoon means parties, marriages and coming-of-age tests. The Fyodoi even seem less fearful of the Galidyn at this time and spend less energy hunting the creatures.

All of the moons are airless chunks of rock, with very little in the way of minerals or other resources. They are devoid of life.

When the moons come into conjunction, a unique gravitational flux is created. This has the effect of agitating the upper atmosphere of Fyodos, producing an aurora borealis effect. This also causes interference with sensors and communications for up to 20 hours.

The biggest event in Fyodoi culture coincides with the conjunction of all three moons, which takes place once every 190 days. The event is called "the Gathering," and features a huge feast attended by all the chiefs and shamans, along with at least 100 members of each tribe. Tests of skill and combat prowess are featured, as well as children's rites of passage into adulthood. The Gathering's commencement is signalled by the aurora borealis that marks the lunar conjunction.

The Tharak Installation

The Tharak installation once served as an orbital control site, monitoring and routing space traffic. Hidden inside a mountain, most of the installation's lightpanels, environmental controls and other machinery still functions. The signal beacon is located at the mountain's peak. Unauthorized intrusion into the installation triggers a silent alarm and a signal relayed to a device carried by the shaman. The shaman will bring the chief and 20 men with him to investigate, as the alarm means that a great taboo has been broken.

There are any number of tools and spare parts here which can be salvaged for use by the characters, including power cells for energy weapons and ammunition for slugthrowers. The installation also comes equipped with comfortable barracks, med facilities and communications gear, which gives evidence of the existence of a base on Deathmoon.

The most amazing thing here is the holo-globe of the planet. This two-meter-wide hologram also shows the exact location of the three moons. Small points of light represent the Tharak installation, the Deathmoon base, the landing strip, the player characters' ship and any other vessel in orbit, all in their correct positions.

The Galidyn have no understanding of what the installation was used for, but they watch over it once the shaman leaves. Because they have a poor understanding of Fyodoi technology (despite the advanced nature of their own devices), they have been unable to decipher the nature of the base. This place is a very likely spot for visitors to meet a Galidyn.

Report from Imperial Scout XX-298-B

Upon achieving orbit around the only habitable planet in the Tatrang system, I immediately began performing the necessary geo/bio surveys. After a few hours, a blip of energy showed up on the primary continent, followed by what seemed to be a response blip from the second largest moon.

I brought my ship to a landing on the moon and found little more than a small observation base, abandoned of all life. I was unable to penetrate the lower levels of the base, but huge power generators, inactive at the time, were detected by my scanners.

Making a landing on the planet, I was amazed to find a squad of primitive men brandishing archaic melee weapons. They seemed agitated at my presence, with their anger specifically directed at my equipment. After dispatching them, I investigated the other base and found an automated communications relay station.

It is my belief that the planet cataloged as Fyodos was once home to a technologically advanced society, which somehow collapsed over the course of time. In my opinion, the Empire has no use for such a place.

I was not sure if I should include this, but when I got back into my ship and took off, I had a near collision with a huge flying lizard. There must have been some actual damage done to the ship's external audio receptors, because it appeared that the lizard turned to me and said, "Terribly sorry, my fault!"

FYODOS DIAGRAM
Ruh Village

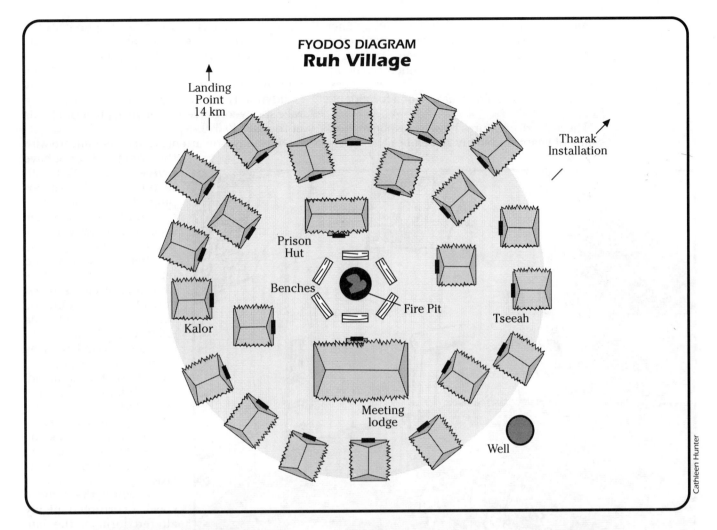

Landing
Point
14 km

Tharak
Installation

Prison
Hut

Benches

Fire Pit

Kalor

Tseeah

Meeting
lodge

Well

Cathleen Hunter

Deathmoon Base

This small base on Deathmoon was built to accomodate 24 soldiers. Besides communications dishes, sensor arrays and telescopes, the base contains enough equipment to make the base the equivalent of a limited services starport. Of course, the base is abandoned, but in excellent shape, since there are no natural forces to produce wear and tear. The base is still functional, and all energy and environmental controls are in working order. There is even fuel still in storage.

Characters must make a Difficult _security_ roll to be able to enter the base's lower levels. Once in these levels, they may learn of the missiles in the base.

Accessing the base computer gives an account of the staff's indecision regarding whether or not to return to Fyodos during the crisis, stay put on the base, or even strike out for other planets. During the Cleansing, they received orders to launch the missiles, but in light of the overwhelming carnage they had witnessed, couldn't bring themselves to launch the attack.

Eventually, some left for the planet (and were subsequently incinerated). After the war ended, it initially appeared that no one on Fyodos had survived. Thus the personnel remaining on Deathmoon abandoned the base for other worlds.

The computer also contains records regarding the missiles present on the moon. Getting that information out is a Difficult _computer programming/repair_ skill roll. The missile silos are located in a crevasse 10 kilometers northwest of the base. The crevasse is eight kilometers deep, but not wide enough to hold anything larger than a light freighter.

The Galidyn

Galidyn are huge, scaly lizards with small prehensile forepaws. Though most Galidyn are about five meters long with a 10-meter wingspan, some specimens grow to only two meters in length, with a four-meter wingspan. Possessed of keen intellects and great curiosity, Galidyns prize ideas and discussion above all else, though every once in a while they "go native" and prey on some of Fyodos' wandering herd animals.

As a rule, the average Galidyn would rather launch into an analysis of Fyodoi combat tactics than actually fight them. However, their keen intelligence and impressive vocabulary should not be considered a sign of physical weakness. When angered, a Galidyn makes for a formidable foe.

These lizard creatures have a lifespan of thousands of years, and many remember the "Great Cleansing," at least well enough to appreciate the irony of that name. The Galidyn avoided the deadly weaponry of the Fyodoi through natural underground shelters not known by the Fyodoi and hibernating for a good century or two. Many Galidyn still perished, but the vast majority of the race survived. Current Galidyn population stands at roughly 40,000.

Nowadays, all attempts to communicate with the primitive Fyodoi have proven futile. With all records of their past expunged, the Fyodoi consider the Galidyn to be heinous, technology-worshipping monsters. In truth, the Galidyn feel sorrow and pity for the Fyodoi, but realize that attempts to re-educate them would be wasted, at least under the current conditions.

When a Galidyn takes flight, it is a majestic thing, indeed. To the paranoid, superstitious Fyodoi, the sight of a flying Galidyn is a terrifying omen of death.

The Galidyn speak the same language as the Fyodoi, except that the lizards speak it in its purest form, while the Fyodoi speak a corrupted, highly altered form of the language. A Galidyn who tries to speak to a Fyodoi runs the risk of having the Human understand only a few of the lizard's words and misconstrue the intent of the conversation (perhaps seeing it as an attempt to lure the Human to his doom).

Galidyns have underground complexes, complete with many technological devices. These communities are located in the mountain ranges north of the Roh village.

The Galidyn reproduce by laying one egg every century. Each young is cared for by its immediate family, then educated in the Galidyn "school system," usually by an elder Galidyn

Mike Vilardi

who teaches history, hunting, mathematics, language, aerodynamics, computers and medicine. The species has a participatory democracy and all Galidyn who complete their instruction successfully can participate.

The Imperials remain unaware of the presence of Galidyn on the planet. When initial probes and scouting parties landed on Fyodos, the Galidyn hid themselves and used their sensor-jamming equipment to avoid detection. The only encounters between Imperials and Galidyn have been accidental in nature, and written off by the Empire as hysteria-induced fiction on the part of their personnel.

Galidyn

Rob Caswell

■ Galidyn

Attribute Dice: 16D
Attribute Minimum/Maximums:
DEXTERITY 2D/5D
KNOWLEDGE 2D/4D+2
MECHANICAL 1D/3D
PERCEPTION 3D/5D
STRENGTH 3D/6D+2
TECHNICAL 1D/4D
Special Skills:
Strength skills:
Flight. Time to use: one round. This is the skill Galidyns use to fly. They begin with a flying speed of 35 and may improve their flying speed as described on page 15 of *Star Wars: The Roleplaying Game, Second Edition.*
Special Abilities:
Armor: +1D energy and physical
Fangs: Do STR+2D damage
Story Factors:
Mistaken Identity: The Humans on Fyodos think the Galidyns are treacherous monsters.
Move: 12/15 (walking), 35/45 (flying)
Size: Up to 5 meters long

Galidyn Society

The average Galidyn community is comprised of a few hundred beings. The communities are located at least one kilometer below the planet's surface, and consist of caverns filled with lightpanels, electronic gear, security alarm systems, environmental control systems, geothermal power plants, fungus parks, and living quarters made of refined metal and plastics. Several communities are often united to form a city. Average Galidyn population in one of these cities at any given time is about 5,000.

There are eight cities, each ruled by a Galidyn whose title is "Steward." The closest city to the Roh tribe has a Steward named Ssseeeeseetek, a 4,000-year-old Galidyn who is clearly the oldest, strongest and most respected member of the species on the planet.

Any off-worlders spotted with high-tech equipment will be escorted to an open meeting place called the "Crater of Debate," and asked to explain themselves and where they have come from. It is very possible that some particularly eloquent heroes may be able to convince the Galidyn to support the Republic, but the majority of the great creatures will not consent to leave their planet. Instead, they will vigorously defend the planet from any Imperial incursions, as well as aid the Republic in setting up a base on one of the abandoned continents. (Some Galidyn may be persuaded to venture out into space, providing they are promised intellectual stimulation and problem-solving.)

Bear in mind that the Galidyn are the truly civilized species on the planet. They can boast of scientists, physicians, philosophers, technicians and the like.

The Galidyn will be absolutely delighted to see manifestations of the Force. Their scientists and philosophers have debated the existence of an "all-encompassing energy field in all things," but have not been able to either prove or disprove its existence.

Lesynn

Lesynn are small avians noted for their gorgeous golden plumage and delicious meat. They nest in the forests of Fyodos, feeding on insects and vegetation. Their song is said to be a cry for peace, one that went unheeded during the "Great Cleansing." Now they sing everywhere they go to remind the Fyodoi of the beauty that can be destroyed by war.

Most Fyodoi value lesynn for their taste and use the feathers for ornamentation. However, a small sect who have turned away from their shaman now worship the birds, believing them to be messengers from the gods. They fiercely protect the nests in their territory, even going so far as killing their fellow Fyodoi to keep them from harming the lesynn.

The birds themselves are harmless and peaceful provided their nests and eggs are left alone. They choose mates for life and females lay two to three eggs a year. Lesynn feathers can occasionally be found in other systems adorning expensive clothing produced by small traders.

The Galidyns also enjoy the company of lesynn, who often fly beside them.

■ Lesynn
Type: Small avian
DEXTERITY 4D
PERCEPTION 1D
STRENGTH 1D+1
Special Abilities:
Beak: Does STR+1D damage
Move: 29 (flying)
Size: 33 centimeters long, 66 centimeter wingspan
Scale: Character

Adventure Idea

The characters are informed by New Republic officials that the Tharak installation may contain key information. It is believed that the Empire once attempted a biological warfare experiment on nearby Tatrang III, and the products of that project may still be alive in the poisonous jungle. The characters must travel to the Tharak installation (hopefully without triggering the alarm) and obtain the information. While there, they will encounter a Galidyn.

Should they set off the alarm, the shaman and his men will arrive in time to see them in conversation with the "demonic" lizard.

Adventure Idea

The Fyodoi group which worships the lesynn have spotted one of the objects of their adoration flying with a Galidyn. Far from losing faith in the avians, they are instead convinced that the demons were attempting to tempt the lesynn.

There can obviously be only one response to this: the Galidyn must be exterminated, once and for all. They lesynn-worshippers are currently trying to convince the rest of the Fyodoi to join them in a "holy war" against the lizards. If they are successful, Fyodos could be the site of yet another bloody conflict. The characters must find a way to defuse this situation before hostilities erupt.

Adventure Idea

A free-trader who landed by accident on Fyodos has been imprisoned for attempting to sell a blaster pistol to a native and plans are moving ahead for his execution. What makes the situation even more dire is that the man carries information of value to the New Republic.

The characters must find a way to extricate the free-trader from this situation, either by negotiating or breaking him out of the crude Fyodoi prison.

Adventure Idea

The Imperial scouting report (see the sidebar above) winds up in New Republic hands, and the characters are sent to investigate Fyodos, particularly these rumors of talking lizards. The mission has the feel of a diplomatic venture.

A possible variation on this theme could be that the characters themselves find the report, perhaps with a drunken scout, trader, or even a pirate. This would be especially useful if the characters are not actively involved with the New Republic.

Adventure Idea

While just passing by this system, the characters' ship picks up the planetside blip, which resembles a landing transponder code. The curiosity factor present is that the ship's nav computer has a planet listing of "low-tech retrograde civilization" for Fyodos.

Adventure Idea

Fyodos can be a great place to have the characters' ship break down, or have some ship that is being pursued by the characters go down here. In either case, a forced landing on the Tharak continent could prove interesting. The landing pad transponder will be one of the primary signals picked up by the stricken ship, and may fool the characters into thinking that there is an advanced civilization on this planet.

Adventure Idea

A seemingly addled eccentric scientist wishes to hire the characters to take him to Fyodos. He is a scholar of dead civilizations. Unknown to the characters, he is also an Imperial lackey and carries a long-range homing device. If he finds anything of great importance, he will call in Imperial help. (Apparently, the Empire was not so quick to dismiss their initial scout's report.)

Adventure Idea

Once on the planet, the characters, if befriended by the Fyodoi, could be told exaggerated stories about the great flying lizards and their alleged atrocities against the Fyodoi. The characters will be approached and persuaded to join the hunt.

In fact, either the Fyodoi corner a wounded lizard, which attempts to speak, or the Galidyn wipe out the party, saving the characters for last.

Adventure Idea

This adventure should be used if the characters befriend a Fyodoi chief. The party incurs the jealousy of the shaman. Since he recognizes technology, he attempts to trick the party into revealing their items. Such attempts may include herding wild animals in the characters' direction, or having someone feign illness and see if the characters use modern medicine. If the characters reveal technological items, the items will be destroyed and the characters seized and forced to undergo trial by combat.

Adventure Idea

The Galidyn, who know of the presence of "something big and disturbing" under the Deathmoon base, alert the characters to some eventual danger to the planet. There should be a tough time in getting down the crevasse where the missiles are located, most likely with the use of *climbing* skill. Disarming the missile system requires a Very Difficult *demolitions* skill roll.

 # Gacerian

Gacerian

Type: Desert Planet
Temperature: Hot
Atmosphere: Type II (breath mask suggested)
Hydrosphere: Dry
Gravity: Light
Terrain: Desert, mountains
Length of Day: 36 standard hours
Length of Year: 375 local days
Sapient Species: Gacerites (N)
Starport: 1 stellar
Population: 27 million
Planet Function: Trade, homeworld
Government: Imperial government
Tech Level: Space
Major Exports: Musical entertainment, gemstones
Major Imports: Foodstuffs, luxury goods
System: Gacerian
Star: Klozar (orange)
Orbital Bodies:

Name	Planet Type	Moons
Tun	desolate searing rock	0
Wei	desolate searing rock	0
Alc	steaming jungle	1
Gacerian	terrestrial desert	2
Tytun	gas giant	8
Rue	frigid rock planet	0

World Summary

Gacerian is a hot desert world of stark beauty. It has very little in the way of remarkable geological features, but the few it does possess are rather unique.

The planet is a frequent rest stop for traders and travellers. What the vast majority of travellers are unaware of is the existence of an Imperial base on one of Gacerian's moons. The planet is run by an Imperial governor, since the Gacerites have dem-

System Datafile

Gacerian system, star: Klozar, orange star. Six planets in system; one terrestrial planet, Gacerian, fourth from the sun. High-tech, near-Human civilization. Music and leisure are largest planetary industries. High demand for luxury goods and foodstuffs. Possible Imperial presence in system.

Please take some time to learn the social customs of Gacerian during your stay. It will show your good manners.

onstrated their incompetence at self-rule.

Gacerian is also known for its high-quality gemstones. The Gacerites mine them using the most advanced known sonic mining equipment. This is probably the most manual labor done by the delicate Gacerites.

Gacerian has always been an Imperial-aligned planet.

System Summary

The Gacerian system consists of six planets orbiting an orange star called Klozar. Of the half dozen planets in the system, only Gacerian and Alc have any sort of breathable atmosphere. Alc has yet to be explored, as current geological reports show that the expense of settling would far outweigh any profit to be made from the natural resources present there.

Gacerian's two airless moons, Tempay and Fortay, orbit the planet once every 37.5 days. The moons are in opposition: located 180 degrees from each other, they are always on opposite sides of the planet.

The Empire has recently established a small base on Tempay. While no great effort has been made to keep this a secret, it is not exactly common knowledge in the area. Since it occurred a mere few months ago, word of its construction has not gotten around yet.

The precious stones of Gacerian are the main reason the Empire is here. The stones are mined by the citizens, and a hefty percentage is willingly turned over to the Empire.

The most important Imperial presence on the planet is the Imperial Governor, his staff of 12, and his 24 stormtrooper bodyguards.

A Planet of Sand

Gacerian is a hot desert planet with two main continents, Elto and An-Elto, plus a small archipelago. Most of the citizenry live in the capital city of Harmonia (the name is a translation from the Gacerian language; in fact, Harmonia is the only city on the planet).

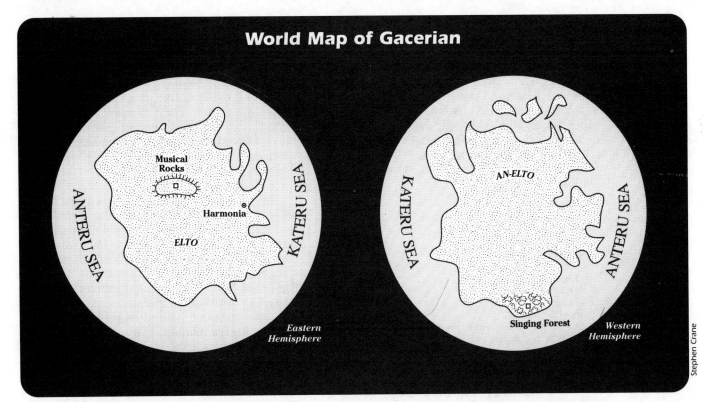

World Map of Gacerian

ANTERU SEA

Musical Rocks

Harmonia

ELTO

KATERU SEA

Eastern Hemisphere

KATERU SEA

AN-ELTO

ANTERU SEA

Singing Forest

Western Hemisphere

Stephen Crane

Due to the planet's very low axial tilt, there are no seasonal variations. The orange sun is so intense that the daytime temperature reaches 30 degrees Centigrade at high noon. When the sun sets, the temperature plummets to five degrees Centigrade.

There are strong winds on Gacerian, which make desert travelling a hazard. Difficult *survival* rolls are required when crossing the desert. If the characters do not come from a desert planet and/ or have never had to attempt survival in a desert, the task becomes Very Difficult. The winds are most common around dawn and dusk, when the air is either heating up or cooling down.

Gacerites

Gacerites average 2.5 meters in height, and are thin humanoids with spindly limbs. They are completely hairless. Gacerite eyes are tiny, in order to protect their optic nerves from their sun's glare. Their ears, however, are huge and exceptionally keen.

The most unusual physiological feature of the Gacerites is their respiratory system. In addition to having a highly efficient pair of lungs (the better to breathe the thin air of Gacerian with), Gacerites have a second set of air-intake holes, located on their necks, right below the jaw. These breathing holes are attached to a third lung. Gacerites make music with these "gills," which means that they can breathe normally and sing without having to pause for breath.

Gacerites live in family units, though their word for family translates more as "ensemble," as in a musical group. All children are raised with musical training.

Music and etiquette are the way of life for the Gacerites, and all aspects of their culture reflect this. In fact, the Gacerite courtship ritual, a series of songs and mannerisms, can take upwards of 10 years to complete. Fortunately, Gacerites have a life span of 150 years.

The average Gacerite loves music and the freedom of expression that it brings. On the other hand, music is made up of notes played to a certain rhythm. Everyone in an orchestra must know their part and when to play it. As a result, the Gacerites have also developed a love of discipline and order. This carries over into their system of etiquette.

Unfortunately, the mixture of the artist's creative mind and the strictness of order make for a rather bad social combination, especially when it comes to government. Thus, the Empire has assigned a governor to rule the planet. Gacerites are rabidly pro-Imperial, since the Empire stands for order, and each player must play his part.

In terms of language, the Gacerites speak in musical tones. The higher the key, the happier the words. Things like war, death, sadness, and displeasure are conveyed by low bass notes and dirge-like melodies. In fact, it is rumored that, prior to his death, Emperor Palpatine had a fondness for Gacerite dirge opera.

Gacerite manners are excruciatingly precise and their social rites are complex and feature long-winded orations. There is a certain etiquette to everything, and each occasion has its own rules and regulations regarding what constitutes standard behavior. Though the Gacerites make it a point to learn the customs and etiquette of other races, this is usually reserved for their dealings off-planet. When on Gacerian, the Gacerites expect visitors who have been exposed to their society to at least make the attempt to conform to their mannerisms.

■ Gacerites

Attribute Dice: 12D
Attribute Minimum/Maximums:
DEXTERITY 1D/3D+2
KNOWLEDGE 2D/4D
MECHANICAL 1D/3D+2
PERCEPTION 2D/4D+2
STRENGTH 1D/2D+2
TECHNICAL 1D/4D
Special Abilities:
Skill Bonus: All Gacerites receive a free bonus of +1D to *alien species, bureaucracy, cultures* and *languages*.
Move: 7/9
Size: 1.8–2.5 meters tall

Gacerite Society

The Gacerites have a classless society which revolves around music and manners. Social customs are tightly regulated and enforced. Politeness is the most valued trait of all, even if it means telling a few white lies or indulging in false modesty.

It is easy to mistake the Gacerite's excessive courtesy for cowardice. Nothing could be further from the truth. Despite their pleasant demeanor and near grovelling attitudes, Gacerites are fearsome in warfare. Their armies are well-disciplined, and are most receptive to the martial music played by the unit Musicmakers. In fact, when the *Aria Callet'dira* is played, Gacerite soldiers erupt into a battle frenzy as the music stirs their passions.

The pleasing Gacerite melodies attract many music lovers from all over the galaxy, enough so that the Gacerites have been able to turn their music into a thriving industry. In fact, sound and the sense of hearing are venerated above everything else here. Silence is equated with death. On the other hand, loud, grating noises or atonal music is considered the equivalent of swearing.

As for etiquette, Gacerites pride themselves on knowing the manners of most known cultures — the more exotic the manners, the more interested the Gacerites become. Gacerites make excellent translators and dipomatic aides. Many travellers who own 3PO units seek out Gacerite programmers to improve their droids.

In addition, the Gacerites have mastered the science of sound, and use sound-based weapons to stun opponents, kill enemies, or even level buildings. Of course, these weapons are useless in space, which is where the Imperials take over and defend Gacerite vessels, in return for continued Gacerite obedience.

Culture and songs are taught to Gacerites from infancy. Many Gacerites have special songs which they sing whenever they get into certain moods. For instance, a Gacerite may have a song for happiness, one for fear, and one for hunger.

As mentioned before, the Gacerites are extremely poor at governing themselves. The Imperial Governor meets once every Gacerian week with a group of Gacerites and goes over routine matters. It is part of Gacerite society to respect the Empire, which includes reporting all suspected New Republic members to the Governor, who in turn calls in reinforcements from the moon base.

Harmonia

The only city on Gacerian, Harmonia, and its accompanying starport take up an area of 520 square kilometers. Most of the city is made up of tall, glistening spires of crystal that vibrate from the offshore breezes, setting up a beautiful resonating music. The orange sunlight reflecting through translucent portions of the crystal buildings produces brilliant colors.

The Imperial Governor rules from and lives in

Gacerite

Rob Caswell

Gacerite Weapons

The following is a list of Gacerite weapons. Weapons with a parenthetical entry under Damage can be used to inflict stun damage, requiring a simple change of a setting.

Weapon	Where	Cost	Damage	Ranges
Sound Pistol	3F	800	5D+1 (4D)	3–5/15/25
Sound Rifle	3R	1400	6D+1 (5D)	3–20/50/100
Sonic Grenade	3X	300	6D/4D/2D	3–5/10/20

Harmonia. An atmospheric shuttle runs from Harmonia to places such as the gem mines, the Musical Rocks and the Singing Forest. The shuttles depart every four hours.

The Imperial Governor

Ulbrek Gostech is the Empire's representative and the Imperial Governor of Gacerian. The Gacerians willingly awarded him the title of *Gacer'grocinga*, meaning "leader of artists." He is a popular leader. He is the first Imperial representative to hold the title, and has been in charge for the past seven years. Fortunately, he is a music lover.

Although Gostech scrupulously adheres to Imperial policy, his rule of Gacerian is actually quite fair. Gostech is smart enough to know that, especially when dealing with a manners-conscious race such as the Gacerites, using the kind and fair approach yields better results than an iron hand could. Of course, if things did get out of control, Gostech could always resort to the iron hand, and would do so without the slightest hesitation or regret. Gostech is a portly man with beady eyes and short black hair. He dresses the part of the Imperial governor. He wants to gain a reputation as an excellent administrator and a tough enforcer of Imperial law. His career within the Imperial bureaucracy has been one characterized by steady competence. Though fanatically loyal to the Empire, many of his superiors felt his tendency towards compassion hampered his ability to govern: Gacerian, with its colonies of docile artists, was the perfect assignment for him.

Gostech is a man of culture and taste. He does not lose his temper easily, nor does he act in haste. Even when confronted by New Republic prisoners, Gostech is civil. However, the governor is curious about the workings of the "criminal mind" and will even invite New Republic prisoners to dine with him so that they may explain their motivations. Gostech is painfully aware that most other Imperial administrators feel he is too soft — he has, in fact, executed New Republic agents in an attempt to dispel this perception.

■ Ulbrek Gostech, Imperial Governor of Gacerian

Type: Imperial Governor
DEXTERITY 2D+2
Blaster 3D, dodge 3D
KNOWLEDGE 4D
Alien species 6D, bureaucracy 7D, culture 7D, Imperial law 8D, languages 7D, planetary systems 8D, streetwise 6D+1
MECHANICAL 3D
PERCEPTION 3D
Command 8D, con 9D
STRENGTH 2D+1
TECHNICAL 3D
Character Points: 9
Move: 10
Equipment: Comlink, hold-out blaster (3D+1)

The Musical Rocks

Also called *Oueee-ha* in the Gacerite language, the Musical Rocks are a group of boulders on the Plateau of Dreams, a huge formation in the middle of the Elto continent.

The rocks got their name from the eerie music that is produced when the wind blows through them. Many Gacerites come here to meditate, and this is the closest thing in the Gacerite culture to a religious shrine.

Unfortunately, the Musical Rocks often attract wild animals, who pose a threat to unwary tourists and pilgrims.

The Singing Forest

Translated as *Keee-s'ae* in Gacerian, the Singing Forest is made up of a dense area of *s'ae* trees. The s'ae tree trunks get as wide as 12 meters at the base, and the average tree height is 100 meters. Since this area is close to the southern polar region, the temperature is cooler and more moisture is found in the air, allowing the huge trees to thrive.

As opposed to the Musical Rocks and the spires of Harmonia, both of which make music because of the wind, the s'ae trees in the Singing Forest are sensitive to seismic activity. The slightest shift in the bedrock, a movement so slight that the average person cannot detect it, causes the trees to resonate like a forest of tuning forks.

In the direct center of the Forest is a spring-fed lake. This is a popular area for swimmers to take their ease.

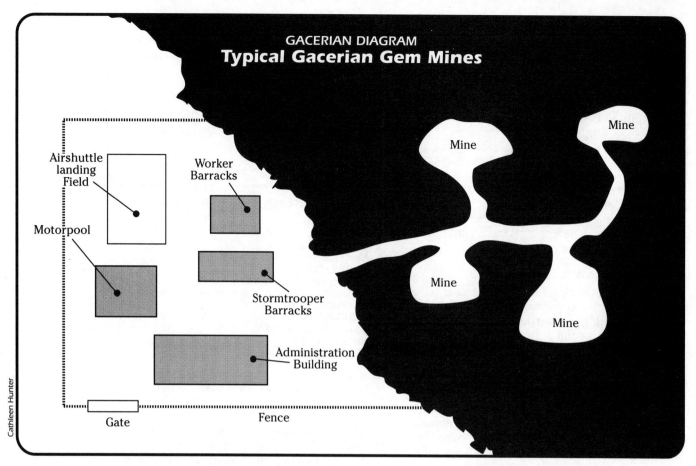

GACERIAN DIAGRAM
Typical Gacerian Gem Mines

Airshuttle landing Field

Worker Barracks

Motorpool

Stormtrooper Barracks

Administration Building

Gate

Fence

Mine

Mine

Mine

Mine

Cathleen Hunter

The Gem Mines

Each gem mine is staffed by 110 Gacerties, 100 of whom do the mining and 10 who handle administrative duties. In addition, there are 20 Imperial stormtroopers stationed at each mine, ostensibly to protect the workers from wild animals and off-world gem thieves. The stormtroopers have been warned not to abuse the Gacerites, since they are working in the mine as normal paid workers, not as slaves.

At any given mine, there is a two in six chance of there being 3D off-worlder miners here as prisoners, usually being held on smuggling or low-level piracy charges. In such instances, the number of stormtroopers present is doubled.

Each mine also has an administrative building, an airshuttle landing field, workers' barracks, stormtrooper barracks, plus a motorpool containing six landspeeders, 12 military speeder bikes, and one cargo skiff.

■ Revirs
Type: Carnivorous mammals
DEXTERITY 4D
PERCEPTION 3D
STRENGTH 4D
Special Abilities:
Howl: 6D stun damage, 10 meter radius
Claws: STR+1 damage
Teeth: STR+1D damage
Move: 14

Size: 1.5 meters long, 1 meter tall at the shoulder
Scale: Creature

Capsule: Revirs are carnivorous mammals who haunt the mountains of Gacerian; they are also known to frequent the fringes of Gacerian's deserts. They are four-legged wolf-like creatures with a glossy ebon fur. Revirs use their piercing howl as a primary means of attack, and while the target has been stunned, make a rapid charge, with fangs bared. Revirs hunt in packs of up to a dozen animals.

■ Mears
Type: Grazing herbivores
DEXTERITY 3D
Missile weapons 4D+1
PERCEPTION 1D
STRENGTH 3D
Climbing/jumping 4D
Special Abilities:
Quilled Horns: STR+2D, ranges 3-10/15/20
Hooves: STR+1D
Move: 9
Size: 2.5 meters long, 2 meters tall at the shoulder
Scale: Creature

Capsule: Mears are six-legged herbivores who make their homes in Gacerian's mountains. They normally travel in packs of up to six animals and are frequent targets of revir attacks (mear meat is also a staple for Gacerians).

They rely on their horns and hooves for defense. Their horns are covered with thick, barbed "quills" which they can shoot at short range. It takes them a week to grow full size quills.

STAR
WARS

The Tempay Imperial Base

The Gacerite moon of Tempay is host to an Imperial scout base. Constructed several months ago, the base is not yet common knowledge.

Tempay always shows the same side to Gacerian, so the base is located on the north pole, at the terminus point between light and darkness. This way, base personnel can keep tabs on both the planet and on space beyond the system.

The base is commanded by Captain Engar Ret, an Imperial Navy officer who is at odds with Governor Gostech. Captain Ret covets the governor's position, and is always alert for any signs of weakness in order to report it to the Empire. Actually, the way Ret has planned it, he will win either way. Either Gostech will not be hard enough on the Gacerites, in which case the governor will be replaced, or Gostech will be too harsh, causing an uprising, which Ret will be there to quell. After ending a rebellion, Ret would file a report indicating that Gostech cannot even control his own population of supposedly loyal Imperial citizens.

The base's complement consists of:

40 Stormtroopers
32 TIE Pilots
32 Ground Crew Technicians
12 Controllers
12 Sensor Technicians
24 Gunners/Weapons Technicians
20 Imperial Intelligence Officers
50 Base Security/Detention Troops
One squadron of TIE fighters (12)
One squadron of TIE/rc reconnaissance (12)
20 miscellaneous vehicles

Any New Republic prisoners captured on Gacerian are sent to the moon in Gacerite light freighters manned by Imperial forces.

Adventure Idea

A New Republic Senator has vanished en route to a conference. The last transmission from his vessel put it in the vicinity of the Gacerian system. From all indications, it appeared that the trip was proceeding normally. The characters are sent to Gacerian to look into the disappearance and hopefully rescue her.

The Senator, named Ala Cornin, is being held under house arrest in the Imperial Governor's crystal tower. Two days after the characters land, she will be transferred to a freighter and brought to the moon base for further interrogation.

Adventure Idea

A variant of the previous idea. Several prominent figures in New Republic politics and industry have disappeared in recent weeks. They were last seen at Harmonia's poshest hotel.

What has happened is that these important guests have been kidnapped from their rooms and sent to the moon base. To add to the drama, a Star

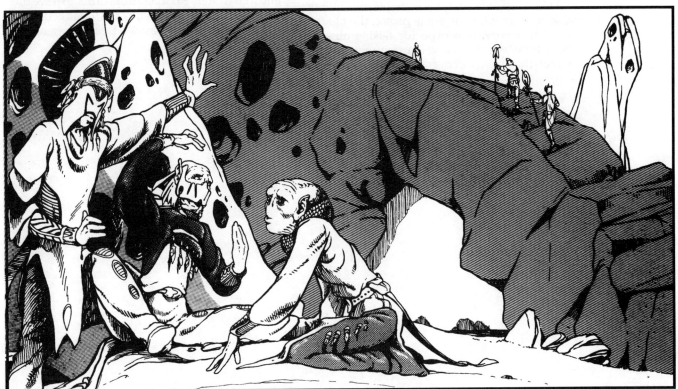

Mike Vilardi

Mike Vilardi

Destroyer is due soon in-system to pick up the prisoners and take them into the heart of Imperial space.

Adventure Idea

(This is a good one for greedy players.) While drinking in a cantina on some planet, the characters hear a grizzled prospector talking about a place where "you can just walk around and pick the gems off the dirt!" The coordinates he gives are for Gacerian.

This is a scam. The grizzled prospector is Dek Anorik, a smuggler who was captured, along with his best friend, by the Imperial forces on Gacerian. In exchange for his freedom, Dek is to assume the guise of an old prospector and try to lure Rebels and free-traders to Gacerian, in order to have them put to work in the gem mines. His friend remains on the planet in order to assure Dek's cooperation.

Korbin

Korbin

Type: Temperate plains
Temperature: Hot
Atmosphere: Type I (breathable)
Hydrosphere: Dry
Gravity: Standard
Terrain: Scrub, urban
Length of Day: 28 standard hours
Length of Year: 380 local days
Sapient Species: Human
Starport: 1 standard
Population: 1 million
Planet Function: Criminal haven
Government: Vying criminal factions
Tech Level: Space
Major Exports: Mining, kyrf
System: Atrig
Star: Atrig (orange)
Orbital Bodies:

Name	Planet Type	Moons
Beneris	searing rock	0
Tollero	searing rock	0
Amrap	desert	2
Torvik	swamp	1
Korbin	terrestrial	1
Grillis	asteroid belt	0
Abatrarg	gas giant	18
Lynaria	frozen rock	0
Altrax	frozen rock	1

World Summary

Korbin is an excruciatingly hot planet with very little to offer. Formerly a successful mining colony, the veins of ore have long been played out. What remains barely keeps the planet's economy going. The planet's secondary industry is the growing of a certain fruit that is used to make a potent alcoholic beverage, but its primary money-maker is a thriving black market.

The planet has no surface oceans. Water is found in small quantities in underground pools and reservoirs. The terrain is mostly flat scrub plains, with a few small mountain ranges and valleys to break up the monotony.

Korbin is the last stop for many in the galaxy whose fortunes and scruples have dwindled to nothing. The Korbin system is located far enough away from normal Imperial routes and patrols

that the Empire sees no point in going in and cleaning the place up.

Planetary government is non-existent. Chaos and anarchy reign. Korbin has never professed loyalty to either the Empire or the New Republic, and the Battle of Endor changed nothing as far as the planet's occupants were concerned.

System Summary

The Korbin system contains a large number of planets, with most of them of little use to starfarers. Four of the planets in the system, Beneris, Tollero, Lynaria, and Altrax, are incapable of supporting life and have no resources to speak of. Only the third, fourth, and fifth planets, known respectively as Amrap, Torvix, and Korbin, are habitable.

The sixth orbit is occupied by Grillis, an asteroid belt, which supports some light mining under the aegis of Cross-Galactic Mining, a small corporation that has mines scattered on a dozen worlds. The seventh world is the gas giant Abatrang, with its poisonous ammonia atmosphere.

All in all, the system is a lawless, dangerous place. The Empire and the New Republic agree on one thing: anyone who goes to Korbin and gets into trouble deserves everything he gets.

Weather and Geography

Korbin has no axial tilt, which results in no seasonal variations. However, the orange sun is very strong and heats things up quickly. Daytime

System Datafile

Atrig system, star : Atrig, large orange sun. Nine planet system. Main terrestrial planet Korbin, principal industry, mining. Black markets in weaponry, ships, and other equipment exist on the planet.

TRAVELLER'S ADVISORY: The Atrig system is not under any political jurisdiction. Anarchy reigns on Korbin. Proceed at your own risk!

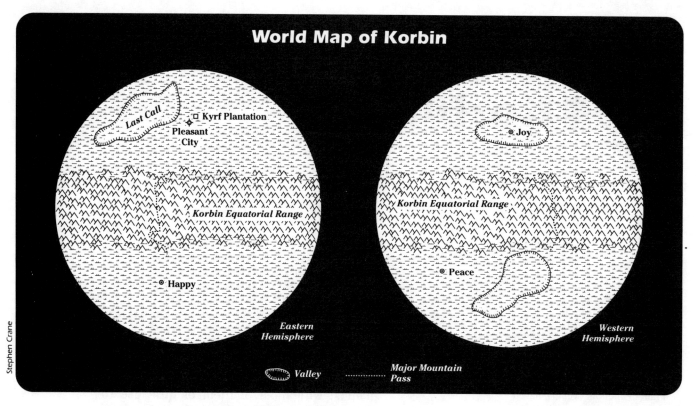

World Map of Korbin

Last Call
□ Kyrf Plantation
◇ Pleasant City
Korbin Equatorial Range
◉ Happy
Eastern Hemisphere

◉ Joy
Korbin Equatorial Range
◉ Peace
Western Hemisphere

🝣 *Valley* .... *Major Mountain Pass*

Stephen Crane

temperatures get as high as 35 degrees Centigrade. When the sun sets, the temperature plummets to as low as five degrees below zero Centigrade.

What rainfall there is normally begins at dusk and lasts a for few hours. On exceedingly rare occasions, Korbin sees snow.

A huge mountain range girdles the planet. The high peaks are often covered in ice and snow and howling winds whip around them, making the going even more treacherous. The only safe means of travel through the mountains are the two passes, Selenfer (linking the cities of Pleasant and Happy), and Refin (linking Joy and Peace). However, the passes have dangers of their own, as bandits often lurk there waiting to ambush travellers.

Redeye

Korbin's sole moon, Redilos was long ago christened "Redeye" by the planet's occupants. The huge moon hangs close to the planet — if Korbin had oceans, the tides would be horrific.

Redeye is an intimidating sight, a huge blood-red disk, pock-marked with craters and ridges. Redeye is barren, and has no resources to speak of.

A World to Beware

The planet Korbin played host to a thriving mining industry for centuries under the Old Republic. Though the population was never very big, it was a productive, industrious place.

But long before the fall of the Republic, Korbin's

resources began to dwindle, with veins of ore becoming harder and harder to find. It soon became evident that the expenses involved in getting the ore out of the ground dwarfed the income generated by its sale. The planet's limited resources would not support terraforming into an agricultural planet, and tourists were not interested in vacationing in old mine shafts. Slowly, the population left for better prospects on other planets.

Eventually, the only people left were some struggling miners working for a few small corporations. A nearby system with overcrowded prisons asked for the Old Republic's permission to resettle 200 dangerous prisoners on Korbin. The Republic agreed, and the prisoners were settled on Korbin and made to earn their keep by working in the mines.

At this point, most of the honest workers left, concerned about how long they would last working side by side with murderers and psychopaths. As the years went by, more planets sent their felons to Korbin. In time, fugitives, dregs of society, and other lowlifes began flocking to the planet in droves, using it as a refuge from the law.

It soon became apparent that the inmates were running the prison, but the Republic did not have the iniative to get involved — other, more important, matters were at hand. The felons were confined to the Atrig system, and the few corporations left on Korbin gave the whole arrangement a touch of legitimacy.

Even the corporations themselves got into the act, by sending their most bothersome, irritating, and incompetent executives and employees to Korbin. In an atmosphere where the rules had ceased to matter, many of these corporates began making a profit on the side by selling goods at vastly inflated prices. This was the start of what is now a thriving black market on Korbin.

With no central government on the planet to watch for smugglers, the transport of goods that are illegal in other systems is acknowledged and encouraged here. Korbin is well known among free-traders and pirates as the place where they can obtain anything, for a price: weapons and other personal equipment, forged identification, Imperial seals of safe conduct, even ships, all can be found somewhere on the planet. (Expect prices for these items to be two to three times that listed in the *Star Wars Sourcebook* — the sellers are, after all, criminals and swindlers.)

Korbin Society

Korbin has only one law: "The one with the biggest blaster makes the rules." Despite this edict, there is a "rough justice;" often, a gang of Korbinites will gang up on someone they feel has done a little too much rule-making. Therefore, survival on this world requires knowing when to be aggressive and when to hold back. Many Korbinites die trying to learn this lesson.

Truly there is no Korbin law. Everyone does whatever they please, though even some of the worst dregs know that running around and destroying everything is a sure way to get one's throat slit. But there is no weapon, no pastime, no substance, no thought or idea, that is considered illegal. In some ways, Korbin can be said to have a perfectly integrated society with no bias whatsoever. Everyone distrusts and dislikes everyone else.

Pleasant City

All of the cities of Korbin were deliberately given cheery names as a cruel joke. Pleasant City is the largest urban area and home to the Korbin Starport. There are no customs inspections at the starport.

In addition, the Pleasant City starport has no truly qualified mechanics. Characters can rent a berth for their vessel and conduct their own repairs. Naturally, Pleasant City will not be held responsible for any break-ins or vandalism done to the ship while it is berthed.

The buildings of Pleasant City are a tumbledown collection of prefabricated houses and old stone structures. Many of the buildings show signs of efforts at repair having been made, but such renovations are half-completed, as if the laborers simply lost interest.

The air is hot and dusty, and smells of garbage, sweat, and some minor industrial emissions. There are few children, and most of them are free-running ruffians. Korbin is not where one goes to start a family.

Since hygiene is not a major priority, diseases are common. For each day spent in Pleasant City, each character must make an Easy roll against their *Strength*, or else contract an airborne disease, virus, or plague (gamemaster's discretion as to damage).

All equipment found in the *Star Wars Sourcebook* can be found in Pleasant City. There are no restrictions on legality codes or licenses, but prices are high, as noted above. Whenever an item is purchased, the gamemaster should secretly roll 2D. On the result of a "2," the item bought is flawed, and will break down at the most inconvenient time. On a "12," the item never works, period. Since most "stores" have at least one violence-loving bouncer, refunds are unlikely (always assuming that the character is still alive to ask for one).

What Pleasant City does have is a huge variety of alien species among its residents. Practically every known species is represented here, and

Pleasant City Encounter Chart

Roll	Encounter
3	Characters witness a blaster fight between 1D+1 city dwellers.
4	Characters witness a brawl with melee weapons, between 2D city dwellers.
5	Characters witness a small conflict with heavy weaponry between 3D city dwellers.
6–7	1D of natives amble up to the characters and offer to sell them services of some kind (gamemaster's choice).
8–9	2D natives are doing some gambling on the street. Characters may feel free to join in.
10–11	A native comes up to the characters and offers to sell them something (gamemaster's choice).
12–15	A group of 2D natives attempts to mug the characters.
16	A madman rushes up to the party and claims to be someone important (e.g. a New Republic spy, Imperial official, Jedi Knight).
17	Someone from an upstairs apartment dumps garbage on the characters.
18	A big, ugly, drunk, well-armed alien mistakes one of the characters for its worst enemy. (Gamemaster option: Alien mistakes character for its girlfriend.)

they mix freely. For every 10 minutes in which the characters are walking the streets of Pleasant City, roll 3D and consult the "Pleasant City Encounter Chart."

Jedi Knights, the Force, and Korbin

Jedi Knights without any traces of the dark side will stick out in Korbinite society like Darth Vader in a field of Imperial stormtroopers. The power, serenity, and honor of the Jedi Knights is practically a tangible thing in this pit of evil, corruption, despair, and dishonor. This will either cause the natives to give the character a wide, fearful berth, or get cocky and indignant and try to pick a fight with the character.

Korbin Careers

There are a number of occupations available to the aspiring Korbinite. The following list covers some of them, and is useful for gamemasters to consult when trying to create encounters.

Miner — There are not many of these left, as most of the mines are played out. They are looked down upon by the unsavory elements on the planet, most of whom have never done a day's honest labor in their lives.

Asteroid Miners — These are the people who toil in the corporate mines in the asteroid belts. The procedure for a worker is 38 days of work on an asteroid, followed by 19 days off on Korbin.

Scavengers — Armed with a ship and protective suits, these vultures travel the system, looting any vessels that might crash on one of the worlds (see below).

Mike Valardi

Gangs — Organized groups of criminals, each gang led by a crime boss. Many gangs have rivalries. This is by far the most well-represented occupation on the planet, since most gangs also dabble in the black market. Gangs also account for most of the robberies and protection rackets operating on Korbin.

Black Marketeers — Sellers of both legal and illegal goods abound on Korbin. Most do their

Mike Vilardi

best to avoid violent confrontation, as it's bad for business.

Mercenaries—Professional soldiers who hire themselves out as muscle. They are the most reliable folks on Korbin, and will keep their word when working for someone, providing they are well paid to do so.

Pirates — Organized gangs with space-going capability, they prowl around both within and outside the system, waiting to attack unwary vessels. The scavengers make much of their income simply by shadowing the pirates and stealing whatever they leave behind.

The Last Call

As might be expected, life is "nasty, brutal and short" on Korbin. Some way of disposing of all of the victims had to be found, and quickly, before the cities grew more diseased than they already were. The natives settled upon the idea of "Last Call."

A huge valley 700 meters deep, the floor of "Last Call" is littered with the remains of Korbinites and foolish off-worlders. Fortunately, the prevailing winds blow to the north, sweeping away any possible unpleasantness.

The Small-Timers

Korbin's cities are connected by a system of roads, but these are rarely travelled, as the cities do not often trade with each other. Each city keeps to itself. Besides Pleasant City, the other cities are Happy, Joy, and Peace. Collectively, the three smaller cities are known as Small-Timers.

Life in the Small-Timers is similar to Pleasant City, only less intense. Also, the mines are located on the outskirts of Pleasant City, so there are fewer hard-working people in the Small-Timers.

The Kyrf Plantation

Besides a smattering of mining and the black market, Korbin is known for an alcoholic beverage called *kyrf*, which is derived from the fruit of the same name. Kyrf only grows in one area of Korbin, and that area is a plantation owned by a less than honest Korbinite, Drelmar Bin.

Kyrf itself is an extremely flavorful and quite powerful drink. A Human drinking one glass of kyrf needs to make a Very Easy *Strength* roll in order to avoid the intoxicating effects. Every additional glass requires another Strength roll, but at the next highest level of difficulty.

Beings drunk on kyrf start misspeaking and slurring words, then lose their coordination, then lose consciousness. Those who fail a *Strength* roll by 10 or more go straight to unconsciousness.

Korbinites love kyrf, because it enables them to escape into oblivion for a while. The effects last for up to 12 hours.

Located a mere 10 kilometers northeast of Pleasant City, Drelmar Bin's kyrf plantation is the closest thing to class on Korbin. The 900 square kilometer plantation is a forest of green trees, all of them bearing the oval-shaped, metallic golden kyrf fruit — the fruit thrives in dry or arid conditions. The plantation is surrounded by a power fence, and the perimeter is heavily guarded by mercenaries who are unflinchingly loyal to Bin. Many of the laborers on the farm are people who owe Bin money and must work to pay off their debt. The plantation also has a small processing plant, which turns out the kyrf liquor.

Cross-Galactic Mining Corporation handles the exportation of the liquor. Bin doesn't trust the corporation, but it seems to be the only organization on the planet sufficiently competent to handle the shipping of the product and business transactions with the purchasers.

Bin lives in a spacious, beautiful home, air-conditioned and filled with every luxury imaginable, including several droids and a few mistresses.

■ Drelmar Bin, Corrupt Plantation Owner

Type: Gangster
DEXTERITY 3D
Blaster 4D, dodge 5D, melee parry 3D+2
KNOWLEDGE 3D+2
Streetwise 8D, value 7D
MECHANICAL 2D+1
Repulsorlift operation 4D, space transports 3D
PERCEPTION 4D
Bargain 7D, command 6D, con 8D, search 5D+1
STRENGTH 2D
Brawling 3D+2
TECHNICAL 3D
Security 4D
Character Points: 6
Move: 10
Equipment: Hold-out blaster (3D), comlink, gaudy jewelry, expensive clothing

Capsule: Drelmar Bin is a gangster who owns the kyrf plantation outside Pleasant City. He is a conniving, scheming, anything-for-a-credit crimelord. He has no scruples, but sees himself as a well-mannered being of elegant taste.

Bin's origins are far more humble. He began his career as a corporate employee, but was caught embezzling funds. He fled before anyone could haul him off to jail and ended up seeking refuge on Korbin. Once there, Bin met a man who had learned how to distill kyrf fruit into a potent liquor — Bin killed the man and took over his plantation. Bin is a pencil-thin, hawk-nosed man with a pinched smile, sharp chin, and slicked-back hair.

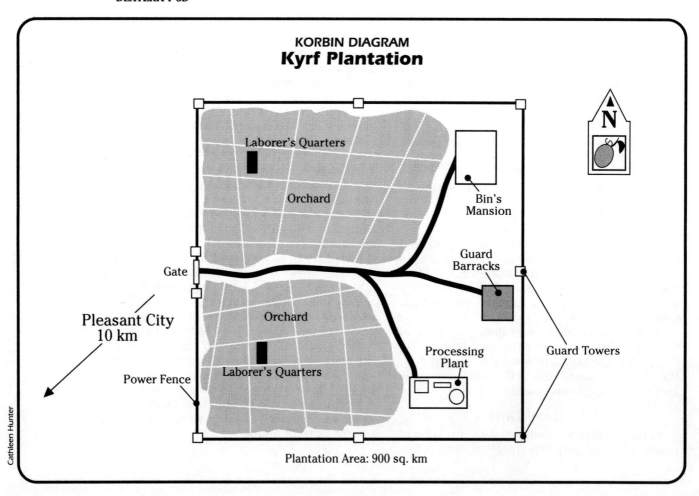

KORBIN DIAGRAM
Kyrf Plantation

Plantation Area: 900 sq. km

Average Mercenary. *Dexterity 3D, blaster 5D, brawling parry 4D, melee combat 6D, Knowledge 1D+2, alien species 4D+1, streetwise 5D, Mechanical 1D, Perception 2D, bargain 4D, con 5D, search 5D, sneak 4D+1, Strength 3D+1, brawling 5D+1, Technical 1D, security 4D.* Move: 10. Bounty hunter armor (+2D physical, +1D energy), heavy blaster pistol (5D), vibroblade (STR+1D+2), comlink, 2 grenades (5D), macrobinoculars.

Scrub Lizards

The predominant native life form on Korbin is the scrub lizard. These large carnivorous reptiles enjoy congregating in the Last Call valley, as well as near the roadways that link the cities. Scale coloration ranges from copper to golden brown. Scrub lizards can crawl flush with the ground, which leads some to mistake them for snakes.

Korbinites enjoy hunting the big lizards for food and sport. The skin and teeth of a scrub lizard make colorful personal adornments. Some of the nastier local gangs take their enemies and "lizardbait" them, which involves tying the unfortunate to stakes pounded into the ground and letting the lizards take him.

Scrub lizards are attracted to kyrf, but are incapable of becoming intoxicated by drinking it. Drelmar Bin has a large force of mercenaries employed to keep the lizards away. Denying the only decent fruit to the scrub lizards does not do much for their temperament, which might explain their aggressive and violent behavior toward humans.

Efforts to domesticate the scrub lizards have met with mixed success, with a few of the species made into mounts, beasts of burden or watch-lizards.

Wild scrub lizards are normally found in groups of two to six animals.

■ Scrub Lizard

Type: Desert hunter
DEXTERITY 2D
PERCEPTION 3D
Search: tracking 5D, sneak 5D
STRENGTH 4D
Special Abilities:
Blood Frenzy: If a scrub lizard can cause a wound when attacking a target, the lizard goes into a frenzy, giving it +1D to *Strength* and *Dexterity* actions.
　　Armor: +1D to physical and energy
　　Teeth: STR+1D damage
　　Trample: Causes 4D damage
Move: 15
Size: Up to 3 meters long, 1 meter tall at the shoulder
Scale: Creature

Korbin Scrub Lizard

Rob Caswell

The Salvaging Crews

There exists a core of people on Korbin who do salvaging for a living.

The total time of most salvage runs, including round trip travel time, is four days. The salvage is either directly used as is, or sold or traded on the Korbin.

The only law of salvage is "finders keepers, providing the keepers can hold on to it." There are some pirates, nicknamed "carrion eaters," who lurk in the spaceways between Korbin and her sister worlds, waiting for a successful salvage ship to come by. These pirates want others to take the risks, so that they may take the loot.

Of course, not all salvagers are rotten to the core. A few, like Kara Saffch and her technician brother, Willi, are willing to take on risky jobs for relatively little money, providing they have some regard for the cause being fought for. Often, these residents of Korbin can be found well outside the system, pursuing their trade.

Kara Saffch

Kara Saffch is one of the best scavengers on Korbin; amazingly enough (at least for this world), she matches her talents with a strong sense of ethics. Kara and her brother, Willi, have traveled the galaxy for nearly a decade (they both left home as teenagers). Somewhere along the way, they acquired their ship, the *Night Havok;* however, they still owe a large debt to the ship's prior owners. They headed to Korbin since they believed it was a world they could lose themselves on. She and Willi have managed to scrape by the past few years, but they are always living week-to-week trying to arrange scavenge missions or cargo hauls.

Kara is a Human female, 27 years old, with brown hair that reaches to the back of her neck. She almost always wears a flight suit and comfortable jacket. She has a cocky grin that comes off as either charming or irritating (and often a little bit of both). Kara tries to act like she is always in control of every situation (which is especially amusing considering how often the *Night Havok* breaks down). She is upbeat, proud and full of enthusiasm.

■ Kara Saffch

Type: Freighter Captain
DEXTERITY 2D
Blaster 6D+1, dodge 6D, melee parry 3D+2
KNOWLEDGE 2D
Streetwise 9D, value: starship parts 7D, value: salvage 9D
MECHANICAL 4D
Astrogation 5D, repulsorlift operation 6D, space transports 7D, starship gunnery 6D, starship shields 5D+2
PERCEPTION 4D
Bargain 6D+2, command 5D, con 6D, gambling 5D+2, search 8D
STRENGTH 2D
Brawling 5D, lifting 4D
TECHNICAL 4D
Space transports repair 6D+2
Force Points: 3
Character Points: 15
Move: 10
Equipment: Blaster pistol (4D), comlink, space suit

■ Night Havok

Craft: Modified Corellian YT-1300 freighter
Type: Modified light freighter
Scale: Starfighter
Length: 30 meters
Skill: Space transports: YT-1300
Crew: 2, gunners: 2, skeleton: 1/+10
Crew Skill: See Kara Saffch
Passengers: 5
Cargo Capacity: 200 metric tons
Consumables: 1 month
Cost: 35,000
Hyperdrive Multiplier: x2

Hyperdrive Backup: x18
Nav Computer: Yes
Maneuverability: 1D
Space: 6
Atmosphere: 330; 950 kmh
Hull: 5D
Shields: 2D
Sensors:
 Passive: 10/1D
 Scan: 25/2D
 Search: 40/3D
 Focus: 3/3D+2
Weapons:
 Twin Laser Cannon (fire-linked)
  Fire Arc: Turret
  Crew: 1
  Skill: Starship gunnery
  Fire Control: 4D
  Space Range: 1-3/7/15
  Atmosphere Range: 100-300/700/1.5 km
  Damage: 6D
 Laser Cannon
  Fire Arc: Turret
  Crew: 1
  Skill: Starship gunnery
  Fire Control: 3D
  Space Range: 1-5/15/30
  Atmosphere Range: 100-500/1.5/3 km
  Damage: 3D

■ Necresh

Type: Rodent
DEXTERITY 4D
PERCEPTION 2D
STRENGTH 1D
Special Abilities:
Teeth: STR+1D damage
Move: 16
Size: Up to 20 centimeters long
Scale: Character

Capsule: Necresh are carrion-eating rodents who infest the Last Call. It's unknown how many thousands live there; fortunately, an ample food supply in the valley means that they haven't spread to Korbin's cities. Necresh are covered in short, wiry red hair. They are skittish and easily frightened and their keen senses of hearing, sight and smell allow them time to scurry away when larger beings approach.

■ Draz

Type: Canine hunters
DEXTERITY 4D
PERCEPTION 3D
STRENGTH 2D
Special Abilities:
Teeth: STR+2D damage
Claws: STR+1D damage
Move: 10
Size: 1.5 meters long
Scale: Creature

Capsule: Draz are extremely vicious canines. They were originally bred as fighting animals, but thousands were turned loose on worlds around the galaxy. Their predatory instincts have made them familiar dangers of the wilderness regions of many worlds. On Korbin, packs of draz frequent the wilds, meaning that solitary hikers must always be on the lookout for an attack.

Some domesticated draz are used as guard animals, especially by some of Korbin's more vicious gangs. They are up to 1.5 meters long, and generally have white, grey or black hair. They are known for their savage and frightening demeanor. Their immense teeth and claws are quite dangerous in combat.

Adventure Idea

A criminal organization based in Pleasant City has begun shaking down the citizens of Happy for protection money. Most of Happy's residents are, of course, criminals as well — but those few who are (relatively) innocent are also being victimized. A collection of Happy residents ask the characters to protect them, promising in return access to a cache of weapons originally intended for shipment to Imperials.

The characters are outnumbered and outgunned. They will have to rely on their wits and make good use of the terrain in and around Happy to defend the city from its larger neighbor.

Adventure Idea

The *Night Havok* has been hired to transport an important cargo of black market medical supplies to a New Republic base in a nearby system. But Captain Saffch well knows that pirates will be waiting to seize the medicines and equipment if possible, and so hires the characters to "ride shotgun" on the shipment. They will accompany her, brother Willi, a New Republic official, and a trio of mercenary "security guards" on the run.

During the course of the trip, the *Night Havok* will have to outrun pirates and avoid some more aggressive salvage crews. In addition, the characters will find evidence that all is not as it seems on the ship. All signs point to the mercenaries having betrayed the ship to Imperials. But in fact, the New Republic official is an impostor who has subsituted poison for the medicine being transported. The characters must uncover the deception before the *Night Havok* reaches the base or else watch tragedy befall their comrades.

Adventure Idea

Ores mined in the asteroid belt are somehow being smuggled out of the system and sold to raise money for fragments of the Imperial army. The New Republic asks the characters to go undercover as miners for the Daedalus Corporation to discover the truth of the matter.

The characters swiftly discover that nothing is how it appears to be at Daedalus. Miners are treated like convicts, many being worked until they drop dead. Disk work is being falsified and corporate officials are seen wearing full protective suits when handling ores. Some of the laborers are afflicted with strange illnesses. The existence of entire digs are being covered up at the highest levels of Daedalus.

The truth is horrendous: using slave labor purchased on Korbin, Daedalus has its miners illegally digging for radioactive ores, to be sold to Imperial engineers for use in weaponry. Lacking the proper protection, the miners are being poisoned by the very ore they're handling.

The characters must find a way to stop the mining operation and expose Daedalus as an Imperial front before they, too, perish.

Adventure Idea

A Corellian Corvette, the *Empire's Twilight*, has been lost. The last signals came from the vicinity of the Korbin system. The Republic hires the characters to search for the vessel and any survivors.

The *Empire's Twilight* was attacked by pirates while passing through the Korbin system, in the vicinity of Abatrang. Captured by the gravity of that planet, the ship went out of control — fortunately, the 45 crewmembers had the presence of mind to eject in an escape module. They are currently living inside this structure on the planet's surface, with enough food, water and air to last for one week.

Salvage crews will inevitably spot the module.

The characters will have to brave the perils of Abatrang to save the crew, and even then their mission will not be finished — "carrion eaters" are waiting in space near the world and may mistake the characters for successful scavengers.

Adventure Idea

While on Korbin, the characters are approached by Drelmar Bin's men and told that he has a business proposition for them. At his plantation, Bin tells the characters that he wants them to capture two scrub lizards, since he wishes to have them trained as attack animals.

Being a generous man, he will pay each character 2,500 credits for each lizard captured. He does not have cages and nets, so the characters are going to have to make do with what they have, or can purchase in Pleasant City. He mentions that the best place to look is "Last Call."

In the valley, the characters will find scrub lizards, all right. They will also find gang members disposing of the bodies of some of their rivals, who will be disposed to attack the characters "so they can't tell anyone what they saw."

Zelos II

Zelos II

Type: Terrestrial Mountainous World
Temperature: Temperate
Atmosphere: Type I (breathable)
Hydrosphere: Moderate
Gravity: Standard
Terrain: Mountains, hills
Length of Day: 20 standard hours
Length of Year: 300 local days
Sapient Species: Zelosians (N)
Starport: 1 standard
Population: 10 million
Planet Function: Trade, mining
Government: Military dictatorship
Tech Level: Information
Major Exports: Raw ores
Major Imports: Weaponry, foodstuffs
System: Zelos
Star: Zelos (white)
Orbital Bodies:

Name	Planet Type	Moons
Keryt	barren rock planet	0
Zelos II	terrestrial mountainous world	4
Rymm	mountainous/volcanic	1

World Summary

Zelos II is located near an important regional Imperial trade route. It is considered a pleasant place to stop by to do some trading, perhaps get some routine maintenance done on one's ship, perhaps even enjoy a little bit of relaxation.

The planet is known for its mining industry, and is a prime source of ores for the Empire, though the Zelosians are not aware to whom their government sells the minerals. The Zelosians believe themselves to be neutral in the galactic struggle but the dictator Nul is allowed by the Empire to retain power.

The planet is covered by hills, mountains, and other rough terrain. There are only a few scattered islands in the Zelosian oceans. Kryndyn, the capital, is located on the primary continent.

Zelos II boasts four moons, upon which many local superstitions center. An inexplicable gravity well also rests at the edge of the system, which is responsible for untold numbers of unexpected visitors to the planet every year.

System Summary

The Zelosian system has a white star and three planets. Keryt, the first planet in the system, is a barren rock that could be terraformed if the effort were ever to be put into it.

Zelos is the second planet in the system. Its four moons have never been explored, as the Zelosians have forbidden others to explore them due to overwhelming ancient superstitions.

Rymm is the third planet, and is a considerable distance from Zelos. The planet is geologically unstable and still going through tectonic shifts, characterized by frequent earthquakes and volcanic eruptions.

The gravity well is close to Rymm, and there is some speculation that Rymm's instability can be attributed to the well. Ships that file a navigational flight plan with the Empire are given the proper approach vectors.

The Gravity Well

This anomaly is a stationary distortion in space, located close to the orbit of Rymm, the third planet in the Zelos system. The Empire has it well-charted and is aware of a means to avoid it.

When a ship piloted by someone who is not aware of the anomaly's presence passes the sys-

---

System Datafile

Zelos system, star: Zelos, white star. Three planets in system, second planet, Zelos II, terrestrial. Good port facilities.

Be warned that there are many nocturnal predators on Zelos II, a source of fear among the populace. Be advised that the population is extremely superstitious.

Loyal citizens of the Empire, be advised that the only safe approach vector to Zelos II is X coordinate 7.5, Y coordinate 4.2, Z coordinate 0.9. Any other course will result in disruption due to presence of a gravity well.

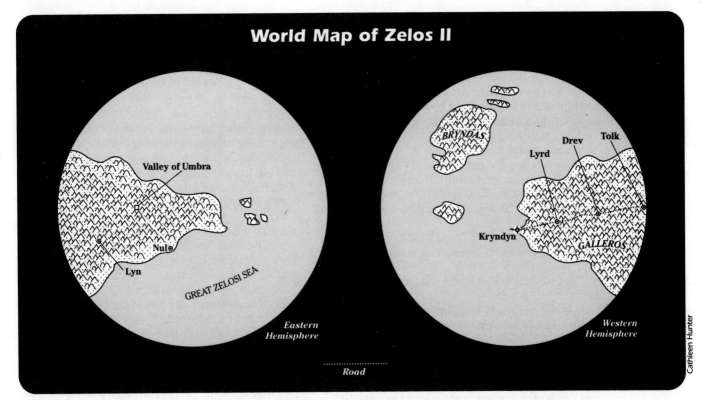

World Map of Zelos II

Valley of Umbra

Nul

Lyn

GREAT ZELOSI SEA

Eastern Hemisphere

BRYNDAS

Lyrd **Drev** **Tolk**

Kryndyn

GALLEROS

Western Hemisphere

Cathleen Hunter

....
Road

tem (or enters it), there is a strong likelihood that the gravity well will capture the vessel and hurl it close to the orbit of Zelos II.

The anomaly's effects are handled as follows:

• The unsuspecting ship arrives within range of the gravity well. Hyperdrive immediately cuts out due to the presence of massive gravitational forces.

• Ship's pilot must make a Moderate piloting roll. Success indicates the ship is stabilized, and may resume its journey, even if the destination is not the Zelos system.

• If the ship's pilot failed his roll, the vessel is caught in the gravity well and begins hurtling uncontrollably into the system. Ship's pilot must make another piloting roll, this one Difficult. Success means the ship is stabilized, and slows down as it arrives in Zelos II's orbit.

• Failing the roll means that the ship was badly shaken during its passage through the system. Roll for damage on the "lightly damaged" table.

Note that hurtling through the system, regardless of whether or not the second piloting roll was made successfully, produces a very bumpy ride, with lots of shaking and rattling. This little trip should produce a lot of dramatic tension as everything inside the ship begins shaking and things are turned upside down, falling off of shelves, and people are tumbling out of bunks, falling out of chairs, etc.

An Outsider's View of Zelos

The light freighter *Night Havok* shuddered out of hyperspace and into sublight with all the grace of a drunken bantha. Kara Saffch, the ship's owner and pilot, relaxed in her seat.

"I don't believe we made it!" exclaimed an older man, seated next to her. Several other people poked their heads into the cockpit from the adjacent room. "But did we really?" a young man asked, not certain that he wished to know the truth.

"Well … considering that we're having this chat and not fighting off TIE fighters suggests that we did," Kara grinned in her ingratiatingly cocky manner. "When you people hired me and my brother to take you out of Imperial space, you hired the best!"

"Maybe we survived, but the *Night Havok* sure didn't," said a voice from the ship's intercom. It was Kara's kid brother, Willi, technical genius and by far the grimmer of the two. "Hyperdrive looks like someone set fire to it, shields are gone, I could swear I heard the hull pop a few times, and I think the ship's power plant is about to _ "

Willi's voice was cut off as ship's power failed and everyone was plunged into darkness. In a few heartbeats, eerie green emergency lighting shone weakly from the lightpanels. Willi's voice returned, but the reception was far weaker. " … Yep, main power just gave out and reserve kicked in."

Kara stared out the window for a few moments, her grin disappearing rapidly. "Willi, meet me at the computer," she barked into the intercom.

"What is it?" asked the older man. "Listen, I hired you to get me and my family away from the Empire, and I have a right to know …"

"Could be nothing. Could be something. Could be the last time this ship ever flies," Kara muttered as she left the cockpit.

Later, as the siblings were busy at work at the computer, the older man ambled over and peeked over their shoulders. When Willi glared at him, he backed away. "But I only want to know what's going on … "

"Fine," Kara sighed. "You paid the fee, you're entitled to answers. The ship is moving toward a star system … "

"But that's wonderful!" the man gushed in relief. "You people —"

" — did nothing," Kara interrupted. "The ship is on reserve power. We shouldn't be moving. Apparently, we are caught in some strong gravity well."

"Which means?" the man prompted.

"Which means that we are being sucked into the Zelos star system, and we can't stop it," Willi finished impatiently. "We're doomed."

"Is the Zelos star system that bad?" the man wondered aloud.

Kara moved aside and let the man approach the console so he could read the data coming onscreen. "Read for yourself," she replied.

The man read the words on the computer screen, his face falling further and further the more he read. Finally, he loosened his collar, cleared his throat, and in a classic example of understatement, mumbled, "I don't think this was quite what we had in mind when we paid for passage."

The Zelosian Moons

Zelos II has four moons, named, from largest to smallest: Bellatrig, Tanatrig, Moratrig, and Nekotrig.

If all four moons ever appear in the night sky together, with at least one moon full, this is enough to send the populace into a deep depression and intensify their fears, even in the daytime. This phenomenon happens once every 120 days.

The worst experience possible for the Zelosians is a solar eclipse which, when the entire sky is darkened, reveals the presence of the other three moons in the sky. Such an event is called the "Day of Sepulchral Night," and prompts mass closings of stores and bars, locking of all doors, and in some instances, temporary insanity or suicide attempts, prompted by abject terror. (In truth, the sky on a Day of Sepulchral Night does look foreboding. When the eclipsing moon moves into position, it almost seems as if the other moons appear by magic.)

The Zelosians

The natives of Zelos II appear to be of Human stock, but with some subtle differences. Their height, build, hair color variation, and ability to grow facial hair is similar to other typical Human races. All Zelosians are night-blind, their eyes unable to see in less light than that provided by a full moon. In addition, all Zelosian eyes are emerald green.

The greatest difference between Zelosians and standard Human stock is that Zelosians are descended from intelligent plant life; there is no concrete proof of this, but many Zelosian biologists believe they were genetically engineered beings since the odds of naturally evolving to this form are so low. Their veins do not have blood, but a form of chlorophyll sap. There is no good way to visually tell a Zelosian from a regular Human, since their skin pigmentation resembles the normal shades found in Humanity. This plant heritage is something the Zelosians keep secret.

The Zelosians' plant heritage does go a long way toward explaining their dislike of darkness, and their transformation into happy, carefree people in the sunlight. Their skin photosynthesizes for them, though they are also able to take nourishment from other sources, including other plants, as well as animal meat.

Zelosians love to drink, though due to their physiology, they cannot become intoxicated. Refined sugar, on the other hand, is something else. A tablespoon of sugar to a Zelosian is the equivalent of strong liquor to a Human.

The entire culture of the Zelosians is built upon the dichotomy of day and night. In their language, "good" is synonymous with bright, light, glowing, and day. "Bad" is identified with dimness, darkness, shadows, and night. Speaking any of the four latter words is akin to swearing in the Zelosian society.

There are dark-skinned Zelosians, but they are not shunned. It appears that the light-darkness stigma is limited to their words and ideas, and excludes colors, as they paint their dwellings all manner of hues and will wear any shade of clothing, including black.

During daylight hours, Zelosians are happy, cheerful, energetic, helpful, kind, open, pleasant people with laughing voices and animated movements. As the sun goes down, their moods sink, and they seek the shelter of their well-locked homes, even to the point of being rude and leaving someone in the middle of a task or conversation in order to get home in time. During the night, Zelosians are fearful, easily cowed, suspi-

Mike Vilardi

cious, and unwilling to help strangers.

Whatever the time of day, the Zelosians are very superstitious people. The following are some of their more interesting superstitions:

• Never leap out of a starship and land on the ground with both feet.

• Never travel in groups of four. Four is an unlucky number.

• If the light of two full moons strikes you, you will die within one day.

• If someone spills water or any other drink, they must be lightly slapped across the face

• Right is an unlucky direction. Shake with your left hand. Right-handed people are more vulnerable to bad luck.

• Never begin a voyage, including a space voyage, at night.

• Never make plans at night.

• Devout vegetarians are bad luck.

Government

Galleros Nul is the charismatic military leader of the planet. Though in simple terms he is a dictator, he dislikes the word, and instead prefers to call himself the "Mandated Commander of the People of Zelos." People may address him as "Commander."

Nul's most amazing talent is his ability to withstand being outside at night without break-

ing into a panic. This discipline came slowly and with much training, but it has paid off by vastly increasing his stature among the people. His evening constitutionals are the only time he travels without his six bodyguards, who have yet to overcome their dislike of the darkness (they are always within shouting distance, however).

The word of Commander Nul is absolute law. The people obey his orders without question. This blind obedience stems from Nul's record of public service. He enlisted in the Zelosian Home Defense Force as a young man and worked his way rapidly through the ranks, eventually being named a general.

Soon after that, a particularly devastating attack on the capital city of Kryndyn by a horde of nocturnal predators resulted in the slaying of the planet's leadership; General Nul declared a temporary state of emergency. He rallied the armies under his command, launched a counterattack, and drove back the hordes of night.

This incident, known as the "Battle of Kryndyn," was fought 10 years ago. Nul has yet to lift the state of emergency and has no intention of doing so.

As for the Empire and the New Republic, Commander Nul has declared Zelos II to be neutral. This is a hollow gesture, since the Empire controls all approaches to the Zelos system, and has in fact established a full sized TIE fighter base in the Valley of Umbra. This is the ideal site for such a base, as no Zelosian, not even Null dares set foot here (see below).

Mike Vilardi

Thus, Nul's absolute rule exists because the Imperials allow it to, largely because it saves them the trouble of keeping the skittish population in line. Besides, there are some in the Imperial ranks who admire Nul's use of power plays and underhanded tactics.

■ Commander Galleros Nul, Dictator-for-Life

Type: Zelosian Dictator
DEXTERITY 3D
Blaster 4D, blaster: blaster rifle 5D, dodge 7D, melee combat 5D, melee parry 5D+1
KNOWLEDGE 4D
Bureaucracy 7D, intimidation 7D, survival 6D, tactics 7D, value 5D
MECHANICAL 2D
Repulsorlift operation 3D
PERCEPTION 3D
Bargain 7D, command 9D, con 6D+2
STRENGTH 3D
Brawling 5D, stamina 5D
TECHNICAL 3D
Security 4D+1
Force Points: 2
Dark Side Points: 4
Character Points: 8
Move: 10
Equipment: Blaster pistol (4D), vibro-blade (STR+1D+2), comlink, swagger stick

Capsule: Commander Nul is the military commander and dictator of Zelos II. He is a handsome man in his 40s, with jet-black hair and piercing green eyes. He almost always wears his military uniform.

Nul has used a variety of excuses to hold onto power — while it is never stated openly (although everyone suspects as much), Nul intends to use any excuse possible to hold power. Currently, the "nocturnal predator problem" is his excuse for maintaining martial law. If he ever felt that his power was threatened, he would not hesitate to commit genocide against his own people to hold power or make sure any future rulers had nothing to inherit.

Galleros Nul was raised to fear the dark, but his curiousity prompted him to make late-night forays to see what terrors Zelos truly had. In time, he learned to control his fear of the dark, although there are still places (like the Valley of Umbra) wehre he will not go.

Nul is a tactical and strategic genius, but he is fully aware of his abilities, so his ego overshadows those talents. His sense of arrogance and self-importance is obvious in even the most casual conversation. He feels that everyone on his world should obey his commands without question. Nul is also a very curious man, and enjoys visiting with off-world travellers — he often expects a few gifts, but will invite spacers to dinner so they may discuss their adventures.

Population Centers

There is only one political unit on Zelos II, based in the capital city of Kryndyn. No other nations exist. In fact, the entire population lives on a single continent, Galleros (renamed in honor of the Commander). The capital city of Kryndyn holds nine million people, while the remaining five smaller cities hold the other million. The largest of these is the coast city of Nul (also named in honor of the Commander).

All Zelosian cities have certain things in common. Each city features a 10 meter-high wall around it, with six gates. The wall is wide enough that sentries may walk on top of it while on patrol. Each small city has a garrison of 1,000 troops. Kryndyn has a garrison of 50,000 troops.

The five small cities have several mines close by, usually within a few kilometers of each city. The cities are connected by a roadway and a railway system. The two lines run parallel to each other. The railways are the only way for the ore to be transported to Kryndyn, from where it is then shipped off-planet on ore freighters. Nul also has an airfield that allows airshuttle landings, and a port that accommodates ships from the capital.

Kryndyn

Kryndyn is the heart and soul of Zelos II. Here, a traveller can find a wide selection of bars, casinos, entertainment centers, libraries, sports events, and hotels.

The natives of Kryndyn are very friendly to off-worlders, especially those that bring shipments of weapons or edible delicacies to sell. There is a thriving commodities market, where traders come to purchase loads of Zelosian ore. The market is dominated by the Empire, though this is not common knowledge.

Commander Nul resides in the old Royal Palace, from which he runs the affairs of the planet. The Palace always has at least 100 soldiers garrisoned within it at any given time.

The Valley of Umbra

This unique geological formation has a valley 500 meters deep, protected by many mountainous overhangs. Despite appearances, there is ample room in the valley for fighter pilots and airspeeder or landspeeder drivers to operate their vehicles

The Valley of Umbra is always in the shadows. Sunlight never strikes it, and consequently it is shunned by all Zelosians. The Empire has taken full advantage of native superstition by creating a fully equipped, fully operational base and Imperial garrison. The base follows the same design and sports the same defenses as the Imperial Garrison detailed on pages 117–121 of the *Star Wars Sourcebook, Second Edition*. The only exception is that this base is occupied by a half-strength garrison, which includes the following:

Stormtroopers	400
Scout Troopers	20
Speeder Bike Technicians	10
TIE Fighter Pilots	20
Ground Crew Technicians	30
Controllers	12
Sensor Technicians	12
Gunners/Wpns Technicians	50
Walker Crew Personnel	25
Walker Technicians	40
Imperial Intelligence	25
Base Security/Detention	75
Perimeter Support Troops	100
Command Personnel	150
Support/Services Person.	250
Technical Personnel	100
Science Personnel	100
Medical Personnel	50
TIE Fighters	20
AT-AT Walkers	5
AT-ST Walkers	5
Speeder Bikes	20
Landspeeders	30
Misc. Vehicles	50

The Imperial Garrison is commanded by Luana Treftite, an ambitious young lady who aspires to greater things than the command of an installation on a backwater planet populated by superstitious sheep.

Though the Zelosians are, of course, aware of the continued existence of the Empire, they have no idea that there are Imperial forces on the planet. Even Nul is unaware of the existence of the base, firm in his belief that the Empire heeded his wishes that Zelos II be left alone.

Treftite will concede that the Zelosians are correct about the potential dangers from nocturnal predators on the planet. The bold, fearsome and plentiful creatures have accounted for a number of losses among her base's perimeter guards.

■ Major Luana Treftite, Imperial Garrison Commander

Type: Imperial Commander
DEXTERITY 3D
Blaster 5D, dodge 5D, melee combat 5D
KNOWLEDGE 3D
Survival 6D+1, value 5D
MECHANICAL 4D
Astrogation 5D+1, repulsorlift operation 6D, space transports 7D, starfighter piloting 8D, starship gunnery 7D, starship shields 5D
PERCEPTION 4D
Bargain 6D, command 8D, con 6D, search 7D
STRENGTH 2D
Brawling 4D, stamina 3D
TECHNICAL 3D
Computer programming/repair 4D, security 5D, starfighter repair 3D+1
Character Points: 13
Move: 10
Equipment: Blaster pistol (4D), comlink

Capsule: Luana is a coldly beautiful, severe-looking woman with very pale skin, pale blonde hair in a tight bun and icy blue eyes. She is always seen in her military uniform, even when off-duty.

Luana grew up with tales of the Jedi Knights. Her

parents were loyal to the Old Republic. Luana attempted to study the Jedi way, but lacked the clarity of thought and pureness of motive — she sought only power and did not have the patience to master her will. As she grew older, her lust for power brought her to the Empire — rejecting the old ways her parents stood for, she embraced the New Order and its evil. She has since risen to the rank of major, but wants far more. She hopes to rise above this assignment and to be assigned to a major command.

Creatures of Zelos

Zelos II is home to a number of dangerous creatures, the vast majority of whom are nocturnal, including the three listed below.

■ Aga
Type: Immense predator
DEXTERITY 4D
PERCEPTION 3D
Sneak 7D
STRENGTH 5D
Special Abilities:
Bite: STR+1D damage
Claws: STR+1D+2 damage
Clubbing Attack: STR+2D damage
Screech: Target must make an Easy *Perception* total or be stunned for one round (-1D to all actions)
Armor: +2D physical, +1D energy
Move: 9
Size: 4 meters tall
Scale: Creature
Orneriness: 5D

Capsule: Aga are tall quadrupeds with grey skin, yellow eyes, fangs and six muscular legs. They often walk on their four hind legs, using the forward legs as arms. They are generally encountered in groups of two to five creatures, although packs of as many as a dozen aga have been encountered.

Aga are dangerous hunters who have been known to hunt for "amusement," as opposed to for food. They show signs of rudimentary intelligence — they have been known to uproot trees and similar objects and use them as immense clubs. Aga attack in groups, often beginning the assault with a terrifying screech which frightens and confuses their targets.

■ Kilit
Type: Hunting raptor
DEXTERITY 4D
PERCEPTION 4D
STRENGTH 3D
Special Abilities:
Beak: STR+1D
Move: 38 (flying)
Size: 1 meter long, 2 meter wingspan
Scale: Creature
Orneriness: 4D

Capsule: Kilits are raptors that are covered with short, oily, black hair. They have razor sharp beaks and hunt other creatures with high-speed swooping attacks. They travel in flights of two to a dozen creatures. There is a legend that says the kilit got its

name when a pack of the creatures attacked a wandering scout. His companion scout, in his excitement, asked, "What is it?" The senior scout shouted, "Kill it! Kill it!" The name stuck.

■ Kro
Type: Small reptiles
DEXTERITY 4D
PERCEPTION 2D
STRENGTH 1D
Special Abilities:
Bite: STR+2D
Move: 32
Size: Up to 1 meter long, 0.75 meters tall
Scale: Character

Capsule: Kro are rodent-like reptiles with wide, scooping snouts and a toothy maw. Their tails are prehensivle and they use them to hang from tree branches or get a better grip on an opponent. Kro have deep red eyes which glow in the dark, lending them a fearsome appearance.

Kro travel in packs of six to 20 creatures. They will normally only attack other creatures if they outnumber them at least two to one. Kro are omnivorous — while they prefer meat, they can survive on roots, scrub plants and berries. They make a distinctive "meep" sound when attacking.

The Walking Dead

Zelos is home to a unique species of nocturnal parasite called "jumpers." This three-millimeter-long creature feasts solely on the dead. However, its feeding produces a rather grisly side-effect. If the body has been dead for a week or less, it is vulnerable to certain enzymes and electrical currents released by the jumper during its feasting. This combination of enzyme and electrical energy "jumps" the brain back into activity. Motor skills are engaged, and the dead get up and walk. Residual memory causes the animated dead to go to the last site visited prior to its death and just stand there, which produces some unpleasant reactions among the living.

The effect lasts for 1D hours, after which the jumper leaves the body, having taken everything it can from that particular corpse. The emptied body then collapses again.

It must be stressed that the so-called revived dead are automatons. There is no consciousness. All functions are reflexive, triggered by the parasite. If the body is attacked by weapons, and given four more wound levels, it collapses and will not move again.

Note that it is the Imperial garrison that has discovered these parasites, not the Zelosians. The Zelosians are convinced that the dead truly walk again. Imperial Commander Luana Treftite is delighted that this phenomenon elicits such a reaction; she wants to keep the population terrified.

Rob Caswell

Adventure Idea

A mysterious figure has begun stalking the capital city of Kryndyn, setting fire to buildings, robbing shops and generally terrorizing the populace. The culprit is an Imperial guard whose mind was broken by too many nights on sentry duty, fending off Zelos' nocturnal predators. Though Major Treftite is aware of the situation, she is unwilling to take steps to stop his rampage, for fear of exposing the presence of an Imperial base on the planet.

At the same time, the Zelosians are unable to stop him because of their fear of the dark. The only possibility of stopping the madman lies with the characters, who must brave the terrors of the Zelosian night to bring him down.

Adventure Idea

The characters learn that a top Imperial official will be passing through the Zelos system, on his way to a secret meeting with some of the galaxy's top assassins. It is believed he will be handing out a contract on a major New Republic figure — but who, and where the meeting will be held, remain mysteries.

The official's ship will be protected by a number of Imperial fighters, and Commander Nul has given his "permission" for them to pass through the system. The New Republic asks the characters to stop this convoy and learn the target of the murder plot.

The characters are provided with ships, though nowhere near enough to stop the Imperials. However, if the Imperials could be lured into the clutches of the gravity well and forced down on Zelos or one of its neighboring planets, the characters might have a far better chance of success.

Once they capture the Imperial agent, they will learn that the target of the assassination is none other than Mon Mothma herself. The agent taunts them that if he does not arrive to meet with the assassins, they have orders to send message back through Imperial spies and await further instructions. Eventually, he says, the Empire will send someone else to pay them their blood money.

The characters have only one chance: if one of them could impersonate the Imperial agent, they could lead the assassins into a trap and save the life of Mon Mothma. But exposure would mean instant death, so the chosen character had best be sure his act is perfect.

Adventure Idea

A group of Imperial agents have been directed to ensure that Commander Nul "keeps in his place" and does not get the idea into his head to challenge Imperial authority directly. Rather than actually threatening him, the agents have decided to use the common superstitions of the Zelosians against him — rigging it so that he travels in groups of four, is (apparently) struck by the light of two full moons, and so forth.

Frightened (though unwilling to admit it), Nul retains the services of the characters to protect him from what appears to be a conspiracy by the Fates to destroy him.

With the characters involved, the agents up the ante. After all, they are prohibited from killing Nul, but not a bunch of New Republic upstarts. Again using the superstitions of the Zelosians as their jumping-off point, the agents scheme to slay the characters using a noxious black gas, hoping that Nul will interpret their deaths to mean that the darkness itself is stalking him.

The characters' own lives depend on their ability to stop this plan from coming to fruition.

Adventure Idea

The most obvious hook is the gravity well, which draws the character's ship into the system, since it is very unlikely that the characters filed an Imperial flight plan.

This hook can then be used in conjunction with any of the following ideas.

Adventure Idea

While on another planet, the characters hear a rumor about Zelos II: "Though the day brings happiness and wealth to all, the dead walk at night on Zelos II." This alone should be enough to intrigue the characters.

Adventure Idea

The New Republic contacts the characters and asks them to visit Zelos II, for two reasons. The first task is to check out the possibility of swaying the sympathies of the population. The second task is to scout the system for Imperial influence.

If the characters meet Commander Nul and inquire about the Imperial presence, it will be met with blustery denials, which may seem phony but are actually sincere. Nul truly believes that the Empire pays heed to his wishes.

The Imperial garrison routinely sends intelligence personnel disguised as traders into Kryndyn to check out visitors to the planet. If they catch wind of New Republic sympathizers in the city, this information will be immediately relayed to Luana.

Adventure Idea

The Zelosians hire the characters to act as security on a shipment of ore going by rail from Nul to Kryndyn. The train ride from Kryndyn to Nul is uneventful, and is used to show the characters the route. The ore train has a crew of four Zelosians. The train departs Nul at midday, and the ride lasts five hours.

After passing Lyrd, four and a half hours into the ride, the train derails and overturns. The crew is killed. The sun is going down. There are no other people on the nearby roads. Walking to either Lyrd or Kryndyn will take two hours.

The characters are about to get a first-hand look at Zelos' nocturnal predators. At least three encounters will suffice. Then all the characters have to do is to go to the walls of a city and convince the night-frightened guards to let them in.

Adventure Idea

The characters are hired by Commander Nul to make a landspeeder courier run to Lyn. They are to stay the night there, then bring back any return packages from the Lyn garrison commander.

The evening they arrive in Lyn, the alarm is raised as several corpses begin to rise and wander about. The wrinkle that should get the characters interested is that two of the dead are Imperial stormtroopers, killed in an avalanche, who are now staggering around the perimeter of the village.

It is possible for the characters to track the dead men back to their compound, which happens to be the Imperial Garrison.

INDIANA JONES™ and the RISING SUN

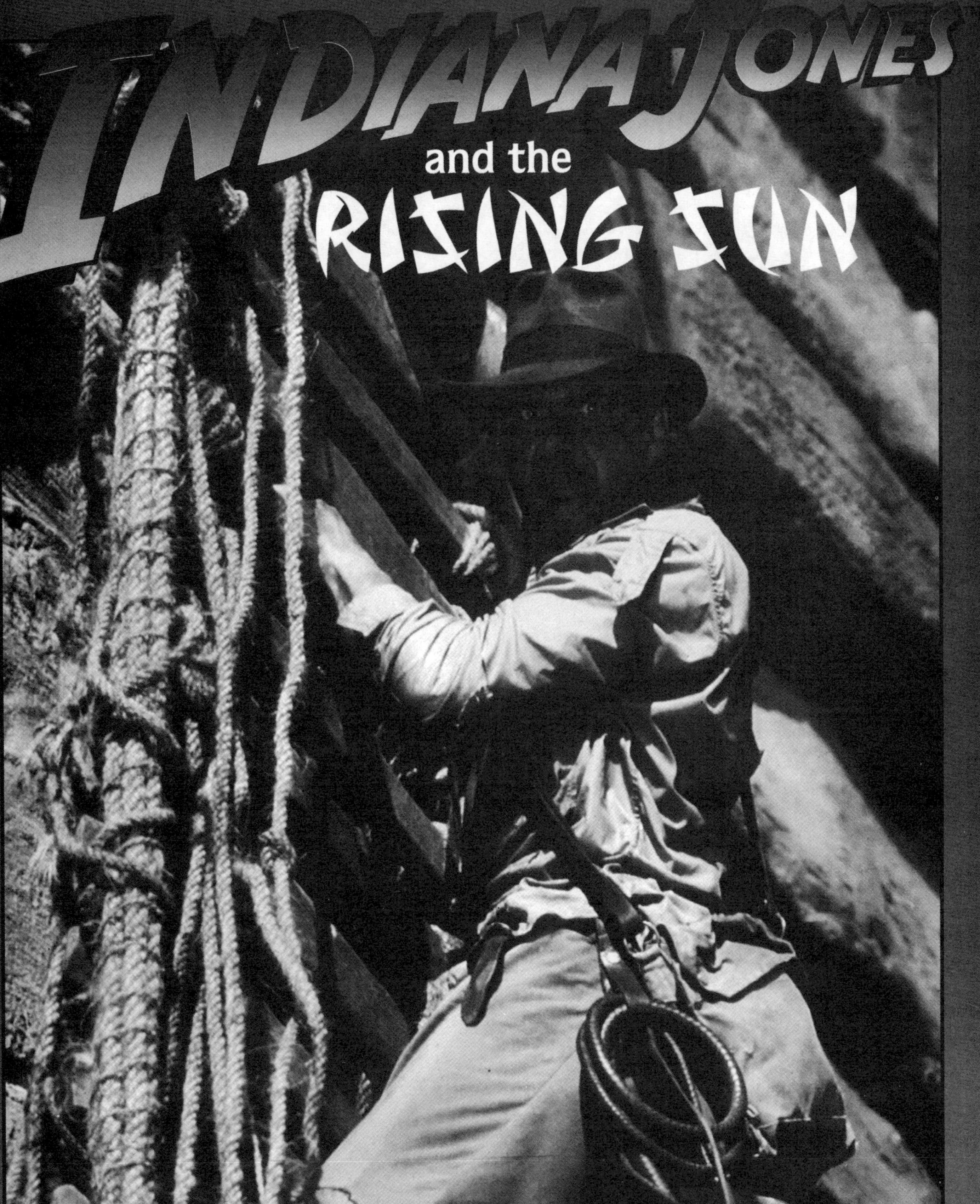

A MasterBook GAME

MEAN STREETS

BAR

CONDITIONED

midnight

Stephen Crane